Death in the West Wind

Death in the West

Wind

DERYN LAKE

This edition published in Great Britain in 2002 by
Allison & Busby Limited
Bon Marche Centre
241-251 Ferndale Road
Brixton, London SW9 8BJ
http://www.allisonandbusby.com

A catalogue record for this book is available from the British
Library

ISBN 0 7490 0588 2

Printed and bound in Spain by
Liberdúplex, s. l. Barcelona

Acknowledgements

So many people have so generously given their time to assist me with this book. First and foremost, Charlie Smith, ropemaker and man of the sea, who told me the other meaning of the word canvas and helped me to get the nautical details correct. Next, fellow crime writers Michael Jecks and Mary Jones. Mike gave me the idea for this story after a very good Sunday lunch at which a great deal of wine had been consumed. Mary went to no end of trouble to take me round Topsham and help with the photography, to escort me to The Bridge Inn and sample the fare, to send me road maps of the period and to make enquiries about the quay master and come up with a name. Next the Devonians; Barbara and Derek Marriott, who introduced me to the Sea Dog and also gave me another idea for the plot; Heather Skermer, always ready for a gin and giggle; Imogen Vance, who masterminds things from a distance. And grateful thanks to those fantastic publicists Beth Macdougall and Tom Templeton whose sheer expertise got me the best publicity I have ever had. Last but very far from least, I would like to thank Madeleine Midgley and the staff of the Devon and Exeter Institution, situated in The Close, Exeter. They are the nicest, friendliest group of archivists I have dealt with and they helped make this book possible.

For Beryl Cross - present when John Rawlings
first stepped out of the archives
and friend of his ever since.

The West Wind

It's a warm wind, the west wind, full of birds' cries;
I never hear the west wind but tears are in my eyes.
For it comes from the west lands, the old brown hills,
And April's in the west wind, and daffodils.

JOHN MASEFIELD

Chapter 1

A few miles beyond Exeter, the sea worked its usual magic and the wind changed, coming from the West. Pushing down the window of his brand new carriage, a smart affair comprising gleaming black bodywork with scarlet trim, a fine conceit of the owner's monogrammed initials upon the door, John Rawlings stuck out his head. Well pleased with what he saw, he sniffed the air, relishing the faint smell of salt, his ears excited by the wild high cry of gulls, his face warm in the gently blowing April breeze. It was springtime, the year 1759, and the Apothecary of Shug Lane, Piccadilly, had left London on honeymoon, those idyllic four weeks immediately following a wedding, during which time he had decided to go on holiday with his bride, Emilia. A European tour not being possible because of the present hostilities, they had chosen to visit Devon, that huge and mysterious county of contrasting moods, to which they had presently ventured with a certain amount of trepidation.

The night before this bright April morning they and their team of elegant horses had rested at The Half Moon in High Street and had watched the departure of the Exeter Stage Coach, leaving for London by way of Dorchester and Salisbury, taking three days over the journey in summer, longer in the other seasons when the ways were more likely to be foul.

"We could have travelled on that," John had said
to his bride, who stood beside him at the window
overlooking the courtyard wearing nothing more
than a nightrail.

Emilia had smiled at him saucily. "It wouldn't
have been half as much fun," she had answered,
referring, though not directly, to the fact that they
had made love, and twice at that, in the dark depths
of their own carriage while Irish Tom, their coachman, had driven stoically on.

"No, it wouldn't," John had answered, holding
her close to him and mentally thanking Sir Gabriel,
his adopted father, who had presented them with
the brand new equipage, complete with horses and
driver, as a wedding gift.

They had departed from town in it the day after
their marriage. John had worn a suit of dazzling
green and gold for his wedding, while Emilia, radiant in white taffeta, had stood beside him in the
glow of the rose window of St. Ann's, Soho, where
the ceremony had taken place. From there the bridal
party, complete with three fiddlers, had made its
way to number two, Nassau Street, in which every
room had been turned over to accommodate the
feast and the dancing that would follow. And though
the house had been full to overflowing, there had
been so much happiness and jollity that nobody had
minded when Samuel Swann, John's lifelong friend
who had acted as bridegroom's witness, had got
very tipsy and high-spirited and danced till he fell
over at the feet of a young lady.

Nicholas Dawkins, the Apothecary's apprentice,

had been allowed to discard his sober gear and dress up for the occasion, being given a plum-coloured suit as a special gift, in which he looked both pale and handsome. While Sir Gabriel Kent, who always dressed starkly in a combination of black and white, emerged in an ensemble of glittering silver brocade with only a darkly embroidered waistcoat to add a sombre note. John Rawlings thought, as he looked round the company, that it was one of the best-dressed marriages he had ever attended, and that his lovely bride looked more like an angel than ever in her bridal array.

The young couple had set forth the next morning, following in the wake of the Exeter Stage, which left from the Gloucester Coffee House in Piccadilly. They had rested at Thatcham and the next night at Marlborough, then on to Bath, where they had lingered a day or two taking the waters. After that they had stayed at Taunton, then made their way to Cullompton, and now they were departing from Exeter, their destination the bustling port of Topsham where John had a mind to look at the great ships of the world and watch their exotic cargoes being unloaded.

He breathed in once more, filling his lungs with salt air.

"You're sniffing," said Emilia from within the confines of the coach.

"Come and sniff with me. This air is so good for you."

"It's certainly like wine. I don't think I have ever slept so well in my life."

"That's because you are married to me," John answered, to which Emilia instantly responded, "Don't be pompous," and the Apothecary, just for a heart-wrenching moment thought of Coralie Clive, his love of many years, who would certainly have replied exactly as his bride had just done.

If Emilia noticed the small silence, she said nothing, and continued to stare out of the carriage window, watching as Topsham appeared in the distance, a forest of masts lining its thronging quay.

"Where to now, Sir?" called Irish Tom from the coachman's box.

"The Globe or The Salutation. Whichever we like the look of."

"Very good, Mr. Rawlings," the Irishman answered, then slowed down as a toll gate came into sight, its little house standing by the roadside, the only attendant a small girl of about eight years old.

"Where's your pa?" shouted Tom in his broad Irish brogue.

The child answered in an incomprehensible drawl of long aahs.

"What's that you say?"

John put his head out of the window again. "She's speaking with a Devon accent, Tom. Just pay her and let's be on our way."

"All very foine, Sir. But I don't know how much."

"Let me have a try."

Eventually, with Emilia's help, it was discovered that the toll was two pennies, somewhat expensive in John's view, and the carriage passed through and into the town.

"Well?" said the Apothecary, watching the expressions of delight that crossed his wife's face.

"It's wonderful. So lively. Why, John, there are even persons of good fashion here."

He laughed indulgently. "Then it will suit you?"

"Very much so. I think perhaps we should stay several days."

"It would certainly make an ideal base from which to see the surrounding countryside."

"Then you can look at the ships and I the shops."

"Women!" said the Apothecary, and laughed again, delighting in her company.

"The Salutation is on our right, Sir," called Irish Tom. "Do you want to stop?"

Gazing at the huge studded door, complete with small wicket, dating from at least two hundred years earlier, John felt instantly drawn to the place.

"The Salutation it is," he shouted back, and the equipage swept beneath the arch, over the cobbles and into the stable yard.

An hour later all was arranged. The newlyweds had booked a fine bedroom at the back of the inn, over-looking the River Exe, and had set out to perambulate before the hour to dine. As it was a Saturday and early afternoon there was a lively market in the town, and the Apothecary was greatly impressed with the array of meats, poultry and other fowl, the mounds of cheeses, butter and fruits, to say nothing of the quantities of cider, beer and wines and spirits on offer. Emilia, on the other hand, was more interested in the laces and gloves, the ribbons, frills and furbelows, and with a man owning a small, sad-faced performing monkey, dressed in a fez and waistcoat.

"Oh look at the poor creature. See it capering to the music. I'm sure it is not happy."

"It is perfectly happy," John answered firmly. "It is well fed and well cared for."

"But look at its eyes. Surely it is not natural for it to dance so."

"It loves it. Monkeys are born comedians."

"Should I offer to buy it off him?"

"Most certainly not. What would we do with a monkey on our honeymoon?"

"It could ride beside Irish Tom."

"Emilia, stop it," said John. "It would be cruel to take it away from its master, believe me. You're not going to try and adopt every sad-looking creature you come across, are you?"

"I married you, didn't I?"

"You impudent young woman!"

But it was love play and they kissed one another, lightly, then continued their perambulation, going towards the river.

It was a marvellous place, the great waterway sniffing the breath of the sea, and stirring its heart because of it. John gazed with enthusiasm at the slipways, docks and yards and at all the warehouses and workshops associated with the river. Sweet perfumes rose from the brandy distillery, the astringent smell of salt from the works on the marshes. Close by loomed a windmill grinding corn for export. And everywhere were moored ships, some with exotic foreign names, others from closer at home, their port of origin painted upon them. The *Violet* of Topsham, *Two Sisters* of Swansea, *Nightingale* of Lymington, *Friends Adventure* from Bridlington.

"Marvellous!" said the Apothecary appreciatively.

"Oh look, there's one from the Colonies," answered Emilia, pointing.

"Hope, Carolina," read John aloud.

"And one from Oporto, the *Charming Molly.*"

"Packed with wine, no doubt."

"Not a very suitable name really."

"What would you suggest?"

"The Drunken Portugese," his bride answered, and pealed with laughter at her own joke.

Once again, John was silent, thinking how similar yet how different were the two women he loved. Yet even as he considered it he recalled that the past tense now applied to Coralie Clive, that beautiful, ambitious actress who had turned him down rather than lose her chance of becoming truly celebrated in her profession. Very quietly, he sighed. His charming bride had everything a man could desire: glorious looks and a delightful personality to go with them. So how was it possible that he could even spare a thought for Coralie?

Old habits die hard, he decided to himself, and with deliberation turned his mind to his new wife and the task of concentrating solely on her.

They had left behind the crowded quays and were now walking through a residential area where gracious houses overlooked the water. One in particular caught John's eye. Older than the rest, it had a charming front door, a shell made of plasterwork creating a hood above.

"Look at that," he said to Emilia.

"How attractive it ..."

But she got no further, for the door suddenly flung open and a girl appeared in the opening, a girl with no covering on her head and her hair hanging in what John could only think of as a cloud of gold. Emilia's hair was beautiful, rich and colourful as ripe corn, but this young woman's looked as if it had been spun from silk. Without meaning to be rude, both the Apothecary and his bride stopped to stare at her.

Almost furtively, the girl glanced up and down the street, then she looked across at the young couple. Clearly relieved that they were strangers, she took a step outside and then from the interior of the house a voice called out.

"Juliana, where are you?"

The girl did not hesitate. She ran like a gazelle towards the quays, not looking back over her shoulder, and disappeared from sight as swiftly as she had come into it. John and Emilia turned to gaze at one another but before either of them could say a word, a man strode into the open doorway.

He was a Dutchman, of that the Apothecary felt certain. Tall, well set up and very fair, he had the traditional looks associated with that country. Though his head of flaxen hair was tinged with grey, there was a similarity between him and the girl which made John Rawlings fairly sure that he was looking at her father.

The Dutchman took a step into the street. "Juliana," he called again. Then he looked across at the two strangers. "Have you seen a young woman?" he asked abruptly.

He was Dutch all right, thought John. The slightly guttural accent confirmed his suspicions.

The Apothecary hesitated. There had been something about the girl's plunging flight that had made him feel she had vital tasks to perform, that she was in trouble of some kind and was hell-bent on sorting it out. "Yes, Sir," he answered, at the same time taking hold of Emilia's elbow and putting the very slightest of presures upon it.

"Did you see where she went?"

"Off into the back streets, I believe. I must confess, Sir, that I wasn't paying full attention. Were you, my love?" He turned to his wife and raised one of his mobile eyebrows.

"No," she answered neatly. "I was staring at the river and the flight of the gulls."

"How poetically put," said John under his breath, and grinned at her. Emilia lowered her eyes demurely.

"Huh," snarled the Dutchman and went back inside, slamming the door loudly behind him.

"Dear me!" remarked the Apothecary, pulling a face.

"I think there's great bad feeling there. Shall we move on?"

But before they could take a step, the door opened again and the Dutchman reappeared, this time looking decidedly contrite. He crossed the pathway in a couple of strides and stood bowing before them.

"Forgive my lack of courtesy, Madam. Allow me to introduce myself, I am Jan van Guylder. I am afraid that I suffer with a wilful daughter and tend to forget the niceties in my efforts to control her. Am I forgiven?"

Despite the fact that he mut be in his fifties, his eyes were the clear bright blue of delftware and John saw Emilia melt, though he personally reserved judgement.

She dropped a deep curtsey. "There is no need to apologise, Sir. I am sure that we all suffer family difficulties from time to time."

John hid a smile and bowed. "John Rawlings, Mr. van Guylder. And this is my wife, Emilia."

The Dutchman bowed again. "You are visiting Topsham for the first time? I do not recall having seen you in the town."

"We only arrived today. We are here on holiday and staying in The Salutation."

"Then please allow me the honour of inviting you to dine. I am a Topsham man by adoption and we are known for our hospitality."

But there's something else, thought John. This man has a desperate need to talk to someone.

Curiosity aroused, he was just about to accept, then remembered that he was married and that there was somebody else who must now be consulted. He turned to Emilia. "My dear?"

But she was clearly as inquisitive as he was. Dropping another curtsey, she gave a delightful smile. "My husband and I would be pleased to take up your invitation, Sir."

"Then shall we say tomorrow at about this hour. We country people tend to eat much earlier than you town folk."

"How did you know that?" asked John.

"That you were from the city? Because of the cut of your clothes, Sir. There is no more mistaking a suit made in London than there is one made in Amsterdam." He fingered his own rather dreary garb. "Local tailor, alas."

"But surely in Exeter there must be some fine fitters. We noticed several fashionable folk when we stayed there."

A slightly odd expression crossed van Guylder's face. "I never linger long in Exeter. I go in on ..." He hesitated very slightly, "... business, then come straight out again. I am a merchant and a mariner and Topsham is my home port." He did not explain further. "However, tomorrow I shall wear some Dutch clothes and see how you like them, for I can tell by your own array that you are a connoisseur of style, Sir."

John bowed his head in acknowledgement. "Then we await the meeting with pleasure."

So saying, the three exchanged salutations and parted company.

"What do you make of that?" asked the Apothecary as soon as they were out of earshot.

"I think that he is frightened."

John gazed at his wife in astonishment. "What a curious word to use. Do you mean it literally?"

"Not in fear for his life, no. But he is very afraid. Do you think it is for his daughter? Do you believe that she has fallen in with bad company?"

The new husband held his bride at arm's length. "What an acute little creature you are. I would never have credited you with being so observant."

"I don't know whether to be flattered or insulted."

"Be neither. Just let me kiss you."

So she did, several times, there in the April afternoon, before she and John continued their walk along The Strand.

At the end of the pathway lay a vast expanse of water, the meeting of two rivers at high tide, the confluence heading out for the open sea and finding it at Exmouth. At low tide there was nothing but mud flats, the Exe reduced to a narrow channel, but seen like this the sight was inspiring.

"What's this place called?"

"Riversmeet. Where the Exe and the Clyst find one another," John answered.

"Rather a romantic thought, two rivers conjoining."

"Yes, I suppose it is."

"Is that a bowling green over there?"

"Yes. I can't think of a more picturesque location, can you? I must have a game before we go."

"And I must see the show put on by the Company of Comedians. I noticed a poster advertising it as we drove in."

John hugged her to him. "Are you enjoying your honeymoon?"

"Yes, let's hope nothing happens to interrupt it."

"What do you mean?"

Emilia looked vague. "Oh, I don't know. It's just that trouble seems to follow you about, John."

The Apothecary laughed scornfully. "Not on honeymoon, it doesn't."

His bride put her finger to his lips. "Don't tempt fate, my darling. One simply never knows what is going to happen next."

Though the exterior of Shell House, Jan van Guylder's home, was obviously sixteenth century, much modernisation had taken place within. Small rooms had been knocked into several large ones and low ceilings had been raised, that of the drawing room adorned by an enriched oval from which hung a magnificent chandelier. Blue delftware tiles from Holland lined the fireplace, which was surrounded by a carved wooden frame, while in the corner was a newly built and extremely elegant wig cupboard. A moulded cherub's head adorned the arch leading into the dining room and similarly that above the stairs. Yet in the midst of all this fashionable comfort there was no sign of a Mrs. van Guylder; in fact the Dutchman greeted his guests alone. After a while John's curiosity got the better of him and he asked the inevitable question.

"Do you live here just with your daughter, Sir?"

Van Guylder shook his head. "No, I also have a son. He is studying at the Grammar School in Exeter. He boards there but comes home to attend divine service in Topsham every Sunday, so you will meet him."

"And Mrs. van Guylder?" asked Emilia.

"Dead, alas. We had a third child, another boy, but my wife was not strong and neither of them survived the birth. She was English, you know. A member of the Gibbs family. I met her through their trading contacts with Holland and decided to settle in Devon. I believe that my daughter's erratic behaviour can be linked directly to the early loss of her mother."

Emilia nodded sympathetically. "I am sure you are right. It is not easy for a man to bring up a girl single-handedly, particularly as she has no sisters."

Jan looked apologetic. "I begged her to join us this evening, thinking different company might enliven her, but she pleads the headache and asks that you will forgive her."

"Of course," said John. He put on his helpful face from the range of expressions that he found he could these days summon up at a moment's notice. "Would you care for me to go and see her, Sir? I am an apothecary by trade and perhaps could prescribe something."

The Dutchman slowly shook his head. "I don't think she would agree. She has already refused a visit from our physician who is an old friend of the family. I doubt very much that she would see a stranger."

"As she wishes, naturally."

"But I do thank you for the offer. I only say no because I know how difficult she can be."

"Indeed," said John, and a notion came to him which firmly took root.

The door opened and a youth of about sixteen

came into the room, pausing in the doorway as he saw the guests, then gazing open-mouthed at Emilia.

Van Guylder got to his feet, announcing, "My son Richard." The boy bowed, his pimply face flushing as he did so. The Dutchman turned to Emilia. "Madam, *may* I present him to you?"

She inclined her head. "Of course."

His father made the appropriate introduction while Richard bowed and flushed more than ever. At Emilia's husband, however, he shot a look of curiosity tinged with something that John thought of as unease. Coming to the conclusion that the entire family was somewhat odd, the Apothecary made small talk until dinner was served.

It was just as they were going in to dine that the unexpected happened. A flustered-looking maid servant appeared and breathlessly informed van Guylder that Miss Juliana was much recovered and would be joining them after all. Swiftly ordering another place to be laid, the Dutchman led the way in, his face grim and set.

She timed her entrance well, waiting until everybody was seated then hovering a moment before making her way to the foot of the table, opposite her father. In the gleam of candlelight the silver-gilt hair shone as if it had a life of its own and John saw Emilia straighten her shoulders as she realised that a beauty to rival hers had come into the room. In fact they were not unalike, both fair-headed and small, with exquisite little faces. But whereas Emilia glowed with newly-married contentment, a smile never far away from her lips, Juliana was molten with secret thoughts, her eyes shuttered lest she should reveal their hidden mysteries, her mouth petulant but provocative. Looking at her, John felt certain that his theory was correct.

"I am glad that you have recovered from the headache, Madam," he ventured. "I make quite a study of that particular complaint."

She shot him an uninterested glance. "Oh really."

"I am an apothecary," John persisted, "and over the years have observed the manner in which my horde of different patients have been afflicted by certain illnesses. From this I drew the conclusion that some ailments, headaches in particular, can be caused by many things. In other words, people are subjected to them for various reasons."

"I would have thought as much," she answered acidly.

Jan shot her a reproving glance. "I, too, have suffered from them recently and in my case the malaise is brought about by worry."

"Certainly one of the causes," John answered pleasantly.

"What are the others?" asked Richard.

The Apothecary shrugged a fashionable shoulder. "There are so many. Tension, eye strain, a surfeit of wine, general debility, to name but a few."

"I get them at school," the spotty boy replied thoughtfully. "I reckon that would be too much studying. Indeed I shall be glad to get out of the academic place and on to Oxford."

Emilia laughed. "Surely that will be equally academic."

"But at least I'll be treated as a scholar and not some grubby little inker."

She laughed again, much amused, and Richard looked suitably gratified.

His sister bent her head toward him, her hair glistening. "Won't you miss all your friends?"

It was an innocent enough remark but he paused, his fork arrested on its journey to his mouth. "What do you mean?" he said thickly.

Juliana smiled. "Simply that. Won't you miss your friends?"

"Yes," Richard answered, filled his mouth, swallowed, then gulped noisily.

What a curious exchange, thought John.

Van Guylder clearly felt the need to explain. "The Grammar School is very good, you know, even though Richard complains of hard work. It was founded in the reign of Charles I for the instruction of the sons of freemen. Now, however, it caters for the offspring of the middle classes. Nonetheless, younger boys from the aristocracy appear there from time to time and I must say that Richard has got in with a very good social set. He is invited to some splendid homes. He has even been to stay with the Rolles."

Emilia looked blank and Juliana, over-sweetly, said, "A very prominent family. John Rolle has been a Member of Parliament for Exeter."

"How fortunate for you," came the equally sweet reply, "that your brother moves in such circles. That must open many doors for you too, Miss van Guylder."

Richard rushed in with all the naivety of youth. "My friends call Juliana, 'the Belle'."

"How lovely," said Emilia, smiling sugar.

To say, thought John, surveying them, that this was a family not at ease with itself was understating the case. Tensions and hidden thoughts bubbled just beneath the surface, particularly emanating from the complex Juliana, whom he had already marked down as a bitch with a secret. So it was a relief when the two ladies retired and he was left alone with the Dutchman and his son. Port was passed and an odd kind of peace descended beneath the blue clouds of good Dutch tobacco smoked in long pipes made in Topsham, the bowls decorated with marguerites, the motif of the town's patron saint, Margaret.

"Juliana is very beautiful," said John, speaking his thoughts aloud.

"Too much so for her own good," Jan answered gloomily.

"How can anyone be too beautiful?" said Richard, sounding just fractionally drunk. "That remark is nonsensical, Father."

"If I may say, you know nothing about it, boy. You are still a child in the ways of the world and if you are going to speak to me so, I would suggest you go to your room and stay there."

His son rose to his feet, his face pale, his pimples on fire. "I know a great deal more about the world than you imagine, Sir. But I shall do as you wish and leave the company. Good night to you, Mr. Rawlings." Richard turned in the doorway. "One day you'll find out just how much I understand about society, my dear father. And I look forward to you doing so."

So saying, he was gone, leaving John to gaze at his host in rather an embarrassed silence.

"I did not enjoy that occasion," said Emilia, stretching out beside her husband in the fresh white linen of their bed in The Salutation. "I thought it was most rude of them to argue like that in front of us."

"It was certainly very difficult for the guests, though the three of 'em didn't so much disagree as make digs at one another. I pity poor van Guylder his situation, I truly do."

"He should enforce greater discipline," Emilia stated firmly. "That girl needs putting in her place."

"I still think she is a victim of circumstance. It can't have been easy to lose her mother so young."

"I suppose you'll be sorry for that silly, spotty boy next."

"Of course I am. He's clearly in with a crowd of demi-rips and choice spirits who are most likely leading him astray. He's probably struggling to keep up with them."

"You're so tolerant," said Emilia with a note of exasperation. "Don't you ever get cross with any-one?"

"Frequently," answered John, and thought of Coralie Clive and how enormously angry he had been with her.

"But not with me?"

"No, not with you."

"Do you love me?"

"Of course I do," he answered and snuggled down beside her in the bed to show her just how much.

Chapter 2

Why John woke quite so punishingly early the next morning he didn't at first understand. Then he realised that he had not slept deeply but had spent most of the night considering the problems of the van Guylders and worrying about how their situation would resolve. For after Richard had left the room his father had truly opened his heart, relating such a tale of sadly failed relationships that John had felt himself at a loss as to what to say that did not sound trite. His instinct that van Guylder badly needed to talk had proved absolutely right. The man clearly longed for the advice of someone outside not only the family circle but also the busybody grapevine of Topsham. And it had been the Apothecary's fate, for better or worse, that he had been the one.

Glancing at his watch, John saw that it was still only half-past five and though there was light in the sky, dawn had not yet broken. Beside him, sweetly serene, Emilia slumbered peacefully, but he was too wide awake to contemplate further sleep. Moving quietly so as not to disturb her, John carefully got out of bed and dressed as best he could in the fitful light. Then opening the bedroom door just enough to slip through, he closed it silently behind him.

The inn's servants were already up and at their tasks but despite the tempting smells emanating from the kitchen, the Apothecary decided to have breakfast with his wife and work up an even greater appetite by walking along the riverbank for half an hour. Consequently he wrapped himself in an enveloping cloak, for it was a sharp morning, put his hat on his head and, turning out of the hostelry, made his way to the quays.

It may have been early but the riverside was already swarming with people. Great ships had come in during the night and now that there was enough light to see, the unloading of their cargoes had begun. Holds stood open and hoists lifted out bundles and barrels and crates which were caught by the brawny-armed dockworkers and carried ashore. In the midst of this activity a coach plied for hire beside a notice reading Topsham to Exeter Return, Runs Twelve Times a Day, One Shilling. Some early travellers were already getting aboard and the Apothecary could not help but glimpse Richard van Guylder, soberly dressed and clearly heading for school before lessons began. However he had not expected to see the beautiful Juliana abroad at this daunting hour. But there she was, being helped into the coach by her brother, clad in a black velvet cloak, pale as a wraith inside its dark folds. Her skin seemed drained, transparent almost, and the expression on her face was so devoid of animation, so lifeless, that she seemed as if she were on the point of death. Judging by her appearance, there could be little doubt that some sort of malaise affected the girl. Desperately concerned for her, John stepped forward.

"Miss Juliana, Richard, good morning."

They both jumped and shot him the most guilty of glances and the Apothecary realised that he should have left them alone, that Juliana was probably going to Exeter without her father's knowledge and the last thing she wanted was to run into someone she knew.

"Good morning," Richard answered sullenly, but though her lips moved Juliana did not utter a word.

John attempted to cover his gaffe. "Just taking the air early, though I must be getting back. My wife will be wondering where I am."

The boy managed a half smile. "Do send her my regards, Sir."

The Apothecary decided to do what he had originally intended. Producing a card from an inner pocket he handed it to Juliana. "If you should ever suffer with the headache or any other condition, please don't hesitate to contact me. I can deal by post and you are probably bored to sobs with all the local apothecaries."

She met his eye and a slight flush came into her ashen cheeks, but her words were forceful enough. "If ever I need you I'll let you know," she said, and taking the card dropped it into the reticule that hung over her wrist.

Richard frowned at this but before he could say a word the coachman consulted his watch and called out loudly, "Any more, if you please? We leave punctually in one minute."

"*Bon voyage*," said John, and raising his hat, bowed a farewell. His last sight of Juliana was looking back at him through the coach's small rear window, her expression restored to its usual cat-like secrecy, as the carriage moved off to Exeter.

"Where shall we go today?" asked Emilia, spreading marmalade upon a thin slice of toast.

John, who was tackling a mound of ham and eggs, indicated that his mouth was full and that he could not speak for a moment or two. Then he said, "Down at the harbour some old sea dog told me that a spell of unseasonably hot weather is coming."

"I thought it felt rather cold."

"So it does, but he explained all that. He said the wind had changed to the north but that it was about to veer westward again, bringing warm weather from the Scilly Isles which, according to him, have been baking hot for the last few days."

"He was romancing."

"On the contrary. He seemed to know exactly what he was talking about. The *Daisy* had just come in from Tresco and the crew had told him all about it. He said they were practically black with tan. So, my darling, in view of this I would like to take the opportunity to swim in the sea, it now being the consensus that sea water is as beneficial to the health as that of a spa."

"You're interested in the properties of water, aren't you?"

"Did I tell you that?"

"No, Samuel did. He said you experiment with putting bubbles into drinking water."

"I have done in the past, though I still can't get it right. I thought I might build myself a little laboratory in Kensington and try again."

Emilia smiled. "I can just see you surrounded by gurgling alembics like a magician of ancient legend."

"Merlin, perhaps?"

She considered. "Grow a beard and one could hardly tell the difference."

"You are a very rude young woman. Now, can you swim?"

"Yes. My brothers threw me into the river when I was very young. It was that or drowning."

"Then we shall take to the ocean together."

Emilia shivered. "Not if it's as cold as this."

"Wait and see. These old salts always know what's going to happen."

"I hope so. I wouldn't like to see you die of a chill."

"I wouldn't relish it much either, come to that."

For some reason John had decided not to tell Emilia about his early morning encounter with Juliana and Richard. Despite the girl's sarcastic manner, he felt that the Dutchman's daughter bore a secret and was perhaps involved in something she could not control, so should be pitied rather than disliked. But aware of his bride's antipathy, the Apothecary chose to keep the latest news to himself and was glad that the present conversation was merely banter. He decided to continue it that way, at least for the time being.

"So where are we going?" Emilia was asking.

"The sea dog told me that Sidmouth was a fine place for bathing and had recently started to become popular with genteel folk."

"Well that won't suit you," his wife commented, roaring with laughter.

"What do you mean?"

"That never in my entire life have I ever met anyone less genteel than yourself."

"I shall take that as the greatest compliment you have ever paid me," John replied with dignity. "Now, my dear, hurry up and pack your things. I want to see this miracle of the changing weather for myself."

An hour later they were on the road, having kept their room at The Salutation open for another few days by paying the bill in advance. Irish Tom, who had been enjoying himself in his own way while his master was out and about, seemed in suspiciously good humour and whistled up on the coachman's box, causing John to wonder whether there was a house of pleasure situated in one of Topsham's back streets.

"Where to now, Sir?"

"To Sidmouth. I think we'll have to go inland, more's the pity. In fact it might spare the horses if we went through Exeter."

And so they did, proceeding out of the city on one of the coaching roads to the West, passing a hostelry named the Half Way House, supposedly because it was halfway between London and Falmouth, then travelling several miles further on before they turned down a somewhat evil track and headed towards the sea.

"There," said John, "I told you."

"What?"

"The wind's changed, can't you feel it?"

"Yes," said Emilia, "I can. Oh let's get out for a

moment, John. I'd love my first glimpse of the sea to be on foot."

The Apothecary thumped on the coach's roof with his great stick. "Stop a minute, Tom. We're going to walk for a while."

So it was that they rounded a bend in the track, strolling hand in hand, and saw, gleaming like silver in the sun, a distant dazzling flash of argent.

"It's glittering," said Emilia.

"Wait till you get closer," her husband answered, putting his arm round her shoulders.

They proceeded on slowly, watching the landscape change, seeing it grow more beautiful by the minute as they went downwards into a tranquil valley. Great cliffs cradled the curving bay in their arms, while whitish sands on which several fishing boats had been drawn up, led down to the sea itself. Emilia drew to a halt, turning to her left, gazing in wonderment at the rugged cliff.

"It's red!" she said.

"Like the soil of Devon. Haven't you noticed? In places the earth is the same shade as terracotta."

"I've never seen anything like it before."

"But look how green the grass is above."

"And how peacefully that river flows into the sea."

They stared at where the Sid, meandering gently past a large rock, met the ocean in a flurry of foaming waves, bounding on top of which were a colony of gulls, their powerful wings as white as the spume beneath.

Together the couple turned in the other direction

and exclaimed. For beyond the mighty cliffs which enclosed the cove on the other side, a promonotory of land, capped by fine green meadows, stuck out as a final defence against the world.

Irish Tom who had been plodding the coach along behind them, let out a shout. "B'Jesus, I haven't seen anything like this since I left Connemara."

John looked up at him. "There's a tiny little village down there, Tom. Let's go and find a place to stay."

"I hope there is somewhere," said Emilia anxiously.

"There's always an inn," the Apothecary answered confidently. And taking her by the hand again, led her down to where some small cottages and a church nestled beyond the beach.

It was a spot made in heaven, there was no doubting that. With the weather seeming to get warmer with every step they took, John and Emilia made their way up the path towards the church, round which were grouped several buildings. And there, sure enough, was a tavern, The Ship. "Just as I thought," said the Apothecary.

"I'm sure there is no accommodation."

"There is only one way to find out. We will go in and ask."

It was not the most desirable of hostelries at which he had ever stayed but John and his bride were shown into a clean, serviceable room with basic furniture and a large bed. He turned to Emilia.

"Will it do?"

"I think it will be most romantic. Listen, you can hear the sea."

The Apothecary turned to the landlord. "Is this fine weather going to last?"

"They reckon it's here for a week or so."

"Then I think I'll go bathing."

"Very healthy, Sir. Folks are starting to stay here just to dip in the ocean. But wait till tomorrow. Give the water a chance to warm up."

"Very sound advice," said Emilia, who clearly did not relish the idea of swimming in chilly conditions.

"I'll heed it," answered John, but for all that removed his flannel bathing drawers from his bag and hung them over the back of a chair.

Emilia made rude remarks about their voluminous size, then went downstairs with her husband to settle Tom in a cottage across the way and the horses in a nearby stable.

They did little after that, strolling up the cliff path, sitting on a canvas sheet and watching the great ships heading for Topsham and Exeter through John's telescope. They saw the tide come in, so far that the sand vanished and only a strip of shingle remained visible. Then, as the sun began to dip in the sky, the fishing fleet returned to shore, heavy with their catch which gleamed silver in the brightness.

"A perfect day," said Emilia, getting to her feet.

John put out a hand for her to help him and was just about to answer that there was no sign of the trouble which she claimed stalked him, when something stopped him doing so. A frisson at his spine, a sensation that he had experienced before in his life, suddenly alerted him to the possibility that somewhere, somehow, all was not well. A vision of

Juliana van Guylder's pale, furtive face came vividly into the Apothecary's mind and for a moment or two he just sat silently where he was, waiting till the illusion was gone. Fortunately Emilia noticed nothing, whirling about on the cliff tops like a dancer.

"I shall remember this day as long as I live," she said joyfully, but even that happy statement brought John no comfort.

Again he woke early and was instantly restless. It was the dark hour before dawn and, as he had on the previous day, the Apothecary rose silently and went down to the beach. The fishermen were setting out, splashing off into the darkness, taking advantage of the tide. He could hear their voices conversing in low tones and envied them their day at sea, men alone with the elements. Not, he thought, that those would be giving them much trouble today. The water was as flat and calm as the proverbial millpond and there seemed not a breath of wind anywhere. The small sails would be hard put to it to pick up any breeze and John imagined that the oars, kept for emergencies, might be forced into greater use than usual.

"Good luck," he called out, he didn't know why. But nobody heard him, the only reply a distant murmur as the fishermen called to one another from smack to smack.

The same odd mood was still upon him and John had to make a conscious effort to shake it off and not spoil Emilia's enjoyment. For she was up and dressed and clearly ready for adventure when he joined her at the hearty but basic breakfast table.

"Shall we take a repast to the beach?" she asked, looking delightful in cool muslin.

"If we do am I allowed to swim? Or will you act like a mother hen and make remarks about catching cold?"

She looked contrite. "Is that what I'm like? An old broody?"

"Just."

"How can you be so cruel?"

But she was laughing and John thought that he had never seen her look so well or so happy. Despite the fact that she protected her angel's face beneath a shady hat, yesterday's sunshine had penetrated the barrier and there was a becoming glow about her skin. He took Emilia's hand.

"I'm making it up. You look absolutely lovely," he said.

"More beautiful than Juliana van Guylder?"

"Why do you say that?"

"Because I noticed you observing her at dinner the other afternoon."

"Emilia, I *am* an observer," he answered. "Mr. John Fielding taught me how to be one, though even before I met him I was very taken with the art of scrutiny. I was looking at Juliana and thinking that here was a great beauty marred by some inner unrest. There is a woeful secret in the background of that girl's life."

"I thought her rude and bumptious."

"I know you did. But take my word for it, there is a reason for her acting the way she does."

"I'll take your word," Emilia answered slowly. "But I'm afraid I am yet to be convinced."

But they could not argue, nor even discuss, on such a day as this. As they stepped outside they saw that the sea and the sky had met one another in a great arc of blue, making it almost impossible to locate the horizon. It seemed that hardly a ripple disturbed the vast expanse of water thay lay before them.

"It's like being inside a bowl," said Emilia as they walked down to the beach, Tom in front of them carrying a basket of bread, cheese and apples, stored throughout the winter in some sweet-smelling loft.

"A bowl called paradise," John answered poetically.

Indeed it was as if they were alone in some seashore Garden of Eden. No one else walked the sands and as far as the eye could see not another human being stirred.

Catching the mood, Irish Tom said, "I'll be off, Sir, to do a little sunbathing meself, that is if you have no further need of me. But should you do so I'll be round the bend in the cliffs."

And he set off, walking barefoot through the shallows, the sun gleaming on his copper head and large frame, looking every inch a latter day Brian Boramha, the great Irish chieftan come back to life.

"Swimming," said the Apothecary, and stripped off his clothes, feeling the sun warm on his skin. Then he ran into the sea and swam naked, luxuriating in the sense of freedom this gave him. If he had been with Coralie, John thought, she would have joined him, rushing into the waves beside him, tumbling and turning in the surf, as bare as himself. But though Emilia did follow him into the water she was clad in long drawers and a flowing chemise.

Even as he compared the two women, the Apothecary felt guilty, sick with himself for doing such a thing. It was cruel to his bride to liken her to the woman whom he had both loved and lost.

"I must never do it again," he said aloud to the tranquil sea, and turned to see that Emilia was swimming towards him. He swam back to make sure that she did not go out of her depth, then took her hand, pointing to the far reaches.

"See, there's more wind out there."

"Is it blowing from the west?"

"It must be. It's still so warm."

"Can we stay here as long as the weather holds?"

But John did not answer, his attention caught by something else. Very faintly, almost as if it were an illusion brought about by the water in his ears, he caught the faint sound of voices.

He turned to his wife. "Can you hear anything?"

She stood listening, the sea covering her breasts, the chemise she wore clinging to them transparently. "No, I don't think so."

But there *was* something, John heard it again, blown inshore by the breeze.

"I must get my telescope."

"But you've got nothing on."

"Neither have you - much."

And he gave her a loving squeeze to make the point, then swam back towards the shore, scrambling

to his feet in the surf and heading for where their
basket sat neatly on a groundsheet. Rummaging in
its depth, John found what he was looking for and
put it to his eye, training the instrument towards the
horizon. Sure enough, two fishing boats were coming into sight, immediately behind them a much
larger ship, a square-sailed schooner under full canvas. The Apothecary adjusted the lens to maximum
strength and saw that the two smaller vessels had
tow ropes leading from them, each fastened on
either side of the schooner's prow. The smacks were
bringing the larger vessel into shallow waters, rowing for all they were worth and straining with the
effort. Of the crew of the schooner there was no sign,
the decks clearly empty and devoid of life except for
the helmsman who John recognised as one of the
locals gone aboard to steer her.

Certain that something was wrong, the Apothecary
threw on his clothes, shouting to Emilia to get out of
the water. But she was already hastening through the
waves. The sight of that size of vessel coming so close
in shore was somehow both menacing and sinister,
and the poor girl was acting as if it were coming
straight for her. She ran into her bridegroom's arms.

"What's happened? Why are they towing it in?
Has there been an accident?"

"I imagine so. Dress quickly. We might have to
help."

So saying, he ran to the water's edge as the first of
the fishermen jumped into the shallows and started
to secure their smack, followed closely by the crew
of the other.

"What's going on?" John asked.

The man turned a taciturn face. "That's what we'd like to know."

"What do you mean?"

"The bastard ship nearly ran us down, came within a few inches. We only saved ourselves by rowing out of its path and by Christ that nearly killed us. Anyway, there's no one aboard. We hailed her, then went alongside and got a rope on a grapple to her. Jeb shimmied up it, but called out that he couldn't find no one, so I went up after him. It was true enough. The whole great hulk was empty yet there was every sign of life. Clothes in the cabins, even a pot of tea warm on the table. I tell you, guv'nor, it fair scared the shite out of me."

"What are you going to do?"

"Anchor her up, then send for the quay master from Topsham. She was probably bound for there so he'll know who the owners are."

"Can I help at all? I'm an apothecary and if anyone is lying wounded I could assist them."

"But there's no devil on there."

"Did you search thoroughly?"

"As best I could, yes." The fisherman eyed John up and down. "Anyway another pair of hands wouldn't come amiss. Can you climb a rope?"

"I haven't done so for some years."

"Well you'll have to if you want to get aboard."

It was one of the most perilous ventures the Apothecary had ever undertaken. Shoes and shirt had to be shed on the beach prior to swimming out to the schooner, whose draught demanded that she

stayed in fairly deep water. Having got out to the
bobbing vessel, the next hurdle was to grab the end
of the rope, which rose and fell with the motion of
the ship, then somehow to heave oneself out of the
water and clamber up it. Puffing and panting and
feeling like some decrepit ancient, John finally managed to reach the top and, grasping the ship's rail,
haul himself over, realising as he did so that his
palms were rubbed raw. A moment or two later he
was joined by three of the others, all come aboard to
get the ship's anchor down.

The man who had first spoken to John now
issued orders. "Let's turn the capstan, lads. You, Sir,
you search the ship. Jeb, who's been steering her, can
help."

It was the silence, John decided, that was so eerie.
Walking through the cabins there was indeed every
sign of recent occupation, and in the dining area
places were set for a meal. The teapot which stood
nearby was by now almost cold, yet by touching it
the Apothecary could feel that it had only lost heat a
short while ago. Cups were out, as was a jug of milk
and a loaf of bread, and there was even some cheese,
rather hard but edible. Yet no voice spoke, nobody
called out, the only sound the lapping of the waves
and the seductive west wind playing in the great
canvas sails. With his spine crawling with fear, John
was glad to get back on deck.

In the distance he could see Jeb searching the
stern, on his hands and knees in order not to miss
anything, while the other three men were heaving
round the capstan with much rattling of heavy chain.

John went to the prow, complete with its mermaid figurehead, to hunt there. Then suddenly he stopped dead in his tracks, his heart beating fast. For the carving of the mergirl was so fine that it seemed to him, just for a moment, that it had a veil of spun gold hair hanging down, blowing in the capricious breeze. Then his brain caught up with his eyes and he realised that no figurehead, however intricately exectuted, could possibly give such an illusion. That there was in fact somebody there.

"Who's that?" he called out, not loudly but fearfully.

Nobody answered and John took a step forward. The curtain of hair was streaming outwards like silver gilt, like silk, like that of someone he had seen only too recently.

"Juliana?" he said, his voice only just above a whisper.

She did not move to reply to him and every alarm bell in Christendom sounded in the Apothecary's brain. Running forward he saw that she lay, face downwards, draped over the figurehead, her arms hanging down on either side of it, the movement of the ship giving them a life they did not possess as they swayed gently, the hands totally relaxed.

"God almighty," said John, and raising Juliana by the shoulders, stared into her face. She looked asleep, despite the terrible bruising and cuts she had sustained and the blood that had dried round her mouth, yet this was a sleep that surely was the deepest of them all. Gently, the Apothecary put his head to her heart - but there was only silence. Very carefully, he laid the shift-clad corpse back as he had found it, swiftly kissing Juliana's brow before turning her face down. Then he walked round to where the fishermen had just succeeded in dropping anchor.

"I am sorry to tell you that there is someone aboard," he said grimly.

They stared at him. "What do you mean?"

"Just that. There's a girl lying on the figurehead."

"What's she doing there?"

"Nothing," John answered sternly.

They gaped at him, open-mouthed, clearly not comprehending a word he was saying.

"Who is she?" one of them asked eventually.

"Her name is Juliana van Guylder," the Apothecary replied slowly, "and I regret to have to inform you that she is quite, quite dead."

Chapter 3

Rather than return down the perilously swaying rope, John decided to dive from the schooner's rail, a daunting prospect in itself but quite certainly the lesser of the two evils. In this way he swam ashore to find Emilia, now accompanied by Irish Tom, waiting for him with obvious anticipation.

"John, is that ship deserted?" his bride asked eagerly. "I watched you go aboard through the telescope but there seemed no sign of life. Was there anybody there?"

He did not answer directly but instead asked another question. "How much could you see?"

"I had it on maximum magnification but some of the outlines were blurred."

"Was the figurehead clear to you?"

"No. I could see it of course, but not in detail."

"That's as well, then."

"Why do you say that?"

The Apothecary took his wife's hands in his. "Do you remember remarking that I was a stormy petrel, that trouble followed me around?"

Emilia looked perturbed. "Yes. Why?"

"It's happened. The ship was deserted all right, eerily so, for there was every sign of recent habitation. But draped over the figurehead was a body. And, my darling, I am sorry to say that it was the body of someone we have met."

She looked stricken. "Oh God help us! Who?"

"The wretched Juliana van Guylder."

Emilia went very pale. "And to think I did not take to her. I feel guilty."

Irish Tom spoke for the first time. "This is a tragic set of circumstances, Sir. What can I do to help?"

"Take Mrs. Rawlings and our things back to the village. I've promised to run on ahead and alert the constable. I should also find a physician. He'll need to look at the body before it is brought ashore."

"Let Tom find the doctor. I am perfectly capable of walking back on my own."

"I've a better idea." John ran his eye over the coachman's Brian Boramha physique. "Let Tom stay here and keep an eye on the schooner. The fishermen are off to quaff ale before they do anything further and we don't want anybody to go aboard and tamper."

The Irishman looked very cheered. "I should enjoy that, Sorrh. There's nothing I like better than a good mill." His accent was suddenly very pronounced.

"Well, let's hope that won't be necessary," John answered, then turned as Emilia tugged at his arm.

"My dear, how did Juliana die?"

"I did not examine her body but her face had sustained a terrific beating. It seems to me that she had been most savagely attacked."

"Enough to kill her?"

"I would imagine so, yes."

"How horrible. I hope the village constable is up to dealing with such a crime."

"He won't be of course, unless he is very

exceptional. I think perhaps a letter to Mr. Fielding might be in order."

"But he is in London."

"Ah, don't forget his two Brave Fellows, ready to set out to any part of the kingdom at one quarter of an hour's notice."

"But they wouldn't come to Devon," said Emilia, amazed.

"Would they not! Since Mr. Fielding inaugurated his Flying Runners four years ago in '55, they have so far visited places as far afield as Windsor, Maidstone, Bristol, Barnet, Faversham, Newark, Maidenhead, Henley, Guildford, Tubridge Wells and Oswestry, to say nothing of a three day pursuit in Hertfordshire and Bedfordshire. My dear girl, if I write at once they could be here in six days."

"I shall never," said Tom stolidly, "get over the pace at which life moves today."

"It is indeed," John answered, "a very sobering thought."

The constable, as it turned out, was far more alert than most of his fellow officers of the law. A detested job, unpaid and compulsory, the duty of acting as constable lasted for a year and was so disliked by many citizens that some paid deputies to substitute for them. This had led to the formation of a class of professional deputies, some of whom had held office for a considerable time. As the money paid to them was poor, deputies were usually ignorant, dishonest and extremely inefficient into the bargain. The little village of Sidmouth, however, obviously scorned such individuals and had for its law man a young farmer by the name of William Haycraft. John found him working in his fields and almost felt loath to disturb such honest labour.

"Mr. Haycraft," he called out, hurrying up to the five bar gate.

"Do I know you, Sir?"

John shook his head. "No, I've come about an incident which involves the constable."

William visibly sighed. "Then you'd best come in and tell me about it."

Inside the small, cool farmhouse, John sat with a tankard of home-brewed cider and related the entire story, leaving out no detail, even telling the constable of his evening spent in the company of the van Guylder family.

"So it's the daughter of the house who you recognised as the dead woman?"

"Yes."

"And you thought her death not natural?"

"I did not examine the body. It was neither the time nor the place to do so. But judging by the cuts and bruises on the girl's face I can only assume that she received a beating at somebody's hands."

"You talk, Sir," said William, "as if you would be quite capable of scrutinising a corpse. Are you by any chance a doctor?"

"No, but a member of a closely related profession. I am John Rawlings, an apothecary with a shop in Shug Lane, Piccadilly."

"And what might you be doing in this part of the world, may I ask?"

"I am on holiday here with my new wife, part of that idyllic four weeks known as a honeymoon."

"Well, bless you, Sir. Congratulations. And now you have stumbled into this. I hope it hasn't spoiled things for you."

"Not at all. In fact Emilia, my bride, half wondered if something might happen."

"How's that then?"

It was not easy to say that in the past he had often worked with John Fielding, the celebrated blind magistrate, without sounding full of himself, so the Apothecary kept the explanation as simple and short as he could. But in that he was wrong. William Haycraft positively came to life before his eyes, almost sniffing the air in dog-like fashion.

"Why, even in this remote part we've heard of him, Sir. In fact I seek out knowledge of the man. For he be inspirational indeed. To do what he does without use of his eyes is remarkable. As a matter of interest, though most detest the role of constable I quite enjoy it, thinking about the Blind Beak in London and how he deals with wrongdoers."

"Then, with your permission, may I send for two of his men to assist you?"

Clearly William had never heard of the pair of Brave Fellows and his honest eyes widened as the Apothecary explained their function.

"And you would have enough influence to bring them here?" he said eventually.

"It's not a question of influence. Anyone can call for them. They are there to serve."

"Then I'd be obliged if you would write straight

away, Sir. I can take the letter into Topsham myself this evening. It will get to Exeter and the London Mail quicker that way." He stood up, a true Devonian with broad weathered features, bright eyes and large capable hands.

"Well, I see that I'll get no more work done today." He sighed again. However keen he might be to follow in the footsteps of the Blind Beak, it was clearly still an irritant when precious labouring hours were lost. "I must get down to the beach and investigate this deserted ship for myself." He turned to John. "In all the confusion, you didn't happen to note its name and port of origin, did you, Sir?

The Apothecary nodded. "I did as a matter of fact. She is the *Constantia* from Christiania, which is, I believe, in the Baltic."

"So it's a foreign crew that's gone missing."

"Is that significant?"

"Could be. There's a lot that goes on in these parts. Smuggling and the like. Why, there was piracy at Topsham a mere hundred years ago. Could be that someone abducted the lot of them for ransom."

"But why should a Topsham girl be found dead on a Baltic ship?"

William plucked his ear lobe, a sign that he was thinking. "That is a very good question. Did she come aboard to meet one of the crew? Or was she with some sort of raiding party?"

"That's what we have got to find out."

"Indeed we must. Now let's to the beach."

"You want me to go with you?"

"I want you to examine the body, Sir."

"But what about the local doctor, surely he should be the one to do so?"

The constable turned a look of amused affection in John's direction. "Bless you, Sir, we don't have one of those. Dr. Hunter rides over from Topsham in his gig weekly. The rest of the time Old Saul sees to people."

"Old Saul?"

"An ancient, Sir. A former seafarer. He spent a lot of time in Newfoundland when the Folletts, a leading family in these parts, were trading there. He claims he was taught the art of medicine by the Indians and Eskimos. And I must say, he's very good. Nothing's beyond him, from setting a leg to delivering a babe."

"I'd like to meet him."

"So you shall, Mr. Rawlings. But first we have our duties to attend to."

The fishermen, who as a body had dived into The Sign of the Anchor, the drinking house nearest to the beach, had obviously consumed too much ale and spoken freely about their extraordinary find. For when John and William Haycraft returned to the water's edge a crowd of sightseers had gathered, all of whom resented the fact that a stranger was keeping guard on the vessel. Indeed, abuse was being hurled, to which Irish Tom was responding without inhibition.

"Enough," shouted the constable in an enormous voice, and silence actually fell. John considered that William Haycraft must be one of the most effective people to hold this much despised post, and his admiration for the man, already quite high, rose in bounds.

"Get about your business," William continued. "There's nothing to see here and I'll charge you with loitering if you don't move on." He turned to Irish Tom. "And what might you be doing?"

"He's my coachman," the Apothecary put in hastily, "and I asked him to make sure nobody boarded the *Constantia*."

"'Twas a job keeping them away, Sir. They'd have been out there like flies if I hadn't been forceful. But now you're here, can I go?"

"I'd be grateful if you'd find Mrs. Rawlings and tell her I won't be long. Explain that the constable has asked me to go back aboard as there is no physician to accompany him."

"I'll gladly do that, Sir. And is it in order if I wet me whistle while I'm about it?"

"Certainly," answered John, only wishing that he could do likewise.

The sun was just beginning to lower in the sky as they clambered aboard the deserted ship, while the warm west wind had started to freshen a little. Without preliminaries, the two men went straight to the corpse which lay just as John had left it, her hair blowing in the breeze, though this time her sad white arms did not swing quite so freely. John laid his hand on Juliana's neck and felt that rigor mortis had begun to establish itself.

"She's starting to stiffen," he said to William.

"What does that mean?"

"That she's been dead at least twelve hours, though, of course, the warm weather would most certainly affect the process so it could well be more."

"So she was killed - if she *was* killed - in the early hours of this morning?"

"As I said, it could have been earlier. Perhaps some time last evening. Now, will you help me turn her?"

The constable did not flinch but helped lift the fragile body and lay it on its back, gasping as he saw the state of the bruising on the neck and face. Disliking the task, John raised Juliana's shift above her breasts so that she lay exposed to the two men's examination. The pale flesh was covered in marks, there were even the weals of a whip to be seen.

"By Christ," said William, "whoever did this must swing for it. Did the beating kill her?"

"I think we can safely presume yes. I imagine that there must be internal injuries which were too severe for her to sustain."

"Poor little thing."

The Apothecary looked very harsh indeed. "I think there may be more than one little thing involved in this."

William gaped. "What do you mean?"

"When I met her I became utterly convinced that the girl was pregnant."

The constable stared at the youthfully flat stomach. "There's no sign of it."

"I did not mean anything advanced. Probably no

more than ten to twelve weeks in all." He bent over the body, running his hands over the wounded abdomen and pressing here and there. "Difficult to be absolutely sure without an autopsy but I am fairly certain that I am right."

"A motive for murder perhaps? If the father didn't want to be involved."

"Quite possibly." John slid his hands lower. "My God, this poor thing has been violently raped. Look at this bruising - and at this."

But the constable's sticking point had been reached. Turning away, he shook his head from side to side. "I can't, Sir. It's not decent. No God fearing creature could do so. Medical men excepted," he added hastily.

The Apothecary felt a slight sense of shame. Along with all his kind, he had come to regard the human body as an object of interest and had forgotten the sensitivities of others when it came to examination. Noting to himself the smears of dried semen on Juliana's thighs, he concealed her privy parts with a swabbing cloth, lying on the deck close to his feet.

"I've covered her up, Mr. Haycraft. But I would like you to look once more at the marks on the rest of the body. When you're ready."

William, somewhat reluctantly, turned back his head. "I'm sorry about that, Sir. It's just that I felt it would be wrong for me to have gazed at her so."

"That's perfectly understandable. But you must realise that the coroner will want a report and I must note every detail. Now then, observe these." John pointed to various marks and discolourations on Juliana's stiffening corpse.

"Yes, I see them, and savage they are too."

"Does anything strike you about them?"

With clear reluctance, the constable bent lower. "They are at rather odd angles."

"Precisely. It seems to me that the blows are coming from different directions, which would suggest to me that more than one pair of hands delivered them."

William looked aghast. "Are you saying that this girl was beaten to death by several people?"

"Horrible though the prospect is, that is exactly what I mean."

The constable's face went dark. "Get ashore, Mr. Rawlings, and write your letter. The sooner the two Brave Fellows get here the better for all of us. If a mob committed this atrocity, then that mob must be called to account, and the more men we have to help, the better."

"But what of the body? We can't leave it here overnight."

"No, indeed. It must be brought ashore and set to rest in a quiet place. Tomorrow she will be taken to the mortuary in Exeter, God rest her soul."

"But how do we get her off?"

"There's only one way. A smack must come out with a net. Then she must be placed in it and lowered over the side."

"I suppose," said John resignedly, "it means more trips up and down that horrible rope."

"I think," answered William with a half smile,

"that the time has come to search for the ship's ladder."

It was dusk by the time John got back to The Ship and the place was glowing with candles, an attractive sight from the lane outside. Even more attractive was the sight of Emilia within. Dressed simply but effectively for dinner, her golden hair piled on her head and secured with a decorative comb, the Apothecary stood for a moment just looking at her. She smiled at him.

"Has it been awful?"

He nodded. "Yes. Sidmouth does not boast its own physician and it fell to my lot to examine the body. So tonight, alas, when we have dined, I must write a report for the coroner while the event is still fresh in my mind, and also a letter to Mr. Fielding which William Haycraft, a really good constable despite all my fears, is taking personally to catch the London Mail."

Emilia's skin was like ivory as she asked, "Where is Juliana now? Not alone on that boat, surely?"

"In a barn at Cotmaton Hall. The owner is an officer in the Guards, rarely at home, but he is there at the moment and has given his permission."

"I will take her flowers," said John's bride with determination.

"I wouldn't advise it. She's not a pleasant sight."

"It's the least I can do. I did not like the girl when she was alive, now I must make amends."

"Where will you get flowers at this hour of the day?"

"I shall go out and pick them."

"It's nearly dark."

"Then Irish Tom can accompany me and afterwards we can drive out to the Hall. It will occupy the time while you write your report and letter."

"Oh, very well," said John with a sigh, for there was no arguing with that logic. He had a momentary flash of the married life that lay before him, in which Emilia, with clear reasoning, would win every point that she so wished. The Apothecary's crooked grin burst forth. "You're not an angel, you're an imp," he said, then set to washing in the china bowl in preparation for dinner.

In the event, John - writing faster and more fluently than he had hoped - finished the report of his findings and his letter to Mr. Fielding just as William Haycraft knocked on the door of his bedroom.

"Is it ready, Sir?"

"It is. Come in, come in."

The constable stood in the doorway. "I won't stop, Sir. I've quite a night ahead. I've decided to take the cart into Exeter and hand your letter to the Mail coach direct. I'll have to delay going to Topsham till tomorrow. And meantime I want to go up to the Hall and pay my respects to the deceased. There's quite a few gone up there already, your wife among 'em."

"You suprise me. Why are they going to see a woman who none of them know?"

William looked earnest, an endearing expression.

"There's some, no doubt, who've gone through morbid curiosity. But there's others, good Christian folk, who wish to say a prayer for the poor lost soul."

John felt slightly chastened. "Then I shall go with you," he said. "It is the least I can do."

The cart awaited in the street outside and they bumped over the track, past the church, and on beyond the village to where, pleasantly situated in its own grounds, stood a Devon long house with a thatched roof. Beyond it lay several outbuildings and John saw that a glimmer of light was coming from one of the barns. Captain Henry Carslake, the owner of the property, which John felt certain dated back to Jacobean times, stood outside the barn, easily distinguishable by his military uniform. He appeared to be in charge of a small quiet queue plodding solemnly within, hats snatched from heads in the doorway as they entered the presence of the dead. Having spoken softly to the Captain, with whom he was clearly on good terms, Constable Haycraft led the way in.

Whoever had swiftly organised Juliana's resting place had done well. She lay on a table top, held in place by two stout trestles, a tall church candle in a holder at each corner. Round her body, which was now dressed in a white linen gown, flowers and green leaves had been placed, so that she looked more like a sleeping May queen than the victim of a cruel and vicious attack. The worst of her facial bruising had been disguised by her hair, which had been brushed forward and lay like a silken veil all round her. John, who had seen the girl at her worst, was strangely moved by the sight of her deathly purity and felt the tears well up behind his eyes.

Ahead of him in the slow procession which walked solemnly round the makeshift bier and out of the barn door, Emilia was weeping and Tom the coachman was looking very Irish and making the sign of the cross. A terrible thought came to John at that moment. At home, in Topsham, poor Jan van Guylder must be going frantic with worry, unaware that his erring daughter was dead, believing only that she must be missing. At this very minute he was probably scouring the streets in the darkness, calling her name. Very quietly, the Apothecary whispered,

"Tom."

The coachman looked round. "Yes, Sir?"

"Wait outside for me."

"Very good, Sir."

They joined one another at the barn door, Emilia already gone to sit in the coach, hiding her tears from the world.

"Tom, we must go to Topsham. It's wrong not to break the news to Juliana's father tonight. It might be his wish to see her before she is taken to the mortuary."

"But ..."

"If we hurry we will still be there at a civilised hour. We must escort Mrs. Rawlings back to The Ship then go like the wind. The horses are well rested and should enjoy some exercise."

"Very good, Sir," said the coachman with an air of weary resignation.

Emilia put her head out of the carriage window. "I heard that and I think I should go with you. A woman's touch would undoubtedly be of help."

"There's no time to argue," said John, mounting the step. "There's a man in extremis who needs our help. Now, no more discussion. Let's concentrate on getting there."

Chapter 4

John could not remember ever feeling quite so deflated. They had rushed to Topsham at full speed, clattering through the streets of Exeter where, despite the fact that the hour was growing late, there had still been a parade of fashionable folk. It had been a small, rather modest attempt to emulate the ways of London's *beau monde* and at any other time the Apothecary might have found it amusing, but tonight his mood was too intense for enjoyment.

Retracing its route of a few days previously, the coach had left the city and headed for the port, bristling with the masts of ships etched against the moonlit sky. Stopping for no one, John had ordered Tom to drive on through the narrow streets until they had come to Shell House. There, bracing himself to impart the terrible tidings, he had leapt from the conveyance even as it came to a halt and pulled the bell-rope, while Emilia peered anxiously from the carriage window.

A man servant had answered the call. "Yes, Sir?"

"My name is Rawlings. I dined with Mr. van Guylder the other night. Is he in please?"

The elderly man had shaken his head. "No, Sir, he's gone to Exeter."

"Do you know whereabouts?"

"No, Sir, I don't."

"Or when he'll be back?"

"Don't know that neither. He left in a great hurry

and gave no indication when he would be returning. I'll tell him you called, shall I?"

"If you would ask him to contact my urgently. I
am staying at The Ship in Sidmouth. If he could
send a boy with a message or better still come in person."

"Very good, Sir."

"You look black as a cloud," Emilia said as her
bridegroom hurled himself back into the coach.

"It's because I don't know what to do. Van
Guylder has gone to Exeter, presumably looking for
his daughter, but it's pointless seeking him there. He
could be anywhere. We've no option, I'm afraid, but
to turn round and go back."

"Have you left a message?"

"I've asked him to contact me urgently. Obviously
I couldn't say what it was about and it's not the sort
of thing one puts in a note. Oh damnation, I'd hoped
to spare the poor chap and now, I suppose, I've
made it worse for him."

"How?"

"He'll worry all the more when the servant tells
him I've called."

"But you had no choice. You tried your best."

It was very pleasant, John thought, to have a wife
who said soothing things in moments of great distress. In fact had he known how comforting it was
he would have got married long ago. Then Coralie
came into his mind and her stubborn refusal to be
his wife, and he felt a sudden rush of guilt, as if even
thinking about her was somehow betraying Emilia.

"Where to now, Sir?" called Irish Tom from the box.

"Back to Sidmouth. We've completely wasted our time in coming here."

"You've left word for the poor man, Sir, so something's been achieved."

"I suppose so," the Apothecary answered wearily, feeling the day's events start to catch up with him and every bone in his body begin to ache.

"You're exhausted," said Emilia.

"I know," and pulling his hat down over his eyes, stretching out his legs and putting his arm round his bride, John fell fast asleep.

He was woken abruptly by a sudden sound, or rather two sudden sounds. Simultaneously, Irish Tom called out, "Christ, what's that?" and Emilia shrieked close to the Apothecary's ear. Startled witless, he sat bolt upright.

"What's going on?"

But Emilia did not answer, instead pointing a trembling finger at the carriage window. Following the line of her hand, John looked out, and the sight that he saw in the vivid moonlight froze him to the marrow.

Presumably tiring of driving across the city, Tom had taken them through the country on an entirely different route, and they were presently passing over some rugged gorse-covered terrain, a bleak and desolate place with not a sign of life anywhere. Yet ahead of them on this God-forsaken heath was another coach. And though there was nothing particularly extraordinary in that, it was the con-

veyance itself and its occupants that chilled John's
spine.

The carriage was all white except for the springs
beneath, which seemed to be blacker than most, like
cruel dark fingers supporting the bodywork. As if
this weren't odd enough, within its shadowy interior
sat several people, if human beings they indeed were.
For large floppy-brimmed hats with a veil in the front
entirely masked whatever face may lurk behind, concealing from the world exactly what these creatures
might be. The hats were white and so were the greatcoats that covered the shoulders with many capes.

"They're skeletons," gasped Emilia.

"Nonsense ..." started John, but his voice trailed
away as his eyes travelled up to the coachman.

He was dressed in exactly the same gear but with
one horrific difference. The head, complete with
shrouding hat, lay beside him on the coachman's
box, and the neck sticking up out of the caped coat
ended in a jagged cut.

"Holy Mary," Tom was shouting loudly, and with
that let off a blast from his pistol.

The occupants of the white coach did not fire
back but sped off into the night, their black plumed
horses, just like those of a funeral cortege, rolling
their eyes and foaming as the headless coachman
urged them on with a snake-like whip.

"Oh my God," said Emilia, and threw herself into
her husband's arms, trembling violently.

"Do I give chase, Sir?" shouted the Irishman.

"No, get us back as quickly as you can," John
called in reply.

Despite the fact that all his attention was taken up by his terrified bride, he himself was thoroughly unnerved. Though up to this moment he had had no belief in the supernatural, he had to confess that what he had just seen had shaken him to the core. That the West Country was full of tales of unearthly occurences was a known thing, though the Apothecary had laughed at the stories when he had been told them. But this ghostly carriage with its terrifying occupants was difficult to discount. John turned to Emilia.

"It was probably just a trick of the moonlight. The whole thing was an optical illusion," he said, more to convince himself than anyone else.

She looked at him quite angrily. "John, please don't treat me like a child. I know what I saw. There were ghastly white things inside that coach and the driver's head lay beside him, his neck bleeding from the cut."

The Apothecary looked perplexed. "There has to be a logical explanation."

"There is," said Emilia shortly. "We have just seen a phantom coach driven by a headless coachman."

And despite the fact that he was longing to deny it, John was forced silently to agree with her.

The landlord of The Ship, Matthew Salter, who had started life as a fisherman but who had saved money and become an inn-keeper, nodded knowingly. "They often come out when there's been a violent death," he informed his audience.

"They?"

"The people from Wildtor Grange."

"What exactly are we talking about?" asked John, feeling himself growing increasingly irritable with fatigue.

"The apparition you saw on the moorland. It's a well-known sight round these parts."

The Apothecary, whose old disbelief was returning now that he was safely indoors, didn't know whether to scoff or to listen, but one glance at the avid faces of his wife and his coachman persuaded him to keep his mouth firmly closed. "Go on," he said.

"The Grange is in ruins now but about thirty years ago it was occupied by a family called Thorne. They were a strange, bad bunch. Five sons there were, a drunken crowd of young rascals, and the father no better than he should be. Old Sir Gilbert, he was, the sire of nearly all the bastards in the county. Anyway, the story goes that the men so mistreated Lady Thorne, his wife and their mother, that she was driven off her head and from then on they kept her captive in a suite of rooms in the East Wing."

Emilia's eyes were wide and her lips slightly parted, while Tom was surreptitiously crossing himself. Inwardly, John sighed.

"Anyway, one night she got out and set off alone into the darkness, wearing naught but her nightrail, her feet bare. Old Sir Gilbert called his sons and his coachman and went off in pursuit of her, and they finally glimpsed her crossing the wooden bridge that used to go over the river Otter. He bore down on her with great haste but what he hadn't realised was that she had stolen an old fowling piece before she left the house. Be that as it may, she fired at the coachman and the force of the blast took his head clean off his body. Driverless, the horses charged the bridge but the weight was too great and the coach descended into the water and all its occupants drowned."

"Tell me, why do their ghosts wear such extraordinary clothes?" John asked pointedly.

The landlord looked wise. "That's because the lads were Angels."

"Angels?"

"A street gang that terrorises the inhabitants of Exeter. It was in existence then and it still is now. They base themselves on the London Mohocks and their mischief is cruel. Old Thorne's sons were members of the pack and that accounts for them wearing the rig, beekeepers' hats and greatcoats."

"And what happened to poor Lady Thorne?" Emilia asked. "Did she drown too?"

"No, bless you, Mam. She returned to the Grange and lived in great style till she died of drink in hopeless debt. The house was ruinous by the time she went so no relative would take it on. After that it just fell into disrepair. She haunts the ruins."

"That family seems to have a monopoly on ghostly visitations," John remarked drily, but nobody was listening to him.

"May I ask a question, Sir?" Tom looked at his employer and the Apothecary nodded.

"Why does sudden death stir up the ghosts?"

Salter shook his head. "I don't know. Perhaps because their own was so abrupt. Anyway, you've seen the phantom coach and the headless driver as many have done before you, though very few outsiders mark you."

"How often do these hauntings occur?" asked John, his mind going off at a tangent.

Once again the landlord looked doubtful. "Most people refuse to go near the heath at night, so who's to say."

"Who indeed," the Apothecary answered thoughtfully. He changed the subject. "Tell me more about the Angels."

"They're very similar to the London Mohocks, as I said. They go round at night terrorising watchmen and women; flattening noses, cutting legs as they make their victims dance. They force females to stand on their heads against a wall, then as their clothes fall back play lewd games with them that cannot be described in front of a lady. They are reputedly the sons of aristocrats and gentry folk."

"As were the London gang, now dispersed thank God."

"The Exeter mob was silent for a while, about ten years in fact. But lately some choice spirits have revived the pack and they're back to all their old tricks."

"Can the constables do nothing?"

"No, and the nightwatchmen are too old to be effective. In other words the lads run riot as and when they feel like it. There's been talk of citizens forming a group to protect themselves though nothing has ever come of it."

"Why's that?"

"Because, in my view, the rumour is true, Sir. The fathers of the Angels are mostly well placed and have powerful means at their disposal to protect their sons."

Beside him, John's bride gave a deep yawn and he involuntarily followed suit. "It's been a long and tiring day. I'm afraid the time has come for me to retire." Emilia smiled. "John, will you accompany me? I can't get the picture of that headless coachman out of my mind and think I might jump at shadows."

He grinned unevenly. "So might I. Come, my dear, we'll escort one another." And slipping his arm round his wife's waist, the Apothecary took her to their bedchamber, wondering with every step of the stairs exactly what it was that they had seen on the moorland that night.

At dawn, long before anyone was up, Juliana van Guylder's body was placed in a plain wooden coffin, the lid loosely secured so that those who needed to look at her could easily do so, then put in a farm cart and driven slowly to the mortuary in Exeter. Accompanying her, in fact driving the cart, was William Haycraft, the constable.

Shortly after their departure, John woke and went to the beach. The *Constantia* rode at anchor, her sails catching the pink glow of morning, her decks as deserted as ever, her very silence echoing the brooding mystery that surrounded her. She had drifted a little in the night and the Apothecary, who had been considering a further exhaustive search of the vessel, thought better of the chilly swim and instead walked for a while, contemplating. Then he returned to the inn, wondering how long he should wait for Jan van Guylder to appear before once more going in search of the man. As it was, Emilia made the decision for him.

"Sweetheart, you must leave for Topsham as soon as you have eaten your breakfast. I shall wait here and amuse myself by looking round. If Mr. van Guylder comes I shall tell him as best I can what has befallen, but I truly think it better if you try to seek him out."

"But what if he hasn't returned from Exeter?"

"Perhaps you should look for him there. After all, his son's school should be easy enough to find. Didn't van Guylder say it was the Grammar School?"

"Yes, he did. And you think the boy might be able to tell me where his father is?"

"He is bound to know his haunts, yes."

John nodded. "You're quite right. I shall go as soon as I've had some food."

His wife grinned at him. "Whatever you do, don't leave without doing that."

Much as he had feared, the Apothecary's call at Shell House produced exactly the same result as on the previous night. Jan van Guylder had not returned from Exeter and none of his servants was able to help at all. Grateful, yet again, that he now had his own coach at his disposal, John set out for the city determined to track down his quarry.

They entered Exeter by the Topsham road and made their way up what was known as Holloway, eventually reaching the narrow confines of the South Gate, through which they entered the original old walled city. To their left lay The White Hart Inn, to their right The Bear. But though Tom looked longingly and tapped the window with his whip, John ignored him and the conveyance continued on through the Large Market to the Carfax, a word derived from the French *carrefours* or crossroads. This was the heart of the city where the main thoroughfares High, North and South Streets met each other, and was marked by a Great Conduit, providing a distribution point for piped water. At the Carfax the coach turned right, passing the massive hulk of the Cathedral and its adjacent buildings.

Ahead of them lay the East Gate, in the shadow of which, so enquiries had revealed, were housed the Exeter Free Grammar School and the Blue School, where the sons of the poor were educated. Feeling that his mission was indeed a delicate one, John was eventually shown into the office of the headmaster, where he sat turning his hat in his hands until the door opened behind him.

A big boisterous fellow with little eyes stood there, puffing and blowing with the exertion of climbing the stairs. Observing John with a narrowed porcine gaze, he demanded, "Are you the constable, Sir?"

Startled, the Apothecary rose to his feet. "No, Sir. I am merely a visitor."

"Visitor, visitor? Am I expecting one?"

"I don't know," John answered, feeling utterly foolish.

"No, I'm not, by God. Are you sure you're not the constable?"

"Quite sure. I'm an apothecary by trade."

"But I didn't send for one of those. Why have you come?"

"Hopefully to see a boy, Sir."

"Boy? What boy?"

"Richard van Guylder."

The effect of those words was extraordinary, from porcine to wild boar, the teacher's tiny eyes glinted and he almost seemed to grow tusks.

"Don't shilly-shally with me, Sir. You *are* the constable, now don't deny it."

John thought on his feet. "Why do you want the constable so urgently?"

"You know why. I told your wife."

"I haven't seen my wife since early this morning," the Apothecary answered truthfully.

"Then she can't have told you," the teacher replied, making John wonder which of them was going mad. "But you're right. It's about that very boy, that wretched pustulated creature."

"Richard? Why, what has happened to him?"

"Heaven knows," answered the master, angrily throwing the book he was carrying to the ground.

"What do you mean by that?"

"I mean, Sir, that the snivelling little beast has

vanished, disappeared. He left school early on Tuesday morning and has not been seen since. For all I know, he could be dead."

"Oh my God," said the Apothecary, and sank back down into the chair, all the breath suddenly gone out of him.

Chapter 5

The Apothecary could hardly believe what he had just heard. He had last seen Richard van Guylder boarding the Exeter coach with his tragic sister. Now it would appear that he, too, had gone missing. A ghastly fear that he had suffered the same fate as Juliana gripped John and he felt himself break out in a cold clammy sweat.

"You say you have called the constable, Sir?"

"Indeed so. Yet the wretch has so far failed to put in an appearance."

"You have sent word to Richard's father?"

"I certainly have, but up until now there has been no response."

"That is because he is away from home. I have been searching for him myself."

The little eyes narrowed again. "Who did you say you were?"

"I am a friend of the family." John adopted his upright citizen face. "Would it help you at all, Sir, if I joined in the hunt for your missing pupil?"

"Shouldn't that be left to the constable?"

"But he's not here and I am."

The headmaster considered, his tight little eyes narrowing then widening in concentration. Finally he said, "Oh very well. Where do you want to begin?"

"Perhaps in Richard's room. There might be some clue in there, possibly the address of one his friends, maybe a hint as to where he has gone."

Regarding him with a look of extreme suspicion, the teacher led the way to an institutional building, not guaranteed to bring a great deal of comfort into the lives of those unfortunate young men who dwelt there. However, John supposed, sacrificing the delights of home must be considered a small price to pay in return for a good education. Richard's cell was spartan, monastic almost, containing a hard-looking bed and chair and a small table. Text books lay open, strewn about the place, giving the impression that the pimply youth rarely spent a moment without study. Small wonder, thought John, that the poor chap makes the journey back to Topsham to attend divine service on Sundays. He would seem to have little else in his life.

Behind him the headmaster was puffing noisily. "Not much here, is there?"

"Perhaps we should look through his clothes."

But again there wasn't much. Two serviceable but good quality suits, a cloak, two pairs of shoes and a battered hat seemed to be the sum total of Richard's possessions. Picking up the cloak, the Apothecary felt in the pocket. A handkerchief, a snuff box - a rather pathetic pretension, John thought - and a calling card was all there was to show by way of contents. He turned the card over in his hand.

'Gerald Fitz,' the Apothecary read, '7, The Close, Exeter.' Over his shoulder, the headmaster was doing the same thing. "Fitz, eh?" he said breathily. "Never knew young van Guylder mixed in such exalted company."

The Apothecary's svelte brows rose in an unspoken question.

"The Fitzes are one of the richest and best connected families in the county. They're related to Lord Courtenay, you know."

The piggy eyes glinted meaningfully and John, to whom the name meant nothing at all, looked intelligent and said, "Ah."

"Of course Gerald Fitz was not educated here; private tutors and all that frippery. However, I believe he is a pleasant enough young man, though quite the beau of fashion if one were to judge by appearances."

John looked round the dismal little room once more, trying to picture the spotty boy sitting at the table, his nose in a book, wishing he were somewhere else. He turned to the headmaster again. "As I mentioned, Mr. van Guylder is not at home. You wouldn't by any chance have knowledge of his haunts in Exeter?"

The porcine eyes gleamed rudely. "You could try a certain house in Blackboy Road."

"Do I take it you mean a house of pleasure?"

The headmaster laughed gustily. "Pleasure, ill repute? What's in a name?"

"What indeed? Does this house have a number?"

"No, but you cannot miss it. Outside hangs a sign portraying a female leg, stockinged and gartered. It is much patronised, so I believe, by the officers stationed at Rougemont Castle." The teacher's face took on a perceptive expression. "So both father and son are out of contact at the same time. How odd."

"It is certainly a coincidence but let it be hoped that by the end of the day each will have returned."

"When," said the headmaster nastily, "I set eyes on young Richard again he can be assured of a sound beating."

A fact guaranteed, thought John, to keep him away as long as humanly possible.

Outside in the street, nestling close to the East Gate so that he might observe the passing parade from the commanding view of his coachman's box, Irish Tom sat patiently, his eyes moving from time to time to The Dragon Inn in High Street, a look of longing on his face whenever he did so. Much as John wanted to get on with his search for the van Guylders, father and son, he simply didn't have the heart to keep his employee, who had after all been born in a hostelry in County Tyrone, away from his ale a moment longer.

"I'll meet you in the inn," he called out, pointing to The Dragon. "I've a lot to tell you."

As soon as he had done this, the Apothecary thought how annoyed his adopted father, Sir Gabriel Kent, doyen of all that was fine and fashionable, would have been with him for familiarity with the servants. Yet it was very difficult not to discuss the matter with someone who had been present from the start of the whole odd affair. And it was odd indeed, John considered, that the family should be so blighted; first the daughter's murder, then the son's disappearance, and finally the father, presumably at his wit's end, wandering the streets of Exeter in search of a girl already dead.

Irish Tom heard the story in silence, supping ale the meanwhile. When John had finished, he finally put his tankard down. "Are you going to the brothel, Sir?"

"Well, I don't suppose for a minute that van Guylder will be there, after all the last thing on his mind must be the delights of the flesh. But perhaps I might get some information about where else he goes."

"And what about these people, Fitz? Are you going to call on them?"

"It's going to be difficult if they're as grand as they sound. But try I must. After all, the disappearance of Richard at the time of his sister's murder is very significant."

"Do you think he had anything to do with it?"

"In what way?"

"I mean could he have killed her himself, Sir?"

"I suppose he might have been one of the people involved, yes. You see, Tom, it's my belief that this was the work of at least two different hands, probably more."

"The van Guylders, father and son?"

"Perish the thought, for she had been raped as well."

"How disgusting. Yet one hears some terrible things on one's travels."

"Further, Tom, I'm certain the girl was pregnant."

"Well, if one of the filthy bastards had done that to her they might well want her silenced for ever, rather than bring shame on the pair of 'em."

John was about to remonstrate, about to say that they were jumping to conclusions and that incest was very far from proven, when a name caught his attention.

" ... Richard van Guylder been in today?"

Both the Apothecary and his coachman turned to look and saw a beefy young man, very fresh of countenance and fair of head, standing at the counter, earnestly questioning the landlord. Realising that he was being regarded, the newcomer stared back then made an awkward bow.

"Do I know you, Sir?"

"No, Sir. But I couldn't help hearing you mention Richard van Guylder."

The young man's rubicund features flushed to the shade of a cherry. "You have news of him?"

It was impossible, for the moment at least, to tell the truth. "I have some," John answered vaguely. "But perhaps you would care to sit here and tell me your connection with the gentleman before I impart it."

The young man crossed the room, his over-tight breeches straining a little as he walked. The Apothecary found him rather a pathetic figure despite his hearty looks.

"Tobias Wills, at your service, Sir." He bowed, his jacket creasing at the sleeves as he did so. "I am betrothed to Juliana," he announced proudly. "We are to be married in the summer. Richard is my future brother-in-law."

John stared at him, stupified, not having a single idea as to how to handle this latest situation. "When did you last see her?" was absolutely the best he could manage.

Every thought process Tobias had ran over his face for even a child to read. Surprise changed to suspicion to worry before he blurted out, "Why do you ask that?"

The Apothecary decided that total discretion was the only way forward.

"Because I believe she might be in Exeter visiting her brother, who has probably taken the day off school. Mr. van Guylder is thought to be in the city looking for them."

Tobias laughed heartily. "How like Juliana. She'll be shopping and has met one of her lady friends, I dare say. I doubt there's cause for alarm."

Poor bastard, thought John, while beside him Irish Tom, clearly embarrassed, got to his feet and said, "I'll be round in the yard if you need me, Sir." The Apothecary managed a smile. "How long have you known the family?"

"All my life," Tobias answered cheerily. "I grew up with them. My father is a great friend of Jan van Guylder's. I think the two of them decided that Juliana and I would be wed while we were both still in our cradles."

"And the pair of you went along with this?"

Suspicion returned to the honest countenance. "These are very personal questions from a stranger, Sir."

"Forgive me. It is just that as I am acquainted with the family I have been entrusted with the task of finding Richard, who is not in school, by his headmaster."

Relief and trust appeared. "Oh, I see."

"But allow me to introduce myself. I am John Rawlings, an apothecary of Shug Lane in London."

Now Tobias was totally perplexed. "You have come all the way from London to find Richard?"

"No, not at all. I am staying down here on holiday with my bride of two weeks."

Tobias looked conspiratorial, man-to-man ish. "Honeymoon, eh," he said roguishly. "Can't wait till mine. Juliana will make a beautiful bride, don't you agree?"

It was heart-rending to hear him speak in that way and yet it could, John considered, be the cleverest bluff of all. If Tobias were not the father of Juliana's child and had discovered that she was pregnant by someone else, could he and a cohort have murdered the girl? Or, even more convoluted but still possible, if it was his child and he had tired of his betrothed, had he killed her to rid himself of both her and his unwanted baby?

Yet, again and again, John found himself coming back to the same stumbling block: the terrible beating and the rape. Could anyone who had once loved Juliana inflict such appalling injuries on her? Could a father, brother or lover be so evil? Then the Apothecary remembered the cruelty he had encountered in the past and decided that anything, however vile, was indeed possible. He stared at Tobias closely, considering whether the jolly but juvenile manner was a clever act.

"I am wondering," he said, "if you might be able to give me any information regarding Richard. As I have been set the task of finding the boy I think I really ought to get on with it."

"While I meanwhile will search for his sister. What a good plan. Should we meet later and compare notes?"

John looked doubtful. "My wife is in Sidmouth and I am most anxious to return to her by dinner time. I shall call on the Fitzes and at the bro ..." His voice trailed away.

"You were saying?" Tobias asked politely.

Oh dammit, thought John, the fellow's a grown man.

"The brothel in Blackboy Road. I am told that Mr. van Guylder frequents it from time to time."

"Oh he does," Tobias answered seriously. "He is a widower but not old, so who could blame him?"

"You obviously know the family very well indeed."

"Well, I am destined to become part of it."

"Even down to sharing their darkest secrets?"

Tobias went crimson. "I don't know what you mean," he said.

"That was terrible," John remarked as he stepped into his coach. "If that chap is as innocent as he looks, then I have most cruelly deceived him."

"Well you could hardly blurt out that his betrothed has met a grisly end and is currently lying in Exeter mortuary, now could you?"

"Not really." John glanced at his watch. "I mustn't be late back, Tom. I think I'll visit the brothel then save the Fitzes for this evening when, finely dressed,

Emilia and I might call. I have a feeling I would stand a better chance of being admitted that way."

"I'm sure you're right, Sir. But what if you find neither Mr. van Guylder or his son today? Will you be content to go home empty-handed?"

"I'll be far from content but I think I have little choice. I don't want my wife to lose all patience with me even before the honeymoon is over."

"No, Sir, that would never do," the coachman answered seriously as they trundled their way towards Blackboy Road and the house with The Sign of the Gartered Leg.

In the event, they never got there. Whether he had been in for a visit or whether it was just by the merest chance John was not sure, but as they turned into the street where gentlemen took their pleasure, he saw Jan van Guylder striding towards their carriage, his eyes glazed and tears pouring down his cheeks. The Apothecary was on his feet in an instant, lowering the window and sticking his head out.

"Mr. van Guylder. Over here. It's John Rawlings. I must have a word with you."

Tom pulled the horses in and the carriage came to a stop. Jan, however, shook his head, applying his handkerchief to his eyes and making a motion with his arm which suggested pushing away. John ignored him and jumped down, fishing in his pocket for the smelling salts which he always carried.

"No, please no," said the Dutchman from the

depths of his hands, which he had placed over his face, apparently to conceal his public shame.

"Get a grip on yourself," John said, as soothingly as he could. "There is much to get through today. Come, sit in the carriage with me."

Van Guylder turned a tortured face in his direction. "What do you mean? Do you have news of my sinful daughter who has strayed from her home yet again?"

"Yes, I have news of her," the Apothecary answered. "My friend, you must prepare yourself for a shock. I beg you to step into my coach where we will be guaranteed privacy."

The Dutchman's eyes bolted in his head and he appeared on the point of collapse.

"She's dead, isn't she? Nothing else could make you look so grim."

"I will not speak until we are hidden from the world," John stated resolutely, and taking van Guylder by the arm he dragged him, protesting but fortunately too weak to put up much resistance, into the conveyance.

Once inside the Dutchman lost all control. "What has happened?" he sobbed, his voice thick with emotion. "Is Juliana really dead? Has she paid for her sins with her life?"

Despite the man's obvious distress, John felt immensely irritated. "You sound like an Old Testament thunderer, Sir. Let he who be without sin cast the first stone, is more my philosophy. Yes, your tragic daughter is dead but through no fault of her own, of that I feel certain. It is others who have sinned against her by taking her young life."

Van Guylder stopped weeping and gazed at the Apothecary transfixed. "Are you saying that she was murdered?"

"It grieves me to agree that I am."

"By whom for God's sake?"

"That," John answered savagely, "is what I intend to find out."

There was an awful pause during which the Dutchman turned ash white and retched violently. John, fearing for his upholstery, opened the window and shoved van Guylder's head out but fortunately it was merely a spasm and the cobbles below remained unscathed. Jan drew his head back in and looked at the younger man.

"I know who killed her," he said.

It was John's turn to gape. "What?"

"She had a lover, here in Exeter. She tried to hide it from me but all the signs were there. I became certain that she was with child and I think she came to town to tell him of it. He killed her to silence her, that is what happened."

"Who is he? Do you know him?"

Van Guylder sobbed and shook his head. "No, she never told me. But Richard, does, I am certain of that."

The fact that something truly sinister might be lying behind the young man's non-appearance at school struck the Apothecary forcibly. He hesitated, then decided that it was better to come out with everything than burden the Dutchman with future revelations.

"Your son is missing from his lessons," he said quietly.

"What do you mean?"

"He hasn't returned to school since his weekend with you."

"But today is Wednesday. He caught the coach on Monday morning."

"Yes, I know. I saw him."

"You what?"

"Mr. van Guylder," said John patiently, "it is obvious that I must tell you the whole story. Answer me truly, are you up to hearing it?" The Dutchman nodded but looked so pale around the gills that John decided on another course of action. Putting his head out, he called up to the coachman.

"Let us take our guest home. He will be better equipped in his own surroundings to deal with all of this. As fast as you can Tom without causing hazard."

It was a journey of pure torture. Refusing to rest or sit quietly, van Guylder bombarded the Apothecary with questions which he felt duty bound to answer. In this way, the story of Juliana's discovery on the deserted ship, though related tactfully, sounded so sinister as to be unreal. Indeed, even as he was telling the tale, John was remembering the ghostly white coach and its terrible occupants and how hard it was proving for him to dismiss the incident as having a perfectly rational explanation. Right at the back of his mind was growing the nasty feeling that there had been something supernatural about the whole affair and that somehow or other the ghost-ship and its solitary passenger might be connected with it.

But he had practical things to do. The Dutchman, who had wept silently since he had got into the coach, collaspsed in a heap as John, omitting all the unpleasant details, described to him how Juliana had been found. Smelling salts were administered, clothing loosened, and a bandage soaked in Common Water Soldier applied to the brow, thus preventing Jan van Guylder from losing consciousness all together. No one had ever been more relieved than when the masts of Topsham came into view and Tom turned the carriage in the direction of Shell House.

Yet here the situation grew slightly worse as Jan, still sobbing, said, "I pray Richard has returned. At least we can comfort one another in this black hour," then rushed into his home calling his son's name.

John did not know what made him so certain that the spotty boy would still be missing, but certain he was. Groaning audibly, he got out of the carriage and went into the house. Van Guylder was now acting like a man possessed, hurling himself from room to room, throwing open doors and demanding of the bewildered servants where Richard was hiding. So terrible was his manner and his look that a young female domestic started to scream, her high-pitched yells adding to the general pandemonium. John, who had brought his medical bag with him even on honeymoon, dashed to the coach to get it and collared Tom to come in and help. Between them they managed to adminster a large dose of Greek

Valerian in the form of an infusion, already prepared, down the throat of the loudly protesting Dutchman.

"What does that do, Sir?" asked the coachman.

"It is very good in hysteric cases and works wonders with the vapours. Give some to that girl while you're at it. I want to question the servants."

Yet, with one exception, this proved fruitless. Much as they wanted to help, for the news of Juliana's death had shocked them into stunned silence, there was little they could add. The young mistress had left the house early on Monday morning and had not been seen since.

"Did she take clothes with her?"

"Yes, Sir," said the dead girl's personal maid, "and a strange selection at that. As well as her travelling dress, which she must have been wearing, she took evening clothes and her very best gown."

"So she carried a large bag?"

"Yes, Sir."

John thought aloud. "Then the coachman will probably remember her."

"Of course he will, Sir. He took Miss Juliana into Exeter quite regular."

"So if anybody met her at the other end he would know about it."

"Most certainly, Sir."

"I must have a word with him."

This information was useful but about Richard there was absolutely none. He had left the house for school early on Monday, behaving quite normally, and not a word had been heard of him since. With a growing sense of unease, John went back into the drawing room to find that the Dutchman was reacting to the infusion and quietening down at last.

It was gone three o'clock and John drew van Guylder's manservant to one side.

"I must return to Sidmouth. I have left my wife alone all day and it simply isn't fair on her to be away a moment longer. As soon as I have quit the house I want you to send for your master's physician. Tell him all that has taken place and ask him to call. I will leave a note for him about the physick already prescribed."

"Will you return tomorrow, Sir?"

"I don't know yet. It depends on what is happening at the other end. The constable took Miss Juliana's body to Exeter mortuary this morning and soon somebody must identify it."

"Oh pray God it doesn't have to be the master."

"It more than likely will be," John answered. "If so, I will escort Mr. van Guylder, that is provided Master Richard doesn't turn up."

"What can have happened to him?" asked the servant, shaking his head.

"I don't know," answered John, but there was an awful leaden feeling in his gut as he said the words.

"I have never," John called out of the window to Tom, "been more glad to get back home in my life."

The carriage was plodding up through the centre of Sidmouth village, heading towards The Anchor, which stood, as before, attractively lit by candles and looking thoroughly picturesque and inviting.

Even more inviting was the sight of the beautiful Emilia, standing in the doorway and staring up the track to see if the oncoming vehicle belonged to her husband. As soon as she saw that it did, she flew towards it, smiling and calling his name.

The Apothecary's heart lurched. I really love this woman, he thought, and realised simultaneously that he hadn't considered Coralie for at least two days.

They went into the inn and sat by the fire. Even though the day had been hot, Matthew Salter had put a tinder to the wood so that its comforting glow might cheer the evening. Sitting on either side of it, each consuming a glass of claret, John in a quiet voice caught Emilia up with the day's events. She looked thoroughly alarmed as the conversation came round to Richard.

"What can have happened to him?"

"I honestly don't know."

"Do you think this is connected with Juliana's death, John?"

"I do somehow, yet I can't quite see in what way."

Emilia drew a breath. "He couldn't have killed his own sister and gone into hiding, could he?"

The Apothecary shook his head. "Again, I don't know. But don't forget that I believe she was killed by more than one person."

His bride's angelic features contorted. "All this weeping and wailing coming from van Guylder, was it an act?"

"If it was, it was damnably convincing. I've never seen a fellow in such a lather."

"I have watched actors on the stage give performances that would wither your soul. They were very convincing too."

"I know, I know," said John. He drained his glass. "Let us change for dinner then let me take you to bed."

"There might be time beforehand," Emilia answered pertly.

"If there isn't I'll make time," John answered, and, slipping his arm round her waist, led her up to their bedchamber.

It was all he could do to stay awake. The combination of a full stomach, a bottle of wine, a frantic day and energetic lovemaking, to say nothing of the sea air, was too heady a mix for John to cope with. Hoping that he wasn't getting old before his time, the Apothecary was only too glad to return to his room as soon as the meal was done, and stretch out beside his wife. He was asleep within two minutes and knew nothing further until at some time in the small hours there came a thunderous knocking on his door. It so startled him that John was out of bed and on his feet before he even realised it. Practically sleep walking he slid back the bolt and opened the door a crack, looking out blearily. In the gap he could see framed the honest countenance of William Haycraft, the constable.

"So sorry to disturb you at your rest, Sir, but I was wondering if you would be able to come with me down to the beach."

"Why, what's happened?" asked John, trying to bring his thoughts into some semblance of order.

"A man's been found in the shallows, pretty far gone but still alive. I wondered if you might be prepared to tend him."

"Where does he come from, do you know?"

"Certainly not an English ship, he's speaking a foreign tongue."

"Give me a minute to get dressed and I'll join you."

"What is it?" said Emilia.

"A man's been washed ashore in dire straits. The constable has asked me to help."

"Do you want me to come?"

"No, darling, I don't. It's going to be unpleasant, I'm sure of it. Stay here and keep my place warm."

She was clearly in no mood to argue for she snuggled back down into the pillows. Pulling on travelling breeches and a shirt, John grabbed his medicine bag and followed the constable down the stairs, thinking his must be one of the most eventful honeymoons a man had ever experienced.

The fishermen were on the beach and the Apothecary realised that it must be time for the fleet to set out. The man they had found, for presumably that was how he had been discovered, had been carried inshore and covered with a pile of old sails and nets to keep him warm. Further, some goodhearted soul had lit a fire out of driftwood to give the poor devil a chance to recover. He was terribly weak, though, thought John, feeling his feeble pulse and looking at all the outward signs of cold and exposure.

In fact if it hadn't been for the unseasonably warm weather the wretched fellow would probably be dead. Reaching in his bag he fetched out a decoction of Agrimony made with wine, a general cure-all for internal wounds, bruises and hurts. This he followed with a dose of white poppy juice to ease the man into a peaceful sleep and relieve any pain he might be suffering. He turned to the constable.

"We must get him inside if he is to have a chance of survival. Can The Anchor take him?"

"They will if I order it. There is still some respect for the law round here."

"Can you fetch a table top or similar. We'll need it to carry him on."

"I'll find something and I'll be as quick as I can." And William set off at speed.

Left alone, John stared at the man brought in from the sea, thinking that he was probably no more than forty years old and certainly not English. Dark hair and a swarthy skin, clearly visible in the moonlight, spoke of different origins.

John had a brainwave. Very gently, close to the man's ear, he said the word, *Constantia*. There was a reaction, for the eyelids flickered and then slowly opened. The Apothecary repeated himself and there was a barely perceptible nod of the head.

So this was a member of the disappearing crew. "Do you speak English?" John asked slowly.

"A little," the man gasped, then came a drift towards sleep.

"What happened? Tell me?" begged the Apothecary desperately.

The man opened his eyes and gave him a look that John would never forget. "Angels come," he said, and then quite quietly and with not another word, he died.

Chapter 6

Despite the earlier fatigue he had suffered, the Apothecary realised there would be precious little sleep for him that night. Between them, he and William had carried the dead sailor back to The Ship where they had placed the body in an outbuilding and firmly locked the door. Then they had gone to sit on the settle by the fire which Matthew Salter, anxiously hovering and wanting to be part of all that was taking place, had thoughtfully stoked up.

The Apothecary and the constable eyed each other over a glass of brandy.

"What do you make of it all, Mr. Rawlings?"

"I truly don't know. But before we discuss it let me tell you everything that happened in Exeter today. To begin with, the dead girl's brother has gone missing. Secondly, quite by chance, I located her father and his grief was terrible to see. Or so it appeared."

"Are you saying it was an act?"

"I'm saying that it could have been."

"Go on. Tell me the rest."

John did so and the constable looked thoughtful. "Is the young man's absence connected to all this?"

"Yes, I think it is. I saw them both get the very early coach from Topsham on Monday morning. The girl was going to Exeter to tell her lover she was pregnant, that is according to her father who is guessing just as we are. Richard was obviously in league with his sister. I have ascertained that she had a large bag with her, just as if she were running away. Her brother must have realised what she was up to and been assisting her."

William took a mouthful of brandy that would have downed a lesser man.

"More than that, he probably helped her plan it."

"Does this suggest to you that he knew who the lover was?"

"Yes, Mr. Rawlings ..."

"John, please."

"Yes, John, it does. But the question remains, why did he vanish?"

"Fearing his father's wrath when the plot was discovered?"

William nodded thoughtfully. "A very good point. And now he's too frightened to emerge."

"You think he's heard about his sister's death?"

"When I drove that cart into Exeter, even though I'd put a tarpaulin over the coffin, there were those who saw it arrive at the mortuary. And there were those who noticed me go to the coroner's office to report the death. Believe me, the fact of poor Juliana's demise would have been common knowledge throughout the city by nightfall."

"But not the gruesome details, surely?"

William shook his head. "Not all, but I wouldn't put it past a loose-mouthed mortuary attendant to describe the injuries of a Topsham merchant's daughter to a crony in a hostelry. That would be enough to inform the world and his wife."

"And what about our present corpse? Will you take him to Exeter as well?"

"There's a mortuary in Topsham so that's where he'll go, then he can lie with the other seafarers." William gave a humourless laugh. "His ship has gone back to harbour as well."

"What do you mean?"

"The *Constantia* was towed to Topsham yesterday. Apparently that's where she and her cargo of hemp were originally bound."

"Will the cargo be unloaded?"

"Most certainly. Whoever bought it will insist that it won't go to waste."

"William," said John urgently, "have you enough authority to stop that happening until the Flying Runners get here?"

"I don't know that I have. Why?"

"I would like that ship searched by experts from prow to stern before a horde of people start clambering all over it."

Poor William, who was clearly wrestling with the most difficult challenge of his year in office, said, "I can only try, John. Maybe if we both had a word with the quay master it might do some good."

"Why should he listen to me?"

"Because you have that way with you."

John smiled in the firelight but said nothing and there were a few minutes of companionable silence before the constable spoke again.

"What do you think the dying man meant by his last words?"

"Angels come? I have no idea."

"Do you think that he was so near death he had glimpsed the heavenly host?"

John, who was something of a cynic, looked at William and saw that he was utterly sincere. "It's possible, I suppose."

But though it could be argued the dying sailor was in a death dream, it seemed to the Apothecary that something entirely different might well lie behind those inexplicable words.

At dawn he walked on the beach to clear his head. The tide was right out and a great swathe of sand glistened rose pink beneath the first shafts of sun. On either side reared the mighty cliffs, the red one an unbelievable shade in that pure clear light, the other stretching its long arm into the sea to hold and protect the bay of Sidmouth against all ills. Yet ill had come, John thought, brought in by that deserted ship whose crew, with the exception of one man, had vanished off the face of the earth, or should it be the sea? What had he meant by 'Angels come'? John wondered for the hundredth time. Was it possible that the crew of the *Constantia* had suffered some kind of breakdown and believed they were seeing things that were not really there? Or was there a rational explanation to the whole enigma? Yet, crazed crew or no, there was one inescapable fact. The body of Juliana van Guylder had been placed aboard their ship, almost certainly by her killers, so what had taken place that could allow honest sailors to witness such a terrible event? Or had they already gone overboard, called into the deep by a chorus of angelic voices?

By the time he got back to The Ship the day was already warm and John thought that he would like nothing better than to spend his time relaxing on the beach. But not only had he promised William Haycraft that he would speak to the quay master at Topsham but there was also the matter of Tobias Wills. For by now the wretched young man must surely have heard of his fiancee's murder and be in a state of despair. Further, the Apothecary thought wryly, he might be sufficiently upset to want to discuss a rival, that is if he had known such a being existed. But whichever way he looked at it, John's honeymoon seemed destined for yet another interruption. Worried that Emilia would get tired of the situation and demand his full-time company, the Apothecary mounted the stairs to their bedroom.

She was awake but not yet out of bed, as pretty as a picture with her ripe corn hair spread over the pillow and her blue eyes bright as the sea.

"You look lovely," said her bridegroom.

She stretched out a hand to him, smiling lazily. "Have you sorted everything out?"

"Not really. The poor man died, too far gone for me to save him."

"Where had he come from, do you know?"

"I mentioned the name of the deserted ship and he nodded." John sighed and put on his most pleasing expression. "Emilia, it is very important that the cargo of the *Constantia* is not unloaded until the Runners get here. So the constable has asked me to go with him to see the quay master - today."

His bride sighed, very noisily indeed. "I thought

this was meant to be a time that we spent together, getting to know one another. At this rate I stand as good a chance of getting to know William Haycraft as I do you."

John was silent for a moment, considering the best way to handle the situation. If he took a chance and offered to give the investigation up, Emilia might easily accept. By the same token he wanted her to enjoy herself and remember the marriage month with pleasure. Being a husband was not easy, he thought. With a sigh, John said, "Sweetheart, I have been working with Mr. Fielding for some years now, indeed that is how you and I met. If I promise to hand over to the Runners when they arrive, will you let me assist the constable in the meantime? He is a good man and true but he hasn't the experience of cases of violent death that I have."

"Put like that you make me sound a regular scold. Will I let you indeed! John, I can't stop you doing anything you want to do."

"But if you don't like me doing it then all the pleasure's gone for me."

He was utterly sincere. To upset this woman who had given her pledge to him was not what he wanted at all. Yet, conversely, he was so intrigued by the case of the deserted ship and the dead girl that he longed to see it through to its finish.

Emilia put out her hand again. "Do you mean that?"

John took it and held it to his heart. "Of course I do. Tracking down villains has been a large part of

my life for some years now. But if you truly wanted
me to give up, I would do so."

"But how could I ask such a thing?"

"Very easily if you had a mind."

A memory of Coralie Clive putting herself in danger in order to assist him came back, and John frowned without realising he had done so. Emilia, who was very far from stupid, looked at him shrewdly.

"Would it help if I befriended the ladies involved? Not that there are any mark you."

John, realising that she was probably obeying her mama's instructions and behaving sensibly and with reason, drew her close to him. "Would you do that? For me?"

She gave him that pert smile which he liked so much. "No, actually I would be doing it for Mr. Fielding. Now I'm going to get dressed. I presume we are on our way to Topsham?"

"I think we should be on our way in every sense and return to The Salutation. With the *Constantia* docked there and the body of the sailor going to Topsham mortuary, it seems to me that is where the investigation will be currently centred. Besides that was the address I gave the Runners and they should be arriving any day now."

Emilia got out of bed, allowing her shift to fall to the floor as she did so.

"Will you assist me with my stays? The chambermaid has no idea how to get them truly tight."

"I would rather assist you to take them off."

"That would be difficult as I am not wearing any."

"I had noticed," said John, turning the key in the bedroom door.

To return to Topsham they were obliged to traverse that same wild heath on which they had seen the phantom coach and its headless driver. Even though in daylight it seemed slightly less eerie, for all that it was a bleak and unwelcoming place, the sort of terrain in which a ghostly visitation would not be in the least unexpected.

John turned to Emilia, who was snuggled up close to him with a contented smile on her face. "Shall we try to find the ruins of Wildtor Grange?"

She looked at him blankly, then remembered. "You mean the place where the wicked Thornes used to live?"

"The very same. If the ghosts ride out from there I would like to have a closer look at it."

"You don't believe they do, do you?"

"I don't know. What I saw the other night truly frightened me but still something tells me there has to be a rational explanation." He knocked on the carriage roof with his great stick. "Tom, we're trying to find a ruined house. Can you see anything resembling one?"

"No, Sir."

"Well, keep looking and shout as soon as you do."

"Very good, Mr. Rawlings."

Five minutes later, the coachman called out and John stuck his head from the window, seeing a bleak desolate sight, though impressive in its gaunt loneliness. The house, or what was left of it, for it was roofless and the windows were gone, stood on a hill, the rough outcrops of rock surrounding it presumably giving rise to its name, Wildtor. In the distance could be glimpsed the sea and the town of Exmouth, where the Exe and the ocean conjoined. Indeed, in its day the Grange must have commanded magnificent views over the water at both sunset and sunrise, for empty windows were everywhere, gazing at the Apothecary and his wife like blinded eyes. The ruin was at once both mysterious and spectacular and John felt an almost compulsive urge to leave the coach and walk there, in fact, as if reading his master's mind, Irish Tom was already slowing the horses down. The Apothecary looked at his bride. "Emilia, I'm going to walk up. Will you come with me?"

"It looks very frightening. Promise not to wander off if I do come."

"I won't leave you."

"Very well then."

They left the coach and started up the drive, which climbed steeply uphill through an avenue of old gnarled trees. The higher they went, the better the views, which really were unbelievably beautiful. Yet the isolation of the place, the only living things for miles being the sheep circling the house, staring as the couple approached, gave rise to an oppressive feeling, as if indeed some terrible acts had taken place within those walls.

The great door at the top of a flight of steps was

tightly closed but a window nearby, or rather the stone embrasure in which a window had once stood, looked invitingly low to the ground.

Emilia turned a stricken face to her husband. "You're not going in, are you?"

"Not without you."

"But I'd be terrified."

"I was rather hoping you'd protect me."

She laughed, despite herself. "John Rawlings, you are impossible. Why, oh why, did I agree to marry you? I wanted a calm and comfortable life and here I am about to enter a haunted house with a mischievous husband. I must be mad."

"All interesting people are," answered the Apothecary, and lifted her through the glassless window, stepping inside himself immediately afterwards.

They were in a huge reception hall, still with faded tapestries hanging upon the walls, off which led several doors, all open. A great and truly overpowering staircase reared to the upper floors, defying anyone to climb it. Looking round, the Apothecary found difficulty in putting a date to the place, for it was most certainly not Tudor, yet lacked the delicacy of anything built in the reign of Queen Anne. Eventually he decided that it must be early Georgian but designed to the specifications of someone wildly eccentric, for who else could have created such a monstrously gothic dwelling.

With enormous courage but for all that scuttling like a nervous mouse, Emilia had started to peer into the various rooms. "They're furnished, John," she called over her shoulder. He went to look and found himself staring into drawing rooms and salons where rotting chairs and couches still stood as if awaiting spectral guests. These chambers in their turn led on to others and John realised that the whole of the ground floor consisted of endless suites of huge rooms, echoing with silence.

They came back into the main hall, daunted by what they had just seen, and the Apothecary found his gaze being drawn to the stairs. "Shall we go up?"

"It looks terrible."

"It can't be worse than downstairs."

But it was, much. For on the first floor the suites of desolate chambers continued endlessly, like some terrible maze, with no furnishings to give them any air of decayed habitation.

"Where was Lady Thorne kept prisoner?" Emilia asked in a whisper.

But John did not answer, instead sniffing the air as if trying to pick up a scent.

"What are you doing?" his wife continued.

"Someone's been in here and not long ago at that."

"How do you know?"

"I can smell woodsmoke. There's been a log fire lit recently."

"You're sure it's not just the aroma of fires long ago?"

"Yes, I'm sure. Come with me. I'm certain it's up on this floor."

And taking her by the hand, the Apothecary led

his wife in the direction of the East wing. Half way there, she remembered.

"The East wing was where Lady Thorne was kept, I recall it now."

"Perhaps her ghost likes to keep itself warm," John answered with a chuckle.

"It's not funny, Husband. This is one of the eeriest experiences I have ever had to endure."

"Well, you're dealing with it very well, Wife." This time he laughed, and the sound echoed round and round the deserted house and seemed to go on for ever. Much like the other suites, the rooms of the East wing were dreary and bleak and endless, the only difference being that there were bars at the windows, presumably to prevent the deranged woman from jumping out to her death. These had the effect of turning something depressing into something sinister. So much so that Emilia suddenly stopped short and said, "Do let's go. I can't bear this stifling atmosphere one second longer."

"Let me look in this last room," John answered. "I'm sure this is where the fire was."

He threw open the door and they both drew breath. A fully furnished salon lay beyond, not only that but tricked out in the most sumptuous and modern style with heavy brocade curtains and elegant appointments. Beyond that again and visible through a partly opened door was the last room in the suite - a bedroom of unsurpassed luxury and elegance. Sure enough a fire had been recently lit in the drawing room grate and, to judge from the warmth of the two rooms, in that of the far chamber as well.

"Zounds," said John, "so there's somebody living here after all."

Emilia, her courage much restored, walked through and into the bedroom.

"It's a woman," she called, "some of her clothes are in the press."

But her husband did not answer, temporarily absorbed in a study of the living quarters, trying to discover whether one or two people occupied these extraordinary premises.

A *duchesse en bateau* very similar to that owned by his great friend Serafina de Vignolles stood before the fire, a very feminine piece of furniture if ever there was one. And though a chair had been drawn up on the other side of the hearth there was no sign of anyone having sat in it recently. Further, on a low table close to the couch, stood a decanter of wine, a small plate of fruit, some consumed, and one glass.

"I think she lives here alone," John called, and walked into the bedroom to find his wife. She was standing by the window, a miniature in her hand, staring at it enraptured. "Look at this," she said admiringly. "Is he not the most handsome creature you ever set eyes on?"

Very slightly offended, John took it from her and moved into the light. The likeness of a young man, probably aged about eighteen, stared back at him from gorgeous eyes, a most stunning colour, almost mauve, according to the artist. It was a truly lovely face, somewhat feminine in its beauty, but for all that, if the miniaturist had been true to his subject, in a class of its own.

"I wonder who he is," said Emilia, taking another look.

"Surely not one of the brutal young Thornes."

"Oh no, there's no cruelty in this face."

"Well, whoever, you'd best put it back where you found it. I wouldn't want the mysterious tenant to know she's had visitors."

"You're sure it's a woman?"

"Certain. And there's no sign of a man living with her."

"But who would choose ..." started Emilia, and then froze as the distant sound of footsteps walking with a hard confident tread over the bare boards of the decaying East wing broke the profound silence of Wildtor Grange.

She looked at John, her face frantic. "What shall we do?"

For no good reason, he lost his nerve. The combination of the frightful house and the legend that went with it, together with the discovery of some unknown person residing within the crumbling edifice, proving too much for him. Grabbing his wife by the arm, John hissed, "We hide."

Eyes darting, they looked round and saw that a small dressing room led off the bedroom. As one they fled into it and into the clothes cupboard that stood inside. With the door open the merest crack, just enough to give them space to see out, the Apothecary and his wife waited in fearful silence.

With a bang the door to the living room flew wide and those confident feet, booted to judge by the noise they made, strode inside. Then came the sound of wine being poured into a glass and someone hurling themselves onto the couch in order to drink it.

John peered wildly but could see nothing, the woman - or whoever it was - being totally out of his line of vision. There was a long silence, then the feet descended to the floor once more and marched into the bedroom. At last their owner came into sight as she sat on the bed to remove her boots. John got the vivid impression of a tall, muscular frame; of a cloud of black hair tumbling to her shoulders as her riding hat went flying; of a terrible scar, long healed, that ran from the corner of the woman's right eye to well below her well defined cheek bone. Then, probably because he was now married and decorum had been thrust upon him, like it or no, the Apothecary turned away his gaze as the supple creature he was regarding slowly began to strip herself naked.

Chapter 7

It was all Emilia's fault, or so the Apothecary kept telling himself. Feeling him turn away and remove his eye from the crack, she tugged at his elbow and silently mouthed the words,

"What is she doing now?"

In the tight fit of the clothes cupboard, John shrugged and mimed, "I don't know."

Without saying a word, his bride motioned him back to his observation post and so, not totally reluctantly, the Apothecary was once more forced into the role of voyeur.

It was an extraordinary body he was looking at. Well above average height for a woman and so muscular that its owner must have spent many years walking, riding and swimming, it was almost masculine in some ways. Lean hips and a flat stomach, totally devoid of spare flesh, long legs and strong arms, would have made the woman he watched totally mannish if it had not been for her bosom. For this, though small, was very beautiful, high and round and, like the rest of her, firm and unsagging. Yet she was not young, probably in her early forties. The Apothecary watched in amazement as this Amazon of a creature put on men's breeches, a man's frilly shirt, a cloak and tricorne, into which she pushed up her netted hair, and a pair of dark riding boots, not the ones she had worn when she had come in. Then, once dressed, she walked back into the salon and was lost to view.

There was a pause while the woman poured herself another glass of wine, John distinctly heard her do so. Then after a few minutes that confident tread left the room and was eventually lost to earshot.

"Has she gone?" murmured Emilia.

"I think so."

"Can we come out?"

"Give it a while just in case she returns for some reason."

They waited in silence but there was no further sound and the Apothecary, cautiously opening the cupboard door, popped out his head. All was quiet and he stepped out, then lifted out Emilia who was caught up in a flowing gown and having some difficulty in moving.

"Who in heaven's name was she?" asked his bride, flushed in the cheeks and definitely looking somewhat the worse for her experience.

"I have no idea."

"And what can she be doing living in a place like this?"

John shook his head. "I get the feeling that this is a bolt-hole, somewhere she comes when she needs to escape."

"Escape what? The law?"

"Sweetheart, all the time we stand here in discussion we are in risk of discovery. Let us get out as quickly as we can and ask Tom what he saw. He's been waiting round the coach all this time. Perhaps he saw her ride past. At least he might be able to tell us in which direction she was heading."

"Was she beautiful?" asked Emilia as they hurried down the overpowering staircase.

"In a strange sort of way."

"What do you mean by that?"

"Well, her bone structure was fine and her hair and eyes both lustrous and dark, but the poor soul was scarred."

"On the face?"

"Yes. A gash ran from eye to cheek, a deep cut that looked as if it had been done with a sword."

"This," said Emilia, suddenly shivering, "is an evil house and brings no luck with it. I worry for her, whoever she might be, that she chooses to dwell here, even if it is only as a place of refuge."

Unsuperstitious as John was, he was relieved to step through the window embrasure and feel the fresh Devon air blowing in his face. His bride was already hurrying towards the coach without a backward glance, but he, just for a moment, stopped in his tracks and looked over his shoulder. Was there really a pale face looking out at him from behind a barred glassless window in the East wing? Or was it just a trick of the light? Whatever the answer, John was glad to clamber into the snug confines of the carriage and shout to Tom to drive to Topsham as fast as he could go.

It appeared that the woman, though Irish Tom would insist that it had been a man who left the

Grange, had ridden off at speed in the direction of Exeter, but further than that he could tell them nothing. He had not seen her arrive, though the coachman had to admit that he had sat inside the carriage and fallen asleep for a while. So there John had to let it rest, though the question loomed large in his mind as to whether the mysterious occupant of Wildtor Grange had any connection at all with the death he was currently investigating, or whether it was all a bizarre coincidence.

Coming from the Grange as they were, John and Emilia found themselves approaching Topsham from an entirely different direction. Hugging the banks of the River Clyst, they passed a mill, then crossed a bridge leading to an inviting hostelry. A foaming weir lay on one side, meadowland on the other, between the two, the Bridge Inn. The Apothecary, longing for something to calm his nerves after his strange ordeal in the clothes cupboard, cast longing eyes in its direction but this time Emilia had the last word.

"I am not going to appear in public in this state of disarray, John. I would like to go straight back to The Salutation and wash and change for dinner. The odour of that terrible house is still upon me."

And the Apothecary had to admit that in truth both of them smelled decidedly musty and reluctantly nodded his head. "I must visit the place another time, though. It is situated in such a pleasant location."

"Yes, another time," Emilia answered firmly, and there the matter was put to rest.

Tom turned the horses down a rough track where they picked their delicate way to Fore Street. The river came into sight, gleaming in the early afternoon sunshine, the masts of the ships thick as a forest. And there, neatly placed on a corner and looking most welcoming was The Salutation. Emilia, clearly very conscious of her dishevelled appearance, rushed upstairs to their room, giving orders as she went for some hot water to be brought, but the Apothecary went straight to the parlour reserved for guests, where he flung himself into a chair and ordered a large brandy.

A figure rose from a settle at the far end. "Well, Sir, you look as if you've been having a few adventures," said a familiar voice.

John gaped, then sprang to his feet, throwing his arms round the newcomer, so very pleased was he to see him. "Joe," he shouted, kissing him on the rugged cheek. "Why, if it isn't Joe Jago."

Mr. John Fielding's clerk and right-hand man, affectionately dubbed the blind Magistrate's eyes, returned the embrace. "Well, Sir, this is a fine how dee do, ain't it? Here you are enjoying your honeymoon, as every man has a right to do, and bless me if you don't stumble across a body. Mr. Fielding had to chuckle ..."

John could almost hear the melodious rumble and smiled.

" ... but for all that he says to me, 'I believe our friend is in trouble'. So here I am, Sir. Setting forth from London into the mysterious West country."

"Are the Runners with you?"

"They are, Sir, and keen as greyhounds. They're in the kitchen at this very moment taking ale with the locals."

John grinned and gave a great sigh of relief. "I'm so glad you're here, my friend. This is truly one of the weirdest situations I have ever found myself involved in."

"If you'll take a bottle of wine with me, Sir, I suggest we sit over there in that quiet corner and you tell me the story right from the start. Then I can make a list if I have to."

Famed amongst his associates for his lists, John could see that Joe had pen, ink pot and paper already standing on a nearby table.

"But I'm forgetting my manners," said the clerk as they sat down. "How is Mrs. Rawlings?"

Just for a second the Apothecary wondered who he meant, then he said, "Emilia is very well, thank you, but at the moment quite taken up with making a toilette. I should say that we have a good hour in which we can talk before she puts in an appearance."

"I'll make myself scarce then, Sir."

"Oh no you won't. She would be mortified. You must join us for dinner."

Telling the story right from the start helped to clarify certain things that John had been aware of but had not yet put into any orderly sequence in his mind. As he spoke he was much amused to see Joe draw paper and pen towards him and start to write. Eventually, when there was silence, Mr. Fielding's clerk looked up.

"Well, it seems to me, Sir, that the most important thing, the item that I have put at number one, is to find young Richard. He probably holds the key to the whole affair. For once he has given us the name of his sister's cicisbeo ..."

Inwardly, the Apothecary cracked with laughter at Joe's pronounciation of the word, though to his credit, his face did not alter..

"... then we have the key to her personal life and, most probably, her murderer."

"Or murderers. I told you my opinion after examining the body."

"Yes, and very nasty too. We are obviously dealing with depraved minds here."

"Which brings me back to something I would rather not dwell on - but must. Was the girl's father capable of such a crime?"

"If his pleasant facade hides a cruel and restrictive parent, then yes."

"And her betrothed, Tobias Wills?"

"A similar reply, Mr. Rawlings. Though I really should reserve judgement until I meet these people."

John stretched his legs in front of him and drank his claret, feeling the soothing benefits of both the wine and Joe's calming presence. "So where do we start?"

"At the quay side. We must make sure that the *Constantia* remains untouched until she has been thoroughly searched."

"I suppose you're armed with letters of authorisation?"

"Yes, for what good they'll do in this Godforsaken part of the country."

"Oh, come now. Exeter considers itself very civilised."

"But Topsham ain't Exeter," Joe replied meaningfully, and winked an eye.

However, his opinion seemed slightly tempered by the excellence of the repast that was set before them when an hour later he, John and Emilia sat down to dine. Looking at the craggy face and the foxy hair that he had grown to love and respect over the years, the Apothecary wondered yet again about the clerk's private life. Other than that there was no Mrs. Jago and that Joe lived in the Seven Dials area of London, he knew nothing further about him. And, considering it, John felt that perhaps he didn't want to. Joe was a character in his own right; utterly reliable, utterly kind and utterly discreet. Let him remain a man of mystery until the day came when he wanted to reveal himself. And if he didn't, then that was a matter for him alone.

"Did you say you were going out?" Emilia asked as they neared the end of the meal.

"Yes, we must see the quay master before sunset. Before we left Sidmouth I told the constable that I would meet him at the man's house at six o'clock."

"Then may I come with you? I should like to see the ships."

Joe raised her hand to his lips, an endearing gesture from such a rugged individual. "Mrs. Rawlings, you are on your honeymoon. If it is your wish that I continue these investigations on my own, then you only have to say."

She smiled, just a fraction sadly John thought. "Mr. Jago, I think perhaps that if I did that my marriage would last no longer than the honeymoon itself."

There was a profound silence, broken by the Apothecary, who said, "I feel so guilty. Why should I inflict all this on you?"

"I married you knowing about it, John. I was aware that you worked with Mr. Fielding." She gave that same wistful smile. "I just didn't think a murder would follow you on honeymoon, that's all."

"Despite your presentiment?"

"I put that down to my own silly superstition."

"Well," said Joe, rubbing his hands together, "do we proceed?"

"Of course you do," said Emilia, and John, leaning across the table in a most ungentlemanly fashion, gave her a smacking kiss upon the lips, which gave rise to a ripple of laughter amongst the other diners.

An April evening by the river and a chilly little wind making wavelets upon the broad back of the Exe, the great waterway reflecting slashes of light from the dying sun, which was sinking amidst a particularly savage sunset. Riding somewhat apart from the other vessels, the *Constantia* looked desolate and alone, its figurehead of a mermaid with long tresses of golden hair too reminiscent of the grisly find that had been placed upon it in what John could only think of as a savage joke.

As was to be expected at this hour of the evening, the quay master was not on duty but at home. Pointed out to them as a house built close to the quay itself, John and Joe Jago, accompanied by Emilia, wrapped warmly against the cold, made their way there. William Haycraft, looking amazingly clean and dressed in a coat of good grey worsted, his best, was already ahead of them and trying his very best to explain to an important individual named Thomas Northmore that the *Constantia* must be thoroughly searched before her cargo of hemp could be unloaded. At the moment of their arrival it seemed that he was not doing terribly well and he cast a look of enormous gratitude in John's direction as the visiting party was shown into Mr. Northmore's parlour. His eyes widened as he saw Joe Jago and realised that the contingent from London had arrived at last.

The quay master, so John thought, epitomised his title, for it was very clear from his attitude that he believed himself governor indeed, not only in his own house but of all those who had anything to do with Topsham quay. He also considered himself a ladies man judging from the leering smile that he gave Emilia, a smile which revealed the most alarming set of false teeth, apparently carved out of whalebone by a whittling sailor from a whaling ship. He was reasonably tall which helped him carry his rather odd figure, somewhat skinny but with a large stomach that sat pudding-like above the fastening of his breeches. This night the quay master had removed his wig and wore an odd arrangement upon his head, not quite turban, not quite hat. However, he obviously considered this the height of fashion and that being thus attired gave him the edge over the people who had come to ask him a favour.

His pale blue eyes, hard as pebbles, gazed from the bags beneath them "And you are?" he said to John, his whalebone dentures clicking very slightly.

"John Rawlings, apothecary of London. And this is my wife Emilia ..."

She curtseyed and Northmore murmured, 'Charming', and kissed her hand.

"And this is Joe Jago, assistant to Mr. John Fielding, the Principal Magistrate of the capital."

"So what is your business with me, gentlemen?"

William Haycraft spoke up. "I have just been asking Mr. Northmore if the unloading of *Constantia*, scheduled to begin tomorrow morning, could be delayed by another twenty-four hours."

"And I have just been answering no," the quay master said down the length of his nose. "The purchasers of the cargo are keen to get the hemp into their warehouse, feeling that they have been kept waiting long enough. And I agree with them."

John was just about to look at Joe Jago to see which one of them should answer first when a woman suddenly scuttled into the room. She had once been a beauty, of that there was no doubt, but now the passing years and her extreme thinness had made her look sunken and sad. She gazed at Northmore nervously.

He glared at her in what could only be described

as a masterful manner. "Wife, go to. We talk men's matters here. This is no place for you."

She stared about at the assembled visitors, her once pretty face pinched. "Yes, Thomas," she said, made an anxious salutation, then fled. John felt like rushing after her and offering her some restorative cordial - or some poison with which to do away with her insufferable husband.

The quay master gave a merry laugh. "Audrey does not understand matters of business, alas. But she runs a tidy house. Yes indeed."

Emilia spoke up. "That must be nice for you," she said innocently, and gave a guileless smile.

Northmore, who was clearly thick-skinned as well as everything else, flashed his dentures at her. "Now, gentlemen, state your business clearly," he said, watching Emilia to see if she was impressed.

Joe Jago, who had been maintaining a heroic silence, broke it. "Sir, I am here on behalf of the Principal Magistrate, John Fielding. Although I am more than aware that his jurisdiction does not extend to this part of the country, I am accompanied on this journey by two of the court Runners, whose duty it is to go to any part of the kingdom in order to apprehend villains. Therefore, an act which could be interpreted as impeding the course of justice would be within their sphere of authority and they are empowered to arrest. As the constable has probably told you, a murder took place on the ship *Constantia*. I am thus asking you officially to impound that vessel until it has been searched by experts, a duty which is scheduled to take place tomorrow."

The quay master attempted to look as if he were considering, narrowing his gaze and pursing his lips, but he was out manoeuvered and he knew it. However, he wasn't going down without a fight.

"May I see your letter of authorisation," he said nastily. "After all, anyone could walk in here and say they were representing John Fielding."

"Indeed they could, "Joe answered, giving him a fox-like smile. He reached into an inner pocket. "Here we are, Sir. Signed by the Magistrate himself."

Northmore scanned the paper. "It seems to be in order," he admitted grudgingly. "I take it you are the Joe Jago that Fielding mentions."

"I am indeed, Sir. Now, what time do you want me and my fellows at the quayside tomorrow?"

"At dawn," answered Northmore, giving a sly grin, clearly thinking that these upstarts from town would shudder at the very thought.

"We'll be there," said Joe. "Now, Sir, let me thank you for your cooperation. If you have any further questions for me I am staying at The Salutation and will be only too happy to discuss them with you."

It had been neatly done and there was no point in lingering further. As one, the company rose and made polite salutations before stepping out into the hallway. There, hovering and pale, stood the skinny wife, wringing her hands and looking generally terrified.

"Is it true that it is Juliana van Guylder who is dead?" she whispered

"I'm afraid so," John answered sympathetically.

"Oh how terrible. I knew her when she was a little girl. I was quite friendly with the family, you know."

"Now, now, my dear," said her husband from the parlour doorway. "This is not a subject fit for womenfolk. Surely you have some delicious meal with which to tempt my jaded appetite. Perhaps you should be seeing to it."

Poor Audrey curtsied. "Yes, Husband."

Emilia pitched in once more. "Would you care for me to call on you, Mrs. Northmore? I am a stranger in Topsham and would much appreciate a little company."

The wretched woman looked at the quay master. "Would that be in order, my dear?"

With the eyes of the other three men upon him, Thomas Northmore had no alternative but to say yes.

"If ever," said Emilia, standing outside in the fitful light of the rising moon, "you become like that, John, I shall run away to my mother."

"And I would help you," he answered. "What an obnoxious fellow."

"He believes himself authoritative," said William Haycraft. "In fact he's known for it for miles about."

"He has very strange teeth," added Joe Jago, and everybody laughed.

It was not late, the interview having been such a short one, and there was yet much to accomplish. It was decided, therefore, that William would head for Exeter and see the coroner at his private quarters,

leaving the others free to visit first, Jan van Guylder
and then, time permitting, Tobias Wills.

"I think, Mr. Rawlings, it might be better if you
undertook those tasks alone," Joe said thoughtfully
as the constable departed. "My presence might well
put the gentlemen concerned off, as people are
always inhibited by strangers. While Mrs. Rawlings,
saving your delightful presence, Ma'am, could
make them omit something that they would readily
say to a fellow. So, if you are both agreeable, I will
accompany the lady back to the inn."

John took Emilia's hand. "Do you mind?"

She shook her head. "Not in the least. The adventure in the clothes cupboard has quite worn me out.
I shall be pleased to retire early."

"But not," Joe said gallantly, "before you have
done me the honour of sharing a few minutes of
your time with me, I hope."

She smiled up at him, looking as angelic as when
John had first seen her. "It will be my pleasure," she
answered, and the Apothecary saw the clerk's
ragged features spread into a delighted smile.

A gloomy transformation had occurred. Shell
House, usually so light and airy and charming, had
become a house of mourning. Black cloth had been
wrapped round the knocker and there was black
hanging where the curtains usually were. Putting
on a suitably sombre expression, John rang the bell
and was ushered into the hall by a long faced servant.

"How is your master?" the Apothecary enquired in hushed tones.

"Taken it very bad, Sir. He has eaten nothing since yesterday when you brought him home."

"What about his son? Has he shown up yet?"

"No, Sir, and that's the hard part of it. If Richard were here to comfort the Master I don't think he'd be in quite such a state. But added to his anguish is the worry over the boy. Oh, it's a truly terrible situation, Sir, truly terrible."

"Do you think he is well enough to receive me?"

"He'd probably appreciate the company, Mr. Rawlings. I'll go and tell him."

But John's lack of sleep on the previous night was beginning to catch up with him and it was almost a relief when the servant returned and said, "The Master begs pardon, Sir, but asks if you would mind coming back in the morning. He was just on the point of retiring when you called."

The Apothecary nodded agreement. "That's perfectly all right, tell him. I'll return. Now there is one thing you can help me with."

"And what's that, Sir?"

"Tobias Wills, Miss Juliana's betrothed. Does he live far away?"

"No, Sir, just a few paces up the street at number 41, The Strand."

"Do you know if he's been told about his fiancee?"

"He has. Apparently he overheard a rumour in Exeter and came back here quite mad with grief. The Master confirmed the truth and the poor fellow

went rushing out of the house like a blinded bull.
He's not been seen since."

"I shall attempt a call."

"Good luck to you, Sir."

Though Shell House was lovely it was old, having
been built in the previous century. But Number 41
was very different, probably, or so John guessed,
dating from the reign of William and Mary and no
more than sixty years of age. From the outside it was
stunning, with a pillared entrance and large gracious windows, including two dormers in the roof
where the servants were housed. With its ordered
gardens and delicate shape, the Apothecary considered it one of the most charming houses he had seen
in a long time.

Again, there were signs of mourning about the
exterior. Black draped the lion's head knocker and
all the curtains had been drawn, though as it was
already dark outside this was hardly surprising.
Wishing that he had a more pleasant mission, John
knocked at the door.

As he stepped into the hall, having produced a
card and explained the nature of his visit, the sounds
of weeping were distinctly audible. From a room
deep in the house's heart a woman sobbed with a
high-pitched sound, while from somewhere close
by a man grieved rather more softly.

"If Master Tobias cannot see me I will quite
understand," John murmured to the footman, the
timbre of his voice respectful. A door flung open

dramatically. "No, I'll see you, Sir," shouted Tobias, rocking on his feet, clearly drunk as a wheelbarrow. "I have words to say to you."

John bowed. "Thank you for dealing with a stranger in your hour of grief."

"Grief, grief!" bellowed the young man. "You don't even know the meaning of the word." And with that he swayed his way back into the small salon, John following in his wake.

Tobias looked absolutely terrible, his face red and blotchy, his eyes puffed up, his clothes crumpled as if he had slept in them and soiled where he had spilled wine down his front. As soon as the door was closed behind them he started to attack agressively.

"Did you know? Did you know when we met that she was already dead?"

John thought rapidly. To tell the truth at this delicate stage would be tantamount to inciting a riot. He lied nobly. "No, Sir, I did not."

A look of drunken cunning crossed poor Tobias's flushed features. "Then why were you looking for Richard?"

"As I told you, because he was missing from school."

"Is that all?"

"Yes, why? Should there be anything else?"

Tobias tapped the side of his nose. "Sit down. Have a drink. I've something to tell you."

The Apothecary took a seat opposite his host's, watching as the sad and wretched drunkard poured out two glasses of port.

"I was betrothed to Juliana," Tobias stated belligerently. "Did you know that?"

"Yes. You told me so the other day."

"I was going to marry her, faithless whore that she was."

"Why do you say that?" asked the Apothecary, feeling that frisson which always heralded the fact that some important information was about to be revealed.

"That she was a whore?" John nodded. "Because she had met somebody else and let him make free with her. I was never free with her, do you know that? I respected her virtue."

Tobias wept again, loudly and blubberingly. John, fearing that the moment of truth was about to pass, leapt to his feet and administered the salts which he always carried in his pocket.

The young man wiped his eyes with his hand. "I loved Juliana, Mr. ... What did you say your name was?"

"Rawlings. John Rawlings."

"I loved her, John," said Tobias, deciding that this was not the moment for the nicety of surnames.

"I'm sure you did. But tell me about her lover. Who was he, do you know?"

"Of course I know. It was that bastard foppish Fitz, that moneyed shite from Exeter."

Memories of the card found in Richard's room came back, together with the fact that though the Apothecary had meant to call on the Fitz family, so far the opportunity had not presented itself.

"And that's not all," Tobias continued thickly, "I also know who killed her."

John felt himself grow tense. "You do? Who was it, for God's sake?"

"Why, Richard of course. That's why he's gone to earth."

John stared at him, uncomfortably aware that the same suspicion had gone through his own mind. "But why should he kill his own sister?"

"Because he was jealous."

"Jealous? Of whom, pray?"

"Of Fitz, of course. Richard was in love with him. You see, John, that was the great irony. The two van Guylder children were both in love with the same man."

"Oh, God!" said the Apothecary with feeling. "And what about Fitz? Did he know all this?"

Tobias burst into most unpleasant laughter. "Know? Of course he knew? You see, my dear fellow, equally he was in love with both of them."

Chapter 8

The spell of hot weather was over. As John Rawlings got out of bed and dressed in the dawning he could feel that the chilly wind of the previous evening was still blowing round The Salutation and in through the cracks of the window that overlooked the river. Turning to look at Emilia, lying fast asleep in their old-fashioned four poster bed, complete with tester, he wanted nothing more at that moment than to crawl in beside her and warm himself up in the nicest way possible.

He had never, he thought as he struggled into his shirt, considered that a honeymoon would involve so little sleep - and for all the wrong reasons. The night before last there had been none at all, while the night just gone had amounted to a mere few hours rest before being forced to rise in the cold and head down to the river to search the *Constantia*. He could, of course, have got out of the job, passed it over to Joe and the two Brave Fellows, but as it had been his idea in the first place, the Apothecary had felt determined to carry it through. However, there was one consolation. As he went downstairs for a hurried breakfast he found that the post boy had brought a letter from Sir Gabriel.

My Son,
    I am Advised by Mr. J. Fielding, at whose House I

stopped to Dine t'other Day, that you are once More
Engaged upon the pursuit of a Murderous Wretch.
My dear Child, is there no End to the Fates that
Befall You? I Hope with good Heart that You find
Time for Enjoyment as well As Effort. Should a
Moment be Found, pray Call upon my Old Friend
Sir Clovelly Lovell in Exeter. I am Writing to him in
this Same Post. Pray give my Kind Regards to Mrs.
Rawlings and Trust I find Her Well. I remain, Sir,
your Affectionate Father and Friend,

    G. Kent.

There was a post script giving Sir Clovelly's address,
which, John noted with interest, was also in The
Close, a mere few doors away from the Fitzes.

"Clovelly Lovell," said John aloud over his ham,
"it has to be a joke. Nobody could call their child
that."

And he was still smiling about it as he walked
down the street to the quay.

It was very dark, only the faintest glow in the sky
showing that indeed dawn was coming up, but the
river itself was as ink black as if it were midnight. It
was at full swell, gurgling and eddying in the darkness, rushing to find the Clyst so that they could
journey down to the sea together. On its back the
great merchantmen rode gallantly at anchor, their
masts creaking in the forceful breeze.

During the night the *Constantia* had been brought
in to the quay side and as John approached he saw
that Joe and the two Runners were already there
ahead of him and negotiating with the quay master

to have a boarding ladder set up. Mr. Northmore, who clearly did not want to make things easy for them, was taking his time about agreeing. The dawn light burnished the clerk's fiery head as he discussed the matter and John could see by the way his body moved that he was starting to run out of patience. Leaving them to get on with it, confident that Joe would win, the Apothecary walked down the quay, staring at the ship that had been brought alongside by the simple means of pulling in her mooring rope and making it fast. Then he saw in the dimness that the *Constantia's* own ladder was in place, hooked over the rail and hanging over the side, merely waiting for someone to secure it to the quay.

"The ladder's already down," he called to the arguing couple.

"Well, there's an end to the deliberations," said Joe snappishly, "if you, Sir, could provide a man to hold it while we go aboard."

The quay master, who clearly liked to look magnanimous on occasion, said, "We'll fasten it in place, Mr. Jago. We cannot have Mr. Fielding in London thinking that we Devonians stand in the way of law and order."

"Quite," Joe answered pointedly.

A few moments later it was done. A burly dock labourer had pulled the lower end of the ladder towards him with a hook and secured it to a pair of stout rings with rope.

"After you, Sir," said Joe Jago and gave an affectionate little bow as John climbed aboard.

It was uncanny, setting foot on that death ship

once more. The dawning cast shadows and pools of darkness over the deck, making shapes which the Apothecary found most disturbing.

"This is not a good light for searching," he said to Joe who was clambering up right behind.

"We'll wait a quarter of an hour or so. Meanwhile, can you show me where you found the body."

They went to the prow where the figurehead stared out sightlessly over the river. "Here. The girl was draped over it, her hair hanging down just like the mermaid's. It was a terrifying sight."

"It must have been, Sir. Now lads," Joe called to the two Flying Runners, "come over here if you would."

The Apothecary had never met the Brave Fellows, though he recognised both of them as the men who had come to Vaux Hall Gardens when a murder had been committed in the Dark Walk several years earlier. On that occasion he had briefly been suspected of the crime and had felt extremely nervous, a state made no easier by the couple of Runners, who by their very professionalism had instantly revealed themselves as being something very special. Now he was to meet them, looking much the same as they had then, hardly a day older.

The Runner whom he had remembered as lively and loud stepped forward and bowed to John.

"Runner Dick Ham," said Joe Jago. The Apothecary bowed back. "We met at Vaux Hall many years ago but you wouldn't remember me."

"On the contrary, Sir," answered Dick in a big, booming voice. "I make it a rule never to forget a face. We escorted you to Bow Street if memory serves."

John gulped. "Indeed you did."

The small, black-haired Runner bowed in his turn. "Nicholas Raven, Sir. We meet again in happier circumstances."

How very well his name became him, the Apothecary thought, as he returned the greeting. The man had a hard avine stare which was enough to unnerve the innocent, let alone the guilty. Remembering how frightened of Raven he had once been, John wondered if he was going to like him. Joe was speaking. "The murdered girl was draped over the figurehead. That's where Mr. Rawlings found her. She had been badly beaten, indeed whipped, and it is the Apothecary's opinion that the injuries she sustained brought about her death."

"Why was she put on the figurehead?" Raven asked.

John replied. "Clearly we will never know. But in my view it was some kind of joke, the spreading of the hair over that of the mermaid was, I suppose, meant to be an artistic touch."

"So we are dealing with a perverted mind."

It was a statement not a question and John nodded. "Either that, or we are meant to think so."

Runner Ham spoke up. "Was the girl beaten by one person, or were several involved? Or don't you know?"

"Obviously I can't be certain but the blows seemed to me to come from different directions. I would say that at least two people had a hand in her death. Maybe more."

"Rum do," said Joe, summing up all their feelings.

It had grown lighter as they spoke and now the sun broke over the eastern horizon, casting a hellish light over the ship that had witnessed so many odd occurences.

"The search can begin," stated the clerk. "Runners, if you will hunt the deck, Mr. Rawlings and I will take the hold and the cabins."

They descended a ladder leading from a hatch, going down into a ghostly world of small passageways and dark wood. John stood a moment, sniffing the air.

"What is it, Sir?"

"I don't know. Can you detect an odd odour?"

Joe stood silently, inhaling. "I can smell something very faintly, but there's another stink drowning it out."

"What do you mean?"

"There's a reek of bad eggs. A gun has been fired down here and recently at that."

"What?" John bellowed in disbelief. "What more can happen on this hell hole of a ship?"

"No time for talk, get searching," Joe ordered urgently.

They raced down the passageway, throwing open the doors of cramped and uncomfortable cabins, seeing yet again in startling detail the fact that this ship had been abandoned at a moment's notice, that clothes and personal items were scattered just as if the owner had merely walked out of the room. Finally they came to the captain's cabin, the larger door indicating that here were quarters of a more generous size. Joe thrust it open, then stood in the entrance, frozen in disbelief. Just behind him, the Apothecary peered over his shoulder through the swirling clouds of blue smoke.

Richard van Guylder was in the cabin, sitting at the captain's table, his back to the door so that he was unable to see the newcomers. But then, of course, Richard would never be able to see anybody ever again. Clutched in his lifeless fingers was a flintlock pistol and scattered over the walls, the ceiling, in fact everywhere that the horrified gaze of the two men came to rest, were Richard's brains and at least half of his head, to say nothing of the blood that had spurted with them. On that ship of ill omen, Juliana's brother had met an end equally as terrible as hers.

Somehow the two men had managed to get back up on deck and take great lungfuls of air and it wasn't until they had done so that John realised he was trembling from head to toe, while Joe had turned ashen white. They looked at one another, very slightly shame-faced.

"Well, Sir, I don't think I've ever run from a death before."

"Nor I. What made us do it?"

"The look of him and that terrible, terrible room."

"Was it suicide?"

"There was a blood-spattered note lying on the table in front of him."

"Then we'd best go and look."

The two Brave Fellows had approached, realising that something was horribly wrong. "I take it there's another body down there," said Raven.

"It's the dead girl's brother and it appears that he's blown his brains out."

"Remorse?" asked Dick Ham.

"What do you mean?"

"That if he had killed his sister for some reason, the guilt became too much for him."

"But what reason could there possibly be?" asked Joe.

"I'm afraid there might indeed be one," John answered with a sigh. "A reason called Gerald Fitz, a blade of Exeter with whom both the van Guylder children were in love."

Joe groaned. "I hate these convoluted love affairs, they never bode any good."

Raven said, quite reasonably, "We might know more when we've read what he had to say."

"Indeed we might," answered Joe, and all four of them descended below deck to examine the scene more closely.

Whatever his reservations about Nicholas Raven, John could not help but admire the man. With admirable calm the Runner approached the body, which had fallen back in the chair, its head, or what was left of it, lolling, and removed the note from beneath the fingers of the outstretched left hand.

Then he had carefully dabbed it with his handkerchief to remove the blood, still sticky and wet, and handed it to Joe Jago.

"I cannot bear the burden of guilt any longer," the clerk read aloud. "Juliana, forgive me."

"Is that all it says?" asked John.

"Yes. It's simply signed Richard."

"Well, that's it then," said Dick Ham. "You've found your murderer. "

Almost as a reflex action, before he had had time to think, John answered, "No, that can't be right."

"Why not, Sir?"

"Because the girl was raped before she was killed and if we are to believe what we are told then Richard would most certainly not be interested, leave alone the fact that he was quite a decent creature and I'm sure would not countenance incest."

"Then are we looking for an accomplice?" asked Joe.

John shook his head. "I have a feeling, though why I simply can't put into words, that it is all far, far more complex than that."

"I think," answered the clerk, "that all four of us should go ashore for a brandy. Then, Mr. Rawlings, I will have to ask you to examine the body before it is removed."

"And the search of the ship?" asked Raven.

"That must continue. In fact it is even more vital in view of this latest development. For how and when did Richard get aboard. That must be ascertained before we can continue any further."

A ghastly thought struck John. "Who is going to tell the poor benighted father?"

"I shall do so in my official capacity," answered Mr. Fielding's clerk without flinching. "Believe me, Sir, he will take it better from an officer of the law than he will from someone that he considers to be a friend."

The morning wore on like a nightmare. The horrible task of examining what was left of Richard van Guylder was one of the most sickening that the Apothecary had ever undertaken. He literally had to step through pools of blood to get at the tragic youth and if it had not been for the very large amounts of brandy that he had consumed, he truly believed he could not have gone through with it. Eventually, though, it was done. Richard had died of a gunshot wound to the head and there was no reason to believe that it had been anything other than self-administered. The fingers gripping the flintlock had not been forced in any way that the Apothecary could see, nor did the position of the corpse at the table look as if it had been arranged.

Yet the suicide note bothered John. Providing that it was in Richard's handwriting, it would certainly seem to point to him as the murderer. Yet, from his very brief acquaintanceship with the poor spotty boy, he simply would not have believed him capable of such a thing. Did the plea for forgiveness and the expression of guilt refer to something else? Was it possible, the Apothecary conjectured, that Richard

had been told of his sister's death and been
unhinged by the news? Or was it even more sinister
than that? The necessity of seeing Gerald Fitz had
now assumed enormous proportions. In fact, John
decided, it must be done this day without fail.

The removal of another body from the ghost ship,
as the inhabitants of the quay had nicknamed the
Constantia, had caused a near riot. A call for some
tarpaulin and a plank had raised the alarm, and by
the time the two Brave Fellows had struggled
down the ladder with their secret burden, securely
wrapped and lashed to the spar but for all that clearly resembling the shape of a human being, there was
a crowd on the quay. Well to the fore, in fact pushing
the throng back, was the masterful Mr. Northmore.
He stopped Joe in his tracks.

"What's that you have there?"

The clerk put on a very severe face. "It is a body,
Sir. There has been another fatality aboard. One of
my Fellows will inform the constable just as soon as
we have arranged carriage to the mortuary."

The quay master barred his path. "This is my
quay, Sir, and all that goes on here is my responsibility. I insist on being told the identity of the
deceased."

John watched Joe think on his feet. If the truth
leaked out now it might well have awful consequences as the gossip spread like wildfire and
reached the wretched Jan van Guylder before he had
been officially informed that he had lost both his
children.

"I do not know the person concerned," the clerk

answered truthfully. "He is a stranger to me. All I can tell you is that it is a male."

"Show me his face. I'll soon identify him for you."

"That would be breaking the law," said Joe with authority. "Until the constable and the coroner have been informed I am not at liberty to let you anywhere near. Good day to you."

So saying, he and the two Runners swept off in the direction of the mortuary, leaving John to return to Emilia.

Two hours later the four men were back together again, seated in The Unicorn, a private room in The Salutation, discussing not only what the search had yielded up but also how and when Richard had crept aboard.

"He couldn't have been there all along, could he?" asked John.

"You mean that when he went missing he was hiding on the ship?"

"Precisely."

Joe considered. "I suppose it's possible. Men would have gone aboard at Sidmouth to fix tow ropes but most likely none of them went down to the cabins. I'll wager you're right there, Sir. That's where the little devil hid out, God rest his sad soul."

"Then if that is the case, the ladder is very significant."

Raven's black eyes glinted. "You mean he had a visitor last night?"

"Well, if not then, at least during his stay. Somebody

lowered the ship's ladder into place to allow another party to board."

"Unless Richard went ashore for some reason."

"That's possible too. Perhaps he was over-whelmed by a need to see Gerald Fitz."

Mr. Fielding's clerk donned a pair of folding spectacles which he removed from a steel case, then peered over the top of them.

"Gentlemen, let us start at the beginning. I have already sent a man with a trap to drive to Exeter bearing a letter from myself to the coroner. In this letter I informed him that I am staying here and can attend his office at any time. While I was busy organising this, the Brave Fellows sought out the constable."

Dick Ham took up the story. "He turned out to be a deputy, much sodden with drink and not enthusiastic about his duties. He was only too pleased to hand over to us; lacking pride, energy and enthusiasm. As a gesture I promised to report any developments to him. And there the matter rests."

"So the task of finding Juliana's killers remains with us and the excellent William Haycraft."

Dick Ham looked doubtful. "I still think it was the brother, begging your pardon Mr. Rawlings."

"It would be the most obvious solution, I agree. But humour me, friends. There is more behind this than we can see at the moment, I feel certain of it."

"There are certainly Gerald Fitz and Tobias Wills to be considered as suspects," said Joe. He was silent a moment, then added, "Mr. Rawlings, do you feel up to going to Exeter after dinner?"

"I promised Emilia that I would take her there this very night. The poor girl is getting bored indeed with being left alone."

"And is it your intention to seek out Gerald Fitz while you are there?"

"One way or another, yes. I may manage an introduction to him through a connection of my father's."

"Very good. Meanwhile, I have the unpleasant task of informing Mr. van Guylder of his further bereavement. That leaves Tobias Wills to be spoken to."

"What about Nick and Dick?" said John, slightly amused by the Runners' names.

"I think they would frighten him. He is more your meat, Sir. Perhaps a call tomorrow?"

The Apothecary shook his head. "No, tomorrow I will spend with Emilia. Just her. This unfortunate happening on our honeymoon has robbed her of my company and I believe she is starting to get unhappy. When I came back this morning she was rather pale and sad."

"We can't have that," said Joe heartily. "I'll deal with young Wills myself. Take her to Exeter, Mr. Rawlings, and let her enjoy what the city has to offer."

"I will certainly do my best," John answered, then wondered if Sir Clovelly Lovell was really the right sort of person to raise the flagging spirits of a neglected bride.

As it turned out, he was. Standing only just over five feet in height and as fat and round as a bursting pumpkin, Sir Clovelly looked like a jolly doll, with his bunched red cheeks and merry water rat eyes.

"Sir Gabriel's son, eh?" he said as John and Emilia were shown into his large salon. "I've been expecting you. Your father wrote that you might call." For no reason he roared with laughter at this, slapping his thigh. John and Emilia caught each other's eye and smiled nervously. "Have you dined?" Sir Clovelly added.

"Yes, thank you, Sir."

"Oh shame. I quite fancied another portion. My wife tells me I'm too damned fat and must cut down my substances." He looked gloomy at the very thought of it. "Never mind, we shall have fruit and cheeses and hams and sweetstuffs. Tell me, what brings you to Exeter?"

Emilia curtseyed demurely. "We are on our honeymoon, Sir Clovelly."

The little fat man positively bounced with delight. "Honeymoon, eh? This calls for a celebration. Bumpers are in order, I feel. Champagne of course."

"Will Lady Lovell be joining us?" John enquired politely.

"Zounds, no. Spoil our fun. She watches every mouthful I take. Can't relax when she's there, damme. Do you know what she said to me?"

"No."

"That it was hard to tell which way up I went. Damn rudeness."

It *was* rude, very, but it was also outrageously accurate. Emilia smiled sympathetically in order to disguise the fact that she was dying to giggle, but John roared with laughter. Sir Clovelly looked slightly hurt.

"It is funny, I suppose. But I don't like being deprived of my victuals." He stuck his lower lip out like a truculent child. "Anyway, she's out playing whist and we've a wedding to celebrate." Sir Clovelly cheered up and let out another roaring laugh. "So, let's to the fun."

He sprang up and enthusiastically tugged at a bell rope, ordering what sounded like a feast from the servant who responded. It was perfectly obvious, thought John, that they were going to be with him most of the evening and hopes of contacting the enigmatical Gerald Fitz began to fade. However, there was nothing to stop him broaching the subject.

"By the way, Sir Clovelly," he said when champagne had been poured and their host had made the appropriate toast, "do you know anything of a family named Fitz? I believe they live quite near you."

"Yes, they do indeed. Strange lot. Father's a taciturn brute, a snarling dog of a man. The wife's a poor bird, beating her wings in her luxurious cage."

"And the children?"

"The eldest is Gerald, an effete ass. Very handsome, of course, and dressed like a fashion plate, but no substance in him. I swear a puff of wind would blow him down."

"Are there any others?"

"Another boy, quite the opposite of his sibling. A big, brawling creature whose very life offends me with its oafishness. And a simpering girl, all curls and poutings. Can't say I like any one of 'em."

Whatever else Sir Clovelly may be, he was certainly a master of the word picture. John felt that he knew these people just from the pithy sentences used to describe them. He decided to take the fat man into his confidence.

"Sir, I need to meet Gerald. I am not allowed to give you all the details, so suffice it to say that he has to be questioned regarding a death. Please advise me, how can I get to see him?"

"A death, eh?" said Sir Clovelly, his water rat eyes strangely sharp and alert, giving John the impression that an acute mind lay behind all the corpulence. "I'm not surprised. Probably some lovelorn female. He has several mooning after him."

"Did you know one called Juliana van Guylder by any chance?"

"Can't say that I did. As I told you, I don't reckon much to the family, albeit they're the richest for miles. All Gerald's women looked similar to me. All beautiful and all damned stupid."

"I see. Anyway, what excuse can I make to see him?"

"Excuse not necessary," said Sir Clovelly, rising once more. "If the fool's at home he'll come here if I ask him."

John stared astonished. "Why's that?"

"Because his father, for all his wealth and show, keeps a poor cellar, Sir. Damme, but he does. And Gerald, limp lily that he is, appreciates fine wine. He has a particular weakness for the champagne that I drink. If I send a footman to say that I am celebrating a wedding with the bride and groom, he will be here in a trice. Greedy bastard."

John, who was rapidly forming the opinion that the roly-poly little man who was entertaining them so nobly was probably one of the best people ever born, laughed joyfully. And he smiled even more when instructions were given for the Honourable Gerald Fitz to be invited to step down the road and celebrate a marriage with vintage champagne. The servant was back in a trice. "He's on his way, Sir, and thanks you kindly for the invitation."

"Told you," said Sir Clovelly, and bent his short bandy legs in a jig. Emilia, really pleased to be out for the evening and wearing one of her best gowns, suddenly rose to her feet and joined him, and thus they were dancing round the room when a footman intoned in the doorway, "The Honourable Gerald Fitz."

John, who was dressed as sharply as he dared for visiting one of his father's friends, could not help himself but raised his quizzer to survey the newcomer who was elegantly drifting into the salon.

He was divinely handsome, of that there could be no question. Tall, slim, yet muscular, forgoing a wig and instead wearing his dark hair rather long and tied with a ribbon, the Honourable Gerald truly had *bon ton*. Age-old elegance oozed from the wretched man and the fact that his nose was long and fine, his mouth passionate, and his eyes large and vivid, paled into insignificance beside the fact that he was an aristocrat through and through. Centuries of privilege were almost tangible as he walked into the room, surveyed Emilia with a more than appreciative eye, disregarded John as a nobody, shot a look of tolerance in the direction of his host, and languidly took a seat close to the fire.

"My dear Sir Clovelly," he said, "how kind of you to invite me. You know I can never resist an invitation to sample your champagne."

"My dear boy," answered his host, affable to the point of deceit, "it is always a pleasure to entertain you. Allow me to introduce the bridal couple. John Rawlings, son of my old schoolfriend, Sir Gabriel Kent, and his charming wife, Emilia."

Gerald made much of rising to his feet again and kissing her hand. "Such loveliness," he breathed. He turned a casual eye in the direction of the Apothecary. "You are a very lucky man, Sir."

"Of which I am totally aware," answered John. "A pleasure to meet you at last, Sir. I have heard so much about you."

"Oh really?" Gerald answered without interest.

"Oh yes," the Apothecary gushed, his impressed face firmly in place. "I have a friend called Tobias Wills. He mentioned you to me."

Gerald raised his quizzing glass and looked John up and down. "Who's your tailor, Sir?"

He was cool, that couldn't be denied. So cool that the Apothecary wondered whether he had ever heard of Juliana's other suitor.

"I go to a fellow in Piccadilly," he answered levelly, watching Gerald all the time. "At the Sign of the Popinjay. Do you know him?"

"Can't say I do," Gerald replied carelessly. He regarded John through his quizzer once more. "Who did you say you were?"

"John Rawlings, an apothecary of Shug Lane, London. My wife and I are in Devon on our honeymoon, and taking full advantage of catching up with old friends. Let me say that you are very well known, Sir. Everyone seems to have acquaintance with you."

Gerald raised a cynical eyebrow. "More people know Tom Fool than Tom Fool knows."

"Oh I would hardly have called you a fool," John answered silkily.

Emilia spoke up. "It's a very good thing we are here at this time, Mr. Fitz. A friend of ours, Jan van Guylder, has just suffered a double tragedy. So fortunate my husband was able to attend him."

Gerald emptied his glass and held it out to a footman for a refill. "Van Guylder?" he said musingly. "I seem to know that name."

"Ah, I recall it now," stated Sir Clovelly noisily. "He's a merchant from Topsham. Had a daughter done to death, so the gossip goes."

"It's true, alas," John answered. "And now his son has been discovered dead as well. What a tragedy for one wretched individual to bear."

Gerald had responded, the Apothecary was sure of it. There had been little more than the slightest quiver as the hand holding his glass had gone to his mouth, but movement there had been. John decided to go for the kill.

"I see you're upset, Sir, and I ask your pardon

for it. I had no idea you were acquainted with the family."

"I'm not," the fop responded briskly, "and your belief that I was disturbed was accordingly quite wrong."

"Then my powers of observation are sadly lacking," John replied, with just the slightest suggestion of a sceptical smile.

"Ah well," said Gerald, and gave an elegant shrug before turning his attention to Emilia, with whom he proceeded to flirt, not altogether discreetly.

John sat seething, angry with himself that he had been unable to draw Gerald out, furious that Emilia was blushing and smiling and generally looking as if she was enjoying the fop's attentions.

Dear Sir Clovelly came to the rescue. "If you'd be good enough to step into my library a moment, there's a book I think you might be interested in. This way, John."

And the Apothecary was out through the door before he could gather his wits.

"Now," whispered the fat man, his dark eyes gleaming, "what is going on? What connection has that silly rakehell with the unfortunate family you mentioned? "

"I've been told that he was their lover, brother and sister both. And now the pair of them are dead. Whether he has any link with the deaths I don't know, Sir. But I am going to make it my business to find out."

"I was watching him closely whilst you were speaking to him. He gave nothing away, in other words he's a clever devil, but I thought he was rattled when you mentioned the death of the boy."

"He was, even though he swore he did not know the family. But in that he lied, Sir Clovelly. I found his card in the bedroom of Richard van Guylder. He must have met him at the very least."

"We'll return in a moment and my suggestion, John, is that you do not refer to the matter again. Let him flirt and frill for all he's worth, sooner or later he'll reveal himself, that sort always does."

But even in drink, and he imbibed plenty of it, Gerald Fitz remained totally in control, never once allowing his veneer of foppish young aristocrat with scarce two wits to rub together, to slip. So much so that the Apothecary began to doubt what he thought he knew, wondering if, after all, Tobias Wills had been mistaken. If the fact that Richard had got hold of Fitz's card was a mere coincidence and that the Honourable Gerald, other than knowing their name, had no knowledge of the van Guylders whatsoever.

The time reached ten o'clock and Sir Clovelly's collection of clocks all began to chime simultaneously. Gerald drew a magnificent watch from his waistcoat pocket and stared at it.

"Is it that late? I really must be going. I'm promised for cards with the Beres at eleven and I'm determined to walk."

"Isn't that a little foolhardy?" Sir Clovelly asked anxiously.

"Yes and no. I'll take a couple of armed servants as escort. I'm damned if I'm going to let a bunch of bullying little ruffians put me off my night time stroll."

Emilia, who had been playing up to him, though whether because she enjoyed it or because she hoped to glean information, looked puzzled. "Bullying ruffians?" she repeated.

Gerald raised her hand to his lips and gave her a scorching glance from his dark long-lashed eyes. "There's a gang terrorising the streets of Exeter at present. I believe they base themselves on the London Mohocks. They enjoy frightening people rather than stealing, though they are not averse to a well-filled purse. They pleasure themselves with woman who they force to stand on their heads against walls ..."

"Really, Gerald, spare us the details," protested Sir Clovelly.

The fop gave Emilia a lazy smile. "Forgive me, Mrs. Rawlings, I did not wish to cause you offence." Though his lips were saying the right words, his eyes were asking her to go to bed with him.

"I'm sure that my husband will protect me," she answered, the merest edge in her voice.

Sir Clovelly came in. "Actually, my dear, no one is advised to try unless they are armed to the teeth and there are several of them. This gang, the Society of Angels they call themselves, are dangerous bastards - language, Sir, language - and are much feared. The *beau monde* of Exeter, or those that consider themselves to be such, clear the streets by eleven because of them. In fact I'll order your coach brought round now so that you won't have to walk a step." He pulled a bell rope.

Emilia turned to John. "That ghost story we heard in Sidmouth. Weren't they meant to be Angels?"

"Yes. The wicked Thornes, now all dead."

Sir Clovelly looked serious. "It's quite an old gang. Went very quiet for about ten years then revived again, more's the pity for us."

"If I could get my hands on the leader I'd string the blackguard up," said Gerald.

"Do men of your social standing do such things?" asked John, straight-faced.

"Of course they do," answered the fop, and looked down the length of his beautiful and aristocratic nose.

It was dark in The Close as they stepped into their coach, yet Gerald strode off into the gloom quite fearlessly.

"He's not as foppish as he makes out," said Emilia, snuggling down into the padded interior.

"That would indeed be difficult."

"You're angry, aren't you?"

"No. If you want to flirt with a fool like that, that is entirely up to you."

Emilia showed enormous good sense and did not argue. Instead, she neatly turned the topic of conversation. "You don't really think Fitz a fool, I could tell that by the way you looked at him."

"I must say he neatly sidestepped all my efforts to draw him out."

"You're very clever, John," said Emilia, and fell cosily asleep. Or at least pretended to.

"The Salutation, Sir?" called Tom.

"Yes, and don't stop for anyone."

"What about these damned Angels the servants were telling me about?"

"It might be a little early for them. Just drive hard and I'm sure we'll be all right."

But even as the Apothecary spoke, the sound of pistol shots rang out from a sidestreet, together with a great commotion of shouts and screams. Drawing his own weapon from his pocket, John stuck his head out of the window.

In the dim light of the carriage lamps, he saw a woman run past screaming, her clothes in disarray. Then came the sound of fast hooves and more shots. John raised his pistol to fire at her pursuer, then realised that the woman's headlong flight was being protected by the horseman rather than the other way round.

"Do you need any help?" he shouted.

"No," came the gruff reply. "I've seen the bastards off."

"Well done."

The horseman turned towards him and raised his gun in mock salute. As he did so the muzzle caught the brim of his hat and lifted it slightly. John stared in amazement at the scar that ran down from the rider's eye to below his cheek but before he could do more than gasp, the horseman had sped away into the darkness.

Chapter 9

He had promised Emilia a day devoted entirely to her whims and wishes and this promise John Rawlings had every intention of honouring. Nonetheless he couldn't stop his brain working and, waking early, he felt compelled to tell Joe Jago of the events of the previous evening. So much so that he got out of bed, pulled on breeches and a shirt, and in his stockinged feet made his way to Joe's room and tapped on the door.

"Enter," said the familiar voice and John went in to find the rugged individual stripped to the waist and shaving himself before a travelling mirror. Joe looked at him through a froth of lather. "Oh it's you, Mr. Rawlings. Good day. You'll have to excuse me while I finish my toilette. I have to go into Exeter early to speak to the coroner. Constable Haycraft came here last night and it seems that two more bodies have been washed up, they think from the *Constantia*. Apparently one of the corpses had some identification which linked him to the vessel. William is bringing them into Topsham early today but is so worried about his farm that I offered to go to Exeter for him."

"Well," John answered, sitting on the bed, "if that is where Emilia chooses to go we can give you a ride in."

Joe applied a viscious looking razor. "Thank you but no, Sir. I intend to be off from here within the next thirty minutes. There are certain lines of enquiry I wish to pursue in that city and so have a full day ahead. Now, how did you get on with Gerald Fitz?"

The Apothecary shook his head. "That's just the point, I didn't. He said that he knew the name van Guylder but that was all. He denied knowing them personally."

"But he was lying?"

"More than likely. Yet he was so good at it that I began to have doubts myself. After all, it is only Tobias Wills's word that Gerald was Juliana's lover."

Joe contorted his face and brought the razor sweeping beneath his chin. "Tobias must be seen when he's sober. That's for sure."

John wriggled his feet and asked a question that had been bothering him ever since he had met Gerald Fitz. "Joe, it isn't possible that the brother did do it, is it? It isn't some puritanical streak in me that keeps telling me he didn't?"

Mr. Fielding's clerk gave a final swipe to his chin, then plunged his face into a bowl of water. He came up streaming like a swimming fox. "Mr. Rawlings, my dear, you were the one who examined the dead girl's body. Did you not point out to William, who confirmed it to me, that Juliana bore marks from at least two pairs of hands, maybe more?"

"Yes, I did."

"Then Richard alone could not have been responsible. You must remember that. And from what you have told me of him, I think he was too ineffectual to be a killer, particularly of his own sister. No, we must broaden our net. My money goes on one or other of the two lovers."

"Or both," said John, and froze at the thought. For could that be the explanation? That despite all Tobias's drunken accusations, he and Gerald were actually working in league. "God's teeth, Joe. You don't think the two of them *are* involved, do you?"

The clerk dried his rugged features with a towel, then lowered it to look at John over the top. "Anything's possible, I suppose. Look, Sir. If Mrs. Rawlings is anxious to go shopping could you send your coachman to escort her while you call on Fitz? We must try and catch him off his guard."

"He'll more than likely show me the street."

"Not as a friend of Sir Clovelly Lovell's, he won't."

John groaned. "I wouldn't wager on it." He got off the bed and headed for the door, turning in the entrance. "If I'm back in time I'll try and ferret out Tobias."

Joe grinned at him as he pulled on his shirt. "Don't you worry about that. Give Mrs. Rawlings a good day. I've got a feeling that soon she'll deserve it."

"Oh dear," said the Apothecary, as he closed the door behind him.

Rather as he had imagined, Emilia did indeed want to spend the day in Exeter, first looking at the shops, then dining out, followed by a visit to the theatre where, so the posters said, there was to be a performance of *The Old Debauchees*.

Resigning himself to the fact that there would be

no work done on solving the mystery of the *Constantia* that day, John put on a husbandly face and escorted his wife round the shops.

There could be no doubt that Exeter was buzzing with the latest fashions and up-to-the-minute household goods. Everywhere he looked there were milliners, habit makers, glove makers, shops selling the newest products from the Potteries, all these jostling scent makers and *friseurs*. Very interested in the perfumeries, the mixing of beautiful scents being a sideline in which he indulged, though this was frowned upon by some of the more old-fashioned apothecaries, John opened bottles and sniffed to his heart's content, despite a few raised eyebrows. His wife meanwhile tried on hats and gloves, being assured that she was looking at the latest modes from Paris or London or Bath, whichever took her fancy. Very pleased with a small shop which described itself as a linen drapery, haberdashery, milliners and tea dealer, Emilia bought muslins and ribbons and one particularly captivating *chapeau*, in which her husband thought she looked absolutely enchanting and insisted she wore straight away. Then, having stowed their purchases in the coach, they went to dine.

The White Swan in High Street having a fine reputation for good food, the couple ate in style before proceeding on to the theatre, which was located behind the Guild Hall in Water Beer Street. Even as he drew near, John had a presentiment that the name he most dreaded to see was going to be displayed on the posters outside the building. And, sure enough, as he got close enough to read them, there it was. *The Old Debauchees by Henry Fielding: Isabella - Miss Coralie Clive.*

The rest of the cast was listed below but their names had disappeared into a blur. The Apothecary stopped dead in his tracks and wished the earth would open up and swallow him.

He must have sighed in anguish, for Emilia gave him a sideways glance. "Are you all right?"

"Yes, fine," John answered, laughing carelessly.

Emilia ran a suspicious eye over the poster. "Oh, Coralie Clive. I see."

"What do you mean, you see?"

"I see that you look daunted and wondered why. Do you still have feelings for her, John?"

"No I don't."

"That denial was a little vehement, wasn't it?"

"Oh Emilia," he said, suddenly feeling annoyed. "It is you I married and you I love. Coralie Clive is part of my past, that is all."

"Yet the sight of her name on the poster made you go pale."

"I am not pale," the Apothecary answered angrily. "Now, do you want to see this play or don't you?"

"Could you bear to sit through it?"

"Of course I could. Coralie means nothing to me any more."

Yet his heart was thudding as they took their seats in the circle where sat the brightest of Exeter's citizens, the *beau monde* of the West Country as John rather patronisingly thought of them. The performance, due to begin at six, had already attracted a large and vigorous audience and the place looked full. In fact the tiers of boxes which rose directly from the pit were all taken, mostly by servants sent ahead to secure their master a place.

It was a very old-fashioned theatre, John thought; a soberly elegant little building with proscenium doors opening on to an attenuated forestage and light provided by overhead chandeliers with tallow candles. A curtain, which would rise and fall only at the beginning and end of the play, was presently lowered to hide the scenery behind. Realising that at this very moment Coralie was backstage, getting herself ready to appear, John found that his hand was shaking at the thought that they were both under the same roof. Furiously, he took himself to task for being so feeble-minded when he had such an exquisite wife.

"Isn't that Gerald Fitz?" Emilia whispered as a bowing servant left a stage box and a beautifully dressed fop appeared in his place.

John raised his quizzer. "Yes, it is. 'Zounds, but he's dressed to the hilt."

"Jealous?" asked Emilia, rather sarcastically the Apothecary thought.

"No. I would say that he's rather overdone for a provincial theatre."

She laughed at this, a shade too heartily, and John felt himself growing quite put out and relapsed into what he considered to be a dignified silence. If Emilia noticed she gave no sign, gazing round and clearly enjoying herself, even going so far as to wave at Gerald Fitz when he looked in their direction, quizzing glass to eye. He stared for a moment or two then clearly recognised them, getting to his feet and giving a most elegant bow. Not to be outdone, the Apothecary rose and returned the compliment.

As he sat down again, there was a flurry of excitement as the curtain slowly went up to reveal a street scene, all painted on flats and lacking the realism of the modern effects used at the Theatre Royal, Drury Lane, by David Garrick. With his heart pounding, John stared fixedly at the stage, scarcely breathing as the cast began to come on and speak their lines. Finally, after a pause for dramatic effect, Coralie made her entrance, running on in an adorable costume of another age, low cut in the front, a swishing train at the back, a fan in one hand and two cheeky feathers on the top of her dark head. There was rapturous applause from the audience and Gerald Fitz shouted, 'Bravo' very loudly.

"Do you think he knows her?" Emilia whispered.

"Of course not. He's simply showing off."

"I'll wager he goes backstage in the interval though."

Sure enough, Gerald Fitz did leave his seat when the intermission came, though that, in itself, proved nothing, for he could have gone to buy refreshments or find a house of easement. Rather than fight their way through the throng, John and Emilia remained where they were and ordered from the various sellers who walked round between the acts.

The play, written by the Blind Beak's late great half brother, Henry Fielding, was both long and funny, so that even more running time was added by the frequent pauses for laughter. Consequently, the audience did not emerge into the street until after ten o'clock. Then, instead of wandering off to have a late supper, the older members of the crowd hurried away, clearly quite anxious to get home. John wondered why, then remembered the Society of Angels who terrorised the streets of Exeter when the hour grew late. He had almost come face to face with them on the previous evening, in fact probably would have done if it hadn't been for the lone horseman who had driven them off with his pistol. Or was it *her* pistol? For that great jagged scar could only belong to one person, surely. It had been the woman who dwelt in Wildtor Grange who had seen the Angels off, he felt certain of it. Was that her role then? A sole vigilante who prowled Exeter in search of troublemakers. A certainty that he must visit the Grange again and try to speak to her face to face was borne in on the Apothecary and added to his mental list of all the other things he had to do in order to find the killer of Juliana van Guylder.

A group of people who were clearly not worried about the Angels were heading purposefully towards the stage door. At their head strode none other than Gerald Fitz.

"Do you want to greet Coralie?" asked Emilia, all innocence.

"Certainly not. I just want to go home and to bed with you," John answered reassuringly.

His wife gave him such a look then, very deep and with great feeling in it. It was so loving and so genuine that John could not help but kiss her full on the lips, regardless of the people hurrying round them.

"Do you love me?" she whispered, close to his ear.

"For ever," he answered, and kissed her again.

It was then that two very different sounds came simultaneously. There was an 'Ooh' as Coralie stepped out into the street and her admirers surged forward. This followed almost immediately by a woman's scream close at hand. John, still holding Emilia closely, looked over his shoulder in the direction from which the scream had come and gasped at what he saw. Clad in long white greatcoats, their heads covered by floppy white hats hung with veiling, a gang of men had approached silently and now stood circling the group surrounding the actress. They were so uncannily like the creatures he had seen travelling in the phantom coach, supposedly the spectres of the wicked Thornes, that John felt his blood run cold.

"Get Coralie Clive," said a muffled voice and as one the Angels started towards her. It was only then that the Apothecary realised that they were armed with swords and bats, not yet drawn but clearly ready for action.

Without stopping to think, he lifted Emilia off her feet and pushed her into a high doorway through which the scenery was obviously brought in and out. Then he took out his pistol and charged into the throng. Simultaneously, Gerald Fitz drew the sword he carried at his side and engaged the Angel nearest to him in a duel. Everything seemed to come to a halt then, and the Apothecary felt as if he were frozen as he watched the dazzling swordplay. It was truly magnificent. Gerald, for all his effete manner, was a swordsman of the first order. Unbelievably, even the other Angels stopped to observe. Indeed the duelling was so fine that it looked rehearsed, as if each thrust and parry had been worked out beforehand. Like everyone else, the Apothecary simply stood, lost in admiration, waiting for some kind of break to come so that he might pitch in.

It happened very suddenly. A wicked thrust from Gerald drew blood from the Angel's arm. There was a cry of, "You bastard," and the Angel fell back clutching his wound. As if released from a trance, John fired at the feet of the Angel closest, forcing the man to jump in the air. At this the younger and more stalwart men present turned on their attackers and in a trice it was all over. The Angels ran off into the dark streets and the whole incident was finished. With a sense almost of anti-climax, the crowd broke up. Emilia came out of her doorway and shot a quick glance in the direction of Coralie, who had remained standing quite still throughout, display- ing no sign of panic. Was it John's imagination or did his wife pull a face before she turned a smile at him?

"Are you going to speak to her?"

"Of course not. She hasn't even seen me."

"I wouldn't be too sure about that."

Before John could answer, Gerald Fitz's voice rang out. "Miss Clive, I am one of your most ardent admirers, having driven to London many, many times in order to see you perform. Allow me to present you with my card." He bowed and handed it over, all the time eating the actress with his eyes.

Coralie took the card in a gloved hand. "The Honourable Gerald Fitz," she read aloud.

"At your service." He bowed again, most fulsomely. "May I have the great pleasure of escorting you to supper? My coach awaits nearby."

She smiled up at him. "As you defended me so nobly it would be churlish of me to refuse. I should be delighted."

Gerald bowed for the third time and John wondered nastily whether he had had lessons in bowing as well as swordsmanship, and decided that he probably had. Disgruntled, he turned away and walked, holding Emilia's hand, to where Irish Tom awaited them.

It was late but The Saluation was still lit by candles and appeared to be full of people. Indeed, Joe Jago hovered in the doorway, peering anxiously into the courtyard as John's coach rumbled over the cobbles.

"Ah, Mr. Rawlings," he said without preamble. "I'm afraid your services are required. There's been an affray. Tobias Wills is very drunk and under arrest. Mr. Northmore, the quay master, is flat on his back, bruised and bleeding. While Mr. van Guylder has taken too much sleeping draught and is being attended by his physician who is unable to cope with all the other problems simultaneously."

"Where would you like me to go first?" said John.

"To Tobias Wills. They have locked him in the cellar where he is attempting to kick the door down."

"Hare and hounds, what a night!" answered the Apothecary and, kissing Emilia swiftly on the cheek, hurried to his room to get his medical bag. As a precaution he put on his long apron just in case anyone decided to vomit in his direction.

Even as he approached the cellar a rumpus could be heard and John, who had been sent down in the company of Dick Ham, the Flying Runner, turned to his companion.

"As we open the door he'll probably come charging out."

"Let him," said Dick cheerfully, "there are ways of stopping a headlong bull." And he indicated both his fist and his foot with a sly wink of the eye.

The Apothecary decided to calm the situation. "Tobias," he called through the crack, "get a grip on yourself, man. You'll achieve nothing by all this drunken brawling."

"Go and piss yourself," Tobias shouted back.

"If that's your attitude you must take the consequences," John answered and, nodding at Dick to stand by, opened the door and stepped back. Much as they had expected, Tobias came flying out as fast as his shambling gait would allow him. Dick acted fast as lightning. Out went his foot and Tobias hit the stone floor with an almighty thud.

"Right," said John, straddling the fallen man. "I've had enough of your stupidity. It's time you sobered up and acted like the gentlemen you're supposed to be rather than an oafish lout. I've got something here that I want you to drink. It will calm you down enough for us to have a rational conversation, tomorrow if not before."

"I'll not have any of your muck down my throat,"

"You'll have it and like it," the Apothecary answered, and turning Tobias over and propping up his head, poured the juice of white poppy into his gulping mouth. Though a great deal was spat out, sufficient went in to have effect, and after a while Tobias dropped into a gentle sleep.

Making absolutely sure that no bottles or barrels were lying round the place, the Apothecary and Dick rolled Tobias onto a matress and covered him with a rather nasty looking blanket, the presence of which suggested that the cellar had been used as a temporary gaol before. Placing a bucket close by in which the wretched young fellow could answer the calls of nature, John and Dick went out quietly, locking the door behind them.

"One dealt with, two to go," the Apothecary said with a sigh.

"Do you want me to stick with you for the rest of the night, Sir? I've precious little else to do."

"That would be an enormous help. You never know with these unhappy tormented people when one of them is going to get rough."

"Just as I thought. Now, who are you going to see next?"

"I presume that Mr. Northmore is somewhere in the inn?"

"They've carried him to an upstairs room, Mr. Rawlings."

"I see. How exactly did he get into that state?"

"He was drinking in one of the snugs, considering himself too fine to mix with the locals, I dare swear, when in comes young Tobias, full of fight, and accuses Northmore of having an affair with Juliana."

"Oh my God, not another one."

"Very much Mr. Jago's reaction."

"Was there any truth in it, do you reckon?"

"That remains to be seen. But the accusation was that it was Northmore who deflowered her when she was a young girl."

"I wouldn't put it past him, considering himself so desirable as he does."

"Again what Mr. Jago thinks. However, Northmore rose up on his high horse and denied it and Tobias hit him in the guts."

"Good old Tobias!"

"Which is just ..."

"... what Mr. Jago said."

They both laughed and went upstairs to one of the smaller back bedrooms. Knocking gently on the door, a voice croaked, "Come in," and the Apothecary and the Runner went in to see an extraordinary sight.

Snatching at what was left of his dignity, the quay master had dragged himself to a chair where he sat in his small clothes, a pair of skinny white legs sticking out before him, his breeches, ripped up the back seam beyond repair, draped over the back. As well as the guts, it seemed that he had been punched in the mouth, for his lips were swollen and bleeding and his whalebone dentures lay beside him on a table with several of their more important components missing. The urge to guffaw was almost uncontrollable and John found himself with an inane grin on his face as his mouth twitched and pulled and his ribs started to ache.

"My dear Sir," he said in a strangulated voice.

The quay master's pebbly eyes glared at him. "Are you laughing at me, young man?"

"Good gracious, what a thought," John answered, and buried his head in his medical bag as his shoulders began to shake.

To his great credit Dick Ham managed to keep a straight face, a trick which he had obviously mastered by means of adopting a forceful manner.

"The accusations that Mr. Wills made against you, Sir, namely that you had robbed Miss van Guylder of her virginity. Is there any truth in them?"

The quay master looked furious, as best he could in his underwear. "How dare you ask me such a question. Who are you to interrogate me? I'll deal with a higher authority, not a common pipsqueak like yourself."

All John's mirth vanished and he straightened up and looked Mr. Northmore in the eye.

"Runner Ham represents Mr. John Fielding, I'll have you know."

"And what is John Fielding to me? He has no fame in Devon, Sir. If I have to speak to a magistrate then I shall make sure that it is one from Exeter, and there's an end to it."

A door opened and closed again quietly and Joe Jago's voice said, "Mr. Northmore, I do not consider it wise of you to take that attitude. I am empowered, when I am on Mr. Fielding's business, to arrest if necessary. But if you do not deem that suitable then the local constable also has such powers. Surely it would be better to avoid unpleasantness and talk to us here in the privacy of this room, out of the earshot of your family, rather than drag your good name through the dirt."

"But I am innocent. I have nothing to fear."

With a coolness that left John without breath, Joe Jago suddenly changed tack. "Sir, I must ask you why you put such obstacles in the way when we wanted to board the *Constantia* t'other morning. Was it because you knew the body of Richard van Guylder was aboard? And was that because you yourself had murdered him and faked the evidence to look like suicide?"

The quay master looked aghast. "How dare you accuse me of such a thing?"

"I dare because it may very well be true," Joe answered calmly, and walked into the room.

"How could it be? I was as shocked as the next man when you discovered Richard's body."

Joe sat down on the edge of the bed. "I have often observed in my career how well rogues and villains assume guises when it comes to protecting their hides."

"How dare you, " Thomas Northmore blustered once more, and then relapsed into silence, perhaps realising that it was not easy to look masterful without teeth.

"These will take some fixing," John said cheerfully, picking up the broken dentures as if to emphasise the point.

Joe came in again. "Now, Sir, do you want to tell me about your relationship with the van Guylders? Or would you prefer to speak to someone local?"

"I would prefer to speak to neither of you."

"That will not be possible. Juliana van Guylder was expecting a child when she died. I have the physician's report here." He tapped his pocket. "Therefore anyone who had any relationship with her in the past will be asked to account for himself. Now, Mr. Northmore, was that child yours?"

The quay master's face went from mottled to pale and back again, clearly shocked. "A child, you say! Did her father know?"

"He guessed at it, yes. Now, Sir, don't beat about the bush with me. Was the baby yours?"

"Of course not. I was an uncle figure to her."

"That's not what Tobias Wills thinks. He told me that you seduced the girl, that you, a man old enough to be her father, robbed her of her innocence. Now, Sir, how do you answer?"

The quay master was silent, clearly thinking through his best course of action. Then after a while, during which the other three men regarded him stony-faced, he adopted a man-of-the-world expression and an almost jovial look came into his eye.

"Gentlemen, I shall be totally honest with you. All of you look as if you know life in its various aspects, so I am sure you will understand the tale that I am about to unfold, indeed even sympathise with it.

Juliana developed a wild girlhood passion for me, disregarding the fact that I was a married man with children. She offered me anything, even a chance to see the funeral cortege of Lord Dalrymple, an event many wished to attend, if I would but run away with her. She offered herself to me, begged me to take her in fact ..." The quay master attempted a man-to-man smile, an effect ruined by his naked gums. "... but I refused because of her youth. But a man's a man, God knows. One day I weakened and she became my mistress."

"And remained so until her death?"

Mr. Northmore looked affronted. "Certainly not. I was constantly persuading her to find a man of her own age and leave me be ..."

Like the devil you were, thought John.

"... and one day she did."

"Was that man Gerald Fitz?"

"I don't know, Sir. Once our association was at an end, that was the finish of all conversation between us."

Joe steepled his fingers, looking at the quay master over the top of them. "I presume you can answer for yourself at the time that Juliana and her brother went missing."

Thomas went purple with fury. "Answer for myself? Why should I? I've told you the truth and there's an end to it."

"Supposing I said that I don't believe you; that it is far more likely that Juliana abandoned you when she suddenly looked at you one day and saw that you were old. And supposing I were to think that you were furious and killed her because of it? Because your self-love had been deeply wounded?"

"Then you'd be a damnable fool."

"That," said Joe Jago in a most sinister voice, "remains to be seen."

They sent him home like that, in his small clothes and with his teeth wrapped in a packet tied with string. As the Flying Runners drove him away in their coach, John Rawlings and Joe Jago turned to look at one another.

"I think, my friend," said the older man, "that we have just done poor Mrs. Northmore the biggest favour of her life. If she has two tuppeny wits about her she'll make this the turning point and never let him forget what a pitiable sight he presented to the world."

"Do you think she knows about Juliana?"

"Of course. Wives have a nose for that kind of thing."

"Did he kill the girl?"

"It's perfectly possible, though who would conspire with him I have no idea. He seems to me to be the sort who would have no friends."

"Maybe she was disliked so much that enemies bonded against her."

Joe turned to the Apothecary. "Find out about her, Mr. Rawlings. Only in that way can we approach the truth."

"Then let's get down to Jan van Guylder's. Perhaps when he recovers he'll be ready to talk."

But there was no possibility of that, the Apothecary saw as he entered the room where the physician attended his patient. Whether by accident or design, the Dutchman had clearly taken a vast overdose of white poppy and was fighting for life.

"My God," said John, running to the bedside.

The physician who knelt there, looked up. "And who might you be?"

"I'm John Rawlings, an apothecary. I was asked to help with the cases you were too hard pressed to attend. Is there anything I can do to assist, Sir? If not, I'll take my leave."

The doctor relaxed a little. "No, you can stay. I've purged him but he's still very weak."

"What about a stimulant?"

"I've nothing on me, alas."

"I have a prepared infusion of Hyssop. It is not ideal but at least it would increase blood circulation and lower blood pressure."

"Let's try it. Damme, the man is hovering on the brink of death. Every effort that can be made, must be made."

"Did he do this deliberately?" John asked as he drew the bottle from his bag.

The doctor looked at him mournfully. "That we'll never know unless he himself tells us. I prescribed him some poppy juice so that he could sleep, for the poor devil has hardly had a wink since the death of Juliana, let alone the double tragedy. Perhaps I shouldn't have done it but I have known Jan for years and he was truly run ragged."

"Was Juliana a little bitch?" John asked suddenly, not quite sure why he had been so forthright.

The physician turned a look of astonishment on him. "What makes you say that?"

"All the evidence is pointing to it."

The other man stood up and stared the Apothecary in the eye. Then he nodded. "Yes, a terror," he said. "Both the children went wild after the death of the mother. But though Richard seemed to settle down a bit after he went to school, Juliana never did. She was sent to Mrs. Simmons' Academy in Exeter, a place with a good reputation, but she was actually asked to leave. After that she had governesses at home. But, damme, Mr. Rawlings, she rode roughshod over the poor women. One of them even had a severe nervous disorder which I had to treat."

John nodded. "Let us get this infusion down the patient and then we can talk further."

They raised the limp and inert form up carefully and while John held him, the doctor spooned the liquid down Jan van Guylder's throat.

"This may well do no good at this stage."

"We can but try," the physician answered, and continued to administer the physick drop by drop.

When the correct dose was fully consumed, the two men drew away from the bed and sat in front of the fire, their heads turned toward the patient so that they could see if there were any change.

The doctor held out his hand. "Shaw is the name. Thank you for your help."

"Let it be hoped that we have saved the poor man."

"We should know shortly. Though not perfect, a stimulant like that will have some effect soon."

Sure enough, ten minutes later Jan van Guylder let out a deep sigh and his eyelids fluttered. Instantly, the doctor went to his patient's side.

"Jan, can you hear me? It is Luke Shaw. Squeeze my hand if you understand what I am saying."

From where he was standing John saw the feeble movement of the Dutchman's fingers and went to the bed, very conscious that he was dealing with another man's patient yet anxious to see what progress had been made. Looking to Dr. Shaw to see if he approved and being given a nod of the head, the Apothecary pulled up one of Jan's eyelids. The pupil of the eye, which earlier had been the size of a pinhead, was starting to return to normal.

The two men looked at one another. "I think he's pulled through," said Luke Shaw.

"The next few hours will be critical. Will you stay with him?"

"He's an old friend. I will not leave his side."

"Can I be of further assistance?"

"No, Mr. Rawlings. You have done splendidly. Return to the hostelry and get a good night's sleep."

The Apothecary gave a wry grin. "Would you believe that I am on my honeymoon and that every day something seems to occur that keeps me from my wife's side?"

"Then you'd better hurry back. There's nothing worse than a warm bed with a bride in it and no bridegroom at her side."

"I know that only too well," John answered rue-fully, and made his way downstairs.

Dick Ham awaited him in the hall, dozing a little by the fire.

"We can go," said the Apothecary. "I think he's out of danger."

"Was it attempted suicide, Sir?"

"There's no way of telling, but somehow I imagine so. He probably feels that there is nothing left to live for with both of his children gone."

"Poor devil."

They stepped out into the April midnight to find it cold and clear and brilliantly lit by the moon. At the quay the *Constantia* rode quietly at anchor, bobbing slightly even though the boarding ramp was still in place. The Apothecary and the Runner looked at one another.

"Did you find anything at all during that search?" John asked. "So much was going on that I lost the thread."

"We came up with very little, I'm afraid. What there was is in Mr. Jago's safekeeping."

"Let's look once more," John said impulsively, and before Dick could even answer had started to clamber up the gangplank.

It was eerie on that ship of death in the moonlight, even eerier than it had been in the dawning. It was with reluctance that the Apothecary felt his feet turn, almost as if they had a life of their own, in the direction of the figurehead. He had no wish to go and stand there, close to the oversized mermaid, her yellow hair streaming, her breasts very white, her blind eyes staring out over the river. Behind him he could hear Dick Ham, approaching slowly, equally unhappy about being in this terrible and haunted place. John glanced down, horribly aware of the small drops of blood that spotted the mermaid's back, horribly aware that a girl had probably died in this very spot. And then he saw it. Caught on one of the figurehead's golden tresses, so small that it could easily have never been noticed at all had the moonlight not been so bright, a tiny piece of white material, probably wrenched from Juliana's shift. Or possibly torn from the clothing of her murderer.

Chapter 10

They were unloading the *Constantia*. Standing on the quayside, looking slightly the worse for wear, Thomas Northmore, displaying his second best teeth, a formidable set of white china that glinted in the sun, was overseeing. Close at hand, saying little but watching with an anxious eye, was the purchaser, a rope maker from Exeter. Also present were Joe Jago accompanied by the long-suffering William Haythorne, whose farm by now must be in dire need of attention, John thought.

The Apothecary, having checked that Tobias Wills was still fast asleep in the cellar, apparently not having stirred at all, had wandered down there with Emilia, prior to setting off for Sidmouth where they had decided to eat outdoors, the weather growing warm again, the wind having veered round to the west. Watching with fascination as the hold was opened and the bales of hemp were lifted out, everyone stood in silence as the cargo was taken from that most haunted of ships.

"What exactly is hemp?" Emilia asked, as a bale was swung aloft and deposited on the quay

"It's a plant," John answered, "that is used to make rope. It can also be used in medicine."

"Oh?"

"The seed is excellent for expelling wind, most vigorously and fully. It is also highly effective for removing worms, both internally and from the ears."

"I don't think I want to hear this."

John grinned. "It is frequently smoked like opium in certain eastern countries with hallucinatory side effects. So really it has triple usage. The inner bark for cordage, its seeds for all kinds of medicinal cures, its leaves and flowers to produce hallucinations. The name of the plant is cannabis satvia and they say that the word canvas, from which sails are made of course, is a bastardised version of the word cannabis."

"I didn't know that," said William, "and I've been round these parts all my life. How did the words come to be connected?"

"Because in medieval times the letters b and v were interchangeable, still are today in some instances. So, cannabis, cannavis. Do you see?"

"I certainly do. Not that I've heard of it mind. It's always been hemp to me."

Joe, who had been listening with interest, shielded his gaze with his hand, his eyes the blue of the river as he squinted at the sun.

"Those bales look a bit thrown together."

"They may not have left the Baltic like that. Though they could have been carelessly retted."

"What does that mean?"

"The soaking of the plants after harvesting is called retting. Retted flax makes linen, retted hemp makes rope."

"What will happen to the cargo if it has been damaged?"

"Presumably whoever ordered it in the first place will still take delivery of it."

"And the ship?"

"No doubt the owners will be written to to send over another crew to sail her back. They're not going to let a good craft like that go to waste."

Emilia shivered. "But it will always be haunted. I would hate to set foot on it."

"Well, you'll never have to."

"Thank God for that."

John turned to the constable. "Have all the crew been accounted for?"

"No, only three's been washed up. God knows where the rest will come ashore."

"Were there any signs of violence on the other two bodies?"

"No, they were like the man who died in your arms, not a mark on 'em. It would seem that they both simply drowned."

"I just wonder," said Joe slowly, "whether Juliana's murderers came aboard and they jumped into the sea in fear." He paused for a long moment to think, then Mr. Fielding's clerk ran his light eyes over the assembled company. "Gentlemen, it's time we three, together with the Runners, held a meeting to pool what information we've gained so far." He bowed to Emilia. "That is if you have no objection, Mrs. Rawlings."

She sighed. "What can I say?"

John felt an enormous rush of tenderness for her. "Sweetheart, I won't do a thing that you don't wish me to."

Emilia shook her head, her bright curls swinging beneath her hat. "I've already told you, I knew that you worked for Mr. Fielding when I married you.

It's simply that I didn't think that you would have to do so so soon after our marriage."

"Then if you agree, Mrs. Rawlings, might I call the gentlemen into one of the snugs this evening?"

"You leave me no option but to say yes," Emilia answered with a touch of asperity, and turned away to find her coachman.

They had a very relaxing day and she was calm again by the time the shadows lengthened over Sidmouth's beautiful bay. Slowly the couple walked back to The Ship, where the coach had been stabled, and set off for Topsham in a mood of great tranquility. But this was not to last for they had not proceeded more than a mile across that strange heathland which housed Wildtor Grange when, with a crunching sound, the coach tipped slightly to one side. With a great many curses, Irish Tom reined the horses in and jumped down from the box just as John opened the carriage door and stepped out. They both stared in dismay at a wheel which had finally objected to the condition of the Devon tracks and worked loose.

"Now what?" said the Apothecary.

"I could do a running repair, Sir, but I wouldn't trust it to get us home. I think I'd best walk back to Sidmouth and fetch the wheelwright. He may only be used to carts but he'll mend it sturdily enough till I can take it to the coachmakers in Exeter."

"What choice have we?" asked Emilia from the window.

"None really, Ma'am. We can't get marooned here overnight."

She shivered. "No, we most certainly can't."

John got back into the coach beside her. "Don't worry, darling. I'll stay here with you."

"But you'd be no match for the ghostly Thornes. Nobody would."

"The ghostly Thornes don't exist."

"Then what was it we saw the other night?"

"Some people playing a prank."

"What about the headless coachman? Was he a prank?"

John was silent, unable to find a ready answer. It had certainly been a horrific sight, yet surely there had to be a logical explanation. He wondered then if these pranksters, whoever they might be, could somehow be connected with the vigilante horse-woman, she of the mighty scar and powerful body.

"You're very quiet," said his wife.

"Just thinking."

"Are you frightened?"

"No," John answered, but for all that he felt in the pocket of his coat for his pistol and experienced a thrill of alarm as he realised that he had left it behind in their room.

It began to grow darker and the sun dipped behind the hills, throwing the landscape into inky shadow. The first star appeared and a faint glimmer of moonshine.

"Dear God, what was that?" said Emilia, gripping the Apothecary's arm.

He strained his ears and, very distantly, identified

the sound of wheels coming towards them. His bride turned a stricken face in his direction.

"It's the Thornes."

"Rubbish," John answered, more vehemently than he had intended, and thrust his head out of the window to get a better look. Then he laughed. "It's two very solid looking ghosts. Tom is here with the wheelwright."

Emilia had the good grace to look apologetic. "I'm being foolish, aren't I?"

"No. We did see something most peculiar that evening. But I will find out what it was before we go home. I promise you that."

"And what about the woman who hides out in the Grange? Will you find her as well?"

"Yes. I'd be on her trail this very night if I hadn't been called to the meeting."

"There's always something," Emilia replied with feeling.

In order to mend the wheel, not only did the horses have to be unhitched but the back of the carriage raised in the air and placed on a special support. With a great deal of sweating and heaving, the coachman managed to lift the carriage while the wheelwright eased it onto the prop. John, meanwhile, held the horses, who were acting in a most uneasy manner, rolling their eyes and pricking their ears and sweating very slightly. Aware that they could probably hear something that he could not, the Apothecary found himself glancing round warily, wondering what it was that was frightening them.

Emilia had wandered off towards a clump of trees into which she had vanished, presumably about business of her own, so it was her shriek that first alerted the three men that something was wrong. John, still holding the reins, started to run in the direction of the sound but as he did so his wife appeared from the thicket, scurrying towards him.

"It's the Thornes," she was gasping, looking over her shoulder, her face pale.

"Where?" said John, but the answer had already come. Hurling into his line of vision came the phantom coach, its occupants still in their spectral white, the coachman, with his jagged neck and his head lying beside him, turning his body in the direction of the four people gaping at him. He raised his whip and shook it menacingly before crashing forward in the direction of Wildtor Grange. With a groan, the wheelwright fell unconscious at the Apothecary's feet, while Emilia let out a long and anguished cry. John, however, lost his temper in the most spectacular manner. Scrambling onto one of the horses, unsaddled as it was, he wrapped its long coaching rein round his arm and set off in pursuit, the other horse, joined by the same harness, following close behind.

"Damn you," the Apothecary shouted at the top of his voice.

There was no reply but the headless coachman stood up and turned his neck, just as if he were looking over his shoulder, then thrashed his horses to greater speed.

"How dare you frighten people like this," John yelled into the wind.

Again there was no answer but now there was
the sound of another pair of hooves coming from
the direction of the Grange. John watched as a
horseman firing a pistol appeared, galloping at full
speed towards the phatom coach. It was the
woman with the scar, the Apothecary felt certain of
it. Slowing his own pace slightly, he observed as
she took aim straight at the headless driver. There
was the crack of a travelling bullet and the coachman slumped, a patch of red appearing at his
shoulder.

"You're no bloody ghost," John bellowed furiously. Then his own horse, tired of the rough treatment
he had been meting out to it, reared in the air in
anger and threw him headlong into a small and
extremely cold stream.

"'Zounds and 'zoonters!" shouted the Apothecary,
and with that momentarily lost consciousness.

He woke to find Irish Tom heaving him out of the
water, uttering oaths that would have made a
Topsham docker blush.

"Did the bastards shoot you, Sir?"

"Not they. That mettlesome brute with the rolling
eye threw me."

"I heard shots and thought they'd got you."

"No, it was the woman who fired."

"What woman?"

"The vigilante who lives in Wildtor Grange. I'll
explain about her later. How are Emilia and the
wheelwright?"

"She's tending him, great fool that he is. He thought they were phantoms."

"So did I the first time I saw them," John admitted reluctantly. "But the woman hit the coachman good and proper and there was a patch of real blood to prove it. Now, I've never heard of a ghost that bled, have you?"

"Well, actually, I have Sorrh," Tom answered, becoming very Irish.

"Not like this, though. The coachman and his passengers are as real as you and I."

"If that is the case, what are they doing driving round like that, terrorising half the countryside."

"That is what I've got to find out," answered John, then added, "As if I haven't enough to do already."

As he walked back to the coach, the two horses having bolted off ahead of him, he found his thoughts turning yet again to the vigilante. First thing in the morning, he determined, he would ride over alone and somehow track her down. There was a great deal he had to ask her and, if luck was on his side, there could well be considerable information she might have for him.

He was late for Joe Jago's meeting, naturally. In fact Mr. Fielding's clerk was in the midst of questioning Nick Raven about his progress in Exeter when John walked in, apologising profusely both for his tardiness and his dishevelled appearance.

"Gracious Mr. Rawlings, you look as if you've been in the wars.".

"I've been having an argument with a coachload of ghosts. But please carry on. I'll explain later."

Nick Raven, having run his dark jewel eyes over the latecomer, continued his tale.

"Juliana and Richard were both seen getting off the coach on the day they travelled into the city together. She was particularly remembered because she was met by a black servant and helped with her baggage."

"Did anybody see where she went?" the Apothecary asked with interest.

"Into the maze of streets by the three conduits. Apparently there are a lot of lodging houses there. After that she was lost to sight. But one interesting feature emerged. Someone who I encountered in an hostelry who knows the man well and has no reason to like him, saw our redoubtable quay master, Thomas Northmore, going into a house in Milk Street in the very area into which Juliana and the negro vanished."

"What about this negro?" asked Dick Ham. "Did anybody know who he was? There can't be too many like him around Exeter surely."

Raven looked pleased with himself. "I struck lucky yet again. He is servant to Lord Hood and was once Lady Hood's little black boy. They kept him on when he grew up and now he is often seen strutting round the city in his scarlet livery."

"What in heaven's name was he doing with Juliana van Guylder?" asked John.

"Clearly he had been sent to assist her, but by .whom?"

"Lord Hood?"

"Or one of his sons."

Joe Jago looked like a fox with a whiff of fat gosling. "Gentlemen, this is a knotty problem indeed. So we must go to our duties. You can leave the quay master to my interrogation. I believe he has a certain respect for me ..."

"Terrified of you, more like," put in John.

"... so I am liable to deal with him better," Joe ended severely.

The Apothecary had a sudden thought. "What's happened to Tobias Wills? He's not still asleep, is he?"

"No, but I have confined him to The Salutation. He woke up late this afternoon and is now nursing a vast headache. I thought perhaps you might attend him, Mr. Rawlings, and sift him for information at the same time."

"Gladly. What else did you have in mind for me?"

"I wondered if you and Mrs. Rawlings might call on Sir Clovelly Lovell and infiltrate Lord Hood's circle if you possibly can. Further, there's the matter of Gerald Fitz. I think he was lying about not knowing the van Guylders. Somehow, he must be made to confide in you."

"A tall order indeed."

"There has to be a chink in his armour."

"I can't imagine what," answered John, and immediately thought of Coralie and frowned.

"What's happening about Miss van Guylder's funeral?" asked Dick.

"The coroner has released the body for burial. I believe the ceremony is to be held very shortly."

"I hope Jan is up to it," said John.

"Ah yes, Jan," Joe answered. "You know, despite all I still have not dismissed him as a possible killer. Runner Ham related to me the conversation you had with Dr. Shaw. It seems the girl was a wild uncontrollable creature."

"It was Richard the brother who murdered her," the Runner answered stolidly. "The suicide note made that perfectly clear."

"My money's on Tobias Wills," said Nick Raven. "A very nasty temper there. He demonstrated quite clearly last night that he can lash out when he feels like it."

"At least two people did it," answered John, rather sharply. He stood up, suddenly tired of this guessing game. "I'll go and see a man who might be one of them right now. Then, gentlemen, if you'll excuse me, I'll retire for the night. Chasing the ghosts led to my being thrown from my horse into a stream and I'm feeling somewhat the worse for wear. Good evening to you

"Good evening, Sir," answered Joe, and made a polite bow as the Apothecary left the room, aware that the conference was likely to go on until late in the night.

Tobias Wills was sitting in The Tyger, a snug normally put aside for visitors of better quality but tonight being used as a place in which to house a prospective felon. Even before John had entered he had decided on shock tactics, and consequently as soon as he was through the door, demanded, "Just what kind of fool are you, pray?"

Tobias looked up and asked, "Am I on a charge?"

"Not yet. But there are witnesses enough to your brawling habits. Mr. Jago has not informed the constable but no doubt the quay master will."

"That filthy old bastard!"

"Tobias, please," said John impatiently, "just stop making accusations. You're under suspicion of murder, you know, and the more you go on hurling insults the more the net closes round you. Now, just answer the questions I am going to put to you and shut your mouth on every other subject."

The other man had gone very white. "I didn't kill Juliana. I swear to God I didn't."

"Save your denials for another time. Now, you say you met her when you were a child. Tell me about that."

A story emerged; rather a pathetic one. Of little sweethearts growing up - and growing apart.

"I truly loved her and we were destined to be married. But then rumours reached my ears; that Juliana had lost her virginity to Thomas Northmore, that she was going to Exeter and meeting other men, that she had fallen in love with Gerald Fitz. The day that I met you in the tavern, the day that you were looking for Richard, I had gone to have it out with her. For an even worse rumour had reached my ears; that she was carrying another man's child. I was going to ask her and if she did not deny it, I was going to break our betrothal and call her the slut that she was."

Tobias let out a terrible sob and put a hand to his aching head.

"You were seen to have a skinful last night. Now, get this down you." And John produced a bottle from his pocket.

"What is it?"

"Carduus Benedictus. That will shift your headache, as well as cure deafness, melancholy and strengthen the memory. It's also reputed to relieve the French or Grand Pox. I can assure you that it is very popular amongst the London beaux who take it on an almost daily basis."

Tobias looked askance but swalled the potion in one draft. "It tastes revolting."

"Things that are good for you always do. Now, listen to me, young man. Hearing what was whispered about Juliana, how did you manage to remain in love with her?"

Tobias looked thoroughly gloomy. "I was besotted with her if truth be known. It was like a fever in me. Do you know despite all I said about calling her whore, I would even have taken on another man's child and brought it up as my own, I loved her so much."

"And did this love suddenly turn to hate one day? Did something inside you snap so that you could no longer bear her cruel treatment of you?"

"If you're saying did I kill her, the answer is no. I swear it."

"Then who did?"

"Thomas Northmore," Tobias said emphatically.

"Why him?"

"He never finished with her, revolting lecher that he is. She no longer wanted him but he was as besotted with her as I was. I believe he still saw her from time to time."

John sat in silence, remembering what Runner Raven had discovered; that the quay master had been seen in Milk Street close to where Juliana and the negro had vanished into the alleyways.

"The negro," the Apothecary said aloud.

"What?"

"Nothing. Just someone else that I have to track down and talk to."

"Oh." Tobias shuffled his feet and looked lost. "Am I free to go now?"

"Yes. The constable may take a statement from you but on the other hand he may be too lazy and ask one of the Runners to do it. And I'm sure Mr. Jago will try and persuade the quay master not to press charges against you. So go, now, while the going's good."

Tobias started towards the door, then turned a flushed and anxious face in John's direction.

"I didn't kill Juliana, Mr. Rawlings. I loved her like a fool, that's true enough, but not like a cruel fool, that's true also."

"Go," said John commandingly, to hide the fact that he completely believed him.

Chapter 11

During the night a mist had rolled in off the sea, obscuring the Devon landscape beneath a cloud of vapour. The hills had vanished, as had the great expanse of river, while nothing could be seen of the sky, veiled as it was by a dense grey shroud behind which the sun was attempting to rise. Riding over that wild heathland where so many strange things had happened recently, John Rawlings knew that he was hopelessly and rather alarmingly lost. In front of him, hidden somewhere in the swirls of fog, lay Wildtor Grange, to his right the town of Topsham, struggling to wakefulness when he had clattered out of it atop a hired horse from the livery stables. To the Apothecary's left was the hamlet of Sidmouth, from which the fishermen had presumably sailed into the mist-wreathed water. Yet to find his way to any of these places would have been an impossibility, in fact John was beginning to think that his only course of action was to dismount and wait until the mist had cleared before proceeding a step further. But the thought of Emilia kept him going slowly forward.

He had left her asleep with a note on the pillow beside her saying that he would be back by mid-morning and would then go with her to Exeter, and he had no wish to break his word. With every day that passed John realised that he was falling more and more in love with his wife, though the glimpse he had had of Coralie Clive had unsettled him, he couldn't deny that. She still had a strange effect on him, an effect of which he was deeply ashamed, for it made his heart speed up and his breath shorten, just as if he were an adolescent apprentice staring at a girl for the first time. Further, he had bitterly resented the fact that she had accepted Gerald Fitz's invitation to supper even though John no longer had any claim on her.

"I'm a fool," he said into the fog, and his horse, a reliable old plodder with an easy-going temperament, moved its ears backwards to listen to him.

It was about seven o'clock in the morning, the journey having taken far longer than it should have done because of the vaporous conditions. Yet much as he wanted to stop and wait for the sun to burn the mist off, John continued to trudge onwards in the somewhat forlorn hope that he would find Wildtor Grange by some lucky chance. Yet nothing loomed out of the mist, no great shape reared on a fogbound hill. Indeed it almost seemed as if he were going in the wrong direction entirely and might, for all he knew, be heading towards the cliffs and the sea.

When he had hired the horse, the Apothecary had been informed that its name was Hicks, a strange title to say the least. Now, John spoke to it again.

"Hicks, you're a local. For Heaven's sake get me out of here. I don't mind whether we even find the Grange. I think the best thing you can do is head for home."

The horse whinnied encouragingly and continued to plod onwards.

"I said home to Topsham," John repeated, but he

never got any further. A movement close at hand
from something that neither horse nor rider could
see, gave the animal a sudden shock, so much so
that it broke into a somewhat laboured canter.

It was very alarming, speeding through the wall
of fog towards the unknown. But what was even
more alarming was the moment when a dark form
suddenly appeared before them and the horse, by
now totally frightened, took off at a tangent as fast
as it could go, only for muffled hooves to follow in
its wake. John peered over his shoulder but could
see nothing, yet the sound of those pursuing fog-
drenched hooves continued at the same relentless
pace. There was only one thing for it and that was to
take evasive action. Seeing a clump of trees loom up
on his left, the Apothecary forced Hicks into them.
Then they stood in silence, horse and rider both
panting, waiting to see what would happen next.

Their pursuer had also drawn to a halt and John
peered into the gloom to see if he could catch a
glimpse of him. But there was nothing. Then, without warning, a hand from nowhere clapped down
on his boot and started to pull him out of the stirrup.
Taken so unawares that he was totally helpless, the
Apothecary felt himself being dragged towards the
ground. Hicks meanwhile was rearing in terror, and
the combination of being yanked from the saddle
and the movement of the bucking horse sent John
hurtling earthwards, flat on his back. His assailant
promptly flung himself down on top of him and put
his hands to the Apothecary's throat.

They fought wildly, John going for the oldest

defence in the world and stretching downwards for the man's testicles. Yet though he reached the crotch of the fellow's breeches, it was empty. It was a woman's anatomy he was feeling. This was no time for delicacy, however. Giving her an almighty pinch which made her catch breath, the Apothecary seized the advantage and threw her away from him and onto the ground. Then he scrambled to his feet.

"Forgive me, Madam. It is not my custom to handle strangers in such a rude manner but I am afraid you left me little choice."

The struggle had knocked her hat from her head and the net which held the thick dark hair in place had become dislodged, so that as she also rose the lustrous locks came tumbling to her shoulders. She took a step towards the Apothecary and at last he was able to see her distinctly, study the strong angular features and the scar that ran from just below her eye downwards to her classically defined cheekbone. She smiled at him through the mist.

"Excuse me, I thought you were someone else."

"Then I don't envy him, whoever he is," John answered, fingering his throat.

She put out a hand. "Have I hurt you?"

"Not so greatly that I won't recover."

"I apologise. Allow me to invite you to my home so that I can tend your wound."

"I would be honoured," he replied, bowing, thinking to himself that he had actually achieved what he had set out for that early morning and been invited to speak with the vigilante.

"You'd best follow me," she said, walking into

the mist then reappearing a minute later astride a black horse.

"I'd be glad to. I am totally lost."

"It was not the best morning to set out, particularly if you are not familiar with the terrain."

She clearly hadn't guessed that he had been looking for her which was a great relief. John, taking advantage of her ignorance, merely answered, "Yes, it was very foolish."

"Well, stay close beside me. We don't want you getting lost again."

With some difficulty, John remounted the sweating Hicks and they set off in a direction that the Apothecary could have sworn led towards Exeter and not Wildtor Grange as he had presumed. Yet the mist was deceiving and it was not until they had been riding for several miles that John became convinced they were heading inland and finally asked, "Where are we going?"

"To my house near Exeter. It is outside the city and overlooks the Exe in rather a fine position."

A few minutes later the Apothecary realised that this was an understatement as, having passed through a pair of imposing gates with a lodge to one side, they began to climb uphill along a drive delimitated by mighty elm trees. So the vigilante, whoever she might be, was clearly a woman of wealth. John's curiosity was at fever pitch as they came to a half-moon carriage sweep, at which the drive came to its end, and hostlers came sprinting round to take the horses. Immensely surprised, he stood stock still and surveyed his surroundings.

An imposing six pillared portico, reached by either of two flights of steps which ran to the right and left of it, formed the central block of the house's grey stone facade. At least fifteen enormous windows wide, these windows and their counterparts above gave light to the four pavilions adjoining the central block. A balustrade with small pillars ran round the beautifully sloping roof, making a perfect setting for the eight large and two small chimneys, while a similar balustrade at first floor level gave outdoor access to every room. In a way it was austere and yet it had such beauty of symmetry and style that John thought it one of the finest houses he had ever seen.

His companion, laughing slightly at his reaction, ran up the right hand steps and, as if by magic, the front door was opened by a bowing footman.

"Ah, Lady Elizabeth, you are back."

"Yes, and I have brought someone with me. This young man was attacked in the fog and has some severe bruising to the throat. Send Jenks in the carriage to fetch the physician and meanwhile order a soothing caudle to be made for the poor fellow."

"Very good, my Lady." And the footman hurried away.

They were standing in an enormous Great Hall, the proportions of which were quite breathtaking. Seventy feet long and about forty feet wide, paired white Corinthian pilasters soared upwards from the floor to a series of shallow arched niches. These, in turn, swept up to a ceiling with an immense centrepiece depicting Britannia with raised spear. The entire gigantic structure had been decorated in an audacious shade of pink.

The mysterious lady chuckled at the Apothecary's amazed expression. "Do you think the colour too much?"

"On the contrary. I think it succeeds."

"Then come to the Blue Drawing Room, you may as well be comfortable while you await medical attention."

"Which I don't agree I need. Madam, I am John Rawlings, an apothecary, quite capable of treating myself. I shall suffer nothing worse than a sore throat I assure you. An examination by a physician will only give rise to a lot of questions which, I believe, neither of us really want to answer."

She looked thoughtful. "Are you certain of this?"

"Yes. Is it too late to stop the doctor coming?"

"It is. But I can always send him away again."

"Won't he think that rather churlish?"

"Yes, but as I am considered a great eccentric, he will accept it."

"And are you? A great eccentric that is?"

She stood up, the shape of her muscular body clearly defined beneath the man's riding clothes she wore, her lustrous black hair tumbling to her shoulders, her scar wickedly revealed by the grey light coming in through the enormous window.

"What would you say?"

"I'd say that you were one of the most outrageous yet one of the most beautiful women I have ever seen."

Her hand flew to her disfigurement. "Beautiful? With this?"

John nodded. "Yes, even with that."

She smiled, throwing open the doors of a large salon, its deep blue walls hung with family portraits. Closing the doors again she turned to the Apothecary.

"I long to kiss you."

He should have felt embarrassed, threatened, guilty, trapped, but none of those emotions came. Instead, knowing that she desired it so much, he folded the woman into his arms and gave her a kiss that electrified them both. In fact so powerful was the feeling as their bodies pressed together that John realised danger lay down that path and gently took a step away.

"Don't you want more?" It was perfectly clear what she meant.

"Had this happened a few months ago nothing would have prevented me from saying yes. But I am recently married. In fact, I am in Devon on my honeymoon," John answered.

She smiled, sphinx-like, and said, "We shall see," then went to sit down in one of the elegantly upholstered chairs.

Collecting his wits with difficulty, John examined the portraits, one in particular of a darkly handome dashing man, very swarthy of complexion and brilliant of eye, clad in a superb red satin coat and breeches, drawing his attention.

"Who's this?"

"My husband. I eloped with him. We fell wildly in love and I shamed my family and went off to Venice as his bride."

"Tell me about him."

"He was the Marchese di Lorenzi, a Venetian nobleman who owned a fleet of ships. In my youth all the countries of the world were trading with Exeter, his amongst them. It was so exciting to go to the harbour and see vessels from Spain and Portugal bringing in fruit, olive oil, indigo and wines. While from the American Colonies came tobacco and skins, and sugar and molasses from the West Indies. Venice exported fine glass, made on the island of Murano, and it was while my husband was here, showing his wares to prospective buyers, for he had no false pride, that I met him. I was seventeen, he twenty-five, and we fell passionately in love. Anyway, my father, who was Earl of Exmoor and full of good breeding, or so he considered himself, thought all foreigners, titled or no, to be less than the dust. He forbade me to wed Luciano but I eloped and was married at sea."

John, still standing before the portrait of the handsome Venetian, said, "So that's why they call you Lady Elizabeth. You're an Earl's daughter."

"Yes, that is so. Anyway, do you want to hear the rest of the story?"

"Please."

"In typical Shakespearean style, my husband lost his entire fleet, partly due to storms, partly to piracy. We were so in debt after that that we were forced to sell up everything and make our way as best we could. We opened a school, my husband teaching fencing and dancing, I needlework and painting to the daughters of former friends."

John laughed. "I can't see you as the needlework type, somehow."

She came to stand beside him. "I wasn't. I was far better at swordplay than sewing."

"Is that how ...?"

"I got my scar? Yes, in a way."

She took his hands and led him to sit beside her on a small, rather comfortless, settee. "A very foolish young man fell in love with me and when I refused him, haunted me night and day. He would be outside in the street when I drew the curtains in the morning, he would be beneath my window late into the night. In the end the situation got so bad that my husband challenged him to a duel. I was twenty and pregnant with my first child."

"What happened?"

"He killed Luciano, ran him through his proud heart and watched him bleed to death."

"How terrible for you. What did you do?"

"I took Luciano's sword and went after my shadow. And then, pregnant or no, I killed the bastard like the mad dog he was."

John could not speak, overwhelmed by what he had just heard.

"Then with the authorities after me I took ship for home."

"So your child was born in England, in this lovely house."

"Very far from it. My father had cut me off when I ran away, changed his will so that I inherited nothing and refused ever to speak to me again. I had to make my way in the world with a baby son to support."

"What did you do?"

"I borrowed enough money to start another school, only this time it was I who taught swordsmanship and dancing. At first the sons of gentlemen refused to come, and then, slowly, the novelty value began to have an appeal. Suddenly I was the rage with all the young bucks and blades in town, and my fortunes began to turn round."

"Was this in London?"

"No, in Bath. Anyway, it seemed that my father had got to hear of my success and one day he sent for me. He had no direct heir, you see, and on his death his estates were going to pass to a remote cousin who, he felt certain, would sell this place of which he, my father, was so fond. It seemed he wanted to leave sufficient money to my son, his grandchild, to ensure that Withycombe House would remain in the family."

"How old was your boy by this time?"

"Frederico was twelve and handsome as day. He had inherited the dark looks of neither of us but instead was as fair and as blue-eyed as an angel. And in that lay his undoing."

"What do you mean?"

"You have heard of the Society of Angels?"

"I have indeed. A gang of young ne'er-do-wells who terrorise the citizens of Exter after dark."

Elizabeth gave a humourless smile. "I'm afraid they are a little bit more than that. They are not just naughty pranksters but something far more sinister."

"In what way?"

"They poison and corrupt. My father duly died and my cousin sold this house to Frederico, paid for with the money left to him by his grandfather. We moved from Bath and took up residence here - and then the trouble started. My son, aged sixteen, frequented Exeter for his entertainment. Monied, with an Earl for a grandfather and an exotic Italian title, he rapidly attracted the attention of the wrong sort. To cut to the bare bones, he joined the Angels and through them learned the noxious delights of opium smoking. Soon my beautiful boy became a craven addict, a wreck of what had been a fine and glorious youth. Then, in some seedy house in the backstreets, he took too much of the filthy stuff and he died, alone and in degradation. It was I who had to bring his body back, it was I who had to deal with the coroner, it was I who swore revenge on them all and who have made it my life's work to hunt the bastards down and get rid of them one by one."

"You mean you kill them?"

"If I can do so safely and without leaving trace, yes. Some I merely wound. Others I frighten into submission."

"I was told that the gang packed up for a while. Was that your doing?"

"Partly. But they were revived again for a purpose, at least that's my opinion."

John shook his head. "I don't understand."

"They're up to something more than assaulting women and terrorising night watchmen. It's my belief that they are smuggling."

"What makes you say so?"

"They've rigged up a phantom coach, complete with headless coachman."

"I've seen it and must admit to being frightened by it."

"Well ..."

But the Marchesa got no further. There was a knock on the door and a footman appeared.

"The doctor is here, Lady Elizabeth, and I have also brought the gentleman's caudle."

"We need one but not the other. Tell the physician that I will pay him for his trouble but that he will not be required today."

"Very good, my Lady." Setting the drink down on a small table, the servant left the room again.

John turned to his hostesss. "You didn't tell me how you got this," and he ran his fingers gently over Elizabeth's scar.

"It was during the duel I fought with my husband's murderer, my so-called admirer. He shrieked at me that if he couldn't have me nobody else would and that he would disfigure me for life, so just before I killed him he did this to me."

"But it hasn't disfigured you."

She was very close to him. "Do you mean it?"

"Of course I do."

"Will you kiss me just to prove that."

"No," answered John very seriously, "I am far too afraid of the consequences."

And with a great deal of determination, he went to sit on the other side of the room to listen to the rest of her story.

The sun was high by the time he rode down the

drive and headed back towards Topsham, his thoughts in turmoil. The Marchesa had told him everything, even down to the fact that she had made herself a hideout in the deserted Wildtor Grange in order that she might spy on the Angels more successfully. The phantom coach she dismissed as a ploy to frighten people away while the gang was about its illegal business.

"They're landing cargo on the Clyst, somewhere round near the Bridge Inn, I'm certain of it. So it suits them well to ride out in that coach and scare people into their houses. I watch for them as often as I can but so far have not discovered their landing point."

Thinking of Joe Jago and the Runners, John had said, "It seems to me you could do with some help."

She had given him the most enigmatic of looks. "I have always ridden alone, my friend. There is no reason why I should ask for assistance now."

"Perhaps because you might then get the results you want."

The Marchesa had smiled at him. "With or without help, I usually achieve those."

Shortly after that he had left her, bowing formally, deliberately avoiding looking into her mocking eyes, wondering when, despite everything, he would see her again.

But now as he headed for Topsham and his wife, he felt guilty that even so much as a kiss had passed between him and the extraordinary Lady Elizabeth di Lorenzi.

Realising that most of the morning had gone,

John encouraged the plodding Hicks to make best speed he could, and finally arrived at The Salutation just in time to see Joe Jago heading down towards the quay with purposeful tread.

"Joe," he called, "where are you off to?"

"I'm going to catch the noonday coach into Exeter."

"Don't worry about that, Emilia and I will take you in. I'll quickly change, then I'll be with you.

Mr. Fielding's clerk looked very solemn though John could have sworn there was a twinkle about the light blue eyes. "I'm afraid that won't be possible, Sir."

"Oh? Why's that?"

"Mrs. Rawlings has already taken your coach and gone."

"Gone? Gone where?" the Apothecary asked in sudden alarm, the terrible thought that by means unknown Emilia had found out about this morning's kiss and left him, uppermost in his mind.

"She's gone into town, Sir. She said that Irish Tom must take the carriage to be repaired and then she had several people to call upon."

"But she doesn't know anybody."

"On the contrary she reeled off quite a few names, Gerald Fitz's among them."

"She mustn't see him. He's a womaniser."

Joe Jago burst out laughing. "I'm sure Mrs. Rawlings is quite capable of looking after herself. Now, if you come as you are we might yet catch the coach and then you'll be able to find her."

Handing Hicks to a hostler and giving the man a

coin to return the weary animal to its stables, John crammed his hat on his head and sprinted down the road to the harbour where the coach that ran between Topsham and Exeter was virtually closing its doors. Clambering on to the roof, John and Joe squeezed into a place normally meant for one person.

"Oh dear," said the Apothecary, all of a twitter, "I do hope I can find her. Tell me, Joe, was she very annoyed?"

"Somewhat put out."

"Exactly who did she say she was going to call on?"

"Sir Clovelly Lovell, Gerald Fitz, possibly Miss Clive."

John groaned audibly and several of the other passengers stared.

"Come now, Sir," said Joe genially. "Let us not waste time worrying. I have much to report to you." And the clerk described how the rest of last night's meeting had gone, ending with, "Dick Ham told me you found a small piece of white material close to the figurehead. Do you by any chance have it about your person?"

John looked apologetic. "I left it in my room. I meant to give it you but it grew late and I forgot. I'm sorry."

"I shall examine it this evening when, by the way, I have the redoubtable quay master to interview regarding his presence in Milk Street on the day Juliana vanished."

"Tobias Wills thinks he did it. Says the old man

never got over his attachment to the girl and was still in pursuit of her."

"Does he now?"

"Yes. By the way, how is Jan van Guylder? Have you any news?"

"He will live, poor soul, for what his life's worth. Richard and Juliana are to be buried side by side day after tomorrow. Apparently all work will cease on the quay as a mark of respect. But how the poor father will be strong enough to attend I cannot imagine."

"Has he any family to support him?"

"No, they are all in Holland and travelling is difficult because of the war."

"The French won't maraud a ship flying the Netherlands flag."

"Perhaps some of them will get here in time," Joe answered. He changed the subject.

"Tell me your adventures, Sir."

John proceeded to do so, leaving out nothing except that one unforgettable kiss which, he knew for sure, it was imperative he did forget. Joe looked thoughtful. "Is there any way in which this woman could be connected with Juliana's murder?"

"I can't think of one."

"Unless ..." Joe looked even more thoughtful. "... she saw something. You say she wanders around the wild heath and has made herself a hideaway up at the deserted house, then she may well have noticed some unusual occurence on the day the girl was killed."

"Would you like to call on her?" said John hopefully.

"No, Sir, as you have made contact with her, I think it should be you."

Inwardly the Apothecary cringed though just a little cold current somewhere was secretly pleased.

The coach rumbled through the South Gate and dropped its first load of passengers at the White Hart Inn, while a few more, bound for the city centre, got on. And it was then, just as they were approaching High Street that John, still on the roof and staring down into the street, saw him. A negro in scarlet livery was strutting along, head in air and whistling a tune.

"Look," said John, nudging Joe in the ribs.

"That's our man, Sir."

"Well, I'm going after him. Please," he shouted to the coachman, just below them on his box, "can you let me out. I've just seen someone I know."

As luck would have it they were travelling at snail's pace behind a slow-moving cart and the Apothecary, with a great deal of assistance from Joe, managed to scramble past the driver and literally drop into the street. However, all this took a few minutes and by the time he had gained the cobbles and looked round, the negro had vanished. Hurrying onwards, John caught a glimpse of scarlet coat and broke into a run.

Hearing footsteps behind him, the negro looked over his shoulder. His eyes widened in panic at the sight of someone pursuing him and he started to lope along the street like a gazelle. Determined to catch him up, John ran all the faster. But there he made a mistake. With his lithe powerful limbs, the negro sped out of sight, leaving the Apothecary puffing and panting and feeling rather foolish as he mopped his brow and fought to get his breath back. Yet there was nothing for it. He had lost his quarry and now had the double task of finding both Joe and Emilia and probably ending up locating neither.

He had run so far that he had almost arrived at the West Gate and there, appropriately enough, John spied a tavern named The Blackamore's Head. Deperately in need of a jug of ale, the Apothecary stepped inside, thinking he would sit quietly and plan his next move. Taking a seat at the nearest table he suddenly realised that from a gloomy corner a large pair of eyes were staring at him. The negro was already in there ahead of him.

The servant made to run but this time John was too quick for him. Grabbing him by the arm, he said, "Don't be afraid. I only want to talk to you about Miss Juliana."

The negro gaped at him, clearly terrified. "I'm not going to hurt you," John said soothingly. "In fact, I've got money for you - " He took a few coins from his pocket with his spare hand. " - if you just tell me about the day you met her off the coach and carried her bags to her lodging house. Do you remember that?" He clinked the coins encouragingly.

The negro, who was probably aged about nineteen or twenty, John thought, cleared his throat. "Yes, Master."

"You needn't call me that. My name is Rawlings."

"Yes, Master Rawlings."

The Apothecary gave up. "And what is your name?"

"They call me Daniel, Master."

"And you work for Lord Hood I believe."

Daniel rolled his eyes wildly. "Please, Master, don't tell him you found me here. He knows that I sometimes go to the inns but today I am running an urgent errand."

John smiled to himself. "I shall say nothing, besides, I am not of Lord Hood's acquaintance. You have nothing to fear from me. Now, tell me about that day. You met Miss Juliana off the coach and her brother handed her into your care. Is that correct?"

"Yes, Master."

"So where did you go?"

"To Milk Street, where she was to lodge until her wedding."

John's jug of ale almost fell from his grip and he stared at the negro in blank amazement.

"Did you say wedding?"

"Yes, Master."

"Who was to be the happy bridegroom? Do you know?"

A look of cunning spread across Daniel's features and he answered nonchalantly. "Oh, yes Master."

John produced a couple of coins and put them down on the table. Daniel scratched his wiry head. "Now, let me see ..."

The Apothecary doubled the amount. "Now, that's all you're getting. I can find out some other way."

"I remember now," the negro said with a grin. "It was old Master Digby-Duckworth."

"Who?"

"Old Sir Bartholomew Digby-Duckworth."

"I don't know who he is. Tell me about him."

"Why, Master, he is a big banker. His bank started long ago with his grandfather. Lord Hood say that Sir Bartholomew is one of the richest men in Devon."

"And Miss Juliana was going to marry him?"

"Oh yes, Master. They were betrothed."

So what price Tobias Wills? thought the Apothecary. And this idea was followed by the notion that if ever a girl was asking to be murdered it was most certainly Juliana van Guylder.

"You say you took her to Milk Street. What number was it?"

Daniel scratched his head again. "Now let me see..."

John produced another coin and the negro grinned broadly. "Oh yes, I recall. It was number three."

"Two more questions.

"Yes, Master?"

"Where does Sir Bartholomew live? And did you see Miss Juliana again after that day?"

"He lives in a big house near Long Brook Street by the castle. And I never saw her again, Master." Daniel's eyes rolled once more. "She's dead, ain't she, Master?" John nodded. "It's the talk of the town that she was murdered. Guess Gerald must have done that."

"Gerald Fitz? How do you know him?"

"Everyone knows me," the negro answered, sticking out his chest. "I'm the best black in Exeter."

"How many of you are there?"

Daniel looked very slightly shame-faced. "Only four. But I'm still the best. Anyway, I call at all the great houses and Gerald Fitz and his friends like me. I play dice with them."

"Do you now. So tell me, why should Gerald kill Juliana?"

Daniel clapped his hand over his mouth and rolled his eyes spectacularly. "I can't say no more. But it's what my mistress call 'Green Eye'".

"Jealousy? He was jealous of Sir Bartholomew?"

The negro shook his head and got to his feet. "I said enough, Sir. Good day to you."

And he had scooped up the money and gone out through the door in one supple, effortless move. Signalling to the girl to refill his jug, John sat in silence, pondering this latest extraordinary development. So who was the father of the child Juliana had been carrying? Tobias Wills, Gerald Fitz, Thomas Northmore or old Sir Bartholomew? Or none of them? Still much preoccupied, the Apothecary left the tavern and headed back in the direction of The Close and the home of Sir Clovelly Lovell.

Chapter 12

It appeared that not only was Sir Clovelly Lovell at home but that he was more than anxious to receive. He came bustling out of his library, smiling and nodding and greeting his visitor as if he were a long lost relative.

"Ah my dear young friend, how very pleasant to see you. You are here in search of your wife no doubt. Pretty little thing, what what? Well, she and Lady Lovell have gone to shop and then to see the play. Which gives us much free time, dear chap, much free time. They asked me to accompany them but I refused. Can't stand the playhouse. Always go to sleep, damme. Anyway, what say you that we go to see the sights and then to dine? Always enjoy a little night life in the company of another male. And being able to eat what I like without the womenfolk butting in."

John smiled encouragingly. "An excellent plan, my dear Sir Clovelly. But meanwhile I have a favour to ask you in connection with a matter that we have discussed once before."

Instantly the jolly water-rat eyes were full of perception. "Are you referring to the death of that unfortunate van Guylder girl?"

"Yes, Sir, I am."

"Do you want to see Fitz again?"

"Him and another. Sir Clovelly, I had the most preposterous conversation today which I would very much like to repeat to you."

"Then step into my library, my boy, and we'll discuss it over a bumper or two. A most valuable asset when it comes to sharpening the brain. Or so I've always found."

Not quite certain that it would have the same effect on him, having breakfasted hours earlier and hurriedly at that, John sipped at his glass as he told his host, who listened in total silence, not only the story of his meeting with Daniel but also about Juliana's connection with Tobias Wills and Thomas Northmore.

Eventually Sir Clovelly nodded. "It is becoming quite obvious to me that the girl was little better than a doll common."

"Reluctant though I am to admit it for the sake of her father, I think you are right, Sir."

"And you say that her brother shot himself and that one of Mr. Fielding's men believes it was he who killed his own sister?"

John sighed. "Yes."

"Do you?"

"No, I don't. There were the marks of at least two assailants on her. But it seems to me she could have made so many enemies, had so many different men on a string, that any two of them might have conspired together to bring about her end."

Sir Clovelly looked thoughtful. "I wonder."

"What, Sir?"

"About old Sir Barty. He wouldn't take too kindly to his honour being impugned."

"Could you tell me something about him."

"Known him for years. Nice chap. Rich as Croesus,

part of the banking family of course. He's retired from business affairs now, though. His son runs the bank and, in time, his grandson will take over I suppose, though I can't say I'd trust him with my money, empty-headed young fool."

"Sir Barty's a widower, I take it."

"Heavens yes. Edith died years ago. He never seemed to be very interested in women after that but obviously this young doxy has wormed her way in."

"How old is he?"

"Seventy-eight."

"And she eighteen. What a situation."

Sir Clovelly shook his head knowingly, his plump cheeks swaying very slightly. "Men with money can buy almost anything. He has bought youth and beauty to warm his bed at night."

"Do you think he is still potent? Could he possibly be the father of her child?"

The older man looked dubious. "You are an apothecary, you should know more about that than I. No, my guess is that someone else has done the deed but that she will foist the infant on to him, much to the old fellow's eternal delight."

"That will cause ructions within the family."

"Won't it indeed." Sir Clovelly sank a bumper. "What say you John that we stroll in that direction and call on the old fellow? Lady Lovell never stops telling me that I need to take more exercise."

"Won't he be in mourning?"

"Privately perhaps but publicly my guess is no. I imagine that the fact of his forthcoming nuptials was shrouded in secrecy. They were probably quietly going to one of those churches where the officiant asks no questions."

"What defeats me," said John, forgetting himself and taking a large mouthful of wine, "is what she intended to do about Tobias Wills. Apparently they had been betrothed for some time."

"I reckon she intended to present him with a *fait accompli* as with the rest of her friends and family."

"What about Gerald Fitz? According to Tobias, Juliana was in love with him."

"Perhaps the cries of her heart were stilled by the chink of money bags."

"How aptly put. And in answer to your earlier question, Sir, I would very much like to call on Sir Bartholomew."

"Then so we shall. I am as anxious as you are to see how this all turns out."

It was a fine afternoon, indeed rather warm, and Sir Clovelly puffed and panted and complained about his legs as they turned out of The Close and, cutting up St. Martyn Lane, made their way into High Street, going towards the East Gate. This they passed through but not before Sir Clovelly had called into The Dragon Inn for rest and refreshment. Then, admitting to feeling somewhat better, he trundled towards Long Brook Street and the fine house built close to the bowling green in which resided Sir Bartholomew Digby-Duckworth.

Outside the city wall there were trees and fields

and a rural aspect, and John concluded that it must be considered a most desirable neighbourhood in which to live, so close to town life and yet in far more pleasant surroundings. Small wonder, then, that Juliana van Guylder had decided that this would be her future home. For though Tobias Wills's house was splendid, Topsham life would inevitably seem dull in comparison with the delights of the city.

As they approached the mansion from the lane, John was frankly astonished to see the scale of the place. Passing through a gateway he found himself in a large courtyard, a garden to his left, most well tended, and built round this area of green, various buildings housing kitchens and pantries together with a brewhouse and larder. A great oaken door lay ahead of them upon which Sir Clovelly most vigorously knocked, probably thinking about the refreshments that lay within.

Not one, but two footmen answered and ushered them inside a long and spacious passageway, to the left of which lay a small reception parlour. Opposite this and leading off to the right was a huge hall in one corner of which was a spiral staircase climbing to a balcony above. This balcony ran all the way round the room and was one of the most unusual architectural features the Apothecary had ever seen. However, he had no time to study it as he and Sir Clovelly were ushed into the parlour while Sir Bartholomew was informed of their arrival. A few moments later one of the footmen returned.

"Sir Bartholomew will receive you in the large

parlour, gentlemen. If you would be good enough to follow me."

They proceeded down the corridor, past a series of windows overlooking yet another courtyard surrounded by further kitchens and storehouses.

"It's like a palace," whispered John. "How many people does he entertain at a time?"

"In the old days of balls and receptions it was dozens. Now he simply sees a few close friends."

"I feel sure his future wife planned to change all that."

"I'll wager she did indeed."

They had turned right down yet another passageway then paused before two large doors which the footman flung open. "Sir Clovelly Lovell and Mr. John Rawlings," he announced.

"Greetings, my friends," said a voice from a high backed chair, and its occupant half rose to welcome his guests.

He was incredibly fragile, John thought, a whispering shadow of a man; thin and old and transparent of skin. He looked as if his stay in this world might be counted in weeks, not months. And clearly, John thought, this had been in Juliana's mind: to marry him, establish herself as his heiress, then simply wait for the inevitable. Why then, he wondered, that air of brooding on the evening when he had first met her? Why that petulant mouth? Could it possibly be that this girl of many lovers had finally fallen in love herself and was wretched because she could not be with the man of her choice?

His mind roamed on. Surely it could not be the

unpleasant Thomas Northmore, who had called on her in Milk Street, that she pined for. Yet John had seen some strange things in his time, the most unlikely people utterly besotted with persons of no apparent appeal. More likely though that it was the handsome Gerald Fitz who, if Tobias Wills were to be believed, was just as capable of loving her brother as he was of loving her. But the puzzle about the father of her child remained. Could it even possibly be old Sir Barty? Looking at him with a professional eye, John doubted it in the extreme.

The fragile fellow was *en deshabille* this afternoon, a blue turban from which protruded wisps of white hair, on his head, a long robe covering his person. Yet even the loose drapes of this could not disguise how thin he was, no flesh upon him at all, just a bag of bones and folded skin. Even while John studied him, his total antithesis, the rotund Sir Clovelly Lovell, was making introductions.

" ... the son of a very old friend of mine, Sir Gabriel Kent, John Rawlings."

"How d'ye do, Mr. Rawlings. Delighted to make your acquaintance." Even his voice was a piping treble.

"The honour is mine, Sir Bartholomew." And John made a powerful bow that clearly gave a good impression.

"Well now, to what do I owe the pleasure of this visit?"

John remained silent, looking to Sir Clovelly for his cue, and was delighted to see the fat man rise to the challenge with aplomb.

"My dear friend," he said sombrely, "you may show me the door if you will, but news has reached me of a grievous sad nature. Do not ask me how I know, certain things must always remain confidental. Suffice it to say that I have heard that someone dear to you, someone to whom you had made a certain committment, has been snatched from your embrace in the cruellest way possible. My dear Sir, I have come to you today to offer you the hand, nay the shoulder, of comfort."

It was pathetic. Sir Barty's face, no bigger than Sir Clovelly's fist, crumpled like a squashed sultana.

"I loved her," he sobbed, tears of distress running down his crinkled cheeks. "I really loved her, Clovelly. It was a secret, the greatest secret of my life. At long last I had met my true love and we were going to be married in the summer. Then the wedding was brought forward because she found herself with child."

Momentarily he stopped weeping and looked roguish, and John thought that men must never give up, that they must carry the illusion of virility and irresistability with them to the very last trump.

Sir Bartholomew's moment of glory was brief. "But she was killed," he gasped. "Most foully murdered, though nobody seems to know by whom. There's a rumour sweeps the city that men from London have come to investigate, the crime is so serious."

John's opening had come. "It's perfectly true, Sir. Mr. Fielding's Runners are here seeking the perpetrator of this terrible deed. And, in honesty, I have to tell you that I am privy to their discussion. I can only hope, Sir Bartholomew, that if we all speak frankly today, as men of the world, we may grow a little closer to Juliana's killer."

He had deliberately refrained from putting the word in the plural, terrified of sending the old man into a dire hysteric from which there would be no rescuing him this day.

Sir Clovelly chimed in. "Let me assure you, Barty, that John Rawlings is a young man of the highest integrity. It is my one wish that not only do we raise your spirits this noon but that we can relieve you of that cloak of silence which it must have been your torture to bear these last few days."

In a gesture unbearably sad, Sir Bartholomew held out a skinny hand to his old friend, who clasped it in his podgy fingers in return. Then the old man cried again as if he would never stop. Rising from his chair, John administered his smelling salts and laid a cooling hand on the hot dry brow.

"Come, Sir," he said gently. "This will do no good. You must gather all your strength to join me in the hunt for the murderer."

Unable to speak, Sir Barty merely looked at him. Sir Clovelly meanwhile had pulled a bell rope and had ordered the servant who responded to bring a decanter of best brandy and three stout glasses. Then he sat down, very calmly and quietly, waiting for his old friend to regain control.

There were several minutes of profound silence, then the bereaved man spoke. "I'm sorry gentlemen that you should have seen me thus. It's just that she came to me like a flower in the winter of my life. I thought that whatever time I had left on earth she would fill with sunshine. But you are right. The evil must be punished and I will do whatever I can to help."

"Then, Sir, if I might ask," John said gently, "how did you first meet Juliana?"

Sir Batholomew looked the slightest bit sheepish. "It was through my grandson," he said.

Sir Clovelly's eyebrows shot up and John stared.

"He, Peter, was at school with her brother Richard, even though he was older by several years. Richard was often invited to socialise with his school friends because he boarded and had little to occupy his free time other than his studies. In this way Richard's sister Juliana was introduced to the group and because of her outstanding beauty ..." The old man caught his breath and said, "Her hair was like spun silk ... she became a firm favourite. I used to invite the young people round here for cards and on one occasion Juliana came with them. Neither of us wished to play and we spent two pleasant hours in conversation. I tell you, my friends, that was all the time it took for me to fall deeply in love with her. I began inviting her here on any pretext and one day I declared myself. To my amazement she did not spurn me but said she would give the matter her serious consideration. I did not see her for two weeks and then she came here, looking so radiant that I knew I had not been rejected."

John and Sir Clovelly caught each other's eye but said nothing.

"The very next time I saw her I proposed."

"Did she accept?" rumbled the fat man.

"Not straight away, no. Juliana said it was an enormous step to take and she needed time."

"When did you become lovers?" the Apothecary asked bluntly.

Again that roguish look. "Soon after that. All the young men had been here for an evening of whist. She was to travel home in one of my coaches but events overtook the pair of us. I remember that Gerald Fitz was the last to leave, walking as usual, for despite all his foppish ways he has the courage of a lion. But be that as it may, he shot her such a strange look as he went through the front door."

"Was he jealous, do you think?"

"Possibly." Sir Barty shook his head. "Yet it wasn't quite that."

"Then what?" asked Sir Clovelly, intrigued.

"I can't specify."

"Who were her friends?" John asked. "Tell me who made up the group."

"Well, there was Gerald and my grandson, of course. Richard van Guylder, James and Charles Berisbrooke, the O'Connor twins, Simon Paris and Brenchley Hood."

Sir Clovelly snorted. "In short, all the rips of Exeter, excluding Peter, of course."

Sir Bartholomew smiled a wintry smile. "My grandson is as wild as the rest. But they're all good-hearted boys, just full of youth and exuberance, that's all."

"They will have to be questioned about Juliana," John said, to himself more than anyone.

"I believe they were all in love with her," her elderly lover said benignly. He turned to his guests. "Is there anything else you need to ask me?"

"When you last saw her."

"On a Saturday, about two weeks ago. She came hurrying in here late, having caught the stage from Topsham."

The Apothecary vividly recalled the Saturday of his arrival in Topsham; the market, the sad-faced monkey, Emilia's excitement and Juliana, slipping out of her house and running towards the quay, from whence, though he had not known it at the time, the Exeter coach departed.

"Why did she want to call on you at such an unusual hour?"

"To tell me that she was with child and to ask me to bring our marriage date forward so that she would not cast shame upon her family."

"So she had agreed to marry you by then?"

"Yes, indeed. It was to be in the summer, a grand affair in the Cathedral. The *beau monde* were to be present, in fact every dignitary in town."

John and Sir Clovelly exchanged a look and the fat man pulled a face. "Surely, though, you had not announced it," he said.

"No, we were waiting a while. But her news changed all that. We were to be married this week, very quietly. But ..." his sad and shrunken mouth trembled, "... I never saw her again. I sent her back home early next morning, my coachman took her, and that was the last glimpse I had of her."

"But you arranged for her to stay in lodgings in Milk Street, Sir." It was a statement not a question.

"Yes. She was to catch the early coach and black Daniel was to meet and help her. He had often come here with Brenchley Hood and I thought him a likely fellow to run an errand."

"But she didn't call on you?"

"No. I went to Milk Street, incognito of course, but when I enquired, I was told that she had only been there one day and had not been seen after that ."

"My dear chap, what did you do?" asked Sir Clovelly.

"I made enquiries as best I could, but considering the secrecy of our liaison it was not easy. However, nothing bore fruit. It was as if Juliana had vanished off the face of the earth. Then rumours began to circulate about a body brought to the mortuary. That it was the daughter of a Topsham merchant called van Guylder. I bribed an official to let me in ..." Sir Bartholomew let out a sudden shriek which made both his visitors jump. "... and it was her. My darling lay on a cold slab, hidden by a sheet. Oh God, let me die too."

And that won't be long, John thought cynically, if the poor old fellow continues in this manner. "Calm yourself, Sir, I beg you," he said.

Sir Clovelly, who had clearly had enough of high drama, stated firmly, "It's time he got drunk. I'll ring for refreshments."

"Not just liquid I beg you, "John answered. "I haven't eaten for hours."

"Leave it to me," the fat man answered firmly, and once more tugged a bell rope. "Sir Bartholomew has invited us to dine," he told the footman who answered. "Meanwhile, my young friend is famished and we require light food and plenty to drink. Be so kind as to see to it. I'm always polite to other people's servants," he added in a loud aside.

John fought the overwhelming urge to laugh that always seemed to come over him when situations became slightly farcical. Sir Clovelly on the other hand had no such inhibitions. "Now come along, Barty," he said, and guffawed.

The poor old man waved a feeble hand, weeping afresh. At this, his friend practically poured a full glass of brandy down his throat. "Don't choke, this will do you good. Now brace up, Barty, do. You'll sire a few bastards yet. All is not lost."

The frail form shuddered, though whether with horror or anticipation it was not easy to tell.

"That's better," bellowed Sir Clovelly. "Ah, champagne." He rubbed his hands together.

"Come on, Barty, let's drink to the future."

The old soul took a glass with trembling fingers and John, not knowing whether to laugh or cry, nodded encouragement. "It won't do you any harm, Sir. Truly."

"God save the King," said Sir Clovelly unexpectedly, and Sir Bartholomew staggered to his feet as they drank the loyal toast.

Before they left they tucked their host into bed, carried there by his servants, undressed by his man,

administered to by John who, without his medical
bag, was left to looking through what physics Sir
Bartholomew already had. Finding a decoction of
True Wild Valerian already made up, the Apothecary
poured a little into a glass to ensure Sir Barty had a
good night's sleep. Not that there seemed much danger of him doing otherwise for he was already snor-
ing. However, the physick also calmed the nerves
and was good for those inclined to an hysteric,
which might prove useful on the day following.
John only hoped that the other effect of loosening
the bowel when all else failed, would not work until
the morning.

"All done?" asked Sir Clovelly, who was in fine
fig after a large meal and plenty of wine.

"Yes. He can sleep in peace now."

"Besotted old ass," said the fat man as they left
the house. "Fancy being taken in by a doll common
like that."

"She was very beautiful."

"That's as may be. But there's no fool like an old
fool, says I. Did he really believe he'd sired her child?"

"He wanted to so he did".

Sir Clovelly looked at his fob watch. "Talking of
women, we must hurry, John. It's nearly nine. We
must get home before the ladies."

In the event they had been back five minutes
before the sound of carriage wheels were heard. John,
full of conscience, went out to meet Emilia and
helped her from the equipage with the words, "Don't
be angry. I'm sorry about this morning. Please forgive
me."

She turned her angelic eyes on him. "I was about to say the same. It was wrong of me to take the coach and go like that. Oh John, you must consider me a spoiled fool."

"No, no, I don't. I could never think that of you. I ruined your day by being longer than I intended."

"But did you track the woman down? Did you get a chance to speak to her?"

"Yes to both."

"I'm so pleased. What was she like?"

"Interesting," answered John, and changed the subject. "Was the play good?"

"Very. Miss Clive took the part of Viola and strutted well in boy's garb."

The Apothecary contrived to look extremely disinterested and was glad when Lady Lovell, a woman twice as tall as her husband yet a quarter of his girth, said, "So you must be the gallant bridegroom. How unfortunate for you that duty calls at such a time."

John bowed handsomely. "Lady Lovell, I'm so very pleased to make your acquaintance."

"And I yours." She turned to Emilia. "Now, my dear, do you wish to come in?"

"No, Madam. I have had a wonderful day in your company but must now devote some time to my husband."

"And he to you," said the older woman pointedly, and gave John a dark and meaningful look.

It wasn't until the morning that the Apothecary

remembered that he had still to show Joe Jago the
piece of white material found on the *Constantia*. And,
even more importantly, there was all the new information about Juliana to share with him. But of Mr.
Fielding's clerk there was no sign and John wandered
round the inn while Emilia sat before her looking
glass making herself even more beautiful. Eventually,
in the yard, examining the horses that had pulled
them from London he found the two Runners.

"Gentlemen, good morning. How goes it with
you?"

"Slowly, Sir," said Dick Ham. "We were in Exeter
yesterday interviewing Richard's school friends."

John gaped. "I was just about to tell Mr. Jago that I
have the names of his cronies. How did you get
them?"

"Through the headmaster." Dick searched in his
pocket. "I have the list here. Would you care to run
your eye over it and see who we've missed, if anyone."

John did so, then read it again, slowly. "There's
one name that isn't here."

"Whose that?"

"Peter Digby-Duckworth, grandson of her elderly intended."

The Runners exchanged a glance. "She certainly
had her share of admirers."

"Was that the impression you got?"

Nick Raven fixed his dark eyes on the Apothecary.
"Several of them freely admitted to having slept with
the girl, although whether that was youthful brava-
do one can't altogether be sure."

An extraordinary idea came to John and absolutely refused to go away. He spoke it aloud.

"You don't suppose that the child belonged to Peter and that he and Juliana were trying to foist it on the grandfather in case there were a family resemblance, do you?"

The Runner considered it, narrowing his gaze and pulling his eyebrows together. "It would make sense."

"Yet somehow I feel she loved Fitz."

"The one man we didn't get to see."

"Oh? Why's that?"

"Because he refused to give us admittance."

"Too grand or too guilty?"

"Perhaps a bit of both," said Nick, and barked a laugh.

At that moment Joe came into the stableyard, dressed very finely in a plum coloured coat, his hair on fire in the morning sun. "Ah, Mr. Rawlings, do you fancy a ride out to Sidmouth? That is if Mrs. Rawlings is agreeable."

"Why do you ask?"

"Because William Haycraft, the constable, has retrieved the shift in which Juliana was killed. Yesterday after I had concluded my business in Exeter, I hired a trap and found him working on his farm. It seems that those who prepared her for lying in state changed her into a clean white gown and were about to destroy the old one. Fortunately he stopped them. I thought you might be able to compare your piece of material with the original."

"As long as Emilia is happy, then so am I. But Joe,

can you spare me ten minutes now? The things I found out yesterday have to be heard to be believed. Intrigue is hardly the word to describe it all."

They went into The Salutation and sat in The Tyger and while they waited for John's bride to come downstairs, the Apothecary told Joe Jago all that had taken place. He listened quietly, occasionally asking a question. Finally, he said, "What a nasty bunch of young people. Small wonder the girl got herself killed when she played fast and loose with all and sundry. Somebody must have tired of her games and decided to end them for good."

"But who?"

"We must narrow the field." Joe shielded his eyes from the sun that poured through the window. "I spoke to the quay master last night. I asked him what he was doing in the vicinity of Milk Street on the day Juliana disappeared. He blustered but finally broke down. He called on her to give her money."

"Why, for Heaven's sake?"

"He thought the child was his."

"God's precious teeth," said John, leaping to his feet. "How many fathers did that wretched infant have?" Joe put his head back and bellowed a laugh that rang through the inn and down to the river.

"Well, I weren't one of 'em."

"Nor I. So the old lecher was still having a sexual relationship with her?"

"Apparently so."

"Poor Juliana. I almost feel sorry for her. It seems the girl was unable to contain herself. Anyway, what else did Mr. Northmore say?"

"That that was the last time he saw her. On the Monday at about two o'clock."

"Do you believe him?"

"I don't know what to believe. I think I'd better make a list to clear my mind." He pulled paper and pencil from his pocket and wrote in his fine hand, Suspected of Killing. Beneath that he put: Jan van Guylder (could possibly have rebelled against nature and struck down his own daughter because of her perfidy); Richard van Guylder (same but motive could be because she shamed him by her behaviour with his friends); Tobias Wills (in love with her but perhaps love turned to hate when he heard of her other liaisons); Thomas Northmore (same reasons as above); Gerald Fitz (tired of her maybe). He handed the list to John. "Can you think of any more, Sir?"

"Well, Sir Clovelly said that Sir Barty would take most unkindly to his honour being smirched. He could have hired an assassin to do the job for him. Yet, Joe, I still can't escape the fact that there seemed to be two different attackers."

"We've gone down that path countless times. If the girl stirred passions then fury might have made strange bedfellows act against her. Even old Sir Barty could have hired two footpads to make sure."

"There's just one thing," said John, thinking aloud. "The baby no longer presented any problem, did it."

"What do you mean, Sir?"

"That if somebody wanted to murder her because he was terrified of being publicly accused of fathering her child and had his reputation to consider, Thomas Northmore for example, the fact that she was going to marry Sir Bartholomew would have removed that motive."

Joe sat silently, thinking that through, then said, "You're right of course. The child was being blamed on the old man so whoever was really responsible could breathe again." Now Joe spoke very slowly as the thoughts came. "So whoever killed Juliana did so for another reason entirely. The fact that she was pregnant is coincidental. None the less, it still leaves a good few suspects."

"Yes," said John, as a glimmer of an idea was born.

Chapter 13

Even while they were dressing themselves in the darkest clothes they had brought with them, the sonorous single funeral bell of Topsham's parish church began to toll its melancholy note. John and Emilia looked at one another and shuddered, for this day would see the last mortal remains of the benighted van Guylder children laid in the earth. Juliana had been brought from Exeter on the previous day, as had her wretched brother from closer at hand, and both had spent the night laid out in the largest salon in Shell House. On these occasions coffins customarily remained open, allowing friends and neighbours and the usual strangers to gaze on the waxen features and shed a tear. But in view of their injuries, their father had decided against this and the lids had stayed securely nailed down.

Arriving home late from their day in the city, John and Emilia in company with Joe Jago and the two Runners, had gone to pay their respects and had been amazed by the size of the throng. It would seem that the entire town was there, all dressed sombrely, many openly in tears as they filed by the coffins in silence. Whatever the faults of his wayward children, it appeared that regard for Jan van Guylder had brought people out in a public show of support for him on this grimmest of occasions.

And now as they left The Salutation to walk the short distance to the church, John saw that it had happened again. The entire town was out, proceeding in a body, four abreast, to go to Shell House and bring the dead to their final resting place. With the tolling bell as accompaniment and no sound except that of the marching feet, the solemnity of the occasion was quite indescribable. Behind the solid press of people were several coaches, unable to get through the throng and forced to go at a snail's pace behind it. Turning his head, the Apothecary had a long hard stare to see if he recognised anybody. Sure enough, Gerald Fitz was there accompanied by several other fops of about his age. It seemed that Richard's school friends had stirred themselves to put in an appearance. Of Sir Bartholomew Digby-Duckworth there was no sign, nor indeed of any of the other older citizens of Exeter. It seemed that all the mourning - or could it merely be idle curiosity? - was being done by the young. The only mature man present was the boisterous schoolmaster who today looked as if all the bluster had been knocked out of him.

The crowd tramped down Fore Street and onto the Strand, where the great black horses with their nodding plumes and glass sided hearses already stood, side by side, outside Shell House, the cortege entirely blocking the narrow street. Immediately behind the coffins waited Jan van Guylder and Tobias Wills, the younger man there because he was officially betrothed to Juliana, John supposed. Thomas Northmore had hidden himself in the crowd, his long-suffering wife beside him. He was attempting to adopt a pious expression but merely succeeded in looking pompous, in fact John longed to shout 'Hypocrite' under the man's nose, just to wipe the smirk from his face.

"I see that all Juliana's lovers are present," whispered Joe in the Apothecary's ear.

"All but the old fellow."

"Shame about that. I would like to have had a look at him."

"Perhaps we can call officially."

But Joe's answer was lost in the melee as the crowd parted like the Red Sea to allow the two hearses to pass through. Walking stolidly behind, supporting one another in their mighty effort to remain calm, came Jan and Tobias, followed by Mr. and Mrs. Wills and all the servants. After them came the throng of Topsham people, still in silence. Swept along by the crowd, John managed to break ranks and make for the back of the church, his favourite place for observing those present. He was followed by Joe Jago, foxy face very alert, but the two Runners remained with Emilia, hidden somewhere in one of the central pews.

The Apothecary lowered his voice. "Tell me which is which of the young men."

"The dark one sitting next to Fitz is Brenchley Hood, the big one on the other side is Fitz's brother. The identical twins are the O'Connors, the two similar-looking are brothers, name of Berisbrooke."

"Which is Peter Digby-Duckworth?"

"I don't know. We didn't meet him. But by a process of elimination it has to be the one on the end of the pew, for the other is Simon Paris."

John stared at a very pretty young man, fair curly hair and large long-lashed eyes giving him a sensitive and girlish look. Dispensing with a wig, Peter had his blond locks tied back with a black ribbon and sported a very smart dark coat. From his vantage point John noticed with amusement that Emilia gave the charming fellow a look of admiration, and thought to himself that Peter was just the type to have women fawning all over him. The rest of Richard's friends, though well set up in their way, were not in the same league of looks. Brenchley Hood was too pointed; chin, nose and cheeks all sharp. The brothers Berisbrooke were too bland, like big, affable, enormously stupid dogs. The O'Connors were Irishness personified; hulking red-heads with dark blue eyes. While Simon Paris, dark and dashing, was spoiled by being unusually short, probably no more than five feet in height. He also had his arm in a sling which didn't help his general presentation.

"What do you think?" whispered Joe.

"That you could find them anywhere. A typical bunch of rips about town."

"And all sharing the same girl!"

"Let it be hoped that her father never finds out."

The service continued, punctuated with sobs and sniffs, for the thought of laying to rest two people, neither of whom had even reached their twentieth year, was daunting for all present. Much to their credit both Jan and Tobias, probably dosed to the eyeballs with a really strong anti-hysteric such as Greek Valerian, managed to contain themselves. But when the coffins were carried shoulder high to the greedy-mouthed double grave, the Dutchman finally broke down and sobbed despairingly on Tobias's shoulder. Thomas Northmore, standing close by, began to sweat slightly, though whether with relief that it was over at last, it was impossible to say.

Emilia found her way to John's side and he saw that she was weeping. "Poor things," she said quietly.

"The living or the dead?"

"Both. John ..."

"Yes?"

"Those responsible for all this suffering will be caught, won't they?"

"We will make every endeavour. Won't we, Joe?"

Mr. Fielding's clerk turned his light blue eyes on her, a worried look in their depths. "It's a terrible tangle, Mrs. Rawlings. I have my suspicions about it all but lack the evidence to proceed. We need something to happen to give us the break through we need."

"Can't you set a trap?"

"The point is exactly who are we meant to be trapping?"

"The killer."

"But who is he? Or they?"

"Do you think everyone should be questioned again? All the people on your list, Joe. And that group of young men into the bargain."

Joe scratched his head thoughtfully, his best wig, which he wore for funerals and making arrests, slipping to one side. "Does Fitz connect you with me, Mr. Rawlings?"

"He can't do. He met me through Sir Clovelly.

There's no reason for him to suspect that I work for Mr. Fielding."

"Then somehow get yourself to a place frequented by him and his cronies. Ask Sir Clovelly's help if necessary. Those young rips will spill more to you when they're in their cups than they ever would to Runners Raven and Ham."

John looked dubious. "Well I can but try. But what about the others involved?"

"We'll see them together and very soon at that. But there's one thing that Gerald Fitz needs to be asked immediately."

"I know what you're going to say. Why, if he denied knowing the van Guylders, did he attend their funeral today?"

"Precisely."

"There's no time like the present," answered the Apothecary with determination. "I'll quiz him here and now, at the side of the grave itself if necessary." So saying, he pushed his way through the crowd, holding a handkerchief to his face as if he were in distress and needed to leave hastily.

People were already wandering away, most too shocked to speak, but Fitz and a big brawny boy who resembled him slightly were already heading for his carriage.

"Mr. Fitz, my dear Sir," said John, hurrying towards him, "how very nice to see you. We met in Exeter t'other day if you remember, at the home of Sir Clovelly Lovell."

Gerald looked at him through his quizzer. "Oh yes, " he said disinterestedly.

"The name's Rawlings, John Rawlings." He bowed to the brawny lad. "I don't think I've had the pleasure."

"Henry Fitz," said the other, sighing with boredom.

John continued unperturbed. Adopting a slightly stupid expression, he said, "I didn't expect to see you here today, Sir. I was convinced you said to me that you didn't know the van Guylders."

Fitz was smooth as satin, there could be no doubting that. "I meet so many people," he said languidly. "If memory serves I said I recognised the name. Then I was reminded that I knew the young man. He was at school with someone or other and would come for cards or dice occasionally. But one gets confused with them all, don't you agree?"

John contrived to look enormously earnest. "That is just what I said to Coralie Clive on the last occasion I saw her. You've heard of her perhaps? She's an actress."

Fitz came to life. "My dear fellow, I saved her from kidnap but recently. She was being attacked by those frightful louts who call themselves the Angels. I swear they would have carried her off had I not intervened."

So he hadn't seen John there, that much was plain. "Oh thank you for that, Sir," he answered, beaming inanely. "Any friend of Miss Clive's is a friend of mine."

"You know her well?"

"We are both members of the same gambling set," John lied cosily. "We often play with the best gamester in town, the Masked Lady. But then I don't suppose you would have heard of her here in Exeter."

"*Au contraire*", said Gerald, steadfastly refusing to be impressed. "The name has been mentioned. Tell me, Sir, do you play deep?"

"Very deep," John answered, glinting his eye. "And I haven't rolled a dice since I left town, more's the pity."

Big Henry spoke. "What say we invite Mr. Rawlings to cards tomorrow? You said it's time we had a game to cheer us after all this sadness."

Gerald smiled at his brother as if he were a slightly simple child. "Would you like that?"

Henry looked enthusiastic. "Shall we send for the others as well?"

"Why not? Time Mr. Rawlings met a few friends his own age. Shall we say seven o'clock? I live in The Close, near to Sir Clovelly. Ask anyone. No wives by the way. It's an all male affair."

John swept a stunning bow. "My dear Sir, I shall be there. You can count on it."

"Well?" said Joe as the Apothecary returned to his side.

"Triumph. He's invited me to gamble tomorrow with the whole nest of vipers present."

"Excellent."

Emilia sighed. "And what shall I do while all this is going on?"

"I wondered whether I might escort you to dine in Exeter, Madam?" Joe asked with deference.

"It would be my pleasure," answered Emilia, and gave John a rather cold look.

Whatever the circumstances, the death of the young before their time and, in this case, even before one of their parents, is such a terrible tragedy that none connected with it can leave the experience unscathed. So it seemed for all the people who had attended the double funeral that day; only the young men of Exeter getting into their carriages and driving off without a backward glance. Yet John thought he detected a certain sadness in the pointed face of Brenchley Hood, whose father employed black Daniel amongst his retinue of servants. Was it possible that through the servant Brenchley knew more about Juliana's condition than the others? Or did some other reason give an extra pinch to that sharp, harshly defined chin?

However, he had no time to ponder it. The flow of people had turned back towards Shell House and John and Emilia found themselves going along with it. But even as they moved, Joe Jago took his leave.

"It is not seemly that I attend, Sir. Besides I have to write a full report for Mr. Fielding tonight which must catch the post first thing in the morning." Joe dropped his voice. "Don't forget that you ought to question that mysterious woman as soon as you can. We need to find out if she saw anything unusual while she was out and about."

"Right," John whispered back, guiltily glad that Emilia had moved out of earshot.

Shell House was sombre indeed, full of sad-faced people, the women weeping, the men taking strong liquor to help them recover from the ordeal. Jan was tightly under control once more, so much so that

John could not help asking Dr. Shaw what he had prescribed.

"A concoction of my own. Some Greek Valerian, one simply cannot better it for any form of the vapours, and a little opium." He saw John's look and hurried to explain, "Not enough to hurt him in any way, nor even to make him sleepy. The merest dash just to help him keep his emotions in check."

John decided to be very forthright. "Dr. Shaw, you remember how you told me of Juliana's bad behaviour."

"One shouldn't speak ill of the dead, of course, but yes, the girl was very wild and unruly."

"Is it possible that her father could have lost his temper with her? Could have struck her a violent blow and accidentally killed her?"

"Never. He was too lenient with her if anything. The poor devil has had a terrible life in many ways, but nothing has affected him so deeply that he would turn into a murderer."

John nodded. "And Richard? Would he have been capable of killing his own sister?"

Dr. Shaw looked thoughtful. "You are asking this because the poor child blew his brains out and left some sort of note?"

"Yes. It said, 'I cannot bear the burden of guilt any longer. Juliana forgive me.'"

"May I ask how you know all this? I thought you were here on your honeymoon, not investigating a tragedy."

"Sir, I told you the truth. I am on my honeymoon and I am also an apothecary with a shop in Piccadilly.

What I did not tell you is that in the past I have worked with John Fielding, the blind magistrate, helping to solve various cases of murder and so, willy-nilly, I have got drawn into this one. I cannot go into all the details with you, it would not be ethical to do so, but let me say that though I personally suspect neither Jan nor Richard of killing Juliana, there are those that do."

Luke Shaw made no comment but asked another question. "And why do you not?"

"Because the girl was raped before she died and I feel neither father nor son brutal enough for such a vile offence."

"Yet his suicide note was rather damning."

"But it could be referring to something else, some other terrible event that he had on his conscience."

"What though?"

"That remains to be discovered. Perhaps he borrowed money off her and gambled it all away."

"He certainly moved with a crowd of choice spirits. I often felt the lad must be out of his depth."

"If he was, he has paid for it very dearly."

"Yes indeed."

Dr. Shaw frowned, clearly thinking things through. "You're sure it was suicide, not murder?"

"The position of the corpse seemed natural enough and the fingers gripping the pistol did not appear to have been arranged."

"So you examined poor Richard, God help you."

"Not only that. I actually found Juliana draped over the *Constantia* figurehead, beaten to death, the most terrible marks upon her body. And yesterday it was all brought back to me. My wife and I went to Sidmouth and while she amused herself on the beach collecting shells, I examined the shift that Juliana was wearing when she was killed."

"Why?"

"Because a small piece of white material was found on the figurehead and I wanted to see if it had come from the victim's own clothing."

"And had it?"

"No, Sir, it had not. It was altogether denser."

Dr. Shaw looked intrigued. "How fascinating this study of murder must be. How you must enjoy following all the paths."

"Only if they lead to the right destination. Frankly, Sir, this one appears to be going straight into a maze."

"Well, I think you can safely rule out Juliana's father and brother. Like you, I cannot believe they would rape their own flesh and blood." He paused, then said, "It sounds more like the work of the Society of Angels to me."

"Why do you say that?"

"They're not beyond a little rape. They stand women on their heads and indulge themselves."

"So I've heard. But why should the Angels pick on Juliana?"

"She could merely have been walking the streets of Exeter for it to happen."

John was silent, then said, "I saw the Angels close to the other day."

And he explained how they had tried to snatch Coralie Clive from the theatre and might well have

done so had it not been for the intervention of
Gerald Fitz and his brilliant swordplay.

"So they're growing more daring. They used to
save their activities for late at night. "

"Perhaps the lure of Coralie drew them out."

"Who knows." The doctor was silent for a while,
finally saying, "I wonder if I'm right about the
Angels."

"You may well be."

"But how in the Devil's name will you ever find
out?"

"By asking someone whose sworn purpose it is to
hunt the Society down," John answered, and
refused to be drawn any further.

He knew he had to see Elizabeth di Lorenzi because
she might well hold the key to the whole mystery,
but how and where were at the moment questions
that he found himself unable to answer. The logical
thing would be to visit her tomorrow when he
would be in Exeter to play cards with Gerald Fitz
and his friends. Yet John had a feeling that this
might well turn into a very late session and to call on
a lady at some ungodly hour of the night was hardly
courteous to say the least. If he had had freedom of
choice he would have gone to Wildtor Grange in the
daylight and sought her in her hideaway, but to
abandon poor Emilia by both day and evening
would have been the height of callous behaviour.
The compromise, of course, would be to take his
wife with him - and yet the Apothecary hesitated.

For some reason that he could not, or would not, put into words, he had no wish for the two women to meet.

Throughout the rest of that dismal wake John had thought about all the doctor had to say and his ideas, coupled with his own belief that Jan and Richard would never have raped Juliana, nor allowed anyone else to do so, had made him positive that they could be crossed off Joe Jago's list. But this still left Tobias Wills and Thomas Northmore to be dealt with, though personally John was equally convinced that Tobias's protestations of innocence were genuine enough.

Looking at the poor creature, now on the brandy and growing flushed, the Apothecary decided to have one more talk to him, and seeing Tobias head for the decanter, he swiftly joined him at the table.

"This has been a terrible day for you," he said by way of opening.

Tobias sighed heavily. "I hope now that I can be free of her at last."

"What do you mean?"

"I told you that she was like an obsession with me, has been ever since I reached puberty. I can only pray for the salvation of my soul that she won't continue to haunt me."

John was very blunt. "Just because Juliana is dead and buried, don't make a saint of her, my friend."

"I don't understand."

"I've seen it time and again. Quite hateful people are sanctified by the very act of dying, particularly by a spouse who never really got on with them when they were alive."

"But I did get on with her."

"Did you? Did you really? She betrayed you in every way possible, she was even pregnant by another man. If I were you, Tobias, I would let today's ceremony draw the final curtain. Only in this way will you be free to live the rest of your life in peace."

"You don't think I killed her, do you?"

"No, I don't."

"It was that bastard Northmore."

"I'm not so sure about that. Tell me, what do you know about the Society of Angels?"

"They are a bunch of stupid young fools who terrorise the defenceless of Exeter. Why?"

"Because someone mentioned them in connection with Juliana's murder and the suggestion is not altogether a foolish one."

"But she didn't know them."

"Do any of their victims?"

Tobias took a moment both to drink and consider, then said, "That's true enough. But how are you going to discover the facts?"

"There's a vigilante after them, someone who watches their moves and probably knows more about them than anyone else, including the constables. I'm going to ask that person."

"Who is it? Would I know him?"

"I doubt it. But even if you did I have no intention of telling you. The vigilante's identity is a secret."

"It all sounds very mysterious."

"It is."

Emilia came over and John stopped speaking, rather abruptly. She smiled up at him.

"My dear, I would like to go back to the inn and dine. I can think of nothing nicer than to spend an evening quietly in your company after a day such as this."

Tobias bowed and moved away, and John flattered himself that there was a more determined air about the poor fellow than there had been of late.

The Apothecary kissed his wife's hand. "Shall we go early to bed?"

She smiled her angelic smile. "What a delightful prospect."

"And what would you like to do tomorrow?"

The smile became just the slightest bit wistful. "No doubt, there will be some call on your time so it is pointless to make plans."

He looked at her very seriously. "Do you hate this honeymoon?"

"No, of course not. Yet I can't say that I'll be sorry to get back to London and start married life without all this excitement."

"Do you long for dull domesticity?"

"I can't say that a great deal of dullness would be unwelcome."

"I promise you that we shall have the dullest life a couple could wish for."

"Oh good," said Emilia, not believing a word her new husband was saying.

The minute that the note was handed to him, John

knew that it was going to ask him to do something, and so determined was he to give Emilia an enjoyable evening - and night - that he hid it in his coat pocket, resolving to open it in the morning and not before. As a result, they had a very good time, drinking too much wine and laughing at one another's jokes, and going to bed and making love by candlelight. Therefore it wasn't until he was halfway through his particularly hearty breakfast - John made it a golden rule always to eat well after a funeral - that he remembered the note and pulled it from his pocket. It was in a laboured, rather poor hand that he did not recognise, but when he opened it he realised why. It had been written by the farmer William Haycraft, presently acting as constable of Sidmouth. The Apothecary scanned the contents.

'Sir', he read. 'With Respect I write You to Ask your Help. A Odd Occur Rance has happened. I Think there might Be a Sir Vivor from the Constantia. Gossip Has It that Widow Sarah Mullins has Rescued a Man from The Sea and Has taken him to Live with Her. He Speaks No English and Was found at the Time of the Sailor Who Died. Can You come and Sift Her as She Refuses to Answer to Me.

Ever Your Obedient and Humble Servant, W. Haycraft.'

"Zounds," John exclaimed loudly. "This could be the key to the whole thing."

"What?" Emilia asked, looking over the rim of her cup.

"It seems that there might be a survivor from the *Constantia*. A man has been found alive."

She put the cup down. "My darling, if this means another visit to Sidmouth, please excuse me. I have collected shells, I have walked on the beach, I have swum in the sea. Unless I am spending all my time with you there is little fun left in the place for me. So, if it is agreeable, I would prefer to take the carriage and go into Exeter with Tom to escort me. Lady Lovell has issued an invitation for me to call at any time and I really would prefer to do that."

He took her hand across the table. "I feel that I have been a great disappointment to you."

She withdrew her fingers. "I admit that I thought we would spend the days together on our honey-moon but that is clearly not to be. However, I am having a good time in a very different way to the one I imagined, so please don't worry."

"But I do worry."

"Then drop the investigation. Joe Jago and the two Brave Fellows are more than capable of seeing it through, I feel certain of that."

"You're right of course. My duty is to you, not John Fielding."

Emilia laughed, just a little wryly. "But how could I be the one to drag you away from your beloved hobby? Whatever you say, resentment would creep in, I know that perfectly well. John, if I succeeded in making you devote all your time to me, it would be a pyrrhic victory indeed."

"But, sweetheart ..."

"There's no but about it. I am telling the truth. You are only upset because I would prefer to go off on my own rather than spend the day with you."

"But you did that so recently."

"Without telling you, yes I know, and I have apologised. But now I am stating the facts to your face. I want to go to Exeter and you want to go to Sidmouth and meet the sailor who survived. So let's forget that we are meant to be on honeymoon and do what we both wish."

It was undeniably sensible, it was utterly reasonable, and yet somehow the Apothecary felt that he was failing her. Yet Emilia was right. If he gave up now, he would hardly know how to contain himself. Juliana's killers had to be found, and to stand by and watch Joe and Runners Ham and Raven work their way through the puzzle without him playing any part would be more than he could stand. John sighed deeply.

"Emilia, what can I say? "

"Nothing," she replied robustly.

"You know I love you, don't you?"

She gave him a tight litle smile. "Oh yes, in your way I'm sure you do, John."

Chapter 14

It was exhilarating to ride at speed across the bare heathland, feeling the wild west wind whip his hair into a tangle of curls, for today John was hatless, his wig in its box ready for the evening, a sudden longing in him to get to the sea and let it soothe him with its magic. He was not happy as he rode, sad that he had saddened Emilia, determined to make it up to her once he had caught the killers. And this spurred him on to ride even faster, as if the sooner he got to Sidmouth, the sooner he met the man whom William believed might have survived that dreaded ship of death, the sooner he would be able to settle down to married life and give his wife all the happiness she deserved.

Because he had felt the compulsion on him to travel swiftly, he had refused the placid Hicks at the livery stable and instead hired a young grey mare with long legs to take him on his journeys that day. And, indeed, he had not been disappointed in her, for she moved like a greyhound and seemed as keen as he to get to the sea and listen to the song of the toppling waves. In fact when he turned inland towards William Haycraft's farm she let out a whinny of annoyance and slowed her pace.

"Just be patient," he said, as they proceeded down the track.

The constable was in the fields, stripped to the

waist and sweating profusely despite the fact that the sun was far from at its warmest.

"Oh, you came, Sir," he said, looking up at the sound of the horse's hooves.

John dismounted. "Just as soon as I could. This sounds an amazing stroke of good fortune, William. Is the man really from the *Constantia*?"

"I don't know, John, and that's the truth of it. The story is this. Widow Mullins lives in one of those little cottages near the seashore neath the cliff and has remained there alone ever since her husband was drowned. He was one of the sailors who went to Newfoundland but never made the journey back. But that's by the by. Apparently she was out walking one evening and found a drowned man in the surf. Or at least, so she thought. But when she pulled him out there were signs of life. To cut a long tale short, she dragged him to her cottage somehow or other and nursed him back to life. Now, he's staying put and likes it. And she's not complaining either! But the heart of it is, is he from the death ship? Cos if he is, Sir, then he might be able to tell us exactly what happened."

"You said he doesn't speak English?"

"He's learning from her - and not only how to talk." William guffawed happily.

"Anyway, she won't take any notice of me. Tells me to be off and leave her man in peace. But we must speak to him. He might have seen who brought Juliana on board."

"Unless he'd already gone into the sea as we first thought."

"Even knowing that would help." William wiped his hand across his brow. "I'd best wash and dress and take you there. Maybe you'll have better luck with her, John."

The Apothecary shook his head. "Don't disturb your working day. You've had enough interruption over this affair. I'll find my own way there."

"But how will you gain admittance?"

"I don't really know. I'll have to think of something."

"Sarah is friendly but likes to keep herself to herself."

"I'll just have to try my best," John answered, and put his foot into the stirrup of the capriciously wheeling mare.

The widow's cottage was most snugly situated, the great cliffs leading towards Jacob's Ladder behind it, sheltering it from storms, the beach in front giving the most beautiful views over the sea but offering scant protection should the waves get rough and come lashing inshore. There were four dwellings in the row, all whitewashed and all tiled rather than thatched, presumably because of their close proximity to the salt water. Putting on his most charming expression, John dismounted outside the last cottage and knocked on the black painted door. There was the sound of approaching footsteps and it was flung open to reveal a simple but very clean interior. But it was not to the furnishings that the Apothecary's eye was drawn but to the woman who stood in the doorway.

She was like sunshine, from her big beaming smile and great mass of red curls that splayed out round her head in whorls and spirals, to her generous breasts, saucily visible above the chemise that she wore with her long brightly coloured skirt.

John grinned in pure appreciation of such a Junoesque beauty. "Is your mother in?" he said.

She smiled all the wider. "Who do you want, young man?"

"The Widow Mullins."

"Then you've found her." The great mass of hair tossed backwards as she laughed.

"Have I indeed. I was expecting someone much older."

"A woman can be widowed at any age. Now then, how can I help you?"

This was the difficult moment and John thought on his feet. "I believe you rescued a sailor from the sea recently."

Sarah didn't look quite so sunny. "So what if I did?"

"Only that I wanted to ask your advice. You see, I am an apothecary, often called upon to attend people who are sick or who have been involved in accidents. I simply wondered what techniques you used to bring the poor fellow back to life. For I must confess to you that while I was in Sidmouth a man was washed ashore from the boat that was towed in, the *Constantia,* but try as I might I couldn't save him. He died in my arms."

The Widow Mullins relaxed slightly. "Yes, I heard about that. They said a gentleman who was here on his honeymoon ministered to the poor soul."

"That was me. Anyway, it wasn't until this morning that I heard of your heroic deed and decided to ask you how you did it. Do you mind?"

She hesitated, then the big grin reappeared. "No, of course I don't. Come in, come in. You can see the patient for yourself."

John stepped into the glowing interior, all stone floors, rag rugs and gleaming brass, and thought how well Sarah kept her house in view of the fact that she must have hardly any money. Then his eyes got used to the brightness coming from the window overlooking the sea and he realised that the survivor of the death ship was in the room, had risen to his feet, and was surveying him with caution.

"This is Dmitri," announced Sarah, and went to stand beside her guest. The raw attraction between them crackled and John wondered how they ever managed to get out of bed, the feeling was so powerful.

The Russian smiled. "Good day to you," he enunciated carefully.

Sarah beamed like a proud mother. "You said that very well."

Quite unabashed, Dmitri kissed her full on the lips. "Thank you."

Feeling something of an intruder, the Apothecary decided to be businesslike. But it was difficult in the presence of two such healthy creatures who obviously found so much physical pleasure in one another.

"Congratulations," he heard himself saying.

"On what?" asked Sarah, mystified.

"On being so natural." He eyed Dmitri up and down, taking in the man's enormous height and breadth, to say nothing of his thatch of blond hair and dark weatherbeaten skin. "Did you come from the *Constantia*?" he asked.

The sailor nodded. "Yes."

"Thank God," said John under his breath. He turned to Sarah. "Mrs. Mullins, you know, of course, that a dead body was found aboard that ship."

"Yes, I do. And I've had that wretched William Haycraft round here wanting to ask questions. I'm sure they think that Dmitri was involved in her death."

John shook his head. "On the contrary, it is perfectly obvious that he wasn't. Otherwise the body would have been in the sea and the sailors aboard. No, the whole mysterious circumstance points to someone else, some outside agency, boarding the vessel and dumping the body there."

"But why? Why do that?"

"I can only imagine that some tormented mind regarded it as a joke." John looked at the widow very seriously. "Mrs. Mullins, so horrible was the crime that I have offered my services to help hunt down the perpetrators. In order to do this I have to find out what took place on that terrible ship. Do I have your permission to question Dmitri about what happened that day?"

She paused, gesturing the Apothecary to sit down, then doing so herself. There were only two chairs and the Russian came and sat at her feet like some enormous wolfhound.

"What did you say your name was?"

"Rawlings, John Rawlings."

"Well, Mr. Rawlings, I don't mind helping you but there are difficulties. If Dmitri should be accused of killing that poor girl, then I should lose him, and that I do not want to happen. Secondly, he knows very little English and we will need help from someone who speaks his lingo."

"Is there such a person in Sidmouth?"

"Yes, Old Saul."

"The medicine man?"

"That's him. He's travelled far and wide in his day and has picked up a smattering of most tongues. Anyway, he sailed on a Baltic ship for a while and so can talk to Dmitri. Do you want me to fetch him?"

"I would be most grateful. Mrs. Mullins ..." John put out a hand and briefly touched her arm. " ... Dmitri will not get into trouble through this. I give you my word on it."

"If he does you'll have me to answer to," she replied, and tossed her great mane of hair in a challenging gesture. John got to his feet. "May I escort you to Old Saul's house?"

Sarah laughed. "If you wish. He's only next door."

"Oh I see. Was he part of your secret? Did he help bring Dmitri back from the dead?"

"Of course. I bless the fact that I'm big and strong because it was me that dragged him from the shallows and half way up the beach. Then I ran for Old Saul, who was at home, God be thanked. He knew what to do with a drowned sailor."

"What?" John asked curiously.

"He turned him on his side and pumped his back with his hands, then he kept raising Dmitri's arms, pushing the water out of his lungs. Then Old Saul and me between us up-ended Dmitri, heaven knows how when you look at the size of him, and what was left of the water came running out of his mouth."

"You must have caught him just in time. I'm afraid I was too late with his fellow sailor."

"At least you tried," said Sarah.

They had reached Old Saul's door but there was no response to the knocker and the widow turned back to her own place.

"He goes out a lot, attending the sick and looking for herbs and things. Do you want to come back later?"

"I can't be too long. I have other things to do today."

"Try returning in an hour."

"I'll do as you say." John swept Sarah a bow which Dmitri studied with interest. "Many thanks for your help. You have contributed a great deal towards bringing wrongdoers to justice."

"Not yet I haven't."

"But you will," said John, and left.

There wasn't enough time to venture to Wildtor Grange, nor indeed did the Apothecary feel like cooping himself up in The Ship. So instead, he mounted the mare and took her for a wild canter in the shallows, both of them getting thoroughly soaked and enjoying every spattering of foam. Then he dismounted and led her quietly along while he looked into the rock pools and examined the seaweed with its lovely moist bubbles, so delightful to pop and squeeze between the fingers.

As he walked John was aware of a distant figure, coming towards him from the direction of the red cliffs, a figure who was beachcombing just as he was, a small, russet-coated figure that matched its surroundings and was so wind-tanned that the skin of the face and hands matched the coat in their turn. Looking at it, seeing it sniff the seaweed and stare into the rock pools just as he was, John knew that he had found his man. Without a doubt, Old Saul was coming towards him.

"Good morning," he called cheerfully when the distance between them had narrowed sufficiently to allow his voice to carry.

"Good morning, Apothecary," answered the other.

John was amazed, wondering if the old man also practised magic, but realised after a moment or two that his presence must have been noted by all the locals when he had stayed at The Ship. He held out his hand. "Old Saul?"

"That's me, Sir. And how be you today?"

"Well, my friend, well. How fortunate that we should meet. You're the very man I was looking for?"

"How's that then?"

"I believe you speak Russian. I've a few questions I want to ask Dmitri."

Old Saul chuckled. "There's a lot would like to do that."

"Oh? Who?"

"Constable Haycraft for one. And that gaffer from Exeter."

"What gaffer from Exeter?"

"Don't know his name, don't wish to. But he come round this way after the *Constantia* was brought in and asked if there were any survivors."

"How interesting. I wonder who he was."

"Don't know, but he went away empty handed. I'd helped to save Dmitri by then, but I never let on."

"Why?"

"Cos I didn't like the cut of his jib. He was smooth as a snake, that one."

"Does the constable know about the man?"

"Don't reckon he do. Too many people asking too many questions, that's what the fisherfolk thought. So they kept their mouths shut".

"But William's a good man. Why hide things from him?"

"Old saying. Least said, soonest mended. Sarah Mullins has been alone a long while, now she's found a good man who'll wed her in time. Nobody wanted to see him taken away."

John scratched his head. "But why should Dmitri be removed?"

"Because the gaffer from Exeter would have snatched him soon as look at him. But he never got the chance."

"I wish I knew who this man was."

"Had a black coach with a coat of arms on the side."

"What did it say?"

"Something about sickness."

"Was he a physician?"

"Not he," said Old Saul seriously. "Not that one." He looked John up and down. "Let us repair to the tavern and talk of healing, Sir."

There was no way he was going to be rushed and John knew it. "I should be delighted," he answered, though he actually detested the delay. "I would be interested to hear some of the things that you were taught by the Eskimos."

"Those that aren't secret you shall learn," Old Saul answered.

John asked the obvious question. "You wouldn't talk to the constable nor to the gaffer from Exeter. Why have you chosen to confide in me?"

"They said you were brave as a lion the day the *Constantia* was brought in, that you did not flinch from looking at that poor creature on the figurehead. I'd reckon from that, Sir, that you've earned a little respect. So I'll help you question Dmitri provided you don't tell what he says to another living soul."

"I can't promise that. It may be so important that it has to be passed on to the authorities."

Old Saul looked deeply concerned. "Does that mean Dmitri will be in trouble?"

"It means that we might be able to find out who the gaffer from Exeter is and put a stop to his games."

Old Saul nodded but said nothing as they made their way into the quiet dimness of The Ship.

He had thought he was going to be bored, would be

chafing at the bit to interview Dmitri and get a little closer to the secret of the *Constantia*. But in fact John had never passed a more fascinating time than he did in Old Saul's company. He hardly said a word as the old man spoke in his soft Devon burr of how the Eskimos had taught him the technique of bringing the drowned back to life, of how they treated burns by pouring cold water over the scalded place, of how they used ambergris from the whale to rub on wounds and heal them quickly. He also spoke of the Red men, the Indians native to the Colonies, who had taught him about their medicine. Had shown him how fat from the antelope could be used as a cooling substance, how ground snakeskin and mint would stave off fever, how a vaginal suppository made from fir resin, juniper and crushed peas was used to help a woman give birth.

The Apothecary listened in wonderment, feeling that he, supposedly the qualified practitioner, had still a great deal to learn, and that Old Saul, supposedly an amateur, probably knew as much, if not more, than he did. Instead of looking at his watch and itching to be off, it was with reluctance that John finally left the inn, realising that two hours had passed instead of one.

Rather surprisingly, the door to the widow's house stood open, letting the west wind blow through the cottage, chilling it a little. It had pulled one of the windows off its catch, so that it occasionally swung wide then banged shut again. It was rather eerie in view of the profound silence everywhere else.

"Sarah," called Old Saul, "we'm be back."

John went to the bottom of the stairs, which led directly out of the parlour, expecting the widow's cheerful voice to call from above, but the silence continued, only the banging window breaking it. A noise from the front door had both men wheeling round to see who was coming in. But it was only a large black cat who stood there, staring at them rather uncertainly.

"Come on, Mab," said Old Saul, bending to stroke her. "She be Sarah's," he added. Then he stopped speaking and straightened up, his face suddenly frozen. "Look!" And he held his hand out to John. It was covered in blood, oozing between the old man's fingers as he spread them. "The cat's got it all over," he said hoarsely.

The Apothecary did not hesitate, leaping up the dark spiral stairs and throwing open the door of the only bedroom. On the bed, entwined in each other's arms, stark naked, were Dmitri and Sarah, both of them covered in that same terrible red and neither of them moving at all.

"Saul," John screamed, "get up here. Quick!"

He heard the old man clambering up and come to stand behind him in the doorway.

"Christ's mercy!" he said softly. "Who's done this to them?"

"I don't know. But we've got to act fast. There might still be a chance. I'll tend the man you the woman."

"No, Sir, t'wouldn't be decent. I know her, you see. Let's go t'other way round."

There was no time for argument. John raised the naked Sarah in his arms and put his head down to her splendid breasts, listening for the beat of her heart. There seemed to be nothing yet the smallest flicker at her wrist revealed that she clung on to life.

"She's alive," John called to Old Saul.

"So's he, but within an inch of it. Whoever beat them round the head practically brained them."

"They're still losing blood. It must be stayed. The plant Adder's Tongue is good but I haven't got my bag with me."

"I have a jar of Indian paste next door."

"Then go and get it, man, and bring some bandages and boiling water with you. I'll try and revive them meanwhile."

John held his salts beneath Sarah's nose, patting her hands and calling her name and pulling the bedclothes round her to keep her warm. She fluttered, no more than that, but at least it was a sign of life. Dmitri was far worse to rouse. Wiping away the blood which still oozed from the poor fellow's head, the Apothecary practically pushed the salts bottle up the Russian's nostrils but with very little effect. Dmitri groaned in pain but there was no response other than that. It seemed to John at that moment that there was very little hope of saving him.

Plodding footsteps on the stairs told him that Old Saul had come back, laden. In fact the poor fellow was weighed down by a great canvas bag from which he proceeded to draw various jars and bottles.

"I had to leave the boiling water at the bottom. I hadn't a hand to carry it."

"I'll go and get it. But before we clean them up, we've got to stop this bleeding. You haven't by any chance got any Clown's Woundwort, have you?"

"Not only the ointment but the syrup."

"God be praised, let's get some down them."

It was John's favourite remedy for inward wounds and ruptures of veins and now he spooned an extra large dose down, first Dmitri, then Sarah. Then he set too with the ointment.

"When you've finished with that I suggest we clean 'em up, so I can apply my special paste."

"What's in it?"

"It is a great secret, known only to the Navajo tribe. But one day I might share it with you."

As they cleaned the blood away from the two inert forms, it became abundantly clear that the lovers had been the victims of a most frenzied and vicious attack.

"Who could have done this?" asked Saul once more.

"My bet would be on the gaffer from Exeter. He wanted to know if there were any suvivors of the *Constantia* and it's my guess that he found out there was one."

"But why would he want to harm them?"

"Because, my friend," John replied quietly, "it's my belief Dmitri knew too much."

They worked throughout the afternoon and when he finally thought it was safe to leave them, John put the couple in the charge of Old Saul and went in search of William Haycraft. Then the hunt was up for a physician to stitch the wounds, which had finally stopped bleeding. As chance would have it, as William, who had saddled up a horse for speed, rode back beside the Apothecary, he stopped short outside one of the larger dwellings.

"That's Dr. Hunter's trap. He's in Sidmouth, Lord be praised. Let me stop a moment or two and leave a message for him."

"Very well, but William, don't be long. Sarah and her Russian lover are not out of the wood yet."

The constable looked considerably annoyed. "I find it hard that this fellow confided in Old Saul but refused to talk to me. It's a conspiracy of silence that should never have taken place."

"But the fact that there really is a survivor alive will finally open this investigation up. For the chances are that he saw something, something which will definitely point to Juliana's killers. Why else should Dmitri be attacked?"

"I can't wait to find out."

"My friend, if I were you I wouldn't even try. I have a feeling that one glimpse of you and all concerned will become silent as the tomb. Because I am an outsider they seem to trust me. Let me get as much information as I can and pass it on to you."

Reluctantly, the constable nodded. "I think you're right. I'll keep away. But as soon as you know something please tell me of it."

"Well, it certainly won't be for several days. They

are both far too ill to speak - that is, of course, if they ever speak again."

It was another hour before Dr. Hunter put in an appearance and exclaimed in horror at what he saw. However, he did his duty and stitched those wounds that would not heal without help, John paying his fee, knowing that Sarah would be far to poor to afford the bill. Constable Haycraft meanwhile made a thorough examintion of the house but could find no sign of forced entry, indicating that the attackers had come in through the front door.

"It was open when we found them, but they were obviously upstairs taking their pleasure at the time of the attack. Wouldn't the door be closed in that case?"

"Not necessarily. Perhaps they had left it open for the cat."

"Oh well, we'll find out eventually I suppose." John looked at his watch. "I was hoping to perform one more errand today but I won't have time now. I'm to play cards with Gerald Fitz and his cohorts."

"Sift them for all the information you can, John."

"That I fully intend to do."

They had been speaking in the parlour but now John and William went upstairs to take a final look at the patients. Dmitri was too deeply unconscious for John's liking, as if he had slipped into a coma.

"If he doesn't regain consciousness tonight I think we'll lose him," he said to Old Saul.

"Don't worry, Apothecary, I'll keep vigil with him

- and with Sarah too. I won't let them go, I promise you."

"I only hope you succeed." John looked contrite. "Saul, I'm sorry but I have to leave you now. I'll come back tomorrow morning to see how they are, that is if my wife is agreeable."

"Is she getting angry with so much interruption to her honeymoon?"

"Not angry exactly. More hurt than cross."

"An Indian love potion might be the very thing."

"I tell you what, Saul," said John, putting his hand on the old man's shoulder, "if the situation gets any worse I'll definitely buy one."

William looked at the couple, still lying side by side in the blood stained bed. "What are their chances, John?"

"Not good at all. The only thing in their favour is their natural strength and energy."

"Well I pray to God that they make it because it seems to me that only the man can answer one truly vital question."

"What happened aboard the *Constantia*."

"That, and whether he, too, saw angels before he jumped into the sea."

He had been planning to go to Wildtor Grange to seek out Elizabeth di Lorenzi, but in view of the day's dramatic events all such plans had been over-turned. For John knew that it was vital he kept his evening appointment. To see Gerald Fitz relaxed, hopefully in his cups, and to find out all he could about his relationship with Juliana van Guylder was too great an opportunity to be missed. Keeping well away from the ruined house in which the extraordinary Marchesa hid herself, John returned to Topsham.

Emilia had been back, had changed for the evening into a fine gown and had gone out again in the company of Joe Jago, Irish Tom had informed him as he clattered into the inn yard on the skittish grey mare. They had travelled in the Runners coach, driven by Dick Ham, Nick Raven acting as guard, all four of them taking themselves off for a night out in Exeter.

"The two Runners are going *incognito*," the coachman had explained, relishing the word so much that he had said it twice.

"What exactly do they mean by that?"

"They will be mingling with the crowd dressed in ordinary clothes."

"That should be fun for them."

"Indeed it should, Sir. Now, I'll just get the coach polished up while you change your clothes. I've been making enquiries and hear that the Fitz place is one of the grandest houses in town. We can't arrive looking shabby, now can we?"

"Certainly not. I shall make an effort."

It being his habit never to travel without at least one superb suit, John fetched his best from the clothes cupboard. Indigo silk embroidered with silver leaf work, an intricate silver waistcoat beneath, was his choice, the ensemble completed by fine white stockings and meroquin leather shoes with sparkling buckles. Fixing a diamond brooch - a gift from Sir Gabriel - to his flared skirt coat, John turned to see it glitter in the light. On his head the Apothecary wore a tie wig with a long queue interwoven with black ribbon. It was undress but considered extremely smart by the younger members of the *beau monde*. Completing the rig with his great stick, John stepped forth for his evening's entertainment.

The Fitz house was indeed very imposing, so large that Gerald and Henry had been given a whole suite of rooms at the back in which to entertain their friends. Ushered down a long passageway by a footman in very stylish livery, John was announced and shown into a spacious salon, lit by a dozen chandeliers. Here a reception with servants carrying round champagne was in full swing.

"My dear Rawlings," said Gerald Fitz, approaching with a languorous air, "how good to see you." He raised his quizzer and studied John's suit, then sighed. "I simply must get back to my London stitcher. One feels quite the frump in comparison to your heavenly costume. Remember to give me your tailor's name before you leave. Now, introductions are in order I believe."

They were all presented, all those young men he had seen at the funeral and a few more beside. John almost had the feeling of being an intruder amongst them, as if this were a community complete in itself who resented strangers how ever well-dressed they might be.

"We drink first, then go in to cards and dice," Fitz informed him. "Then we play for an hour or so before supper. Then sport is resumed once more and goes on till dawn, or later. Have some more champagne, my friend, it will do you good."

As his glass was being refilled, John heard the distant peal of the doorbell, at which Fitz clapped his hands together for silence.

"Gentlemen, our last guest has arrived. I know our golden rule is that no women are allowed but in this case I have been so bold as to make an exception. I ask you to welcome her with much good show."

There was a dramatic pause and every eye turned to the door which was suddenly flung open. The elegant footman stood there, completely concealing the figure that waited behind him. John felt a sudden surge of excitement.

The servant cleared his throat. "Lady Elizabeth, the Marchesa di Lorenzi", he announced in ringing tones as every man in the room bowed low in greeting.

Chapter 15

She looked sensational, dressed entirely in scarlet trimmed with black roses, her sacque back dress, which fitted tightly in the front but flowed in a full train at the back, made from a fabric called chine. The Apothecary, with his love of high fashion, recognised it at once as being woven in the materials satin and flowered velvet, both together in one piece, having a waistcoat of similar cloth in his clothes press in London. Round her neck the Marchesa wore a simple black choker adorned by a velvet red rose in the centre of which, like a dew-drop, glittered a diamond. This night she was fully wigged, her head piece a stylish cocncotion of loop-ing white curls. While high on her cheekbone, almost flaunting her scar to the world, Elizabeth wore a black patch in the shape of a galleon.

Gerald Fitz raised his quizzer and walked towards the new arrival, and John knew by the fop's very gait that he desired her.

"Exquisite, Madam, truly exquisite. Now may I present the company to you?"

"Delighted," she said, and flashed her eyes round the room.

They fastened on John and he saw her brief look of surprise turn into something else, a small cloud-ing, a tiny warning which he could not interpret. But at that moment it seemed as if all the beaux in Christendom were bowing before her and it was with impatience that the Apothecary waited his turn, wondering what it was that she had been trying to signal to him. His opportunity came at last. "May I present a visitor from London, Ma'am? John Rawlings, a man of medicine I believe."

"How d'ye do?" said Elizabeth grandly, and extended a haughty hand.

So that was it. They were to act as if they were perfect strangers. John gave quite the most elaborate bow in his repertoire, then raised her fingers to his lips.

"Delighted to make your acquaintance, Ma'am. Your reputation as the most beautiful woman in Exeter precedes you."

"Not as far as London, surely?"

"Even as far as London," John replied solemnly, and gave another, smaller, bow.

He moved on, letting the next sycophant take his turn, wondering what she was doing here and why she should be friendly with Fitz, of all the repellant people. But his train of thought was broken by a tug at his elbow and John, looking round, saw a young man with the sleeve of his coat hanging loose, and that of his shirt barely disguising the fact that he was bandaged from shoulder to wrist.

"Sir, may I present myself? Percival Court's the name. I overheard Gerald say that you were a man of medicine."

"Yes, I'm an apothecary."

"Oh, are you? Then I wonder if I might seek your advice regarding my arm."

Wishing that people wouldn't do this to him at social gatherings, John gave a noble smile.

"Certainly. What seems to be the trouble with it?"

A very sheepish grin crept over Percival's features. "Well, I've received a wound but have not dared consult a physician about it."

"Why not, damme?"

"Because word would be bound to get back to my father. It's from a sword."

"I presume you've been duelling?"

"Precisely. And if he knew I swear my revered sire would disinherit me. He's damned strait-laced about that kind of thing."

"But surely you could go to a doctor who doesn't know him, someone who would be utterly discreet?"

Percival sighed. "The trouble is everyone knows him - and me - for miles around. You see, he's Lord Clyst."

John looked blank, the name meaning nothing to him. "None the less ..."

Percival's expression changed and he suddenly appeared desperate and haunted. "Please, Sir, I really do need help. The damn thing is terribly painful."

"You realise I haven't got my bag with me."

"If you could just advise."

"Then let us step somewhere where we can be private and I'll take a look at it."

The wound had become infected, that was the trouble. John stared in horror at a severe gash which should have been stitched immediately but was now inflamed and oozing with pus.

"This mustn't be left a moment longer," he said. "You are to get into your coach and go to a physician now."

"But ..."

"There are no buts, you life might well be at stake. Have you heard of blood poisoning? Sepsis? It is fatal. For God's sake, Percy, who did this to you?"

"A friend."

"Some friend indeed! What were you quarreling about? A woman?"

"In a way."

He wasn't going to be drawn further, that was obvious, but the fact remained that the silly creature had to be persuaded to go for immediate treatment.

"Don't move!" said John with sudden authority. "There's someone who should see this."

Percival opened his mouth to object but the Apothecary gave him such a dark look that he closed it again without saying a word. Glaring at him, John left the room and went to seek out his host, explaining as briefly but as clearly as he could that one of the guests was in dire peril if he did not get to a doctor very quickly indeed.

Fitz raised his quizzer to stare. "And to which of my many foolish friends do you refer,

"To Percival Court."

A truly extraordinary expression momentarily crossed Fitz's features and John was immediately struck with the notion that his host knew far more about the incident than he was going to admit. "I see," he said slowly.

"I must impress on you, Gerald - I may call you that, mayn't I ...?"

Fitz nodded.

"That Percival could die if he isn't treated swiftly.

Sepsis will set in and will kill him, there's no doubt about that."

Fitz went pale. "I'll speak to him at once."

"I've left him in the small ante-chamber. Please do your best to persuade him."

They went into the passage together but at the door, Fitz turned. "No offence, John, but I would rather speak to him privately. He'll take more notice if no one else is present."

"Of course," the Apothecary answered, and turned to go as the door closed behind Gerald Fitz. However, he did not hurry about returning to the reception, instead lingering in the corridor for several minutes. The voices coming from within were muted but just for a moment Fitz's became distinctly audible. "I order you to go - now," he said.

Puzzling over the use of the word 'order', John returned to the party.

It seemed to be the night for wounded men, for the first to accost him as he went back into the throng was the dashing little Simon Paris, his arm still in its sling. Half smiling, John stared at the injured limb.

"What happened to that?"

Simon looked casual. "Fell over and hit myself on a boulder. Damn nuisance, can hardly get a glass to my lips." He roared with laughter.

"I take it you've been to a doctor?"

"Of course. Someone had to extract ..." He stopped short.

"Extract what?" John asked politely.

"A piece of rock that splintered," Simon answered patly, then laughed again.

The Apothecary changed the subject. "I saw you at the funeral the other day. A very sad affair that."

Simon seemed relieved to talk about something else. "Yes, bad business. Rumour has it that Richard murdered his sister then shot himself. Is it true?"

"Not in my opinion."

"You seem convinced."

"That's because I'm certain that is not what happened."

"You give the impression of knowing a great deal about it."

"Well, I'm staying in Topsham at the same inn as the men who have come from Bow Street and, obviously, we chat about it."

"Oh yes, I'd heard some big-wigs from London were investigating." Simon Paris flashed his dark eyes. "Ridiculous, in my view. What could they possibly know about local affairs?"

"I'm sure they have their methods," John answered enigmatically.

Simon looked bored and waved to someone across the room. "Excuse me, Sir. I've just seen an old acquaintance. If you'd forgive me." He bowed and departed.

"So," said a soft voice in the Apothecary's ear, "you are a friend of Gerald Fitz's. I am greatly surprised."

"I am equally surprised to see you here," he answered, smiling, and turned to see Elizabeth looking at him, very quizzically he thought. "And just for your information," he added in the lowest tone possible, "Fitz is no friend of mine. I am here to snoop on him."

"But I thought you were in Devon on honeymoon. Which reminds me, where is your bride?"

Without thinking, John took Elizabeth by the hand. "I am indeed on honeymoon and my bride is out with friends. But meanwhile I have become involved with the case of the girl found dead aboard ship. Have you heard about it?"

"Of course. Everyone has."

"As an apothecary I was asked to examine her body. She had been raped and beaten to death. One of the suggestions put forward, though this is by no means proven fact, is that it was the work of the Society of Angels. Because of that I wanted to ask you if you had seen anything unusual round about the time of her death."

"Which was when?"

"Roughly two weeks ago. She was last seen alive in Exeter on a Monday but exactly what day she died is not quite certain."

Elizabeth put her fan to her face. "There are ears everywhere here. Come to Wildtor when this evening ends and we can discuss it. It would be far safer."

"Very well."

"One final question. What has Gerald Fitz got to do with all this?"

"He knew the girl, in fact he was probably her lover. Further, most of the young men in this set admit to having slept with her and, to crown all, she was about to marry Sir Bartholomew Digby-Duckworth on the pretext that she was carrying his child."

Instead of looking askance, Elizabeth laughed. "I wonder what she did in her spare time."

"Heaven knows."

At that moment came a call for silence, then Gerald Fitz spoke. "Lady Elizabeth and gentlemen, the grand saloon is set for gambling. Let us to our pastime." He made much of walking through the company to escort the Marchesa in, nodding his head to John and whispering, "He's gone to see our family physician," as he did so. The Apothecary bowed by way of acknowledgment and made his way into the gambling room.

The next hour was one of immense concentration as John, who was not a truly accomplished card player, fought his way through an intense game of whist during which Peter Digby-Duckworth, a gambler to the very bone, executed a stunning Bath coup and won a dashing rubber. It was a relief in view of all this to hear the supper interval called. With an ingratiating smile on his face the Apothecary fell into step with the winner.

"Well played, Sir, well played."

"I get a fair amount of practice."

"How I envy you that."

Peter turned his ravishing lilac eyes on to his companion. "You're the man from Topsham, ain't you? The one who's here on honeymoon?"

"I am indeed, Sir. Rawlings is the name, John Rawlings."

"Peter Digby-Duckworth."

"Digby-Duckworth!" John trilled. "Why, I met your delightful grandfather only t'other day."

Peter looked at him coldly. "Really?"

"Yes, really. But he was much in gloom, alas. It seems that his betrothed was one and the same as that poor unfortunate girl whose funeral you attended recently."

"That poor unfortunate girl was a whore, Sir, and my grandfather nothing more nor less than a besotted old fool."

"Oh come now."

"Come now nothing," answered Peter, tossing his golden queue, his tongue obviously loosened by drink and success. "In case you have any illusions left, Juliana van Guylder had jigged the feather bed with practically every man in this room."

"Including yourself?"

"Yes, even including me."

"Was it your child she was carrying?"

Peter shrugged. "Who knows, it could have been anyone's."

"Your grandfather's perhaps?"

"No, that's for sure. He might flatter himself but the poor old chap was utterly wrong in thinking so."

"How do you know?"

"Because I lied just now. It's mine."

"You're certain?"

"Pretty sure. She'd been Fitz's for a while, but he tired of her when she started to talk about marriage. So, hearing of her splendid reputation as a lover, I took her on."

"And it was during her liaison with you that she conceived?"

Peter's eyes danced mischievously. "Yes, but that doesn't prove a thing. Not with a girl like Juliana. However, in case it was mine, it was a splendid notion to palm it off on my grandfather, don't you think?"

"I think you're amoral, the whole damned bunch of you."

"Fun though."

"Not for your victims," John answered, and walked away.

The supper was superb. Indeed, whatever else one could say or think about Fitz, he was a splendid host. Clearly, though, he was making some sort of play for Elizabeth, probably hoping to amuse himself with a much older woman, John thought. She, however, though charming and courteous, gave him not a whit of encouragement. Nor did she anybody else, contriving in the most clever manner to be attentive yet at the same time remain somewhat aloof. The Apothecary found himself lost in admiration of her stylish behaviour. Eventually, though, it was time to leave the repast and head back for the gaming saloon and it was then that he found himself walking beside her.

"Is your coachman here?" she asked quietly.

"Yes. Emilia, my wife, has been driven by somebody else."

"Head for Wildtor as soon as we have finished

here. I have remembered something that might be
relevant to the girl's murder."

"Will you get there ahead of me?"

"Yes. I shall leave in an hour. Follow me after a
discreet interval."

She could say no more for Fitz, flushed with
champagne and carnality, was bearing down on her.
Elizabeth made the tiniest of curtsies in John's direction and moved away.

He had never been lucky with dice and tonight he
seemed worse than ever. In danger of parting with a
great deal of money, the Apothecary bowed out of
the game and took to wandering the room, pretend-
ing to be tipsy but in fact observing the company.
The Berisford brothers, looking more like large and
foolish hounds than ever, were playing deep and
losing. Little Simon Paris, however, was doing well,
as were the O'Connor twins, who were making a
great deal of Irish noise about it. Brenchley Hood
had also given up and was sitting quietly in a corner,
glass in hand, staring pensively into its dark red
depths. His pointed face in repose was set in harsh
lines that made him look thoroughly wretched. John
decided on bold tactics.

"May I sit beside you, Sir?"

The other looked up and nodded half-heartedly.
Carefully adjusting the skirts of his coat, the
Apothecary took a seat.

"Allow me to introduce myself. My name is John
Rawlings and I am visiting from London. I saw you
at the funeral the other day and marked your sadness. My condolences."

Brenchley stared at him blankly. "You have the advantage of me, Mr. Rawlings. I am afraid I didn't notice you. But then I didn't notice much that day."

"You were very attached to the deceased?"

"Not so much to Richard, but to Juliana, yes."

"She was indeed very beautiful."

"You met her?"

"Only twice. My wife and I were invited to dine by her father. What a tragic thing that she should meet her end in so brutal a manner."

Brenchley Hood blanched white. "Don't even mention it, I beg you. The very thought makes me sick to my gut."

Sensing blood, John persisted. "But who could have done such a vile thing? What tortured mind could have conceived of such an end?"

Brenchly stared at the floor, totally silent, shaking his head.

"I mean, my dear Sir, to have raped the poor girl like that. Why, it's atrocious."

Hood jerked upright. "What did you say?"

"That Juliana was raped before she died. Did you not know?"

"No, I didn't. My God, are you sure of this?"

"Absolutely certain. I apologise. I see that I have upset you."

The other man lurched to his feet, his eyes wildly dilated. Then he clutched his hand over his mouth and dashed from the room, clearly headed for the plunger closet, a vast wooden edifice with gleaming brass handles, drop holes and gurgling cocks, the delights of which John had already sampled.

The Apothecary stared after his disappearing form thoughtfully. "The only one to have a good word for her," he said quietly, and wondered to himself if he had finally discovered the true paternity of Juliana's child.

Exactly as she had said she would, the Marchesa departed a short while later. John waited a good thirty minutes, then followed suit making an excuse about not wanting to disturb his wife by being too late. Fitz bade him farewell, clearly disappointed that the Apothecary had not played.

"I thought you said you were a gamester, Sir."

"So I am," John answered benignly, "but tonight my mind was on other things."

"What, pray?" Fitz was more than a little drunk.

"On Percival's wounded arm, for one thing. On the misery of your friend Brenchley Hood for another."

"Both too high strung for their own damned good," Fitz answered. "A pair of flaps those two."

But despite his words his face had hardened and his eyes grown just a fraction tight. Clearly the evening had not gone entirely to plan.

John gave a charming bow. "I am sorry not to have played a better hand but despite my poor performance let me assure you that I have passed a most enjoyable evening."

"You did not find us too out-of-town for your liking?"

"Not at all. The company was as elegant, sparkling and fine as any London salon."

He had said the right thing and Fitz allowed himself a small smile. "I am glad that we were able to please."

"My dear Sir, had it not been for the fact that I am newly married I would have stayed all night."

"I take that as a compliment."

"Please do." John gave another elegant bow and made his escape, glad to leave before tempers grew frayed through drink.

Outside it was cold, the temperature having dropped dramatically while John had been in the house. Irish Tom stood in a huddle with the other coachmen round a small brazier than had presumably been put there for their benefit. He looked up as the Apothecary approached.

"Going so soon, Sir?"

"What do you mean, soon? It's well after midnight."

Tom looked jovial. "And it wouldn't be right to keep Mrs. Rawlings waiting, now would it, Sir?"

John rolled his eyes. "We're not going back yet. I've another call to make."

The coachman sighed. "Where are we going now?"

John lowered his voice. "To Wildtor Grange and I don't want any protests."

"Protest? Me? Taken off the streets by the kindness of your father's heart and given a chance to make something of myself. Though nothing was said at the time of my appointment about driving a young madcap hither and thither in pursuit of murderers and the like."

"Are you giving notice?" John asked, his tone acid.

"Not me, Sorrh," Tom answered Irishly. "For if truth be told I'm having the time of my life."

"Funnily enough," said John, "so am I. Now set to. There's still much to be achieved this night."

With that he clambered into the coach and they set off towards the wild heathland, the Apothecary smiling to himself in the darkness.

Chapter 16

By night Wildtor Grange was even more terrifying than by daylight. Its black shape, silhouetted against what little moon there was, reared skywards like some haunted ruin, and John had to summon every ounce of his nerve to enter through the broken window and make his way through the pools of shadow to where the monstrous staircase disappeared upwards into the darkness. Step by step he crossed the enormous hall, then started to ascend silently, afraid to make a sound, foolishly feeling as if the house were listening to him, waiting to pounce should he so much as cough. Desperately wishing that Elizabeth would appear from her suite and greet him, he crept through the dimness, his heart plummeting at every creak of the floorboards.

That she was there ahead of him, he had no doubt, for lighted candles had been left in niches to help him find his way. He had seen their glow from outside and thought that they had made the house look even more unearthly rather than less. In fact Irish Tom had crossed himself at the sight and uttered some incomprehensible chant aimed at keeping off evil.

"Will you be alright going in there, Sorrh?"

"I have to meet someone. I'll be perfectly safe. She's on our side."

"She?" Tom had said, and raised his eyebrows.

But John had ignored him and entered the eerie

mansion where he was certain Elizabeth di Lorenzi awaited him.

He reached the top of the stairs and looked round, not certain in the darkness which endless corridor he should go down. But as his eyes adjusted to the deepened gloom he saw that a row of candles had been placed on the floor of one of them and made his way to that one, his ears alert for any sound. There was none but a smell was beginning to fill his nostrils; a smell of deep rich perfume, the sort that could madden a man with its aroma.

"Marchesa," he called quietly, and in the distance came an answering, "*Si.*"

The door to her rooms stood very slightly open and through it John could see the comforting gleam of both candle and firelight. It seemed that Elizabeth had had time to put a tinder to logs before he arrived. Not only had she done that, he saw as he tapped lightly then made his way inside. She had already poured him a glass of wine from a claret jug, while her own stood close beside. Of the lady herself, however, there was no sign.

"Marchesa," John called again.

"Yes, Mr. Rawlings," she answered, and came to stand in the bedroom doorway.

She had changed, removing her beautiful gown and wig. Now Elizabeth wore a silk robe, tied loosely at her waist, while her dark hair tumbled over her shoulders.

"I'm glad you came," she said, and walked into the room.

John was seized by the thought that she had

nothing on beneath the robe and felt his heart quicken at the very idea of it. Carefully placing himself in one of the two chairs, he watched as she elegantly curled onto the sofa and smiled at him.

He cleared his throat. "You said you had some information for me."

He must have sounded strained for the Marchesa laughed. "You appear nervous."

John had had sufficient to drink to give him a little courage. "That's because I am."

"Why?"

"A combination of things. This frightening house - and you."

She laughed again and her hair rippled in the shadows as she did so. "Me? I make you nervous? Surely we are fighting for the same cause. Anxious to see justice done and villains punished."

"That's not quite what I meant."

John leant forward, his elbows on his knees. "I find you terribly attractive, my Lady, and I am a newly married man. I fear the power you have over me, if you want the truth."

She laughed aloud. "How ridiculous. I am old enough to be your mother."

"I doubt that. I am twenty-eight in this June coming."

"And I am forty-three."

"There you are then."

"There you are then nothing. I could easily have borne a child at fifteen."

"But you didn't, did you." It was a statement not a question.

"No. Now, are you too afraid to come and sit next to me?"

"Yes," said John, but he did so for all that.

As soon as he was beside her he was done for. The kiss was as electrifying as the first, if not more so, and the fact that her robe had slipped open and his hands could stray beneath was almost too much for him. He swept her body to his and would have made love to her there and then had he not thought, with a wrench of his heart, of Emilia's face as she had made her marriage vows and the sweet look she had given him when he had pledged his to her.

"Elizabeth, I can't," he said, moving away.

"Don't you want to?"

"More than anything, but I'm married. I love Emilia."

"Then why are you here?"

"Because you enthral me, you witch."

Her dark eyes looked into his. "John, if you were single would you follow me anywhere I asked?"

"To the ends of the earth if need be."

"Then with that I must be satisfied," she answered, and sat up straight, pushing him away from her, indeed forcing him off the sofa and back onto his chair. "We shall not speak of this incident again. But just know, John Rawlings, that I, too, would come to you if you were to require it of me."

"Then my happiness is complete," he said simply, and sat silently, as they both did, watching the flames leap and reflect in the crystal of the claret jug.

Eventually she spoke. "Do you want to hear what it is I have to tell you about the girl?"

He looked at her, thinking how lovely she was. "Yes, of course. I must return to London soon but have vowed to find Juliana's killers before I do so."

"You say you last saw her on a Monday roughly two weeks ago?"

"Yes, catching the stage into Exeter in company with her brother."

"Well, I believe that I caught sight of her the next day."

John reached across and took her hand, kissing it briefly before she slowly removed her fingers. "Tell me of it."

"Not far from Topsham there is an inn called The Bridge."

"I've seen it. It stands right by the River Clyst and there is a weir nearby."

"That's the place. Anyway, I've been watching the entire area because it is my belief that the Angels are dealing in contraband goods and landing them somewhere round there. At high tide there is a vast expanse of water where the two rivers, Clyst and Exe, meet. Smuggled goods could be landed from an ocean going ship then taken up the Clyst in a smaller vessel. Then stowed away awaiting sale. "

"What has this got to do with Juliana?"

"I'm coming to that. Sometimes, dressed as a man, I have called at The Bridge Inn, just to see what I could see. Inside, the place consists of a series of small snugs, each one quite private in itself, so I have got into the habit of going into each, then apologising if the party inside was clearly conversing in confidence. However, on that particular Tuesday, I walked into one and there sat a girl I had never seen before."

"What did she look like?"

"Very beautiful indeed with fine blonde hair. But - and this is the interesting part - she was not alone."

"Who was with her?"

"Two young men, one of whom I knew, the other I saw for the first time last night."

John was agog. "Who were they?"

"Peter Digby-Duckworth, as handsome as ever. In fact I could not help thinking what a golden couple they made. The other not so attractive, rather dark and saturnine."

"Brenchley Hood?"

"The very same. Now, does this help you?"

John poured her some more claret, then refilled his own glass. "Yes and no. As I told you, Juliana was pleasuring herself with both of them, yet it is still interesting to have a sighting of her on the day she died."

Even in the firelight he could see that the Marchesa had gone pale. "Did those young men murder her?"

"It's certainly possible."

Elizabeth shook her head but said nothing and once again there was a profound silence. A million thoughts teemed in John's brain and eventually he spoke them out loud. "Do you think Fitz and his friends are the Society of Angels?"

The Marchesa nodded. "It has been my belief for some while but so far I have been unable to prove it."

John frowned. "Yet there's a flaw in that argument. I actually saw Gerald Fitz fight one of them off. They made a daylight attack on the actress Coralie Clive and he was there, amongst the crowd. He drew his sword and wounded one of them badly. At that the men present turned on the Angels and they ran for it, the injured man with them."

The Marchesa stared into the fire, clearly thinking. "Yes, that does rather ruin the theory."

"Unless ..."

"Unless what?"

"I don't know. I can't even put the notion into words. Yet a thought nags at me that there is something I should have seen, something that is just out of my reach, something I am really aware of, would it but come to the forefront."

"It will in time," the Marchesa said softly. She stood up. "Is there anything more I can tell you?"

"Did you overhear any of their conversation?"

"No, alas. After observing them for a moment or two I left the snug and went to another."

"If only you'd stayed." John got to his feet and looked at her, their eyes almost on a level because of her unusual height. "But then that's easy to say in hindsight, for the world is full of if-onlys, isn't it?"

She nodded. "Indeed it is. And speaking of that, I think you had better go. Your wife will be waiting for you."

"Yes." He was longing to embrace her for a final time. "Will I ever see you again?"

"Who knows?" she answered, then melted into

his arms as their lips met in one last passionate kiss before John turned on his heel and walked away.

The Salutation was both dark and deserted except for a skinny little skivvy who was scrubbing the floors, presumably to avoid the hours when the customers tramped about. She looked up, startled, as John came past her, walking in his stockinged feet.

"Oh, Sir, I didn't hear you coming."

"You weren't meant to," he whispered. "I'm very late and must creep into my room so as not to disturb my wife."

"Then be careful on the stairs, Sir, they tend to creak a bit." John gave her a sickly grin by way of reply and continued on his way, avoiding her pail by a hair's breadth.

Upstairs, the corridor leading to his bedroom, with its fine river view, was completely deserted and dim, the only light thrown by a candle tree, complete with eight tapers, which had been set on an oak coffer to light latecomers to bed. Glancing round to check that he was completely alone, John stripped naked. Then, leaving his clothes folded outside the door, he crept inside and slipped straight into bed, hardly daring to breathe as he slid down beside his wife. But she merely sighed and turned over, her back now towards him, while the Apothecary stared at the ceiling and wondered about himself and his extraordinary character. Glad that he had had the strength of mind not to make love to

Elizabeth, sorry that such a profound experience would now never be his.

How he did it he never afterwards knew, but John woke at the same moment as Emilia, feeling as fresh as if he had spent the entire night lying beside her.

His wife looked at him wide-eyed. "I didn't hear you come back."

"I stole in, in order not to disturb you. I'm sorry I was so late but that wretched Fitz takes it as a personal insult if one does not gamble all night with him."

Emilia yawned. "It seems like ages since I last saw you."

"I apologise, sweetheart, but there were some interesting developments in Sidmouth yesterday. A couple were attacked, one of whom was a survivor of the *Constantia*. It is all highly suspicious."

She yawned again, this time rather pointedly. "Quite honestly, I'm getting a little tired of the whole affair. I just want to spend some time with you."

"And I with you," said John, really meaning it. "Now, tell me, what did you do last evening with all your admirers?"

"The two Runners disappeared into the city but Joe and I went to the playhouse. It was the last night of Miss Clive's season. She played Juliet and was very good, though a little old for the part I thought."

"To get a Juliet the right age is impossible."

"Be that as it may, your friend leaves for Bath this

morning, or so the theatregoers said. And to think you never even got to greet her."

"No," said John, and reflected that since his meeting with Elizabeth he had not spared his former mistress even a single thought. Rapidly coming to the conclusion that he must be a base and worthless human being, he felt a mood of depression coming on him, out of which was born the conviction that he must somehow become an exemplary husband.

"Are you sorry?" asked Emilia, startling him.

"For what?" John said nervously, thinking that somehow she must have found out about himself and the Marchesa.

"For not seeing Coralie Clive."

"I did see her."

"Oh, don't be irritating. You know what I mean. Alone, privately."

"I no longer wish to see her privately. I am married to you."

"Sometimes, John," Emilia answered, "I think you have to say that just to remind yourself."

And she disappeared into the small dressing room which led off their quarters where she splashed about very noisily at the bason-stand.

Fortunately the ordeal of an angry breakfast was broken by the arrival in the parlour of Joe Jago, resplendent in dove-grey with a pink flowered waistcoat. For the thousandth time since they had met, John found himself wondering about the man's private life. That Joe must have come from the streets, for his knowledge of cant was tremendous, indeed he often spoke it when resident in London,

John was certain. He also knew that Mr. Fielding's clerk lived in Seven Dials and was unmarried, but other than for those facts his knowledge of the fellow was scant. Yet there was a certain dignity about Joe which precluded questioning of any kind. The Apothecary had always had the feeling that if ever Jago wanted to confide in him, he would do so.

If the clerk was aware of any frostiness between the newlyweds, he certainly didn't reveal it. In fact he beamed a smile at them both. "Good morning to you."

"Do come and join us," said John, glad of an ally. "I've much to tell you and I want to spend today with Emilia so now would be a convenient moment."

She could hardly argue with that and Joe, rubbing his hands at the prospect of what the Apothecary had to tell him, drew up a chair.

"Relate your tale, Sir. Relate your tale."

"First tell me how you got on with Thomas Northmore."

"Not at all, I fear. Our masterful friend has been avoiding me. I called at his home but his wife said he was in Exeter on business and would not be back until this evening, when I intend to visit once more, though I took the precaution of not saying so."

"Very wise. Now I'll tell you all that has happened to me."

Even Joe, who ate like a trencherman, put down his fork as the Apothecary told the story of Dmitri's rescue from the *Constantia* and of the subsequent attack on both him and the Widow Mullins.

"You see what this means, Sir? That whoever put

the body on board thinks that he was seen and now wants to kill the one person who could give evidence against him."

"But why attack the woman?"

"Because the assailant probably thought Dmitri had confided in her."

"But he speaks hardly any English. Only Old Saul, the local medicine man, can truly converse with him."

"Whoever attacked them might not have known that. On the other hand he probably wanted to kill her because she could identify him. But whatever the reason, the Brave Fellows and I must get over to Sidmouth promptly. There's much to be done."

John frowned and sighed. "I hope the pair of them survived the night."

"I've a mind," said Joe, more to himself than anyone else, "to leave one of the Runners standing guard there. If the would-be killer finds out that he has failed he might decide to strike again."

"Yes," answered John, very thoughtfully indeed.

Joe remembered his manners. "And how are you today, Mrs. Rawlings? I hope I didn't keep you out too late."

"Not too late for my husband," she answered, smiling sweetly. "He was at cardplay nearly all the night."

"Observing Fitz and his cronies," the Apothecary explained.

"Anything to report on that front?"

"Nothing definite. Only a feeling in the air."

"And what might that be, Sir?"

"That despite other evidences, they could be the Society of Angels. Yet there's no proof, Joe, that's the devil of it."

The clerk nodded slowly. "It would make a terrible sense. All young, with too much money and too much time on their hands."

"It could explain Richard's suicide, if he had got in over his head."

"It could indeed."

Emilia interrupted, giving John the same dazzling smile. "And what delights do you have planned for me today, my dear?"

"I thought a drive to Dartmoor, though it will take us most of the morning to get there."

"But what would be the point? As soon as we arrived we would have to turn round and come back."

"It would make a change, though."

"Then I'll go. I fear that we are starting to run out of things to do here and I rather fancy a few days in Bath before we return to town."

"Then we'll have to solve this case quickly," Joe said jovially, but his voice died away as Emilia turned on him an extremely stony face. "No offence, Ma'am," he added hastily.

"I had rather hoped my husband might be allowed to terminate his interest," she said.

Joe gulped. "At any time, Mrs. Rawlings, at any time. He only has to say the word."

The Apothecary squirmed uncomfortably, not wanting a confrontation at the breakfast table. "I think, Emilia, that you and I should talk about this in private."

He had not meant the words to come out quite so severely, indeed he had wanted to placate rather than inflame, but his wife shot him a black look. "I would suggest immediately after breakfast." And she turned a cold shoulder towards him and concentrated her conversation entirely at Joe. Horribly aware that this was a bad situation at any time but particularly so on honeymoon, John chomped his way through the meal in silence.

Mr. Fielding's clerk, clearly uncomfortable, finished his food in haste then made the excuse of needing to check the situation in Sidmouth and rose from the table. As soon as he was out of earshot, John turned to his wife.

"Emilia, we can't go on in this atmosphere. Please complete your breakfast so that we can discuss the matter."

"I have completed it, if you had bothered to look. It is you, husband, who are still eating."

"Not any more," he answered, and putting down his irons, took her by the hand and led her from the parlour.

"Now," he said, as soon as the bedroom door had closed behind them, "tell me exactly what is bothering you."

"Isn't it obvious? This is meant to be our honeymoon yet all you do is chase round the countryside after criminals, spending as little time with me as possible."

"It was your choice to go to Exeter yesterday. I did not force you to."

"What else was I expected to do? Sit on the beach

all day twiddling my thumbs? Be fair, John. We might as well be strangers for all we see of one another."

She sat down on the bed angrily, then suddenly started to cry. With his conscience raging because of the deadly allure that Elizabeth di Lorenzi held for him, the Apothecary could have wept as well. Kneeling before her, he put his arms round his wife, comforting her as if she were a child.

"I do love you, sweetheart. I will drop the case now if it will make you happy."

She looked at him through streaming tears. "But if you do, you will always resent me for asking."

"No I won't. I would understand."

"Would you? Would you really? Oh John, I don't know what to do. I've never been a wife before."

"Nor I a husband. It's not easy, is it?" he answered heavily.

She laughed a little at that. "My mother said there would be tears along the way."

"Oh darling," he said helplessly, and kissed her, somewhat damply. Elizabeth's face came to haunt him but he pushed it away ruthlessly. "Kiss me again," he asked hopefully.

Emilia did so and then it was the easist thing in the world to lie back on the bed and indulge in the oldest healing magic of all.

"I know what we should do today," John whispered into his wife's ear.

"What?" she whispered back.

"This," he answered, and pulled her down beneath the sheets.

"So Mrs. Rawlings was quite happy that you should come with me?" asked Joe Jago.

John gave a cat-like grin. "We have discussed the whole matter and she is totally in agreement that I should complete this case."

"Well, thank God for that, Sir. I thought this morning that you might well be leaving us."

"So did I frankly."

"But you talked your way out of it?"

"Yes," said John, and grinned again.

They were sitting by a window in the Passage Inn, from which spot they could clearly observe the quay master's house and all the comings and goings therein. So far, however, there had been no sign of Thomas Northmore, only of his nervously scuttling wife. Yet John fervently hoped the man wouldn't be late. Peace had been restored between himself and Emilia but he did not want to push his luck by causing further trouble. When he had gone out, following dinner, he had said he would be an hour and not much more, and this was a promise that he intended to keep. Surreptitiously, the Apothecary looked at his watch.

"He shouldn't be long," said Joe, seeing the movement.

"Is there time for another drink?"

"I should think so."

"Then let's toast the recovery of Dmitri and Sarah."

The couple had lived. Old Saul had been as good as his word and kept the night's vigil with them, probably invoking Red Indian magic while he did so. But whatever ritual he had enacted had been succesful. Against all the odds, the pair had regained consciousness. In the morning, so Joe had told John, the doctor had come and professed himself amazed to find them not only alive but recovering.

"There's more in that man's medicine than I care to admit," the physician had confessed to Joe.

"I believe that," John said now as the clerk repeated the remark. "I must write down Old Saul's remedies before I quit Devon. He has told me so much that I really need to take written note in case I forget."

"A sensible idea, Sir. By the way, I've left Runner Raven at the house, along with the old fellow. I've a feeling that the widow and the Russian might still be in danger from an outside source."

John nodded but said nothing, a vague idea now beginning to take definite shape in his mind.

Joe stared out of the window then made a small sound of triumph. "He's here, the old bastard. Let's give him ten minutes then go in."

"That would suit me perfectly."

Joe rubbed his hands together and winked. "But will it suit him I ask myself."

"I very much doubt it," answered John, and laughed.

He was not pleased to see them, that much was certain. Thomas Northmore flashed his whalebone teeth, carefully restored to their former glory, in a snarl, and led his visitors into the parlour without saying a word.

"Now what is it?" he asked wearily. "I've told you all I know."

Joe Jago came straight to the point. "It's about your visit to Juliana van Guylder when she was lodging in Exeter. You said you thought the child she was expecting was yours. Yet my feeling is that she stopped having sexual relations with you some months back. So how is this possible?"

Thomas lowered his voice. "I've already told you. We were still intimate."

"I don't believe you. Subsequent information leads me to assume she had met someone else with whom she had genuinely fallen in love. I think she had already dropped you. So why did you give her money?"

The quay master wrestled with himself, obviously longing to keep his image as a great lover intact yet probably realising that it would be safer to tell the truth.

"All right," he said eventually, "she had left me for someone younger and richer than I, a callow boy."

"Did she tell you his name?"

"No. But the child was not his. She told me that it was mine, that she was several months pregnant and it had been conceived at our last encounter." He looked coy. "She said she needed to go to a physician in Exeter but that it would cost money. She said that she must do this or her new lover would not accept her."

John and Joe exchanged a look of pure amazement, both thinking of Sir Bartholomew Digby-Duckworth's immense glee at the thought of being a father. So Juliana had just wanted money to spend on gowns. The Apothecary, who did not like the quay master at all, suddenly felt very sorry for him.

"Did you kill her?" asked Joe in a quiet, even voice.

"Certainly not. How dare you even suggest it."

"Because it would make perfect sense. An elderly lover jilted for a younger man is just the sort of person to lose his temper and kill the former object of his affections."

Thomas Northmore went purple in the face with fury, indeed he started to tremble with rage. "How dare you! How dare you!" he shouted, teeth gnashing.

"Don't upset yourself," Mr. Fielding's clerk answered calmly. "These questions are routine in a case of murder."

Thomas exploded into speech. "Damn your accusations and damn you, Sir. I'll have you know that I am not elderly, by God. The fact is that I am in the very prime of my life."

"Oh dear, oh dear, whatever next," said John Rawlings and lowered the tone of the entire proceedings by starting to laugh.

Chapter 17

The fine weather had returned and as they approached Sidmouth they saw that the sea and the sky had performed that magical trick of blending into one, obscuring the horizon into a brush-stroke, turning the whole of that glorious seascape into a bowl of immensely delicate blue china.

"It really is entrancing here," said Emilia. "I shall miss Sidmouth when we have gone."

John could have replied that twenty-four hours ago she was bored to sobs with the whole place and was tired of walking the beach and collecting shells, but he was learning, or trying to.

"It was so kind of you to offer to befriend the women in this case. I am sure Sarah Mullins will be delighted to see you. She has had a very hard life, you know, and yesterday was within an inch of losing it."

"Poor thing. Who would do such a thing to a harmless female?"

"Someone who was ruthless enough to rape and beat Juliana to death."

Emilia shivered. "Will you catch him?"

"Yes. I think he is on the point of betraying himself."

"I hope you won't be in any danger."

"With Joe and the Runners to protect me I hardly think that that will be the case."

"I pray not. I'm still not used to being a wife, let alone a widow."

"I can assure you," said John, with a twisted smile, "that I intend to be around a great deal longer yet."

They had driven across the wild heathland, passing within distant sight of Wildtor Grange, and now had started the descent into the fishing hamlet. On every side of them, encouraged by the sunshine, daffodils had opened in abundance, so that the track seemed to weave through a carpet of yellow, while the air was filled with the sound of birds' voices. John thought he had never known a lovelier spring in his life and called to Irish Tom to stop the coach for a moment so that they might look around them.

"Do you like wild Devon?" he said to his bride.

"It is a place to which I will always return," she answered simply, and took his hand as the carriage slowly trundled forward again and they heard the wild high call of the sea.

It seemed that Old Saul was still maintaining his vigil, for he answered the door to the little cottage nestling beneath the cliffs.

"Oh, it's you, my friend," he said to John. "I thought it might be the man from Bow Street."

"He called on you, I believe."

"Yes, and he left one of his men here. He seemed to think that Sarah and Dmitri could be attacked again."

"They might well. Where is the Runner?"

"Asleep in my place. He was awake all night so is snatching a few winks now. He told me to shout for him at the slightest sign of trouble."

"And Mr. Jago and the other Runner?"

"Asking questions in Sidmouth about who saw what and when."

"Did you tell them about the gaffer from Exeter?"

"I certainly did. After they've finished here they plan to go into the city to see if they can identify his coach."

"What exactly was written on its side?"

"There was a coat of arms and some Latin words. It said something about sickness."

"Extraordinary," said John, shaking his head.

Emilia interrupted. "Shouldn't you be looking at the invalids?"

"Of course I should. "John picked up his apothecary's bag. "How are they this morning, Saul?"

"Much improved. Some while ago a sailor brought me some Moringa and from the plant I compounded an oil. There is nothing like it for rapidly healing wounds."

"What recipe did you use?"

"Wax, ox fat, honey, barley, the oil and a little pulped leaves of Herb Robert. I boiled all together, made a poultice, and have bandaged them up with it. They will have healed in a few days, mark my words."

John put his bag down again. "Is there any point in my taking this?"

"If you have a good tonic in there I am sure they would much appreciate it."

The Apothecary laughed. "You make me feel like a novice, Saul."

"Only because you are younger than I," the older man answered kindly. "Now, Sir, which of them would you like to see first? I thought they might heal better if they had separate quarters so Dmitri is in my house - in my bed in fact."

"Then I think a quick look at Sarah, after which I'll leave her in the company of my wife. It is the man that I really need to talk to. Is he up to answering questions?"

Old Saul shook his head. "Not really. But I know the matter's urgent so he'll have to put up with it. After all, he's young and strong."

John turned to Emilia. "Let me examine Sarah privately, then I'll call you up. You won't mind sitting with her, will you?"

"I told you I wanted to be involved."

He kissed her cheek. "It's good of you to offer help."

The wounded woman lay on her bed, as pale as the linen surrounding her, her flaming hair almost shocking against the white pillow that framed her face. Round her head where she had been so savagely hit, Old Saul had wound bandages, so that she looked like some extraordinary Egyptian relic, a body being prepared for mummification. Therefore it was almost a shock when the bright blue eyes opened suddenly and she stared at John, first in terror, then more calmly as recognition returned.

He sat on the end of the bed. "Sarah, how are you feeling?"

She could hardly speak but a faint whisper came in reply. "I lived, Sir, and for that God be thanked."

"I won't bother you with a lot of questions, just tell me one thing. Did you see who attacked you?"

"I caught a glimpse of him, yes. He was clad all in white and had a veiled hat upon his head which made his face invisible."

"The Society of Angels," John answered. "It was one of them."

"I think it must have been, Sir."

"But you saw nothing of him, nothing that could be used to identify the man?"

Sarah hesitated, then said, "Yes, Sir, there was one thing, though I certainly did not see his features."

"What?" asked John eagerly. "What was it?"

"It was a mark of some kind, like a tattoo. It was in a strange shape and it was on the inside of his wrist where it would never normally show."

"What did it depict? Can you remember?"

"Oh yes, I can remember all right. It was an angel's wing, just one, furled up as if prior to flight."

The Apothecary stood up. "It must be their insignia. By God, they must be stopped, and stopped fast. They've done too much damage to too many people to be allowed to continue any longer. "His voice changed. "Now, would you like my wife to sit with you for a while? She'll keep you company while I go next door to Dmitri."

"How is he?" whispered Sarah.

"Improving every day," John answered, just hoping that what he was saying was correct.

As it turned out, he told the truth. Indeed Dmitri, tough sailor that he was, was actually sitting up in the truckle that Old Saul used for a bed. Before the Apothecary had gone up to him, he had woken jolly Dick Ham, the Runner whom Joe had left on duty, and sent him next door to protect the two women, then he and the medicine man had climbed the narrow stairs to the floor above. With Old Saul acting as interpreter, John, after asking a few general questions about the Russian's health, came to the most vital part of the interview.

"Dmitri, what happened that day aboard the *Constantia*? Can you remember what took place?"

The Russian spoke rapidly to Old Saul.

"He says, Sir, that it was very hot and that there was no wind. They were virtually becalmed. There were six crew in all and they were all up on deck waiting for a breeze." Dmitri said something else and Old Saul added, "He said even though there was no wind it was a relief to get some fine weather because they'd hit a terrific storm in the Channel and both the vessel and the men had been thoroughly soaked."

"What happened next?" John asked.

Once more there was an exchange in Russian, then Old Saul said, "He's going on about how lovely it was at sea, what a wonderful aroma there was in the air. Then, he said, he saw an angel float out of the sky and land on deck."

"What?" John exclaimed, flabbergasted, remembering all too vividly the man who had died in his arms with the words, 'Angels come.'

"That's what he said, my friend."

"Can you ask him to explain."

Old Saul rattled off in Russian once more.

"He says he can't. But he saw angels, more than one. They all did. They went flying with them, right over the side of the ship."

"Oh 'zounds," answered John wearily. "Ask him how these angels were dressed."

More Russian was spoken, then Saul said, "They had long white robes and huge white wings, that is all except the ones that came last. They had white coats and hats and carried in their arms the most beautiful angel of all."

"Dear God, was this all an hallucination or were they seeing Juliana and her killers?"

"Perhaps a little of both," Old Saul replied. He stopped speaking, deep in thought. "It almost sounds as if they had been smoking opium."

"Ask him if they had."

But Dmitri knew enough English to answer this. "Opium no smoke. Not good."

"Then what is the explanation?" said the Apothecary, and relapsed into a baffled silence.

It was Old Saul who asked the key question. "What cargo was the ship carrying?"

"Hemp. It was sold to a ropemaker in Exeter."

"I see. Well, that doesn't get us much further."

But John wasn't listening to him, instead repeating the words, "Hemp for making rope and canvas. Cannavis, cannabis. By God, Saul, that's it!"

"What?"

"It was the cargo. If it was badly retted in the first place, which I suspect, then soaked in a storm, it would emit fumes as it dried out. And cannabis is an hallucinatory plant. The whole crew would have been affected. It's a wonder they didn't see the entire heavenly host with the power of those vapours.

Small surprise that they jumped into the sea. The poor bastards could quite easily have believed they could fly."

"So the attack was all for nothing. Dmitri was too far gone to identify those who brought the dead girl aboard."

"Absolutely. He wouldn't have known what was going on. But whoever assaulted him doesn't realise that, does he."

"Obviously not."

"And therein lies our strength, my friend. For that is how we will find him, by laying a trap into which he is going to blunder well and truly."

"I hope I will be able to play my part," said Old Saul stoutly.

"You, my friend, may well prove to be the lynch-pin."

The light thrown by the fire which blazed cheerfully in the snug known as The Tyger, turned Joe Jago's hair into a burnished halo as he nodded enthusiastically to the plan that the Apothecary had just proposed to him.

"Yes, Mr. Rawlings, it is indeed a masterly idea. But are the two wounded people up to such an ordeal - or should I say ordeals?"

"Fortunately they were both fine physical specimens before they were attacked, and this strength has stood them in good stead. If we treat them carefully I am quite sure that they will be able to cope with the situation."

"But the first plan necessitates them leaving home and coming to Topsham."

"I will send Irish Tom to drive them and Old Saul and I will be with them if they should feel at all ill."

"But the fact that the man was hallucinating? That he couldn't, in reality, give reliable evidence?"

"As he speaks very little English, Old Saul will translate. He can hold our audience in suspense, mark my words. But, Joe, don't forget the woman. The tattoo she saw may hold the key to the identity of Juliana's murderer."

"Then, Mr. Rawlings," said Joe Jago, "I suggest we put both schemes into action as soon as possible. Tomorrow, in my official capacity, I shall invite Jan van Guylder, Tobias Wills, Thomas Northmore and Sir Bartholomew Digby-Duckworth to attend us here at The Salutation, on the evening following."

"I think you should add Sir Clovelly Lovell to that list. He can look after poor old Barty, as he calls him, and will add weight to the occasion."

"In every way."

John smiled. "Yes, in every way."

"And the other plan?"

"We must be more subtle about that and set it up with care."

"Indeed we must, for that night we should catch a murderer."

"No more talk of murder," said Emilia, coming into The Tyger, looking very lovely in her dining gown. "Tonight we must celebrate my clever husband's ingenuity in solving the riddle of the *Constantia*."

"Well said, Mrs. Rawlings," answered Joe. "I think we can indeed safely forget why we are here and devote ourselves to having a thoroughly good evening."

"Did they really believe they saw angels?" asked Emilia as the three of them went in to dine.

"Who knows?" answered John. "It is even possible that they actually did."

Chapter 18

It was bizarre, considered John. Seated side by side, neither ever having cast eyes upon the other, were two men both of whom laid claim to being the affianced husband of Juliana van Guylder. Further, the man who thought himself to be the father of her child was sitting on the other side of the old chap who confidently believed that he himself had sired it. What a tangle of manners - or rather lack of them - the Apothecary thought. As convoluted and corrupt as those of any London belle of fashion. For what a promiscuous little bitch the dead girl had been. It was only tragic that this night her father would be subjected to the ordeal of hearing just how unsavoury her behaviour had become in the time leading up to her murder. Yet, despite that, Jan van Guylder was himself one of the suspects and therefore could not be excluded from the meeting.

Somewhat to Joe Jago's surprise, everyone he had requested to attend the gathering had done so, even old Sir Bartholomew braving the night vapours and setting forth. And now the gentlemen in question were all seated in The Tyger, looking somewhat bemused, clearly wondering what was going to happen next.

In another room, being nourished and cherished, were Dmitri and Sarah, Old Saul, wearing an extra-ordinary ensemble which John concluded must be the medicine man's idea of good dressing, at their side. The two Runners, wearing their court uniforms to give them an air of authority, hovered close at hand, ready to deal with trouble at whoever's instigation it might occur. All it needed now was for Joe Jago to start the proceedings off.

This evening Mr. Fielding's clerk was clad in sombre black, a colour he often adopted for formal occasions. His hair shone in the light of the many candles that lit The Tyger as he stood up and cleared his throat.

"Gentlemen, what I have to say to you tonight will, in varying degrees, be painful to each and every one of you. All of you, with the exception of your good self, Sir Clovelly, were closely connected with Juliana van Guylder and for that reason everyone present must answer for himself as regards her murder. Let me make myself quite clear. A woman such as she, capable of arousing great emotion in the hearts of men, might cause even a father to raise a hand to strike against her, or a brother for that matter. So there is not one of you who has not fallen under suspicion."

Jan van Guylder looked at Joe wearily and it occurred to John that all divine spark had departed from the man and he was now little more than a burned-out shell.

"You think I killed my own child?" he said.

"Such things have been known, Sir," the clerk replied with dignity. He cleared his throat again. "Gentlemen, to publicly list the reasons why all of you have fallen under suspicion would be both embarrassing and unfair. For that reason I will be brief. Mr. van Guylder might have grown angry because of Juliana's wilful ways. Tobias could have lost all patience on learning that she had many other suitors. Mr. Northmore might well have wished to silence her before the truth became known. Sir Bartholomew could easily have become incensed if he believed she had been unfaithful to him."

"What do you mean unfaithful?" Tobias asked angrily. "Who is this old gentleman?"

Sir Bartholomew raised a wizened hand which shook as he wagged his finger. "I was her betrothed, I'll have you know."

"Oh what rubbish! She and I were promised since childhood."

It was going to get ugly, John felt sure of it. Obviously Joe had come to the same conclusion for he held up a hand.

"Gentlemen, please. This behaviour will get us nowhere. Mr. van Guylder, I had hoped to spare you this but I'm afraid the truth must be told. However, I shall stick to the basic facts. The rest you must fill in for yourselves."

"It's the only way," said Sir Clovelly. "Out with it, man."

"Very well. I believe that Juliana's behaviour deteriorated after the death of her mother and she started to run wild. Despite the fact that she was engaged to Tobias Wills, she started a love affair with Thomas Northmore."

The quay master would have protested but John fixed him with such a glare that he closed his mouth again, the whalebone teeth snapping shut as he did so.

"Filthy bastard," yelled Jan, coming to life again, while Tobias leapt up and took a swing at Northmore which was deflected by Nick Raven who had quietly come into the room.

"Control yourselves," bellowed Joe, "or I'll have the lot of you up before the Beak tomorrow morning." He stared round menacingly. "Tiring of Mr. Northmore ..."

"Who wouldn't?" asked an unidentified voice.

"... Juliana fell in with a bunch of choice spirits from Exeter whom she met through her brother, who was at school there. Unfortunately, they led her down unfortunate paths and she became pregnant."

"I was responsible for that," announced Sir Bartholomew proudly.

"You dirty old lecher," screamed Jan, pouncing forward and straight into the arms of Nick Raven, who held him very tightly indeed.

John, thinking that this situation was just the thing the Dutchman needed to put some life back into him, had to restrain himself from laughing at the look on Thomas Northmore's face, dying to boast of paternity but too terrified of the consequences to do so.

Joe angrily broke into cant. "I'll flap the lot of you with a fox-tail if you don't shut this gagarino. Bunch of rum coves," he added for good measure. Then he scowled round the room until there was eventual silence. "Right," he said, "you've asked for this. As I've already said, Mr. van Guylder had the motive of outraged papa; Mr. Wills, the cuckolded fiance; Mr. Northmore, the rejected elderly admirer; Sir Bartholomew, the even more elderly rejected one."

There was an indrawing of breath prior to protest but Joe pre-empted them. "So be careful one and all. New information has come to light from a source close to my colleague, Mr. Rawlings."

John tensed very slightly as Elizabeth came into his mind.

"This information is that Juliana van Guylder was seen in the company of two men on the very day that she was killed. It was a Tuesday, two weeks ago. I will give you a few moments to collect yourselves, gentlemen, and then I want you to tell me precisely where you were at noon and for two hours thereafter on that occasion."

There was a stricken silence during which somebody farted nervously. John, hating his sense of humour, kept his eyes well down, not daring to look. Eventually Sir Clovelly gave a burst of laughter and said, "Better out than in, what?" and everybody tittered.

Joe remained impassive, the craggy face not moving a muscle. He was, John thought, one of the most controlled men he had ever met. "Well?" he said.

Tobias Wills spoke first. "I was working in my father's office. He imports and exports goods and is training me to take over the business one day. I was there and witnesses can vouch for me."

"You did not leave at all?"

"Briefly, to visit a client. He was out, however, and I returned almost immediately."

"How long were you away?"

"No more than an hour."

"I was entertaining friends to sherry and whist," piped up Sir Bartholomew. "Sir Clovelly can stand up for me. He was amongst them."

"That is correct," boomed the fat man. "I remember it because Lord Hood spilled drink upon his breeches."

The Apothecary watched Joe weigh up his next words, aware as both of them were that the old fellow could never have committed the crime in person but would have had to hire a ruffian to carry out his will.

"I'll accept that, Sir Bartholomew. Though I may have to question you further about your associates, should it come to it."

"What does he mean?" Sir Barty asked, cupping his ear in Sir Clovelly's direction.

"Stap me, how would I know," the other answered, and roared with laughter once more.

"Well, I was working at the harbour," said Thomas Northmore. "I was in my office as is my wont and there are dozens who can swear to that."

"You did not depart at any time? Perhaps to take a stroll?"

"I am constantly on the move, of course. After all, I am the quay master."

"Prat," said Tobias loudly.

"How dare you."

"Be silent," thundered Joe. "Did you leave Topsham at all that day, Sir? Remember that I am an officer of the law and it would be dangerous to lie to me."

"I did take a brief ride out to quench my thirst, yes."

"And where did you go?"

"To the Bridge Inn. Not far from here."

John and Joe exchanged a glance. "Did you see anyone you knew there?"

"No. Why?"

"Because as chance would have it, Sir, that is the place in which Juliana van Guylder was last seen alive."

"Bloody murderer!" yelled Tobias, and leapt in the quay master's direction, his breeches straining slightly as he did so. Yet again, Runner Raven was too quick and the young man found himself with one arm behind his back, held in an iron grip.

Joe's hair appeared to catch fire as he lost his temper in a sensational way. "Mr. Wills," he thundered, "control yourself. Who are you to accuse others and attempt to assault them in my presence? I swear to God I'll have you on a charge if you so much as make another move."

"Wretched young man," said the quay master nastily.

Joe rounded on him. "That'll be enough from you, Sir. You are in no position to criticise another. Now, tell me about your visit to the Bridge Inn. Did you meet Juliana there? Had you gone by prior arrangement? And have a care when you answer."

Thomas gulped noisily. "I did not even see her. The place is a warren of small snugs. I sat alone, supped my ale, then left."

"Can anyone confirm that?"

"A girl served me. I am sure she knew who I was."

Joe looked at John. "Mr. Rawlings, would you be good enough to ask Runner Ham to escort Mr. Northmore to the inn when this meeting is over and there question witnesses as to exactly what transpired. To be in the same place as a former object of your affections on the very day she is murdered and swear you did not even glimpse her, seems to me to be stretching the arm of coincidence to breaking point."

The quay master had gone very pale. "But it's true I tell you," he blustered.

Joe turned away from him and his tone became kinder. "Mr. van Guylder, where were you two weeks ago?"

The Dutchman looked stricken. "That is something I do not want to tell you."

"Why?"

"Because it is a matter personal to me."

"Would you prefer to discuss it in private?"

"If I must, then yes."

"Very well. But first there is one more thing that I would like all you gentlemen to do."

"Now what?" said Tobias, sitting quietly enough but still surly.

"Recently two people were attacked and left for dead by someone who thought they knew the identity of Juliana's murderers. But though that someone had disguised himself he did not think to hide the tattoo on his wrist, a tattoo which can very easily be identified. Runner Raven, would you bring in the two witnesses please."

"What do we have to do?" asked Sir Bartholomew peevishly.

"Roll back your shirt sleeves, gentlemen, and show us the inside of both your wrists."

"Me too?" asked Sir Clovelly, and looked rather disappointed when Joe shook his head.

The door opened and the Widow Mullins, still swathed in bandages which she had disguised by use of a black veil, made a dramatic entrance, leaning on Nick Raven for support, while Dick Ham followed closely behind, Dmitri holding on to his shoulder. In their wake came Old Saul, staring ominously at every man in turn, particularly at Sir Bartholomew who looked fit to drop with fright.

Joe drew himself up, his ragged face set and serious. "Dmitri," he said very slowly, "do you recognise anyone here?"

The Russian took his time, studying every face in turn, then he said something to Saul.

"What's he telling you?"

"That that man there ..." He pointed at Thomas Northmore, "... looks familiar."

What happened next was highly theatrical. The quay master made a gurgling sound then fell sideways out of his chair, crashing onto the ground, totally unconscious. For a split second everyone stood frozen, then John dashed to kneel beside him, loosening the man's collar and pulling out his formidable teeth.

"Has he had a fit?" said Joe.

"No, just fainted."

"Serve him right," muttered Tobias defiantly.

"While he's unconscious let Mrs. Mullins look at his wrists."

Sarah did so but there was no tattoo and she shook her head. "This man is more heavily built than my assailant. Whoever attacked me was flat about the stomach. It's not him."

Nor was it anybody else. Slowly, the injured woman walked from person to person but there was not a tattoo to be seen. On that evidence it seemed that everyone present was in the clear. Yet thoughts of a hired assassin from amongst the Society of Angels could not be ruled out, particularly in the case of Sir Bartholomew Digby-Duckworth. Aware of this, Joe took the only course of action open to him.

"Gentlemen, thank you for your cooperation. Everything that you have said will be checked. Kindly leave the names of the witnesses who saw you on that fateful day, and also details of where they may be contacted, with Runner Raven. You are free to go except for Mr. van Guylder with whom I shall have a private word."

It was over and slowly the company began to break up, stepping over the inert form of the quay master as they made their way out of the door. Joe turned to John who was administering smelling salts.

"I'll leave you to bring him round, my friend, but I don't intend to spare the man. He will be taken to The Bridge as soon as he is fit to travel. What an extraordinary story he told us."

"Strangely, I think it's true," John answered. "If

he had met Juliana there that day he would have been crazy even to mention that he went to the inn at all."

"Would it be possible for you to ask your contact if she saw him?"

John felt himself flush. "I had not planned to call on her any more."

Joe did not pick up the nuance. "I think it would be worth trying." He turned to Jan.

"Now, Mr. van Guylder, would you be so good as to step into The Unicorn, which should be empty, and I will join you in a moment so that you can tell me your tale."

"Can we go now?" asked Sarah Mullins plaintively as the Dutchman went out.

Joe swept her a wonderful bow. "My dear Madam, I do beg your pardon. In the heat of Mr. Northmore's faint I had rather forgotten my manners. Runner Raven will take you all home. You have helped us enormously."

"It wasn't any of them, you know."

"I realise that. The only question that remains is whether any were in league with the Society of Angels."

"The old man could be," said John, dragging the quay master into a sitting position as signs of consciousness began to appear. "If the Angels are who we suspect, then he knows them all - and their fathers."

"I wonder," answered Joe, "I just wonder."

"What?"

"Exactly how involved with Juliana the Digby-Duckworths really were - and if either of them, grandfather or grandson, actually did sire that child of hers."

"A very interesting thought," said John, and slapped Thomas Northmore's cheeks, not altogether gently, as he began to come round.

It was late, very late, but in The Tyger a fire still burned and Joe Jago, his feet stuck out before him, was thinking out loud to a yawning John Rawlings.

"I suppose we're a little further forward. At least we'll be able to find out whether they were telling the truth about that Tuesday." He took a sip of port. "Pity Northmore was too poorly to be taken to The Bridge. I'd love to catch him out in a lie."

The Apothecary said, "I'll escort him there tomorrow. Nick and Dick will presumably be too busy checking alibis."

Joe nodded. "They will indeed. Thank you for that. Perhaps you could interview the vigilante at the same time. She may have seen Northmore skulking about."

"I will if I run into her."

Joe turned a bright eye in his companion's direction. "You've told me very little about her. In fact all I can remember you saying is that she watches the Society of Angels, has a hideout in Wildtor Grange, and that when you last saw her she reported that she had seen Juliana on the day of the murder."

"There's nothing else to tell. That's it."

"She presumably has a name."

"I believe it's Elizabeth," John answered vaguely.

"Ah," said Joe, and poured himself another port.

Chapter 19

The Bridge Inn had been built in a truly delightful situation. Surrounded by verdant pastureland, the hostelry stood on the very edge of the River Clyst, a tumbling weir of sparkling water behind it, the ancient bridge that gave the place its name, to its right. On the other bank, just to give the scene a look of total rustic charm, a delightful mill threshed its wheel in the foaming stream.

John had ridden there on a hired horse, not wanting to be confined to the coach this day. But Emilia, who had seemed determined to accompany him, had confessed that she was not a good horsewoman and had ordered Irish Tom to drive her. So the Apothecary, feeling almost as if he were an outrider to some regal personage, had ridden beside the carriage, constantly glancing over his shoulder to see if Thomas Northmore were anywhere in the vicinity.

Very early that morning, before he had set off on his many and varied tasks, Joe Jago, looking stylish in dove-grey and lavender, had called at the quay master's house and ordered him to be at the inn by noon without fail.

"How did he respond to that?" John had asked as they said their farewells.

"Quite meekly. I think the man is actually nervous."

"I'm not altogether surprised."

"However, you're probably right about him. The

very fact that he admitted going to The Bridge surely means that he didn't see Juliana. But get all you can, Mr. Rawlings. He deserves nothing better."

John, with one foot in the stirrup, had held fast to his wheeling mount. "In view of what Dmitri said about the angels in coats and hats carrying the most beautiful angel of all, together with the piece of white material I found that most certainly did not come from Juliana's shift, don't you think it was members of the Society who killed her?"

"Very probably. But why, Mr. Rawlings. Why? They may well be a bunch of hooligans but there's no motive."

And John had had to agree. If the Society of Angels had struck against Juliana, why had they done it? Indeed she had been doxy to them all but that in itself was no reason for killing her.

Emilia put her head out of the carriage window. "What a lovely place. I would like to spend some time here. Can we?"

"Once I've interviewed Thomas Northmore's witness, the day is ours."

"Shall we walk by the river?"

"I'd like that very much."

John's bride withdrew her head and he was left to look at her profile through the glass and think how beautiful she was and how he must do his very best to make her happy. Then his attention was drawn by the sound of hooves and he saw that the quay master was approaching on a large horse with a somewhat boring face, not unlike that of Thomas Northmore himself.

"Good morning to you," said the Apothecary politely.

"I don't see much good about it," the quay master answered gloomily. "I mention the fact that I attended this inn two weeks ago and immediately I am treated like a criminal. I tell you, Mr. Rawlings, that I did not murder that wretched girl. Oh, that I had never set eyes on her," he added theatrically.

"I imagine there are quite a few gentlemen thinking the same thing," John said drily.

"But none so sad as I. My wife has heard rumours about my liaison and is starting to act in an intolerable manner. She has even begun to contradict me."

"Gracious."

"I just wish that the wretched killer would be caught and we can all be left in peace."

"Don't worry," said John, giving the quay master a most sinister smile, "the net is closing in on him - fast."

Thomas's Adam's apple bobbed but he said nothing further until they had reached the inn and the horses and the carriage had been removed to the stables. Then he attempted a jaunty manner. "Shall I lead the way?"

"Please do. Neither Emilia nor myself know the place at all."

The quay master opened the door, taking them into a corridor from which led several other doors. At a glance John could see how accurate the Marchesa's description had been. It would be perfectly possible to sit in a snug and be totally unaware of anyone sitting in one of the others.

"Which room were you in on that Tuesday, Mr. Northmore?"

"This," said the quay master, and threw open the first door on the left. The Apothecary gaped, for sitting inside, his head in his hands, racked with sobs, was none other than Jan van Guylder. Positive that the last person the Dutchman would want to see was the one John was standing next to, he motioned Northmore towards another room.

"Go in there and try to find the girl that served you," he whispered. "Emilia, come with me."

They stepped into the snug, finding themselves in a small dark room with a log fire burning in a somewhat undersized grate. Other than for the grieving man, it was empty.

"Mr. van Guylder," the Apothecary said in a quiet voice.

Jan looked up, startled, his face blotchy with weeping. "What are you doing here?"

"I've come as part of our investigations. But may I ask the same of you?"

"I wanted to see where Juliana spent her last few hours on earth. Poor wretched girl." He held out a hand in a pleading gesture. "John, I didn't kill my child. I loved her for all her bad behaviour. It wasn't really her fault, you know. The loss of her mother was what caused all the trouble. Poor, poor Juliana." He wept again.

It was Emilia who went to him. Taking a seat beside him and putting her arm round his shoulders, she produced a dainty handkerchief and gave it to Jan. "Here, use this. Dry your eyes. I would so like to talk to you. My father was murdered, you know, and I feel that we have much in common."

John was lost in admiration. She had said something that had drawn the Dutchman's attention away from himself, and after stealing a glance at her to see if she was in earnest, he had dried his eyes as instructed. Deciding that to leave them alone for a while might well be the best policy, John signalled to his wife that he was going and went off in search of Thomas Northmore.

He found him in a somewhat lighter snug with a fine view over the river. As the Apothecary went in, Thomas was in earnest conversation with a pot girl but he looked up as he heard the door open.

"Ah, the very man. Now, Suky, tell the gentleman what you remember."

The girl looked nervous. "Mr. Northmore often comes in for an ale, Sir."

John decided that kindness was the best approach. "I'm sure he does, my dear. But can you tell me if he was in here recently, about two weeks ago, on a Tuesday?"

"Oh yes, Sir. He was here."

The answer was far too pat and prompt, the poor creature had clearly been bribed. "And how much did he give you for saying that?"

"A shilling, Sir. Ooh!" She clapped her hands over her mouth, realising what she had done.

"You're a fool, Mr. Northmore," John stated angrily. "I believe you were probably telling the truth but now you have to go and spoil it all. You are the sort who absolutely invites suspicion."

The quay master went white. "I swear to God I didn't see Juliana that day. I beg you to believe me."

The Apothecary turned to the girl. "Tell me something, Suky. Do you remember a very beautiful young lady coming in here, a young lady with fair hair? She would have been in company with two young men, a Mr.Digby-Duckworth and a Mr. Hood. Did you see them at all?"

Her answer was prompt. "Yes, Sir. I do remember them, very well indeed. I had seen the gentlemen before but never the lady."

"Can you recall anything they said?"

"We were busy that day and I didn't have much time for eavesdropping."

"But while you were serving them," John asked encouragingly.

"They said something about taking the boat out."

"The boat? Did they say where it was kept?"

"The only thing I heard them say was Red Rock." John looked blank. "What does that mean?"

Suky smiled, clearly feeling more relaxed. "Why, bless you, it's a place, Sir. Where the river bends round. Not far from here."

"Is there a boathouse there?"

Northmore spoke up, glad that the pressure was off him, if only temporarily. "There's a rather ruinous one. I believe it used to belong to the Thornes. It's not that far from Wildtor Grange as the crow flies."

"Well, you can make amends by taking me there." John got to his feet. "Now don't stir from your seat. I'll be right back."

He strode out of the snug, leaving the quay master looking both nervous and penitent. Despite his grim expression, the Apothecary felt elated by this latest turn of events, certain that the vessel which had taken Juliana out to the *Constantia* was about to be revealed.

Jan and Emilia were sitting where he had left them, this time with a glass before each of them from which they occasionally sipped. The Dutchman had stopped crying and was listening intently to every word John's wife was saying, obviously finding at long last someone who could empathise with the terrible situation in which he found himself. They stopped their conversation as the Apothecary came in.

"Please don't let me interrupt. Emilia something of great importance has happened which means that I will have to leave you for a while. Jan, could you be a good fellow and look after my wife for an hour or so?"

A hint of the courtly man they had first met reappeared. Jan got to his feet and gave a stiff little bow. "Sir, it will be my pleasure. She will be perfectly safe with me."

"Emilia, do you mind?"

"Of course not. I am so enjoying talking to Mr. van Guylder. I think perhaps we will go for a walk by the river if the sunshine continues."

"I would like that very much," Jan answered, using John's same words.

Pleased that his wife was doing the bereaved man so much good and appreciating how clever and tactful she was, John returned to Thomas

Northmore, who appeared not to have moved a muscle since he had left.

"Right, we'll go now. Time is of the essence."

"Certainly," said the quay master, and bustled out, conspicuously trying to make up for earlier misdeeds.

Beyond the inn the river ran straight for a little way, then looped round, and it was on the bend of the loop that John saw what he had come for. A dilapidated boathouse, very run down and in need of repair, stood there, its doors firmly closed against the world. John started towards it then reined his horse in, motioning Northmore to do likewise, as the sound of approaching hooves became distinctly audible.

"Keep quiet," he hised at the quay master, "I want to get a look at him before he sees us."

Then he nearly fell off his horse as a familiar figure came into view. Dressed in her man's clothes, Elizabeth di Lorenzi appeared from out of the trees, riding straight up to the boathouse, swinging easily from the saddle, then disappearing from sight as she walked round the ruinous building.

John turned to the quay master. "You can go."

"I beg your pardon?"

"I said you can go. I shall report everything that has happened to Mr. Jago but for the time being there is nothing further I have to say to you."

Thomas Northmore opened his mouth then closed it again, said, "In that case good day," and disappeared as fast as the boring horse could carry him.

Somewhat amused, John dismounted and walked towards the boathouse, very quietly calling Elizabeth's name. Then he rounded a corner and found himself staring straight down the barrel of a pistol. He put his hands in the air. "I'm not armed."

Her eyes widened. "What are you doing here?"

"The same as you I imagine. The pot girl in the inn told me that this place was mentioned on the day Juliana was last seen. I've come to have a look at it."

The Marchesa put her gun away. "It's in use, John. I'm sure that there's a boast in there that belongs to the Angels. The one they use for smuggling."

"And the one they used to transport Juliana to the *Constantia* I shouldn't wonder."

"Let's go inside."

"It's bound to be locked."

"They're not many locks that can resist an accurate shot from a pistol."

"What a woman you are," said John, laughing, and wished that the fatal fascination she held for him would go away for once and for all.

A moment later the lock was a mess of twisted metal and the doors were already starting to open as John and Elizabeth heaved at them. As they finally swung back, the Marchesa paused in the entrance.

"What's that smell?"

"Urine - and blood."

"My God, why?"

But the Apothecary already knew, with a certainty that made his stomach wrench. "I don't think you'd better come in."

"Why not?"

"Because I believe that this is the place where Juliana died."

Elizabeth turned stricken eyes on him. "John, I must see it for myself. I have sworn to be the avenging angel to their demonic ones. What I witness will only strengthen me in my resolve."

"I beg you, please don't enter."

"But I insist."

"Very well."

Together they crept forward into the darkness, their eyes gradually adjusting to the dimness within. It seemed huge as a cavern, for it was a big boathouse, built out over the river on stilts, able to accomodate quite a large vessel. And this indeed it did. As his vision became more and more accustomed to the gloom, the Apothecary made out the outlines of a long boat with five seats athwart, giving enough space for a rowing team of ten, which meant that the entire ship could hold at least a dozen men.

Alongside the boat was built a wooden jetty on which were piled ropes and barrels and various nautical artefacts. But it was not to these that John's eyes were drawn, but to the far end of the jetty where stood the boathouse wall. Attached to this wall were the doors leading to the river, through which the boat would be launched, and hanging from it were a pair of chains, secured at shoulder height. Even at a distance they seemed horribly reminiscent of the kind of manacles used to secure prisoners in a cell. With his heart pounding, John, with a terrible kind of reluctance, made his way towards them.

There was blood splashed upon the brick, and another pool of it on the decking floor. There was also another dried pool where whoever had been secured had lost control of their bladder while they were being beaten. This much was obvious, for the whip responsible for the blood lay casually tossed into a corner like a toy with which a child had grown bored. There was also something else in the corner, something which brought the bile into the Apothecary's mouth to see. An old mattress, stained with blood and the whiteness of dried semen, lay slightly removed from the whip, beside it a man's breeches, also stained with seminal fluid.

"So this is where they raped and beat her to death," said Eliazbeth in a voice that did not even sound like hers.

"Mr. Fielding would tell me that is only conjecture but my gut tells me yes, this is the place."

"I swear to God I'll kill them all."

John shook his head. "No Elizabeth. Only those responsible must die. If the Angels *are* Gerald Fitz and his mob, I do not believe they are all capable of such an act. Besides, you must stop taking the law into your own hands."

"Why? Why should I?"

"Because you put yourself in danger. Justice could be meted out on you as well."

"I don't think I would care very much about that."

The Apothecary turned to face her. "No, but I would care."

"For what reason?"

"Don't ask me that in a torture chamber like this. Simply accept the fact that I would."

She laughed humourlessly. "Then what are we going to do about these evil people?"

"We are going to trap them. Do you want to hear how?"

"Of course I do."

"Then step into the fresh air. The atmosphere in here is beginning to choke me."

"I'd like to set fire to the whole damnable place."

"That must wait until it has been seen by Joe Jago and Constable Haycraft. If it is torched now there would be only our word that it contains the evidence that it does."

John turned again to take one last look at the mattress, the chains and the whip. "Go on, Elizabeth. Go ahead of me. I'm just going to make a quick drawing."

"You have paper and pencil?"

"I always carry some. It's a habit I got into after working for Mr. Fielding."

"Strange young man," she said with a smile of great sweetness, then turned on her heel and hurried into the daylight.

Alone in there, John felt touched by such a sense of horror, such a clutch of fear, that he could barely execute his sketch. It seemed to him, unsuperstitious person though he might be, that Juliana's restless shade was trapped within the boathouse walls, that she lived again and again that last terrible time on the mattress, where she had suffered the horror of careless violation, then the chaining and beating that had ended her short and reckless life. A thought occurred to him. There had been no significant marks on the body's wrists. Loath though he was to touch them, John crossed the decking and picked up one of the chains, finding what he had suspected. The wrist pieces were made like bracelets and were lined with velvet. These were no ordinary chains but those made especially for lovers who enjoyed the use of physical restraints. The presence of the whip suddenly made a great deal of sense. Wondering where this sink of depravity was going to lead him next, the Apothecary made his way into the fresh air. He found Elizabeth sitting on a tree stump, paler than usual. She had removed her hat and the net that bound her hair, so that it sprang free around her shoulders. She looked up as he approached. "Are you alright?"

"Just about."

"What a terrible place. How could you bear to stay in there?"

"I couldn't really."

"Do you want to come back to the Grange for a moment?"

"I shouldn't. My wife is waiting for me."

"But I have something to show you."

"What is it?"

"The phantom coach."

John was all attention. "You've found it?"

"Yes. I've never really paid much attention to the stables up till now. I've kept my horse in a loose box but never investigated the coachhouses. Then yesterday for no real reason that I can explain to you, just a twitch of my nose, if you understand me ..."

John nodded.

"... I decided to go inside them. The first was amazing, filled by an old rotting coach that must have carried the Thornes around in their hey day. But the next was simply astonishing. For there, looking as ghostly as ever in the shadows, was that awful white carriage, just as fearful close to as it is from the distance. Anyway, I climbed on to the coachman's box and guess what I found there."

"What?"

"A pool of dried blood, shed, no doubt, when I shot the headless coachman."

"I wonder how that trick was done."

"By using a very short man with a fake neck on his head."

John Rawlings's thoughts danced a jig as his pictorial memory strove to bring something to the surface. Then he gave a wild cry of elation.

The Marchesa looked startled. "What is it?"

"Do you remember the assembly at Fitz's place?"

"Of course."

"And do you recall the little man, Simon Paris?"

"The one with the wounded ..." Elizabeth suddenly realised what she was saying and her eyes dilated. "Of course. It was him. So they *are* the Angels."

"Without a doubt. The only thing I can't quite understand is Fitz himself duelling with one of them. Unless ..."

"What?"

But the Apothecary shook his head. "I'm not sure yet. There's something at the back of my mind about that incident but I haven't quite worked it out."

"Could it have been staged in some way?"

John stared at her, then let out a yell. "Of course, of course. I see it now. Look no further than Lord Clyst's little boy."

The Marchesa stared at him, nonplussed. "I don't understand you."

"Never mind." John glanced at his watch. "If I come with you I must be very quick. My wife is waiting for me at The Bridge."

"How long will it take you to tell me your plan to capture the Angels?"

"Elizabeth," said John, seizing her by the shoulders, "I don't think Joe Jago wants anyone else involved in this."

"There is no force on earth that would keep me out of it," she answered vigorously, and with that put her foot in the stirrup and set off at speed in the direction of Wildtor Grange.

He caught up with her at the stables, a massive block of buildings surrounding a cobbled courtyard, lying directly behind the big house but slightly to the north east, thus ensuring that the moist west wind would carry the smells away from the residence. Here, once, had struggled hostlers and coachmen and tack boys, all busy about the task of keeping the place running. Now it was empty and silent, only the stamp of the Marchesa's horse as it moved in its loose box breaking the intense quiet. Elizabeth saw him coming and directed him to a mounting block and held his reins for him while he dismounted.

"The most beautiful hostler in the world," said John.

She gave him another smile of great charm but did not answer, merely taking his hand and leading him over to the second largest coachouse. For the second time that day the pair of them tugged on massive doors, then walked into the dim interior that lay beyond. But this place was as nothing compared with the boathouse of torture and despair, even though the white coach gave John a chill when he first looked at it.

"So this is how they travel the countryside frightening everyone to death."

"Yes, the little beasts."

"Have you looked inside?"

"No," Elizabeth answered boldly, and, marching over, climbed onto the coach's step and peered through the window. Then she screamed and stared at him in anguish. In a second John was at her side, gazing in over her shoulder. Just for a moment he thought he had seen the most horrible sight that day, for a decapitated head, still wearing its hat, lay on the floor, a jagged and bloody cut at the neck where it had been severed from its body. Then he laughed.

Elizabeth gazed at him in horror. "What are you doing?"

"Laughing, my dear Marchesa, at a bit of pure

theatre. It's the thing that the coachman had sitting next to him. Allow me." And with that he opened the carriage door, went inside and picked the head up. "Ugly looking brute," he said, staring into its sightless eyes.

"Show me."

"Here. I've a mind to send it through the post to our friend, Simon Paris."

"I'll do better than that," Elizabeth answered determinedly. "I'll deliver it to his house tonight and leave it sitting on the railings."

"How can I ever stop you putting yourself in danger?" John asked with a note of despair.

"That you never will," she answered, and it was her turn to laugh at his aggrieved expression.

Very slightly annoyed with her, the Apothecary began to examine the coach's interior, not really hoping to find anything but feeling that it was sensible to look while he had the opportunity to do so. Without much enthusiasm, having found nothing of interest on his initial search, he raised the coach's seat, only to discover that it was hollow beneath. Putting his arm in, he felt around, and his fingers came in contact with a leather bag. Grunting slightly, he pulled it out.

"What have you got?"

"I don't know yet." With a feeling of trepidation John opened the bag and looked inside. Another bag lay within, this one filled with tiny white grains. Dipping in a finger, the Apothecary licked it.

"Well?"

"Opium. No doubt to be sold to those seedy

houses in which it is smoked or for those who wish to take it to try its odd effects for themselves."

"So that is what they are smuggling. Would it be worth a great deal of money?"

"A considerable amount, certainly."

"Then they will come back here for it."

"If you are planning to catch them in the act, forget it. I intend to remove it straight away."

"But they won't know that."

"Elizabeth, stop it. Promise me you won't set a trap for them. It's too dangerous for a woman on her own."

"I promise on one condition. That you tell me of your plan to catch Juliana's murderers."

"You are blackmailing me."

"Yes, I know." She kissed him, very lightly and without passion. "So?"

"Well," answered John, whispering in the coach's gloomy interior. "It's going to start like this ..."

Chapter 20

It was a very public farewell. Drawn up on the quay, quite close to the stagecoach that ran between Exeter and Topsham on a regular basis, was the coach that had carried Joe Jago, Nick Raven and Dick Ham to the West Country. Standing beside it were its three passengers, long-faced at the prospect of leaving a job unfinished, obviously sad that they must depart from friends old and new, clearly uncomfortable that they had failed in their quest to find the killers of Juliana van Guylder.

For the return journey the carriage that had journeyed all the way from Bow Street in London had been cleaned, removing all traces of the good red earth of Devon, while the horses, well-rested and groomed, jingled their harness as they awaited the order that would start them on their way homewards. But first the ritual of leave-taking had to be carried out.

Joe Jago, suitably solemn in sage green, a colour that became his vivid hair, was bowing to all and sundry.

"Mrs. Rawlings, gentlemen, I cannot tell you how distressed I am to abandon you like this. But, alas, the call for return has come from Mr. Fielding himself. To leave a case unsolved is a slur on the reputation of the Runners and myself." He sighed deeply. "But there is no help for it. Go we must and go immediately."

John spoke. "This is a very worrying development because Emilia and I must also depart, probably tomorrow or the next day. My shop can no longer manage without me." He turned towards William Haycraft, who was wearing his best suit of dark grey serge for the occasion.

"But we know that we can rely on you, my good Sir, to bring the guilty to book."

The constable looked dubious. "I'll do my very best. The trouble is that I have no men at my disposal."

Joe gave an over-hearty laugh which rang out so loudly on the morning air that several people looked round. "A man of your calibre, Sir, is worth a dozen, believe me."

William appeared uneasy. "It is kind of you to say so but I am only too conscious of my limited resources."

There was an uncomfortable silence broken by Jan van Guylder, who hovered on the edge of the little group. "This is a sad day, Mr. Jago. I had thought in my simplicity that the great men of London would solve this terrible crime. But it was not to be." He turned to the constable.

"Believe me, Mr. Haycraft, I will do everything in my power to assist you."

There was another lull in conversation, broken by Joe Jago, whose voice this morning seemed unusually loud. "Gentlemen, we waste time. We have many miles to cover today. I apologise once more and bid you all farewell." He bowed and the other men did likewise, then the clerk raised

Emilia's hand to his lips. "Mrs. Rawlings, what can I say? Your company has been a delight. My only wish is that this wretched business has not ruined your honeymoon. Runners Ham and Raven, we must away."

Moving together, the two men, clearly keen to take the road, ran to the coach, one climbing onto the coachman's box, the other holding the door open for Mr. Fielding's clerk. At this Jan van Guylder let out a cry of anguish which he attempted to muffle as passers-by stared. Richard Ham, the driver, cracked his whip and Joe Jago stuck his head out of the window.

"May good fortune attend you," he shouted, and waved his hand until the coach had vanished into the distance on the Exeter Road.

The next day, almost at the same time of morning, the scene was repeated, only on this occasion it was the turn of the Apothecary and his wife to leave the town of Topsham. Again, William Haycraft, looking mournful beyond belief, was there to wave them farewell, as was Jan van Guylder and Tobias Wills, both of whom, despite the troubles that the pair had brought in their wake, seemed sorry to see them go.

"Does this mean that the mystery will remain unsolved?" Tobias asked in disbelief.

"No," John answered cheerily, "Constable Haycraft is still on the case."

"But he is one man against so many."

"I am sure he will manage," the Apothecary

replied with a confident air, and handed his wife into the waiting conveyance.

"Where to, Sir?" called Irish Tom at the top of his voice.

"To London," John answered with gusto, and stepping into the coach, waved his farewells until he, too, was just a small speck in the distance.

Looking bereft, Jan van Guylder and the man who would have been his son-in-law had affairs turned out differently, walked into a nearby hostelry and there discussed the departure of all those who had been investigating the murder of the girl who had been so dear to both of them not even noticing the slight young man who rose from his place in the corner and headed outside in the direction of the Exeter coach.

Once a week the London to Exeter stagecoach carried foreign mail bound for Lisbon, which was then taken to Falmouth and shipped out on a Saturday morning by packet, should such a vessel be waiting in Falmouth harbour. Consequently, passengers bound for the wild reaches of Cornwall could either change at Exeter and wait for this weekly stage, or catch it in London, preparing themselves for a monumentally long journey when they did so. Leaving the Gloucester Coffee House, Piccadilly, at four a.m. they could, if they were agreeable to sleeping in the coach and not putting up at an inn, reach Exeter just before ten o'clock on the following evening. However, this was not for the faint hearted and most passengers preferred to travel at a more leisurely pace, even though it took longer. Further, there were not many who elected to undertake the treacherous journey to Cornwall and the coach usually cleared out at Exeter. As for the return, the stage was often empty.

On this particular day, however, a Cornish sea captain and his wife, who desired to shop in Exeter, were aboard, and at Newton Abbot three more people got in. They were men, all rather rugged looking, in the driver's opinion. None wore wigs, one having a head full of tight red curls, another very dark and slightly foreign in appearance, the third a big, blond, jolly fellow. When asked if they were going to Exeter the reply was negative.

"Put us down at the Half Way House inn. We're to meet someone there."

So they were duly dropped off, their dues having been paid in advance, and were last seen heading into that remotest of hostelries, carrying no luggage whatsoever. Sometime later, in fact during the morning of the following day, a young couple came by trap, hired from a Honiton farmer, and were deposited at the same place, where they paid the farmer off and went within. The landlord, delighted by this sudden rush of custom to his out-of-the-way establishment, supposedly situated half way between London and Falmouth, though nobody really believed that, was pleased when this group of strangers appeared to get on well together. Indeed, such a good companionship was struck up that they ordered refreshments to be served in his one and only private room, where he could hear them chatting whenever he passed the door, though the words themselves were not audible.

"Well, so far, so good," said Joe Jago, rubbing his hands together.

"Were you seen at all?"

"Definitely not. We turned off the road just outside Exeter and proceeded to Newton Abbot via the rough country near Dartmoor. We crossed the river by horse ferry, one big enough to get the carriage on."

"Where have you stabled it?"

"In Newton Abbot. What about yourselves?"

"We left the coach in Honiton in the care of Irish Tom. He's a good man but gets too carried away in a mill so I thought it best to keep him at a safe distance," John answered. He leant forward. "When do we put the plan into action?"

"Tonight. It's my guess that they won't hold fire once they think we're all gone. You, Mr. Rawlings, and Runner Raven are to protect the widow, Dick and I will remain with Dmitri. Old Saul is to act as decoy by leaving the house and walking towards the tavern in a marked manner."

"Supposing he is attacked?"

"Constable Haycraft has agreed to pose as a drunken fisherman sleeping it off on the beach. At the first sign of trouble he has been instructed to go to Saul's aid."

"Have we enough people? The Angels in force represent quite a lot of armed men."

"We will have the element of surprise on our side. And remember that they can't crowd into those fishermen's cottages in a body. The buildings are far too small. With any luck we will be able to pick them off one by one."

"I hope it happens tonight," John said. "I want to get it over."

"As do we all," added Emilia with feeling. "You will be careful, won't you. Every one of you I mean."

There was a chorus of not altogether convincing agreement, then her husband asked another question. "Jan van Guylder was aware of what was going on. You don't think he will show up, do you?"

"I doubt it," the clerk answered him. "He is only vaguely aware of the details. He knew that our leaving was a blind but was far from certain what the next step was. By the way, he has seemed much better of late."

"That's since his talk to my wife, who has had as good an effect as any tonic I could have prescribed him."

Runner Raven, sipping canary, his dark eyes gleaming over the rim, said, "What did you say to him, Mrs. Rawlings?"

"Actually he did most of the talking. He was telling me about a Mrs. Kitty, a sailor's widow who works in the brothel in Exeter because she has three young children to rear and has no other source of income. He told me that he loved her but could not make her his wife by reason of losing the good opinion of the society in which he mingles. Oh, in case you didn't know, he was with her on the day Juliana was murdered."

Joe grinned. "He did admit as much to me, under some duress I might add. Anyway, what did you advise him?"

"To marry her and take her and her children back to Holland with him where nobody would know anything about her. He has business interests out there, so I don't see why not," she added a shade defiantly.

"Good plan," answered Joe succinctly. "It would give him something to live for. Let it be hoped that he has the good sense to defy convention and follow through."

"He's certainly thinking about it. He says there is nothing to hold him in Topsham any longer."

Dick Ham spoke up. "What are our instructions if the attack happens, Mr. Jago? Do we shoot to kill?"

"No, to wound only. We must get statements out of them. We still don't know if somebody financed Juliana's killing. Further, light must be thrown on Richard's suicide. A dead man can tell us nothing, remember. The only circumstance in which you can kill an attacker is if he is about to kill you. Now, as soon as it is dark we set forth. So not much more to drink, lads. It might spoil your aim."

"How are we going to get there?" asked John.

"All arranged. William Haycraft is coming for us with his largest cart."

"I think it's exciting," said the Apothecary.

"I think it's frightening," answered his wife.

It was a little nerve-racking, John had to admit, as they left the hostelry aglow with candles and plunged

down the treacherous track and into the darkness.
Overhead, the great sweep of sky which seems to
stretch forever in the mysterious county of Devon,
was the colour of stained glass, the deep blue that
comes just before it turns to ebony. The first star was
out and other pinpoints of light were beginning to
appear. In the distance he could hear the slow murmur of the sea, which, in his fancy, was singing to
the stars, the mermaids joining in, calling on them
to shine and light the waves. He was in far too poet-
ic a mood, John felt, for a night that could, if the
attacker rose to the bait, end in death and bloodshed. For despite all that Joe Jago had said, the
Apothecary knew that his finger would tremble on
the trigger if he discovered which of them had tortured a helpless girl and beaten her to her death.

They spoke in whispers, lying on the floor of the
cart, concealed by sacks, these last pulled over their
faces as William drove down the single street, past
The Ship and habitation. Then the wheels crunched
the shingle and drew to a halt.

"Best go on foot from here," murmured the constable. "If the cart is parked too near the cottages it
might arouse suspicion."

"Is there anybody about?" asked Joe. "Anybody
at all?"

"No, the place is deserted. The fishing boats are
beached and they are all in the alehouse."

"There's nobody hiding?"

"No one at all."

"Then, my lads," ordered Mr. Fielding's
representative, "let us go."

They piled out of the cart, landing on the wet sand, which clung round their feet. The tide was going out and there was driftwood and seaweed on the beach. Picking their way through it, the five men silently walked to where Sarah's cottage and that of Old Saul blazed with candlelight, gleaming far more than they normally would, hoping to attract those sinister moths of the night who might later come out to see what was afoot.

Joe spoke very quietly. "Now, each of you to your post. William, where are you going to be?"

"Over by that rock. I've borrowed some clothes and have hidden some fish to rub on my skin." He chuckled, a rather odd sound in the tension of that night. "I have to smell right if I am to convince anybody."

"Indeed you do. Now, the rest of you round to the back. Sarah and Old Saul have left the doors open."

Despite this, John gave a friendly whistle as he entered the widow's house, not wanting to frighten her out of her wits.

"Is that you, Mr. Jago?" she called softly.

"No, it's John Rawlings and Nick Raven, Mrs. Mullins. It is our pleasant duty to look after you this evening."

"Then I'll draw the curtains. Just wait a moment then step into the parlour."

She had brought every candle she had into the room so that even through the drapery it would be obvious to anyone watching that she had not yet gone to bed, and John saw that she had prepared the table with bread, cheese and ale for a frugal supper. Knowing how poor she was, his heart went out to her.

She spoke quietly. "What is the plan?"

"Soon Old Saul will say goodnight to Dmitri, making some noise about it. Then he will come in here as is his usual custom. After a short interval he will be on his way again, heading across the beach in the direction of The Ship. Should he be set upon, William Haycraft is out there hiding, ready to defend him. Once he has gone you are to blow out the candles and take one with you up to the bedroom. If the cottages are being observed, that is the moment when they will strike, when they think that both you and Dmitri have gone to bed."

"Will it be the man with the tattoo, do you think?"

"He and his cohorts, I should imagine."

"Do you have any idea who he is?"

"None, other than that he comes from Exeter and drives a coach with an inscription on the side, which puts him in the upper echelons of society. But then as the Angels seem mostly to be the sons of rich men, there is little surprise about that."

Sarah smiled. "And to think he fears Dmitri so much that he is prepared to kill both of us."

"It is the age-old situation of believing someone knows too much. Have you never, Sarah, been shunned by a person you once thought of as a friend because on some occasion they confided in you and now they fear you?"

She shook her head. "I can't say that I have."

"Well, I have observed it several times and have wondered at the stupidity of such behaviour."

"Folks are very peculiar," she answered.

"And can be very dangerous," put in Nick. "Best keep our voices down."

Duly reminded, they took to speaking in whispers, eating their simple supper quietly, John sitting on the floor as Sarah only had two chairs, two plates and two mugs, which they were obliged to share between them. With the meal finished they waited in almost total silence until they heard Old Saul's voice ring out.

"Well, goodnight to you, Dmitri. I'm delighted with your progress but you still need plenty of rest. Don't wait up for me. Get to bed soon. I'm going to The Ship for a while."

His feet crunched over the pebbles that the sea had deposited on the path outside and a moment or two later the knocker on the widow's front door sounded noisily. "Sarah," they heard Saul call.

"Coming," she shouted back and drew the bolts to let him in.

"Ha, my dear," said the visitor heartily, then dropped his voice to nothing. "I saw a light flash briefly on the cliff. I think I'm being observed."

"Excellent," Nick Raven whispered.

"How kind of you to look in," Sarah said loudly.

There then followed the most extraordinary conversation. In booming tones, Sarah and Saul discussed her health and progress and his plan to go to the alehouse for the evening. At the same time, in quiet murmurs, the Runner was briefing the old man as to exactly how he should behave if he was attacked.

"You are to call for help at once. William Haycraft is close at hand and will be at your side in a second."

"Don't worry, Sir, I have the means to protect myself should he be delayed."

"I'd prefer you not to fire a gun which would frighten off the others."

Old Saul chuckled. "No, this way is silent." And he produced from his pocket a small knife shaped exactly like an arrow, the head of which had been smeared with some dark substance."

"What's that?" asked the Apothecary, pointing.

"A method used by the Red Indians for disposing of an enemy without making any sound. It never fails."

John and Nick looked at one another and shook their heads, silently admitting that Old Saul had the answer to everything.

The medicine man raised his voice. "Now, Sarah, my dear, I suggest you retire early, as I have advised Dmitri to do. You are still weak from the attack and need all the rest you can get. I shall look in on you on my way home, just to check that all is well."

"I'll leave the key under the big pebble."

"Very well. Good night, Sarah."

"Good night, Saul."

She saw him to the front door, candle in hand, while John and Nick vanished into the dark scullery at the back. Glimpsing her through the crack of the door, the Apothecary thought that she looked like a goddess, tall and strong with her mass of red hair emblazoned round her head. And notions about powerful women brought Elizabeth into his mind, and he wondered where she was at this precise moment, then felt intuitively that she wasn't far away.

Sarah returned and now not one of them spoke a word, sure that if the attack was going to happen they must certainly be under observation by this stage. Just as if she were on her own, the Widow Mullins took the supper things into the scullery, then started to snuff out the candles. John was moved to see that the snuffer had been made out of shells, presumably by her dead husband, long ago, and that she touched it with a kind of love.

Her chores done, Sarah took one candle and asked by sign language if this was the right moment for her to climb the stairs. Runner Raven nodded yes, and the two men settled down to wait in the darkness. Over their heads they could hear her moving about, then finally there was the sound of the widow climbing into bed. After that there was silence broken only by the crackle of the flames as the small fire began to go out.

The noises of the night became more acute, every whistle of the west wind clear as a bell. The sea began its wild song in which the shift of shale and the topple of rollers formed a desolate melody. Without knowing why it soothed him so, the Apothecary closed his eyes and felt himself drift into a sea dream. Then suddenly, inexplicably, he was wide awake, and close by he sensed, rather than saw, Nick Raven becoming alert. Somebody had either heard Sarah say where she had hidden her key or had previous knowledge of it, for the lock was turning and the door was silently opening. Just for a second the figure outside was etched against the starry sky and John saw a long white coat and a veiled white hat, then the man stepped within and there was only a faint glow of his clothing in the darkness.

Moving soundlessly, the intruder crossed towards the stairs and put his foot on the bottom step which creaked loudly. He was so close to John that the Apothecary could hear his breathing. Then he must have sensed that he was not alone for he whirled round.

"Who's there?" whispered an urgent voice.

Neither John nor Nick moved a muscle, frozen in silence, and after a moment or two the man continued his climb. It was only when he got to the top and Sarah screamed as he threw open her door that they were released from their catalepsy. Charging up the stairs, they hurled themselves into the bedroom.

She had no curtains at these windows and they could see in the moonlight that he was kneeling on the bed, crouching over her, his hands at her throat.

Nick Raven released the cock on his pistol and put the barrel to the man's head. "One more move and I'll blast you to eternity, you little bastard."

"Damn you," shouted the other, and whirling round fast as lightning knocked the Runner's weapon clean out of his hand.

"So it's going to be my pleasure, is it?" asked John, and shot him straight through the left arm.

The roar of the blast started a barrage of noise. From the cottage next door came the sound of further shots and the cry of a man in distress. Unable to restrain himself, the Apothecary tore down the stairs, out into the night and in through the open door of Old Saul's place. Somebody had lit a candle and in its flickering light John could see that two of the Angels were fighting hand to hand with Joe Jago and Dick Ham. Without stopping to think, the Apothecary came up behind them and snatched their hats from their heads, revealing the faces of Gerald Fitz and one of the O'Connor twins.

"One move from either of you and you're dead men," snarled John nastily, meaning every word.

"Thank you, Mr. Rawlings," said Joe, calmly picking up his pistol which had been knocked to the floor. "I'm afraid they caught us unawares and managed to disarm us. Most inconvenient. What about you?"

"I've winged one of them. He's in Sarah's bedroom with Nick Raven holding a gun to his head. "Now ..." He turned to Gerald Fitz, "...was it you who killed poor Juliana?"

"No, it damned well wasn't. I'd had a bit of fun with her, we all had. I'd even given her a bit of a slapping, which was no more than the silly whore deserved, but it was not I who picked up the whip."

"What about you?" Joe looked fiercely at the O'Connor twin.

"I had a nug with her but left it at that. Hitting the woman didn't appeal to me."

"Was her brother present?" John asked curiously.

"No, we'd sent him and Brenchley on an errand. Hood imagined himself in love with her and would only have got in the way. They didn't find out till afterwards."

"Was that why Richard shot himself?"

"I have no idea," Gerald Fitz answered languidly. "Perhaps he was the father of her child. I wouldn't put anything past that girl."

"You foul-mouthed bastard," said a voice from the doorway. "By God, I'm going to get you for that."

Wheeling round in astonishment, John found himself knocked sideways by yet another white coated figure. Scrambling up from the floor he watched as the figure flung itself at Fitz, then the blade of a knife gleamed in the candlelight.

"Stop it!" screamed a different voice again, and with a reek of fish that made everyone gasp, William Haycraft hurled in from the beach and threw himself on the attacker. But it was far too late. Gerald Fitz's white coat was starting to turn red as blood pumped down the front of it.

"Damn you, Brenchley Hood," hissed the once elegant fop, then collapsed as the pool of blood widened around him.

"Good riddance," yelled Hood, punching the constable in the guts and pulling off his hat in one simultaneous movement. "She loved you and you betrayed her, like the cur that you are. But I loved her too and now she is avenged." Then he would have turned the knife on himself if Dick Ham had not snatched it from him.

"Is Fitz dead?" Joe asked the Apothecary.

John knelt down beside the inert figure, feeling for his pulse. "Yes," he said. "He's gone. A life for a life, it would seem."

O'Connor gave a bitter laugh. "But Fitz didn't give her the death blow. You'll have to search a little harder for the man who did that."

"Enough gab, you Irish clown," said Joe, grabbing the young man by the scruff of the neck and shaking him till his teeth rattled in his head. "Which one was it? Which one actually killed her?"

"Make a move and I'll shoot the whole cull sucking lot of you," said someone from behind them all, and John turned to see that the Angel he had shot in Sarah's bedroom had somehow overpowered Nick Raven and had arrived at Old Saul's cottage, once more armed with a pistol.

"Come on O'Connor, come on Hood," he ordered. "We'll dispose of these four prats then join the others at the Grange."

"I'm not coming," Brenchley shouted back. "I've had enough of you, you bastard. I've got my suspicions, indeed I have."

The Angel gave a cynical laugh. "Have you now? And what might they be?"

"That you were the father of Juliana's child and that it was you who applied the whip and killed her."

"But she enjoyed it. It was one of our little pleasures together."

Hood spat on the floor. "You filthy shite. By God, I wish I had killed you along with Gerald."

"Well, that's something that you will have to regret for what is left of your miserable life. For they'll have you for killing him. They must have all seen you do it, these officers of the law." He sneered. "You'll swing for Fitz, you stupid turd."

Brenchley thrust away the gasping William and leapt in the Angel's direction but was forcibly restrained by Runner Ham. "Did you kill her?" he shouted, clearly in an agony.

"Yes, I did, you prick. I gave her the final blow and watched her die, just as the bitch deserved. She was going to marry my grandfather and foist my bastard onto him, disinheriting me totally. On the old man's death the estate would have come rapidly to me, my father being but a frail creature and not reckoned to live more than a twelve-month. But with the arrival of a second son the terms of the entail would have seen it pass to him. So I got two for the price of one when she breathed her last."

"And talking of breathing your last ..." said a strangely musical voice.

Yet again John turned to that invitingly open front door and his heart lurched to his stomach. Dressed as a man, her hair netted, her hat pulled down, her scar livid in the candlelight, was the Marchesa di Lorenzi, Lady Elizabeth herself.

Peter Digby-Duckworth spun round, but not fast enough. Putting her left hand to her shoulder, Elizabeth steadied her right on her arm and shot him clean through the head which - in terrible imitation of poor Richard van Guylder's - disintegrated, spattering brains and blood everywhere.

She lingered for one second longer. "Until we meet again," she said, looking straight at John, then she was out through the door and off in a thunder of hooves.

Joe gazed across all the horror to where John Rawlings stood. "And that, I take it," he said, with just the merest hint of his old wry humour, "was the vigilante."

"Yes," answered John, smiling despite everything, "that indeed was her."

Chapter 21

John had found a towel of sorts in Old Saul's scullery and as dawn broke walked with it in his hand to the edge of the sea. The first rays of the sun were slashing the horizon with shards of light and the water was the soft pink of a shell, an harmonious ending to a night of bloodshed and death, the sticky evidence of which was still on the Apothecary's hand and clothes. Stripping himself naked, he plunged into the cleansing waves. The water was so cold that it took the breath from his body, but still he relished it, watching as all the blood, both from the living and from the dead, was absorbed by the sea and somehow purified. Trying to sort out his thoughts, John swam.

The most difficult part had not been the sordid clearing up, the scraping of death's detritus from the cottage walls, nor even the frantic dash to get Runner Raven to a physician with a bullet lodged in his shoulder. The worst ordeal had been shielding Elizabeth's true identity from Constable Haycraft, that most honest of citizens who had eye witnessed her shoot to kill a man and whose bounden duty it was to hunt her down, albeit her victim was a reckless murderer holding officers of the law at gunpoint. It had been Joe Jago, with his knowing light blue eyes, who had spoken to William sensibly.

"You knew there was a vigilante in Exeter, Constable. I told you about him. For reasons of his own he was sworn to avenge whatever wrong was done to him in the past by the Angels. Well now he has."

"But he has committed murder in so doing."

"He actually rescued officers of the law, including yourself, who were being threatened with death. If he had not shot Peter Digby-Duckworth, that young criminal would most certainly have shot us."

"I do realise all that, but it is still my responsibility to try and find him."

"Indeed it is."

William had turned to John. "Sir, how much do you know about this person?"

The Apothecary had stared Joe Jago straight in the eye, then said, "I have spoken to the vigilante. It is as Mr Jago says. A wrong was done in the past, revenge was sworn. That revenge has been exacted."

"But what do you know of him? Have you a name? An address?"

"No," John had answered shortly, and when no contradictory noise came from Mr. Fielding's clerk, had continued with his job of tending the wounded.

A sudden sandbank quite far out to sea gave him the chance to stand up for a moment and observe. The constable's cart had been drawn up close to Old Saul's door and two shapes, covered with sheets and carried on planks, were being loaded into it by Saul and William, prior to being driven to Exeter mortuary. Joe, who had spent a great deal of the night writing a report for the coroner, appeared outside and breathed in the morning air as if it were nectar. Dmitri, who had been locked in his room for his own safety, came to join him, stretching as if he were released from genuine captivity. Then he blew a kiss to Sarah who was waving to him from an upstairs window. The only people missing were the two Runners and the two Angels, both of whom were in a makeshift gaol in the charge of Dick Ham. Runner Raven was presumably still resting after the ordeal of bullet removal, an operation he had had to face in the middle of the night at the hands of a somewhat weary Dr. Shaw at his house in Topsham. In an extraordinary way the Apothecary was looking at a scene of enormous peace, almost of contentment, after a night of such violent discord.

Joe, spotting John standing in the sea, began to stroll down the beach, and the Apothecary, realising how cold he was getting, swam for the shore. They met in the shallows and John was glad of the towel, however inadequate, that the clerk handed him. But as he rubbed himself down and put on his stained and not altogether pleasant clothes, he knew that the freezing swim had done him good. His skin felt clean and refreshed and he was ready to face the world once more.

Joe sat down on an upturned boat. "Well, then, it's over."

"Yes, A grim story that ended with equal grimness. What will happen to rest of the Angels? The ones not involved in last night's attack."

"They are in mighty trouble. I named names to the coroner as well as to the excise men when I took the opium to the Customs House. The Riding Officers were preparing to set a trap for them in the coachouse at Wildtor Grange, waiting till they came to collect their booty, then making arrests. For those who escape that, the coroner is duty bound to hand the information about Juliana's murder to the constables. I think we can safely say that the Society of Angels will shortly cease to exist."

"I feel somewhat sorry for Brenchley Hood."

Joe shrugged expressively. "His father is Lord Hood so he will have the finest barrister that money can buy."

"But he killed Gerald Fitz, another family with connections."

"Then it will be the battle of the Titans. But I agree. Hood and Richard van Guylder seemed to be the dupe of others, the creatures sent to perform menial tasks."

"Was Peter Digby-Duckworth the leader of the gang, do you think?"

Joe considered, running his fingers through his tight bright curls. "I had suspected Fitz from all you said about him, but Peter was the one with the tattoo on his wrist. Furthermore, he must have been the gaffer from Exeter that Saul described. His carriage bears the family crest and beneath it the legend 'Sic transit gloria mundi'. Now didn't the old man tell you it had something to do with sickness?" He laughed harshly.

"So passes away earthly glory," John translated. "Well, his has certainly gone, though for sure there was no glory in him. As far as I am concerned he was one of the most foul individuals ever born. To kill the mother of his child because she stood in the way of his inheritance."

"Murder has been committed for far less." Joe answered starkly.

John did up the final button on his shirt and sat down beside the clerk. "I should have guessed that Fitz and his friends were with the Angels far sooner had it not been for the duel I witnessed."

"The one in which he rescued Coralie Clive?"

"Yes. You know, at the time it struck me as very theatrical, very staged and rehearsed-looking. But even when Percival Court, Lord Clyst's son, showed me his sword wound at Fitz's party I still didn't put two and two together. It wasn't until Eliz..." The Apothecary stopped speaking.

Joe turned on him a totally blank face. "You mean that a chance remark by another party gave you the clue you needed."

John stood up and swung his arms as if he were cold. "Yes, precisely."

Joe also got to his feet. "That's often the way of it," he said, and then he winked.

A few miles out of Exeter the wind changed and the song of the sea was no longer audible. The wind blew from the south east and spoke of towns and cities and the great heaving metropolis of London.

"We're going home," said John, with a tinge of regret in his voice.

"Are you sorry?"

"In some ways. Are you?"

"No," said Emilia firmly. "I can't wait to move into Nassau Street and set up residence in town."

"What about the Kensington house?"

"Our country retreat, to be visited when Sir Gabriel invites us."

"It will be an open invitation."

"Then I shall go whenever you wish, my dear."

Moving to the window, John stared back over his shoulder. "Goodbye, Devon. It has been a most interesting experience."

Emilia laughed. "Are you referring to the adventure we had or our honeymoon?"

"Both really." He looked at her seriously for a moment. "Did you enjoy yourself or did the death of poor Juliana ruin it all for you?"

His wife looked at him gravely. "I enjoyed most of it, which, I suppose, would be a fair thing to say about one's life in general."

"You're a wise little thing," he said, and kissed her hand.

She smiled at him. "So John Rawlings, apothecary of Shug Lane and married man, returns to London and domesticity."

"Of course. To a quiet, respectable married life."

Emilia's smile broadened. "Don't you think that sounds rather dull?"

"Horribly so."

"Then why don't you rephrase it? To a rather noisy, sometimes extraordinary, frequently exciting state of matrimony."

"Will it be like that?"

"It might."

"What do I have to do to achieve it?"

"Occasionally go mad in the wild west but never stop loving me."

"Never," said John, knowing that from now on his future was entirely bound up with hers.

Then he held her close to him as, unbidden and unwanted, there ran through his mind's eye a vivid picture of a solitary rider, cantering through daffodils as the gulls wheeled above and the shifting tide boomed upon the shore.

Historical note

John Rawlings, Apothecary, really lived. He was born circa 1731, though his actual parentage is shrouded in mystery. He was made Free of the Worshipful Society of Apothecaries on 13 March, 1755, giving his address as 2, Nassau Street, Soho. This links him with H.D. Rawlings Ltd. who were based at the same address over a hundred years later. Rawlings were spruce and ginger beer manufacturers and in later years made soda and tonic waters. Their ancient soda syphons can still be found, these days usually in antique shops. I was recently presented with one by my favourite French readers, the College La Millaire of Thionville, and am tremendously proud of it.

It may seem incredible to us in the twenty-first century to realise that the famous Sweeny, the Flying Squad, was actually founded by John Fielding, the Blind Beak, in the eighteenth, and that the two Brave Fellows were the forerunners of characters similar to those played by John Thaw and Dennis Waterman. Yet from 17 October, 1754, onwards, an advertisement worded as follows appeared regularly in *The Public Advertiser*:

> WHEREAS many thieves and robbers daily
> escape justice for want of immediate pursuit,
> it is therefore recommended to all persons,
> who shall henceforth be robbed on the

highway or in the streets, or whose shops or houses shall be broke open, that they give immediate notice thereof, together with an accurate description of the offenders as possible, to JOHN FIELDING, Esq. at his house in Bow Street, Covent Garden ... And if they would send a special messenger on these occasions, Mr. Fielding would not only pay that messenger for his trouble, but would immediately dispatch a set of Brave Fellows in pursuit, who have been long engaged for such purposes, and are always ready to set out to any part of this town or kingdom, on a quarter of an hour's notice.

The list of places that the Brave Fellows visited as quoted by John to Emilia in the text is perfectly genuine and has been taken from the records.

The interchange of the words cannavis and cannabis is historically correct. So is the description of the effects of a carelessly retted cargo of hemp. Finally, the use of *Cannabis sativa* in medicine is recorded by Culpepper, though he does give this warning: Too much use of it dries up the seed for procreation. So, sailor beware!